J

Uneasy Spirits
A Victorian San Francisco Mystery

A Novel

By M. Louisa Locke

This book is a work of fiction. Names, characters, places, and incidents are either the product of the author's imagination or are used fictitiously, and any resemblance to actual persons, living or dead, business establishments, events, or locales is entirely coincidental.

Uneasy Spirits

Dedicated to all the family and friends who gave their support during the writing of this book. Special thanks to my writer's group, Ann Elwood, Abigail Padgett, and Janice Steinberg; my friends Jim and Victoria Brown, Sally and Cecil Hawkins, and Terry Valverde; and my loving husband, Jim, and my daughter, Ashley, and her family, who have given me such joy.

A special thanks goes to my father, Joseph H. Locke, who has provided me with the model of how to grow old with grace, courage, and good humor.

Acknowledgements

First I would like to express my appreciation for all the indie authors whose guidance, support, and enthusiasm have made my career as an author both possible and successful. A special thanks goes to April Hamilton, Joel Friedlander, and the members of the Historical Fiction Authors Cooperative, particularly to Martha Marks and Iva Polansky.

Next, I would also like to acknowledge all the people who bought my first book, wrote reviews, and sent me personal words of support, since they have made this whole business of writing and self-publishing a complete joy.

Finally, I would like to give a special thanks to Catherine Coyne, Wendy Cregan, William Drescher, Dottie Huber Engel, Pamela Lyons, Pat McClintock, Gloria Robinson, and Kay Zoldos, fans of my work who graciously agreed to be beta readers and vastly improved the final product. Errors that remain are my complete responsibility!

Unless otherwise noted, all chapter tags are quotes from the 1879 *San Francisco Chronicle.*

M. Louisa Locke's Victorian San Francisco Series

Maids of Misfortune (novel)
Uneasy Spirits (novel)
Bloody Lessons (novel)
Dandy Detects (short story)
The Misses Moffet Mend a Marriage (short story)

Prologue
San Francisco, 1879

Why hasn't that good-for-nothing boy come up to get me ready for bed yet? The hall clock just chimed quarter past nine! Eighty-four years old and I can still hear everything that goes on in this house. There! Sounds like he just knocked something over, down in the parlor. Probably he's smashed up all my pretty treasures by now. Counting on me never making it downstairs again. Hah! Well, son, you have a surprise coming to you. Next fine day, I'll holler down to the garden for Manny and get him to come up here and use those muscles of his to carry me all round the house. See what mischief you've been up to. I'll make you pay for everything you've damaged.

Won't I make you pay! You and that young wife of yours, too. Haven't seen hide nor hair of her since noon. A blessing, really. Watching her gallivanting around the place like she owns it. Makes me sick. She can't keep house worth a damn. Lets the tradesmen and that thieving cook take advantage of her. That's why the housekeeping money don't last! Between the two of you, robbing me blind.

I never should have let you move back in when your pa got so sick. That was a mistake. But he wanted his son nearby, didn't he? Wanted to keep an eye on how you were running the company is more like it. If just one of the other boys had lived, oh things'd be different. Six sons, and the sorriest one of them all is the only one that outlasted their pa. If Zeke just hadn't gotten killed in that brawl. Now that was a man who loved his mother. He wouldn't have left me up here all alone. It's time for my heart pills, and I want to go to bed!

Wedged in a massive wing-backed chair facing the fireplace, the old woman fretfully moved her head from side to side. The few glowing embers in the grate left the room in near darkness, except where the glow from the gas fixture in the hallway showcased the porcelain figurines of shepherds and shepherdesses preening across the top of a mahogany dresser. Ropes of pearls cascaded down the front of the stiff satin dress that stretched over the woman's colossal frame. Wispy white hair capped a face of concentric soft circles, from her multiple chins to the drooping round hole of her mouth. But the pale cold eyes that glittered in the faint light ruined any illusion of amiability.

She suddenly raised an elegant wooden cane and began to pound furiously on the floor, setting every piece of jewelry and china to prancing. Just as abruptly, she stopped and cocked her head, the silence filled by her ragged breathing.

There, I hear you coming up the stairs. Forgot me, didn't you, sonny boy? Left me to freeze up here. How many times have I told you my poor feet can't take the cold evening air? But now you've let my fire go out, and it will take forever for me to warm up. It's Nurse's night off and good riddance to her, sneaky thieving woman, but that means you or that good-for-nothing wife of yours will just have to rub my feet for me tonight, won'cha!

What are you waiting for? Think I can't hear you standing out in the hallway? You know it's past time for my pills; I can hardly breathe. Dr. Hodges told you how important it is to give them to me on time. Too scared to come in by yourself, are you? Want me to say 'pretty please?' I wouldn't give you the satisfaction.

That's better, come right on in and quit trying to sneak up on me. I know that trick, always trying to frighten me to death. There you go, ran right into the end of the bed, you clumsy oaf. Now, why are you just standing there breathing down my neck? Irritating boy. You just come around in front where I can see you, and I'll rap you one with my . . . What are you doing? Stop it! No, no, get that away, I can't brea . . .

The pillow was carefully placed on the floor, the clock in the hallway struck nine-thirty, the last ember snuffed out, and the Dresden figurines stared silently as hundreds of tiny pearls clattered softly to the carpet.

*****

Across town, a young girl sat in the attic in a large armchair, her face in deep shadow. A shaft of moonlight from one of the two eastern facing windows cut diagonally across her chest, revealing multiple loops of colored beads that fell down to her waist. Her feet dangled, not touching the floor. In her arms lay a china doll, whose painted frozen features exhibited more life than could be found in her own face.

A song issued tunelessly from those rigid lips.

"Hot cross buns, hot cross buns! One ha' penny, two ha' penny, hot cross buns. If you have no daughters, give them to your sons. One ha' penny, two ha' penny,
 hot cross buns! Hot Cross . . ."

The girl straightened and pointed, her index finger contorted in a grotesque fashion. "You stop it right now." Her voice, despite a quaver, was sharp and strong, and its force twisted her face into a mask of fury. "I see what you did. I see everything. You can never hide from me . . . stop . . ." The girl clutched at her chest, and the beads broke, cascading to the floor. The girl slumped, again immobile, humming.

"Hot cross buns, hot cross buns, one ha'penny . . ."

Chapter One
Saturday Morning, October 11, 1879

Madam Sibyl, Clairvoyant, specializing in business and domestic advice. 436 O' Farrell Street. Consultations by appointment only, fee $2.

Annie Fuller leaned across to stare at the woman's hands resting palms up on the dark green velvet tablecloth in front of her. She picked up the right hand and slowly traced the client's heart, head, and life lines, struggling to find some words of comfort to extract from these faint creases that crisscrossed Mrs. Crenshaw's plump palms. Stalling, she picked up the left hand. She turned the hand over, noting that the gold wedding band and modest diamond engagement ring were becoming embedded in the flesh of the ring finger and the hand was cold and dry.

"You are still having trouble breathing, aren't you, Mrs. Crenshaw? Did you try the extra pillows as I suggested last week?" asked Annie.

"Oh yes, Madam Sibyl, I did and, just as you foretold, have slept so much easier," Mrs. Crenshaw replied.

Annie glanced up, sudden suspicion sharpening her voice. "You did return to see Dr. Hammersmith, didn't you? Remember what I told you; the science of palmistry is not incompatible with the science of human physiology. What I learn from reading your palms and what Dr. Hammersmith learns from listening to your heart with his stethoscope can both be of use to you."

Mrs. Silas Crenshaw, a fashionably dressed woman in her late sixties, turned her head away for a moment. She then sighed and said, "I saw him, but he doesn't do me any good. He just tells me to be patient. He says a woman my age shouldn't expect to come back quickly from a bout of pneumonia. What he won't tell me is when I can travel to Iowa to meet my new grandbaby. You know how I long to see my daughter and that precious child. He will be six months old in December. My husband is quite determined we should wait until my cough is entirely gone, and Dr. Hammersmith refuses to advise him that I am well enough to travel. So I need you to tell me what is going to happen. There are arrangements to be made; Mr. Crenshaw can't just leave for a month at a moment's notice. Please, when will I be well enough to visit my daughter?"

Annie turned Mrs. Crenshaw's hand back over to trace her Mercury line, which if she really did believe in palmistry would reveal information about Mrs. Crenshaw's future health. Annie, however, didn't believe in palmistry, and it didn't take clairvoyance to tell her that the woman in front of her was unlikely to get well enough to spend Christmas in Iowa with her new grandson. But clairvoyance is what Madam Sibyl promised in her newspaper advertisement, and clairvoyance is what Mrs. Crenshaw expected for her $2 fee. This was a problem, since Annie Fuller, in addition to being a respectable widow and boarding house owner, was also Madam Sibyl.

After her husband John's death, she had spent five wretched years being shunted between various branches of his family back east, finally coming west to settle in San Francisco, where she had inherited a house from her only remaining blood relative, her Aunt Agatha. Despite turning this grand old home into a boarding house, she found she still wasn't financially independent, and Annie had turned to the only other way of making a living she knew, giving business advice. Although she had been trained by her father, one of the most successful stock brokers in New York or San Francisco history, Annie had discovered the only way a twenty-six-year-old female was going to get paid for her knowledge and expertise was if she pretended she got her information from reading her clients' palms or casting their horoscopes.

Hence the invention of her alter ego, Madam Sibyl. She had added domestic advice to Madam Sibyl's offerings, hoping she would also attract female clients. For the last year, she had been gratifyingly successful in not only helping a number of local businessmen begin to recoup their losses from the panic and depression of the seventies, but also helping a number of women better manage their household finances, their domineering mothers-in-law, and their neglectful husbands. Mrs. Crenshaw, however, was different, and with each visit Annie felt increasingly uncomfortable with the charade she was playing.

The wig of intricate black curls she wore as part of her Madam Sibyl disguise felt unbearably tight and hot. Normally the small parlor in which she and Mrs. Crenshaw sat, with its velvet curtains and dim lighting, provided an inviting haven of coolness, but not today. As it was nearly noon, the fog had burned off, and, although it was the middle of October, the unusual heat of early fall persisted. The incipient headache that had hovered all morning finally attacked as Annie anxiously searched for an appropriate answer to Mrs. Crenshaw's question.

She touched the barely visible horizontal lines along the outer edge of Mrs. Crenshaw's palm that detailed a person's travels and said, "Mrs. Crenshaw, I believe the difficulty I am having in reading the answer to your question is that it is really two questions. First, you want to know when you will regain your health. You also want to know when you will get to see your daughter and grandson."

This is ridiculous, Annie thought. *How can she come week after week, asking the same questions, getting the same vague answers from me? That damned doctor should have told her the truth; she isn't getting better. She is getting worse.*

Mrs. Crenshaw's hand trembled, and Annie could hear the soft liquidity of her shallow breaths as the older woman said, "Please, Madam Sibyl. I need to know. I've told you about how Mr. Crenshaw and I had become resigned to never having children when we were blessed with our lovely prairie rose, Sharon. Such a miracle and delight, though she worried us when she was young, seemed each winter she was so poorly. I hated it when Silas decided we needed to move out here, leave the farm to Sharon and her new husband, but he promised we could visit whenever I wanted. And now with the new baby ... I just need to be there!"

Mrs. Crenshaw had first come to see Madam Sibyl last June, right after she got the letter from her daughter announcing she was nearly eight months pregnant. If Mrs. Crenshaw had had her way, she would have gotten right on a train to be with her daughter during the last month of her confinement. Yet her husband had told her that she shouldn't risk infecting her daughter or the new baby with one of her persistent colds. Mrs. Crenshaw had sought out Madam Sibyl, hoping she could foretell if her daughter would have a successful delivery without her.

At the time, Annie had wondered if her daughter's delay in notifying her mother about the pregnancy and her husband's reluctance to let her travel reflected their belief that Mrs. Crenshaw's anxious personality would make her more of a burden than a help during this delicate time. Now she believed the real reason was the family's concern about Mrs. Crenshaw's health, because Annie was convinced it was a dying woman who sat before her, a woman whose heart had probably been failing for a good many years.

"Madam Sibyl, what do you see when you look at my palm? Why aren't you telling me what you see? I deserve the truth," Mrs. Crenshaw said, pulling her hand from Annie in order to scrabble for a handkerchief to press against the coming cough.

Annie watched helplessly as the older woman struggled to regain her breath. She thought about the distressing number of dying women she had attended in her peripatetic shuffling from one in-law to another after her husband John's death: the ninety-year-old grandmother whose last days were a peaceful shutting down of each organ, the twenty-two-year-old new mother whose body burned itself out from a puerperal fever, the aunt of enormous appetites whose life had seeped away through her gangrenous extremities.

However, Mrs. Crenshaw's blue-tinged lips, the swollen hands that contradicted her loss of weight, and the labored cough . . . these she had observed only once before, when she was twelve and her own mother lay dying. No one had been willing to tell her the truth fourteen years ago, and so Annie had agreed to leave her mother and travel up north to San Francisco to visit her Aunt Agatha. Her mother had died and been buried in the hot dry Los Angeles winds before she had been able to make it back home.

With searing clarity, Annie knew she couldn't lie anymore to this woman. She rose and went over to the small sideboard, where she poured Mrs. Crenshaw a cup of tea, putting in the three lumps of sugar the older woman liked. After Mrs. Crenshaw had sipped her tea and gotten her breathing under control, Annie again leaned over and picked up the left hand, beginning to speak in the low, singsong tones Madam Sibyl often used when "giving a reading."

"Mrs. Crenshaw, the truth I see written in your hand is one I believe you already know. Your Mercury line confirms what your life line foretells: that your heart is wearing out, and death, as is true for us all, is your fate. As with any glimpse we are given into the future, the timing is not precise. Yet you have been given the gift of foreknowledge, and your character is such that I know that you will embrace this truth to shape your own destiny."

Mrs. Crenshaw's hand clenched hers, and Annie's words faltered. She squeezed the hand she had been holding, placed it gently down on the table, and took up the right hand, finding the light horizontal lines that intersected with the vertical Mercury line.

"I do not see any more travel in your future, but I do see visitors. I see your daughter sitting beside you in your parlor, which is all decorated for Christmas. I see you holding your adorable grandson, all wrapped up in that lovely blue blanket you have been knitting for him. Finally, I see your bravery in accepting your illness, thereby permitting your family to come together to celebrate every moment you have left in your life."

Annie found both of her hands clasped spasmodically between Mrs. Crenshaw's own as the woman's soft sobs filled the room.

What have I done? Annie shifted nervously in her seat. *Poor woman, I'm not a doctor, and I am certainly not clairvoyant. I have to tell her I am a sham; I can't possibly know what the future holds for her.*

She forced herself to look up, but Mrs. Crenshaw's face stunned her. The older woman was certainly crying, but there was a watery smile emerging as her sobs stilled, and the pinched frown that usually marred the genuine sweetness of her expression had disappeared.

Mrs. Crenshaw pulled her hands from Annie's, blew her nose, and began to talk excitedly. "Madam Sibyl, thank you. Of course I know I am dying. That is why I so wanted to make this trip. It might be the last time I can see my daughter. But I was afraid to tell Silas this. I have found men don't deal well with bad news; I am sure in your business you have found this so. I just don't know why I never thought of asking my daughter to come here! But of course she will be able to come; it will be good for her and the child to be out of Iowa during the worst winter months. Her husband, Stephen, such a good man, will not begrudge me this visit. Perhaps he can get someone to take over the farm for a month so he can be here for Christmas, too. Oh dear, there are so many plans to be made. Silas will grumble at the expense, but how can he say no to his dying wife? I must get home. I swear, this has given me a new lease on life!"

Later, after the boarding house's cheerful young Irish maid, Kathleen, had ushered a still animated Mrs. Crenshaw out of the parlor, Annie stood at the small washstand in the back room and jerked the wig off of her head, hoping to release the pressure that had built to an intolerable level. She poured water into a plain white enamel basin and, dipping a washcloth into the water, began to pat at her face. She longed to plunge her whole face into the water, but she couldn't afford to let the precious elderberry paste she had used to darken her eyelashes and eyebrows be washed away. She tugged down the bodice of her severely cut black silk and tried to ease the restrictive tightness of her corset. She had two hours to rest, but then she had three more clients to meet today.

Annie stared at her reflection in the mirror, poking ineffectually at the mess she had made of her braided hair by pulling off the wig so precipitously. *How pale I look*, she thought as she tucked a reddish blond curl back into place. *You would think I was the one who was at death's door. What if Silas Crenshaw comes here demanding to know how I could tell his wife she is dying? What do I say? I don't even have the excuse that I believe in any of the rigmarole I spout. How much longer can I keep all this up? I'm just not sure what I am doing anymore, and I am so tired.*

Chapter Two
Saturday evening, October 11, 1879

"A. J. WELSH, ATTORNEY-AT-LAW, 434 California street—Divorces, insolvency, probate cases, etc.; prompt action and low charges, no charge for advice."—*San Francisco Chronicle, 1879*

The clatter of wooden planks as the train traversed the Mission Creek Bridge alerted Nate Dawson to the fact he was almost within the city limits and the train would reach the Townsend Street depot in just a few minutes. He put away the copy of the *Chronicle* he had been reading in preparation for arrival. After hours of seeing nothing but sun-seared brown hills, he welcomed the glimpses of the narrow, rectangular houses silhouetted in the evening twilight. He was home.

Odd, he'd never thought of San Francisco as home before. Not in the four years he had boarded in town while attending Boys High, nor the last six years he had spent working in the city in his Uncle Frank's law firm. Home had always been his family's ranch, nestled among tall oak trees in the hills due west of Santa Clara. That's where he'd been for over a month, helping with the fall round-up, something he'd done almost every year since his family had moved west when he was fourteen. Even the years when he'd been back east at college and law school, he'd still thought of the ranch as home and longed to be in the saddle gathering up the stock every September. But this year had been different.

This year, he had become increasingly restless, anxious to come back, come home to San Francisco, and he knew the reason was Mrs. Annie Fuller. He wished he had the nerve to go straight to her home tonight, but his Uncle Frank was expecting him. Nate knew there would be, as usual, a hundred and one tasks that needed to be completed immediately, but tomorrow was Sunday, and maybe he would be able to break free and go see her. For a brief instant, he could see Annie's laughing face, the light sprinkle of freckles across her nose, the soft curve of her mouth.

The squeal of brakes emerging through the hissing steam and the simultaneous slowing of the car wrenched Nate's attention back to the train's arrival at the depot. He stood up and pivoted into the aisle, keeping his right hand firmly on the seat back in front of him, waiting for the inevitable jerk forward and back as the train stopped. He then swung down his leather valise, feeling the contents slide to one end. He never brought much with him to the ranch, since he left his comfortable work clothes there, along with all his saddles and tack. Instead, he had brought the bound copy of the new state constitution, all twenty-two articles of it, as well as a number of law journals. He couldn't say he had spent as much time reading as he had hoped. He always forgot how physically exhausting ranch work was, and this year the demands were even greater, because, hard as it was to admit, his father was slowing down. His younger brother, Billy, had been his father's right hand since the age of twelve, and every-one knew that in time he would inherit the ranch. But this fall, Nate could see that something had shifted. Billy, not his father, had been in charge.

Nate opened up the latch on the valise and stuffed the newspaper in, meanwhile thinking about why this had bothered him so. He had never envied Billy's position on the ranch, never wanted to take his place. But taking orders from his father was one thing; taking orders from his younger brother was quite another. It had irritated the heck out of him. Yet his father had seemed fine with the shift.

Nate had even tried to talk to his mother about the situation, but he never seemed to find a time when they were alone together. That was another reason this visit had been a cause of dissatisfaction. Billy's new wife, Violet, had clung to his mother's side the whole visit. She was very obviously in a "delicate" condition, which was embarrassing enough, but he didn't understand why this meant she had to follow his mother around like a shadow, trying to help when it was clear she should be sitting down and resting. She must be carrying twins, to be that huge. *Won't Billy be insufferable then!* Nate thought as he began the slow crawl down the aisle towards the back door of the car.

He stepped down to the platform and hurried through the crowd to snag one of the hansom cabs waiting on Townsend. He was sorely tempted to give the driver Annie's O'Farrell Street address but squashed the impulse and directed the driver to his boarding house on Vallejo instead. Truth be told, he wasn't entirely sure if he would be welcome at her home, even if it weren't this late. Annie was one of the topics he had wanted to discuss with his mother. *If I'd gotten a second alone with her*, he fumed.

He'd naturally told the whole family about the part he'd played this summer in solving the mystery surrounding the death of his client, Matthew Voss, but when he had tried to explain to them about Annie and what she'd done . . . well, that had been a fiasco. Violet had expressed shock, Billy teased him about getting mixed up with a "female detective," and even his mother had frowned. His little sister, Laura, would have understood. But she was up near the Santa Cruz Mountains in her first teaching job, another reason the ranch hadn't felt quite like home. He might have even been able to tell Laura about Annie's work as Madam Sibyl. Laura was a strong champion of women's rights, and she would have sympathized with Annie's decision to use her business skills to support herself. But he couldn't have told his parents or Billy about this. They just wouldn't have understood. He was uncomfortable enough about her work as a clairvoyant, and, if he had his way, she would get out of that business before they got married and his family ever found out.

When they were married—that was the problem. How could he even think about marriage when he could barely support himself on what his Uncle Frank paid him? *He says I'm a partner, but I don't make much more than a clerk!*

His mother had been telling him for years that her brother planned to retire soon, and then Nate's income would increase. But he was nearly thirty, and, even if his income went up, it could take years of saving to be able to afford a home and servants, everything a woman like Annie Fuller deserved. He just knew if he had been able to explain to his mother how important Annie had become to him, what his plans for the future were, she would know how to approach his uncle. But that hadn't happened, and now he was back in San Francisco, in the same limbo he was in when he left a month and a half ago.

Even worse, what if Annie didn't want to see him? Their last meeting hadn't gone at all well. He knew he had been at fault. He'd stopped by, unannounced, and had had to wait while she finished up with one of "Madam Sibyl's" clients. By the time she entered the formal parlor, two of her boarders, the ancient seamstresses Millie and Minnie Moffet, were staunchly entrenched on the settee, sewing on an elaborate pile of lace. Annie and he had had to sit across from each other in the two stiff wing-backed chairs, with no privacy. The evening had been insufferably hot, and Annie had looked so tired, but all he'd done was sulk because they weren't alone. He'd hoped to recapture the precious bond they'd developed during those weeks in August as they worked together, but events had seemed to conspire against them. First, there was the buggy ride he had planned, which was ruined by a freak late-summer storm. Then Annie had canceled because one of her clients had requested a last-minute emergency consulta-tion. And of course he'd had to say something asinine, like, "Casting someone's horoscope couldn't possibly be any kind of emergency."

Then, as if fate was determined to pay him back for demeaning her work, he'd had to cancel their next assignation. Annie had agreed to an evening at the theater with him, but at the last minute his Uncle Frank had ordered him to write up a complicated will that he wanted to review that night. He'd sent word that he wouldn't be able to come, and she had sent a note back that she understood that "of course his work had to come first," but he had no doubt she was being sarcastic.

What he should have done that last time they met was take her in his arms and tell her how much he'd missed her. Hang the old ladies and their lace! What he had done instead was grumble about being kept waiting, complain about how overworked he was, and make snide remarks about Madam Sibyl. Annie's responses, in turn, had gotten more and more terse. If only she had lost her temper, ripped into him the way she had several times when they first met! Then they could have had a glorious fight and cleared the air. Maybe she didn't think he was worth losing her temper over anymore. Maybe she never had cared as much as he did. That was what he feared.

No, he refused to believe that he had misread her—the warmth of the few precious kisses, the way she had burrowed her face into his shoulder, smiled at him. She'd just been angry about how he had acted. Then, to make matters worse, the next day he had gotten the telegram asking him to come a week early to the ranch, and all he had been able to do was send around a short note informing Annie that he would be gone for the next six weeks. He'd every intention of writing a long letter once he had gotten to the ranch, begging her forgiveness for his rude behavior. In fact, he'd written a letter, several to be exact, but never sent one. He couldn't get the tone right. With each passing week, it became harder, until he had finally decided it would be better to ask her forgiveness in person.

But what if she won't see me? Nate thought as the cab pulled up in front of his boarding house. *What if I have ruined everything?*

*****

The girl, wearing a long white nightgown, went to the door to the hallway and listened. She then pulled out the long cord that hung down her chest, revealing a key. She crept over to another door, used the key to unlock it, and began the long climb up the narrow set of stairs. With difficulty, she opened the trap door when she reached the top and emerged into a room, dark, airless, with only one shaft of moonlight that revealed the large armchair. She moved confidently to the chair, picked up the china doll that lay there, which she began to rock. After several minutes passed, she began to sing.

"Hot cross buns, hot cross buns! One ha' penny, two ha' penny, hot cross buns. If you have no daughters, give them to your sons."

She stopped singing and whispered, "Mama, where are you? You need to save me from the bad man, 'cause I'm the baby, and I sleep with the angels."

Chapter Three
Sunday, late afternoon, October 12, 1879

"The last section of the Sutter Street Road, terminating at Central
avenue…has been completed and is in running order."
—*San Francisco Chronicle*, 1879

Sunlight fled before the shadows sliding up the hill to where Annie
Fuller stared down at the avenue of graves. The wind, fresh from the
Pacific, freed a strand of her hair and wove it through the three small
feathers that jutted from her navy straw hat.

"Why, Mrs. Fuller, whatever are you doing here?"

Annie started, turned, and for a moment couldn't place the tall, neatly
dressed, middle-aged brunette standing on the path beside her.

"Excuse me, I'm afraid… Oh, my word, Miss Pinehurst! I didn't…I
mean, how nice to see you!" Annie gathered her scattered wits and smiled,
embarrassed that she hadn't immediately recognized a woman who lived
in the room next to her.

Although Miss Lucy Pinehurst had moved into Annie's boarding
house over a year ago, she remained a bit of a mystery. She had moved
into the O'Farrell Street house because it was so close to Market Street and
the restaurant where she worked. Nevertheless, her job as head cashier and
bookkeeper for Montaigne's Steak House, which billed itself the "Delmonico's of the Pacific Coast," meant Miss Pinehurst left the house a little
before noon, when Annie was usually busy at work as Madam Sibyl, often
returning well after midnight, when Annie had already retired for the night.
Consequently, there were few opportunities for Annie to converse with her.
In their brief encounters in the hallways, Miss Pinehurst had been polite,
but Annie always imagined she left a faint chill of disapproval in her wake.

She was surprised her boarder had decided to approach her this afternoon at Laurel Hill Cemetery. Miss Pinehurst appeared to be almost as surprised as Annie by her behavior.

"I am so sorry, Mrs. Fuller, I shouldn't have disturbed you. It's just I didn't expect to see you here. I suppose you must have family, I just ... I mean, I often come here on Sundays, and I never encountered ..." Miss Pinehurst stopped short and began to back away. "Please excuse me, Mrs. Fuller, I didn't mean to intrude. I will just be on my way."

"Oh, no, there is no need to apologize," Annie said. "My aunt and uncle are buried over at the Masonic Cemetery, so I don't come to Laurel Hill very often. Today I came to visit an old friend." As she pointed down the hill, Annie realized she was still holding the small bouquet of chrysanthemums she had brought with her to put on Matthew's grave. "But, before it grows too late, I need to finish paying my respects." As if to punctuate this comment, the light suddenly dimmed, the sun sinking behind the bank of clouds piling up over the western horizon.

Miss Pinehurst nodded, then thrust out her hand as if to stop Annie, saying, "Mrs. Fuller, I don't mean to keep you, but I was wondering, when you were done, if you would take a walk with me. I have something I would particularly like to speak to you about."

Startled by the intensity in her boarder's voice, Annie paused and then said, "Certainly, Miss Pinehurst, I won't be but a moment. If you would wait for me here."

Taking the other woman's slight nod as a sign of acquiescence, Annie gathered up her skirts and walked quickly down the hill to stand in front of a grave's white marble headstone, whose crisply chiseled message showed little passage of time.

Matthew Voss 1811-1879
Beloved husband, father, brother
"And He has filled him with the spirit of God,
in wisdom, in understanding and in knowledge
and in all manner of workmanship"—Exodus 35:31

For a moment she was swept up in memories of the past summer, when her attempts to find out the truth behind the death of the man buried here had catapulted her into a few hectic weeks of intrigue that had almost cost Annie her own life. As she leaned over to place the bouquet on the grave, she whispered, "Oh, Matthew, I miss you so."

She smiled, remembering the picture Matthew's sister had displayed in her room. Matthew Voss proudly holding the woodworking tools he had used to build a successful furniture business; Miss Nancy holding the large account ledgers that represented her contribution to the company as its bookkeeper.

A bookkeeper, just like Miss Pinehurst, who was probably waiting impatiently for her up at the top of the hill. She gathered her wool shawl more tightly around her shoulders and made her way up the path, surprised again at how little she knew about her boarder, beyond where she worked and that she had a sister and brother-in-law living in town with whom she usually spent Sundays. This was another reason she hadn't gotten to know Miss Pinehurst, since Sunday dinner was the one meal Annie usually ate with all of her boarders. This would be a good chance to further her acquaintance with Miss Pinehurst, and she wondered what her boarder could possibly wish to speak to her about.

When she regained the top of the hill, she smiled and said, "Miss Pinehurst, thank you for waiting. It has been such a lovely afternoon, and I do believe we have at least another hour of daylight."

Having apparently regained her composure, Miss Pinehurst replied, "I should think we have sufficient time. Perhaps we shall miss the press of people who will be trying to catch the five o'clock car to town. I have never seen Laurel Hill quite as crowded as it was today." She then turned and began to walk briskly down a path that led away from the entrance, deeper into the cemetery.

As Annie caught up with her companion, she remarked, "You are quite right. I was obviously not the only person who read in yesterday's *Evening Bulletin* that the Sutter Street line had finished its cable all the way west to Central. I don't know that the investors will be happy with the paper calling it the 'cemetery run,' but it certainly does make it easier to visit Laurel Hill, and the other Lone Mountain cemeteries as well."

As they came out from the trees and looked down at a little clearing, Annie paused to observe the view. She could still make out the bulk of Mt. Tamalpais across the Golden Gate and could see the tip of Angel Island across the entrance to the San Francisco Bay. A faint tang of salt water teased the air. At this height, the wind from the Pacific tossed the tops of the oaks on either side of them, causing small reddish oval acorns to plummet downward, some rolling to land at their feet. Annie leaned over and picked one up, saying, "You mentioned you come to Laurel Hill often. Are your parents buried here?"

"Yes, Mrs. Fuller, both of my parents," Miss Pinehurst replied. "My family came to San Francisco overland in '57, and my mother died just three years later. She had a hard time on the crossing, never really recovered. My father died in 1865. That left my little sister, Sukie, and myself. Sukie was only seven when mother died, so you could say I raised her."

Even younger than I was when Mother died, Annie thought. *Why have I never even considered going back down to Los Angeles to visit Mother's grave since I've been back?* She didn't know if she could even find her mother's grave. And then there was her father, dying up in that small Maine town while on business and John burying him there without her permission. Would it have brought her any peace of mind to see his resting place? Made his death any more real? She realized she just didn't feel any connection to where their bodies were buried. Yet being able to visit Matthew's grave today had been comforting.

Miss Pinehurst interrupted her reverie, saying, "You mentioned you were visiting a friend. I am sorry if this is a recent loss."

"Why, thank you, yes, very recent. I don't know if you heard, but one of my clients, well, one of Madam Sibyl's clients, Mr. Matthew Voss, died this summer. He was a dear friend."

At her mention of Madam Sibyl, Annie felt rather than saw Miss Pinehurst stiffen. She had explained to her, as she felt she had to do with everyone who chose to live in her boarding house, that the small down-stairs parlor was devoted to the business of Madam Sibyl. She had also explained that she, Mrs. John Fuller, was Madam Sibyl, and this was a kind of business alias she used to keep her professional and personal lives separate. She assured her potential boarders that her work was respectable and very discreet. Some of the residents, like the two elderly seamstresses, Minnie and Millie Moffet, really didn't seem to grasp what she was saying but also didn't seem to care. Others, like Mr. Chapman, one of the two clerks who shared the small room at the back of the second floor, seemed to think it was a good joke.

Miss Pinehurst, on the other hand, had made it crystal clear that she found the whole idea distasteful and that only the strong recommendations from the wealthy and socially prominent Mr. and Mrs. Stein had convinced her that residing in Annie's boarding house wouldn't ruin her reputation. Herman and Esther Stein occupied the two-room suite across from Annie, and it had actually been Mr. Stein's suggestion that Annie start her clair-voyant business as Madam Sibyl.

Annie, squashing her inclination to say something in defense of her occupation, returned to the apparently safe subject of families and said, "You mentioned raising your sister; I believe I heard her husband is a clerk in a bank, such a promising occupation. And that she has a little . . ."

Annie gasped as she realized the enormous mistake she had just made. "Oh, Miss Pinehurst, I am so sorry, your little nephew, I had forgot-ten. Mrs. Stein told me he died suddenly this summer. Such a tragedy. I would not have distressed you for the world."

The older woman gave the tiniest of shrugs and stared down at the graves below. In the waning daylight, her normally pale skin looked ghostly white, and Annie could see that she clenched her hands to her breast as if she was in pain.

Heavens above, how could I have forgotten? Annie thought. *And from what Esther said, she simply doted on the boy. Of course that's why she is here, to visit the boy's grave.*

Miss Pinehurst turned abruptly towards her and said, "Mrs. Fuller, do

you believe in spirits? I have looked at the advertisement you have in the
Chronicle, and it doesn't say anything about Spiritualism or mediums, like
most of them. I wondered . . ." She stopped speaking, as if she didn't know
what to say next.

After a long pause, Annie replied stiffly, "You are correct that as
Madam Sibyl I don't claim any ability to communicate with the spirit
world. What I offer people is advice. This advice is actually based on my
experience and skills in the world of business and finance, as well as a
modest understanding of the human condition. Unfortunately, I found I
was taken more seriously if I said I was aided in obtaining that advice
from palmistry or astrology. May I ask why you want to know if I believe
in spirits?"

Miss Pinehurst reached out to Annie, grabbing her arm. "My sister
does. Sukie believes she talks to the spirit of our dear Charlie, as if he
would come to her while she sits in a dark room with a group of complete
strangers. I went with her once. It made me ill. If she is conversing with
anyone, it is the devil himself. Mrs. Fuller, do you think you could help
me? I am at my wit's end. I fear so for her sanity, for her very soul."

Chapter Four
Sunday late afternoon, October 12, 1879

"Prof Cohen, Celebrated astrologer, fortuneteller, clairvoyant, slate writer, etc, gives important information and help; it is not necessary to give age; fee $1. Removed to 425 Kearny"—*San Francisco Chronicle, 1879*

Annie found herself being pulled down a path by Miss Pinehurst, who seemed to be caught up in some sort of frenzy. Abruptly, they stopped at a group of graves. Two headstones, side by side, looked as if they had stood in position for some time. The grave on the left was that of Mr. Charles Pinehurst, with his wife, Susan, resting on his right. The dark marble headstones were elaborately carved with matching weeping willows and hopeful inscriptions about the "pure of heart" getting to see their "Heavenly Father." There were fresh flowers in small vases in front of each, and Annie surmised Miss Pinehurst had already been to visit these graves today.

Two unmarked headstones stood a little in front of the graves of the departed Pinehursts, and Annie realized with a start that these were probably destined for Miss Lucy and her sister. She wondered where Miss Pinehurst's brother-in-law was supposed to spend his eternal life. Then she looked at the headstone that stood right in front of these empty graves, the humped earth and the sharp letters on the stone screaming out that this was a recent interment.

Miss Pinehurst, still clutching her arm, pointed to the headstone and said, "See there, that is what I wish to speak to you about."

The headstone showed a carving of two cherubs surrounded by roses, followed by the simple but heart-rending words, "Charles Lucas Vetch Born November 26, 1872 and Entered into his New Life on June 3, 1879." Puzzled, Annie peered at the inscription below, hard to read in the failing light, that said, "Our dear, innocent son is not dead, but liveth, in the

Perpetual Garden of Summerland."

Miss Pinehurst continued. "Sukie's husband had put up a wonderful headstone, with the Bible passage 'Suffer the little children,' but then Sukie started seeing those awful people. She told Mr. Vetch, her husband, that Charlie had revealed to her that she didn't need to mourn because he had never died but had been *translated*. Whatever that means. And she ordered a new stone put up, with those silly words about Summerland. She hasn't even been back since the stone was put in place. She also stopped visiting our parents' graves, so it is up to me to bring flowers, and every time I do, I am forced to look at . . ." Miss Pinehurst gulped convulsively and then began to weep.

Annie pulled out a handkerchief, handed it to Miss Pinehurst, and, putting her arm around her, urged her to walk on down the path to where some grieving relative had conveniently placed a bench, which faced a tall, black marble mausoleum. Noticing that the two cadaverous angels that flanked the entrance to the vault seemed to be treading on piles of skulls, she had Miss Pinehurst sit so that their backs were to this monument to the macabre.

Speaking softly, while Miss Pinehurst regained her composure, Annie said, "Am I to gather that your sister has been attending some sort of séance and that she is convinced that she is communicating with her dead son?"

Miss Pinehurst nodded, wiping away her tears.

Annie thought for a moment, trying to find the right words. "I can understand why this might be distressing to you, but I don't think it is at all unusual for a grieving mother to look for some solace in Spiritualism. It is my understanding that Spiritualists believe there is no heaven or hell, and I can only imagine for a mother who has lost a child that this is a comforting thought. What I don't understand is why you feel that this is a threat to her sanity and what you think I might do about the situation."

Miss Pinehurst gave a last sniff. "Mrs. Fuller, at first I thought as you do, that this was just a temporary reaction to her loss. Sukie has always been very sensitive, and her husband has been too indulgent. Charlie's death was so sudden; it was devastating for us all. You see, we thought at first he had a summer cold. Sukie had never been good when Charlie got sick or hurt; she would exhaust herself crying. I came every night after work, sat up with him, gave him his medicine, and rocked him. His throat was so sore he couldn't sleep. After three or four days, the rash and fever he had developed began to disappear, and we thought he was getting better. Then on the morning of the fifth day, his heart just stopped." Miss Pinehurst paused, again overcome with emotion.

"Scarlet Fever?" Annie asked, knowing that her own mother's ill health had started with a childhood attack of this dreaded ailment. Only scarlet fever hadn't stopped her mother's heart for another twenty years. *Poor Charlie Vetch, to think of his young life snatched away so early.*

Miss Pinehurst continued haltingly. "Sukie just fell apart. I tried to share with her my conviction that Charlie was with his *Heavenly Father*, that he had eternal life, but Sukie has never had a very strong faith. For weeks she wouldn't leave her bed, wouldn't eat, even threatened to harm herself. Her husband became afraid to leave her alone during the day, but he had to go to work, as I did. Consequently, Mr. Vetch hired a nurse to take care of her, get her to eat, take some air. We were both relieved when we began to see a marked improvement."

Shaking her head, Miss Pinehurst said, "What we didn't know was that Mrs. Hoskins, the nurse, was taking Sukie to attend séances run by this couple, Simon and Arabella Frampton, and that Arabella supposedly had established contact with Charlie. One day, Sukie announced to her husband that she had talked to Charlie and that he said he was in a wonderful place, 'but he missed his mama and papa so.' She went on and on about how she knew it was Charlie because he knew her pet names for him and kept asking after his purple ducky. Finally, she told her husband he could talk to Charlie if he would just come to the next séance."

"Oh dear," Annie said. "And the nurse, Mrs. Hoskins, could she have been the source of information about the pet names and the purple ducky?"

"Of course she was," Miss Pinehurst snapped. "The evil woman had spent weeks with Sukie as she clutched that toy and sobbed out all her favorite endearments. But, see, this is why I thought you could help me. I knew you would understand right away the kinds of tricks people like this would get up to, how they could ensnare a simple woman like my sister.

"I went to a fortuneteller once when I was young and foolish myself, and I saw immediately that he was just feeding my own words back to me. You must have to do this sort of thing as Madam Sibyl. Make someone think you have gotten special information from some supernatural source, when all the time it would just be good common sense."

The heat of anger suffused Annie's face as she reviewed what devastating retort she should make to point out how very wrong and insulting Miss Pinehurst had been, to lump her with people she obviously thought were criminals. However, a small niggling voice intruded, reminding her that what Miss Pinehurst had said contained a kernel of truth.

Miss Pinehurst couldn't know it, but Annie already had some experience with fraudulent mediums, during the time after her husband's death when she had been forced to live with her in-laws. John's maternal aunt, Mrs. Lottie Vanderlin, recently widowed, had been the only one of his relatives who had treated her with kindness, and Annie had found herself watching with growing concern as Lottie made the rounds of local mediums, trying to contact her husband, Frederick. He had been a devout Spiritualist and promised her he would reach out to her from the afterlife.

Since Annie often accompanied the older woman to these séances, she'd seen how skillfully the mediums extracted information from Lottie, which they turned right around and fed back to her through table raps, badly accented Indian Spirit guides, and planchettes swirling around a spirit board.

Annie's response back then was to create the first iteration of Madam Sibyl, figuring that it would be better for Lottie to listen to her advice than continue to squander her inheritance on unscrupulous mediums. Could she fault Miss Pinehurst for wanting to save her own sister from a similar fate? No matter how insulted she might feel by Miss Pinehurst's assumptions, her own experience, including her work as Madam Sibyl, did mean she was better qualified to recognize what tricks the Framptons were employing than most.

Sighing, Annie said, "Miss Pinehurst, I assume from what you have said that both you and your brother-in-law have attended these séances with your sister, and you are convinced that this spirit of your nephew is a fraud."

Taking an indignant snort as a yes, Annie continued. "What I don't quite understand is why you felt you needed to speak to me *now*? You said her health improved, but earlier you mentioned your fears for her sanity."

Miss Pinehurst turned and looked straight into Annie's eyes and said, "I don't know what your beliefs are about the afterlife, and I know that the fact that I believe that Sukie's actions are threatening the possibility of her salvation may not concern you. But let me assure you, Sukie's delusion that she is speaking to her son has become dangerous to her health and her sanity."

"In what ways?" Annie asked.

"Her whole world now revolves around visiting the Framptons. She insists on attending séances twice a week and then meets for private sittings another two afternoons. I think she would go everyday if she could find the money. Mr. Vetch may have a very responsible position at the Gold and Trust Bank, but his salary isn't enough to support this kind of constant drain on their finances.

"When he refused to keep giving her money to attend the séances, she simply spent the household funds, so that within two weeks there was no food in the larder and their servant had quit because she wasn't being paid. Mr. Vetch then stopped giving her money for the household expenses, but he found that she had started to pawn her jewelry and even her clothing, so he was forced to relent."

"Besides the obvious problem of finances, has attending the séances brought her peace of mind?" Annie asked.

"If only that were true, Mrs. Fuller, I might find it in my heart to be able to be reconciled with her behavior. But the complete opposite has occurred. She can't be bothered to eat or sleep, and she paces frantically around the house, oblivious to the complete disarray around her. When either her husband or I try to reason with her, she lashes out at us, saying we are just jealous because Charlie has chosen to speak to her. The next minute she will begin to cry hysterically, saying that Charlie can't understand why we won't visit him and that we are making him so sad. I don't know how much longer she can go on this way. She is the only family I have left, and I can't stand by, knowing she is putting her life and her soul in mortal danger. Please, you must help me."

Annie shivered, haunted by memories of a time when her own losses had caused a similar kind of dangerous derangement. For a moment, she smelled the curdled milk and rotting meat in the servantless kitchen, felt the clammy sheets that entangled her sleepless body, heard the low humming that filled her mouth, as she had worked to suppress the wails of grief that constantly threatened to overwhelm her. Annie shook her head as if to shake the memories away and thought, *I gradually came to my senses, but then I wasn't the target of some unscrupulous mediums playing on my grief. Poor Sukie Vetch.*

Startled by the sound of a flock of black birds swirling up from the grove of oaks, Annie noticed the wisps of fog sliding through the trees. She realized that it was soon going to be hard to see their way to the cemetery entrance. Annie shivered again. She most definitely didn't want to be in this place in the dark with the ghosts of her past so fresh to mind.

Turning to Miss Pinehurst, intending to request that they depart, she was struck by the tired lines etched around the older woman's mouth, the dark shadows under her eyes, and the slump of defeat in her shoulders. She found herself wondering just who was taking care of Lucy Pinehurst, who had lost a child who was clearly as precious to her as if he were her own?

With a sudden sense of conviction, she said to Miss Pinehurst, a woman she didn't know very well and didn't particularly like, "I'm not exactly sure what I can do to free your sister from her delusions, but I give you my word, I will do everything in my power to help you save her."

*****

The girl stood looking at the smudged window and frowned. She looked around the room until she found the basket of old rags, which she sorted carefully through until finding a soft square of flannel. She then went back to the window and began vigorously cleaning off the accumulated dust and spider webs from each pane. When one window was done, she moved to the next, slowly making her way around the room until all four sets of windows were clean of debris. She stood at the last window for a long time, staring out at the setting sun. Suddenly, she noticed the now filthy rag in her hand and dropped it as if it were on fire. Sinking down until she was sitting on the floor, she silently began to sob.

Chapter Five
Monday evening, October 13, 1879

"ROOMS TO LET: 423 O'Farrell--HANDSOMELY FURNISHED sunny
rooms, suite or single, with or without board."
—*San Francisco Chronicle*, 1879

"Annie, my dear, I can hardly believe that Miss Pinehurst, our own
Miss Lucy, asked if you believed in ghosts. Then she wanted you to help
her, to do what?" said Beatrice, a frown narrowing her clear blue eyes as
she dried her hands on the white apron that went round her ample waist.

Annie chuckled affectionately, feeling, as always, the sense of well-
being she got from sitting in her own kitchen, speaking to her dearest
friend. Beatrice O'Rourke had never quite lost the lilt of her birthplace in
County Cork, even though she had arrived in America at age eighteen and
immediately started working for Annie's aunt and uncle as a maid-of-all-
work. She later accompanied them in '51 when they made the long,
dangerous voyage around Cape Horn to get to San Francisco.

Beatrice once told Annie of her decision to come west. "None of the
other girls would go. But I wasn't afraid. Besides, I was that set on finding
Mr. O'Rourke, who'd gone overland to the gold fields the year before. The
fool said he would send for me when 'he made his pile,' but I wasn't
willing to wait. He might've died out here. Plenty did those first years.
Mercy, I might never have known what happened to him. Your aunt, she
was so kind. The whole trip she kept saying he'd be here waiting for me.
Wouldn't you know, second day we were in town I stopped a constable to
ask the way to a dry goods store, and it turned out to be my Peter's older
brother, Andrew. Such a scamp, but bless him, he was the one who convinced Peter to join the police. I still says, no matter what happened, he
was safer as an officer of the law than if he'd stayed in those mine fields."

Annie admired Beatrice's lack of bitterness over the death of her husband ten years ago, when Peter O'Rourke had been killed in a gun battle with a local Barbary Coast gang. Widowed after fifteen years of marriage, she had returned to work for Annie's aunt and uncle as cook and general housekeeper. When Annie came to San Francisco to take possession of the house when her aunt died, Beatrice had taken her under her wing, helping her set up and run the boardinghouse. Though over sixty, Beatrice managed to do all the cooking for nine boarders, supervise the one servant, Kathleen, and be a friend to Annie, all with unfailing good sense and humor.

"So, dearie, are you going to tell me what Miss Lucy wanted with you, or are you going to just sit laughing at me?" Beatrice said as she sat down at the kitchen table, groaning a bit from the hours of being on her feet.

"Oh, Bea, it isn't really a laughing matter," Annie replied. "I know you remember when her nephew, Charlie, died this summer."

"Yes, it happened the first week in June." Beatrice nodded. "Miss Lucy had just come to the kitchen for a cup of coffee when Kathleen brought down the message. She'd been staying nights at her sister's to help nurse the boy, then coming home to change for work. Such a shame, she had just left his bedside when he must've died. She didn't cry out when she read the note. More like turned to stone. It was terrible to see. She surely loved that boy as much as if he were her own."

Looking over at the older woman, who was busy paring apples for tomorrow's fruit compote, Annie knew her friend had a personal reason for understanding how important Charlie had been to Miss Pinehurst. Beatrice and her husband hadn't had any children of their own. However, with four brothers and three sisters between them, Beatrice now had enough nieces and nephews to fill a quarter of the pews in St. Mary's, and she mothered every one of them.

Annie continued, "It appears that, in her grief, Miss Pinehurst's sister started going to a trance medium who claimed to have contacted Charlie," going on to repeat the details Miss Pinehurst had poured out to her the day before.

"Heavens be, who are these Framptons?" asked Beatrice, scowling as if the name referred to some dockside gang.

"Simon and Arabella Frampton are a married couple who are originally from England. They arrived in San Francisco last April and have taken up permanent residence here. They seem to have been quite successful since, like Madam Sibyl, they don't take walk-in business. All day today, between clients, I have been looking through back newspaper issues and my clippings. The *Chronicle* did a long article on them in May, part of a series one of their reporters wrote on Spiritualism in San Francisco. I'd remembered reading the series because he'd not been very complimentary about clairvoyants and fortunetellers. Thank goodness he didn't mention Madam Sibyl. The Framptons, on the other hand, came off pretty favorably in the story he did on them. The reporter, Anthony Pierce, wrote that Simon Frampton was a 'world-renowned mesmerist' and his 'lovely wife, Arabella,' was an 'unusually skilled test medium.'"

"What in the world does that mean? She tests what?" Beatrice asked Annie.

Annie laughed. "A person tests the medium, not the other way round. A test medium is supposed to be able to give answers to questions that only the departed could know, proving they are indeed in communication with the spirit world."

She continued in a more serious tone. "From what Miss Pinehurst told me, this is how the Framptons convinced Sukie Vetch that Arabella was communicating with her son, since the spirit knew the pet names she had used for her Charlie, as well as his favorite toy."

Beatrice put down her paring knife and tilted her head. "Gracious me. No wonder the poor dear believed them."

"Now, it isn't as strange as you might think," Annie said. "The nurse who brought Sukie to the Framptons was probably working with them, getting a small 'gift' for every new client she brought to them. She could have given the Framptons all sorts of information about Charlie, which would convince Sukie that she was really communicating with her son."

"That's terrible! The nurse, you say? I hope you told Miss Lucy to have her brother-in-law fire that wicked woman this instant! Now I understand why Miss Lucy told you about all this. How clever of her to realize you would know what to do. They need to get rid of the nurse. But first they need to get her to admit to the shenanigans she has been up to, threaten to tell the police. I can tell you, they don't take kindly to this sort of swindle," Beatrice said, taking up her knife again and slicing each quarter of an apple with ferocious intensity.

"I wish it were that simple. Mr. Vetch did fire Mrs. Hoskins as soon as he realized the role she had played, but that was over two months ago, and his wife refuses even to consider that the Framptons are frauds. Miss Pinehurst said they have tried everything."

Annie stopped speaking, interrupted by the bell that signaled that there was someone at the front door. She looked over at the clock on the wall and said, "It's past eight. Who could that be at this hour? Mr. Harvey probably forgot his key again. Isn't this about the time he comes home? Well, Kathleen will get it."

Beatrice stood up and took the apple parings over to dump them in the waste-bucket, saying over her shoulder, "If it is Mr. Harvey, Kathleen will give him what for. Last Monday he forgot his key, and she was elbow deep in soapy water when he rang the bell. Poor man, I swear he works the longest hours. I heard him go out before seven this morning. He can't be making all that much clerking in a dry goods store."

Annie nodded. "He told me he hopes that old Mr. Johnson will eventually take him in as partner. Then he could afford to bring his wife and children down to San Francisco to live with him. I understand his wife suffers from some sort of lung problem, and she and the two boys live with her folks in Sacramento. Such a shame. Mr. Harvey must miss those two boys terribly." And that melancholy thought brought Annie back to Miss Pinehurst and her sister and brother-in-law and how much they all must be missing Charlie.

She sighed and said, "Beatrice, I wish I knew for sure I could help Miss Pinehurst."

"But Annie, dear, I still don't understand what more she figures you can do. You'll not be telling me she thinks that you would have any truck with one of those charlatans? 'A penny to shake hands with your sainted mother.' Such foolishness."

"Oh, Bea! That is exactly what Miss Pinehurst thinks. She feels my experience as Madam Sibyl makes me particularly suited to prove to her sister that the Framptons are frauds. Miss Pinehurst seems to believe in the old adage that 'It takes a thief to catch a thief.'"

"Well, I never! It is certainly a shame if her sister's being made a fool of, but that don't mean Miss Pinehurst has the right to go insulting you."

Annie smiled at the picture of outrage Beatrice made, her arms all akimbo, her blue eyes snapping. Then Kathleen, Annie's maid-of-all-work, burst into the kitchen, dancing in excitement.

She sketched a brief curtsy, shoved back some of her dark brown curls, which had escaped from her cap during her precipitous rush down the stairs, and said, "Ma'am, you'll never guess who's come to visit. I put him in the front parlor, thinking you would want some privacy. Mrs. Fuller, it's Mr. Dawson come to call!"

*****

Damn, she is more beautiful than I remembered, Nate thought, as Annie entered the parlor. The whole time he'd been away he'd tried to picture the exact shade of brown of her eyes, and now he remembered that they changed, depending on her mood. In the lamplight, against her skin, which was as pale as old ivory, her eyes looked coal black and angry.

Bowing, Nate took a deep breath and said, "Mrs. Fuller, Annie, I am so sorry to call this late. I arrived back in town night before last, and I hoped to come yesterday, but my Uncle Frank has kept me completely tied up with business . . . never mind my excuses, I just hope you don't mind the late hour."

Annie gave him a chilly smile and said, "Mr. Dawson, please don't apologize. If your uncle needed your expert legal advice, I have no doubt it was over a serious matter."

Nate's stomach clenched. She clearly hadn't forgiven him for suggesting his work was more important than hers. He fell back on the polite formula of strangers, saying, "I hope you have been in good health, and Mrs. O'Rourke? I almost came to your place right from the train station on Saturday, thinking about those wonderful oat cookies she made for me last time I visited."

"Mrs. O'Rourke is well, although I am afraid that she is finding the long hours standing in the kitchen more and more difficult. She won't admit it, but I can see she hurts at the end of the day. I wouldn't be surprised if she is downstairs right now, making up a batch of those cookies for you," Annie said in a slight tone of disgust. "*She* has missed having you to cook for."

"And Miss Kathleen, is she still being courted by both the butcher's boy and Patrick McGee?" asked Nate, feeling as if he were leaping from one conversational stone to another, hoping not to fall.

"Oh, yes, although I would say that the butcher's boy is a very distant second at this point. I think she strings him along just to make Mr. McGee jealous. Shall we sit by the fire? The night has grown rather chilly," Annie remarked, nodding to the two chairs next to the fireplace.

"If you wish," Nate replied, relieved at this sign that she expected their conversation to be of some duration. After having sat down, he searched for something else neutral to say. Finally returning to that old standby, the weather, he said, "Such a change from yesterday, when we were having a touch of Indian summer. My uncle tells me that the fall has been unusually mild."

"Yes, yesterday I took the new Sutter Street line out to Laurel Hill, to visit Matthew's grave, and the grounds were awash with people picnicking." Annie looked up at him and said, "But then you haven't been in town, have you? So how was the weather down the peninsula? And your parents have been well, I hope? They seem to have kept you very busy this fall."

Nate knew it was now or never if he hoped to explain his failure to write.

He leaned forward. "Please, Annie. I know I should have written. And yes, I was busy, but that is no excuse. You have every right to be angry with me. I just felt like such a fool after the last time I saw you, I . . . nothing I wrote down seemed adequate."

"Nate Dawson, don't be ridiculous. You are a lawyer. You make your living communicating. Don't tell me you couldn't write and at least tell me how you were doing?" Annie said, glaring at him.

"That's just it. I didn't feel I could write to you about the weather, or the number of new calves; I had to try to explain why I acted so childishly that last night. But everything sounded like a legal brief."

"Well, you *were* behaving like a child."

"I know. It was unfair of me to be angry with you because you were working, after I had had to cancel because of work myself. I was angry with my uncle for ruining our plans earlier in the week and disappointed, so I took it out on you."

There was a pause, and Nate looked at Annie, hoping to see some sign of softening. She was staring down at her hands, frowning.

She glanced up at him and said, "And Miss Millie and Minnie Moffet! You were so rude to those dear souls."

Nate, frustrated, blurted out, "Hang the Misses Moffet; I was rude to you, and for that I apologize." He pressed his lips together and looked away, upset that he had let Annie goad him into losing his temper.

There was a very long silence, and then he heard Annie say, "My goodness, Mr. Dawson. Your language, sir. I am *shocked!*"

Startled at this display of outraged femininity, he looked up and caught sight of dimples peeping out from either side of her mouth, as Annie appeared to be trying, unsuccessfully, to stifle her laughter. In that moment, the iron band that had been constricting Nate's heart simply vanished.

Chapter Six
Wednesday afternoon, October 15, 1879

"Spiritualism—Mrs. Eggert Aiken, trance and test medium, 313 Geary Street, Sittings daily from 9A.M. to 9 P.M. Séances Sunday, Tuesday, Friday at 8 P.M."—*San Francisco Chronicle*, 1879

"Ma'am, I'm terribly glad you asked me to come with you to see these Framptons. I can't but think that, with such shady characters, having a respectable maid with you will make sure they mind their manners."

Annie smiled down at her maid, Kathleen Hennessey, who walked beside her. The young woman was nearly eighteen but so petite you could mistake her for a child. Annie knew those looks were deceptive. In fact, from what she knew of her history, Kathleen had never had the luxury of being a child, and the slight frame contained a tough, tireless dynamo who kept Annie's home spotless and her boarders very satisfied.

The two of them had taken a Central Rail horse car, getting on at Taylor, just a half a block from the boarding house on O'Farrell Street. The car crossed Market and went down Sixth. They got off at Harrison, the street where Simon and Arabella Frampton lived. She could understand why the couple might have chosen to live in the Rincon Hill district, which was now a far cry from the fashionable district it once was before the Second Street cut had decimated the neighborhood and sent all the nabobs north to the heights. Some of the streets still clung to their old glory, and it was well serviced by both the Central line they were on and the South Park line that went down Third, making it easy for clients from practically anywhere in the city to get to them.

Kathleen said, "Ma'am, while I'm glad to accompany you, I'm just not sure what you expect of me."

"What I am hoping is that someone in the household will try to pump you for information while I am having my interview with Simon

Frampton, who seems to be the business manager of the operation. What I want you to do, if that happens, is make it clear I have money, that I am gullible, and that some of my boarders might be good pigeons for the plucking as well."

"Oh, ma'am, to be sure they won't have any trouble believing you're a woman of wealth, your new navy polonaise is that elegant. Miss Millie and Miss Minnie did a fine job. But what if they ask me personal information, I dunno, maybe about your past? What should I say?" said Kathleen, tilting her head to the side.

"You can tell them I'm a widow, that you believe my mother died when I was young and that my father also passed away fairly recently. That's no more than I will be telling them myself. But remember, if you get a chance, I want you to hint that I had a child who died young. All the other information is true, of course, and I suspect that Simon Frampton and his wife Arabella have already spent the day finding out as much as they can about me and my father, Edward Stewart. My father's reputation in this town is still pretty well known, and I made sure to mention his name in the letter I wrote asking for an appointment. However, it is with this fictional dead child I hope to trap them. If I can get them to produce the spirit of a child when none existed, maybe I can use that to convince Miss Pinehurst's sister that they are frauds."

"Yes," Kathleen nodded earnestly. "I will try to tell someone you had a little boy that died, just like Miss Lucy's nephew."

Annie thought about Kathleen's questions and hoped that she was not depending too much on the young woman. She was nervous enough about her own coming interview with Simon Frampton. She had written a fairly long letter, begging him to accommodate her attendance at his Friday night séance. She needed to avoid attending the same evenings as Sukie Vetch, who attended both Tuesday and Thursday evening séances, since she might realize that Mrs. Fuller and her sister's boardinghouse owner were one and the same. Annie currently only had one regular client scheduled for Friday nights, at six, so she wouldn't have difficulty attending the evening "circle," as Frampton called it, at eight.

Simon Frampton had written back immediately saying that there was an opening Friday but that he would need to meet with her Wednesday afternoon to see if her "essence" would be compatible with those of the other members of the circle. According to the newspaper article she had read, Simon and Arabella Frampton hadn't arrived in the States until 1876, three years after her husband John had wiped out her fortune and killed himself. Her father-in-law had been pretty successful in keeping that information out of the press, so she was hoping they wouldn't suspect she wasn't a well-to-do heiress, prime for the plucking.

In any case, Annie felt sure her "essence" would be found very much acceptable once she dropped the name of her "good friends the Steins," who were certainly wealthy enough to impress someone who was looking for a new group of people to fleece. She had said in her letter that she hoped to contact her parents, which seemed safe enough. However, at the interview she planned on playing up her status as both an orphan and grieving widow. *First time John has actually been of use to me,* she thought with some surprise.

Annie calculated that two dead parents and a dead husband should give the Framptons enough to work with. She hoped they wouldn't feel the need to investigate her further. The last thing she wanted was to have them sniffing around her neighbors or boarders for information, on the off chance that they would discover that Annie Fuller and Madam Sibyl were the same person.

The late afternoon sun, which was dipping down towards the Twin Peaks, felt good on her back as she and Kathleen made their way east down Harrison. The south side of the street was a hodgepodge of small, well-maintained businesses, offering a miscellany of services. In this one block you could get your shoes shod, your watch repaired, your chairs caned, your teeth removed, and your thirst quenched. Across the street, a wall of tall hedges obscured all but the top floors of what were clearly a series of stately mansions left over from Rincon Hill's heyday.

Coming to Fifth Street, Annie noticed a small puddle next to the curb, left over from yesterday's shower, and she raised her skirts to nimbly skip over it, uttering, "Be careful," to Kathleen, who grinned and jumped over it as well.

"That would have been a shame, ma'am," Kathleen laughed.

"I don't know if Miss Millie would have forgiven me if I had splashed mud on this new dress the first time I wore it. She worked so hard getting the flounce at the bottom right. I wish fashion permitted day dresses to be a little shorter. It's one thing to be able to sweep the floor with a long train if you are going to a ball, but city streets are another thing completely."

"Seems to me I remember that you were quite happy with short skirts at St Jo's Ball when you were dancing with Mr. Nate Dawson," Kathleen teased.

"Now, Kathleen, you promised not to bring him up. And if I remember, Mr. Dawson did not at all approve of the length of my skirt that night."

Annie looked over and saw Kathleen biting her lower lip and continued, "That's right, not a word. I know you and Mrs. O'Rourke don't think I should have sent him off so quickly Monday evening. But really, the nerve of the man! He acted like a rude schoolboy the last time I saw him, then ran off down the peninsula. Not a word for nearly two months and then he drops in, unannounced!"

"But ma'am, he was visiting his parents," Kathleen blurted out and then put her hand over her mouth.

"Whose ranch is in Santa Clara County, not Timbuktu. He could have written! He could have even taken the train back to the city and visited for a day if he wanted to see me badly enough. No. He should be happy I agreed to see him at all."

Monday night, when Kathleen had told her Nate was in the front parlor, all she had been able to think of was the last time they had met, in that very parlor, and how angry she had been then. She should have been angry Monday as well, but, to her surprise, her dominant emotion had been relief, and she'd been forced to admit how afraid she'd been that she would never see him again.

When she'd entered the parlor and saw him standing there, his long overcoat accentuating his height, his deeply tanned skin, hawk nose and prominent cheekbones lending him a slightly dangerous quality, and his warm brown eyes pleading with her for forgiveness, she'd had to work hard not to run into his arms. But it seemed wrong not to make it clear to him that his behavior had hurt her. So, instead, she'd pretended to be angry and gotten no little satisfaction from watching his efforts at an apology.

Then he'd made her laugh, and she knew she had better end his visit soon before she lost any of the high ground she had obtained. Consequently, she told him briefly about Miss Pinehurst's request for help, asked if he could look into the Framptons on her behalf, pled tiredness, which was true, and then requested that they meet again on Saturday. She did hope he could help her with her investigations, but she also wanted more time to consider exactly how she felt about resuming her friendship with him. And she had refused to discuss those feelings with either Beatrice or Kathleen, who she knew would argue on his behalf.

Looking over at Kathleen, whose lips were resolutely pressed together, she relented and said, "You know, I was hoping to wear this outfit when Mr. Dawson and I meet on Saturday, so it is doubly important to keep it clean. I hope that he will have had a chance to look into the Framptons. If he comes up with useful information, I may just forgive him."

Kathleen laughed.

"Oh, my stars," Annie exclaimed as they crossed Fifth Street. "What a difference a block makes!"

On this stretch of Harrison, the small businesses had a decidedly melancholy air. Peeling paint, grimy windows, and boarded up doors provided a definite contrast to the prosperity in evidence the block before. When they had reached nearly the middle of the block, trying to find an address that wasn't obscured, Kathleen stopped and pointed across the street.

"Ma'am, you said the Framptons lived at 525 Harrison, didn't you? It must be that large place in the center of the block across from us. It's ever so fine! I didn't think they would have such a grand place."

Kathleen was pointing at a large dark brown house, which was indeed an imposing edifice. This classic Italianate, with the usual flat roof supported by thick brackets, was topped by a short squat cupola, whose arched double windows gave the odd impression of eyes peeking out at the top of the house. The front doorway was framed on each side with narrow double windows, a pattern repeated in the three windows on the second story, and each window had buff-colored shutters that matched the color of the brackets and the cornices along all the edges of the house. Unlike her own home that sat cheek by jowl with its neighbors, this house sat gracefully in the middle of a large lot, set a bit back from the street, a carriage drive on the left and a garden on the right.

My, the Framptons must be doing quite well to be able to afford such a house, Annie thought to herself. *Such a shame that this prosperity has been built on the pain and delusion of men and women like Sukie Vetch!*

The brown and buff paint on the Framptons' house looked fresh, in stark contrast to the paint on the rest of the houses on the block. The house to its left, although equal in size, had stripes of what must have been its original pale yellow paint alternating with the gray weathered boards, reminding her of a butterscotch tabby cat she had when she was a child. The slightly askew shutters, the missing shingles on the mansard roof, and the padlock and chain around a rusting front gate advertised this as an abandoned house. The house to the right of the Framptons' was in better repair, and the smoke rising from its chimney testified to occupancy, but its landscaping had run amok. The house was covered with half-dead vines, tall weeds were cheerfully destroying the front walkway, and a row of shaggy firs menaced the fence between this house and the Framptons' residence.

Annie, checking to see that there wasn't a wagon or carriage coming down the street, grabbed Kathleen's gloved hand and pulled her across Harrison to stand at the foot of a short flight of steps that led to a gate in the low wrought iron fence. She glanced over and saw Kathleen pat at the small straw hat sitting at a jaunty angle amidst her curls and then square her shoulders under the tight bodice of her neat herringbone wool dress, as if going into battle.

"Kathleen, you look the perfect lady's maid. You will puff up my consequence with the Framptons splendidly. Is the hat new? It is really quite fetching."

"Thank you, ma'am. I bought it with last month's wages." Kathleen smiled up at her and said, "Let's go in before I lose my nerve."

As Annie pushed through the gate and walked toward the small porch at the entrance to the house, she noticed that on closer examination the front of the house revealed a slightly different picture of the Framptons' prosperity. She could see the glossy brown paint had been hastily applied over the previous un-sanded layers, producing the texture of a scabrous reptile that would most likely begin to peel away with the first storm of winter. To her right, a break in the neatly trimmed hedge dividing the front yard from the side yard provided a glimpse into a garden badly gone to seed, a tangle of weeds and vines that were choking whatever flower beds had existed previously. Even the front door, while a lovely polished oak glowing in the afternoon sun, was marred by a series of long raw scratches above the brass door handle. Unbidden, she saw the image of a decaying corpse, cosmetically enlivened by the embalmer's arts. Annie shivered as she raised her hand to pull on the doorbell.

Chapter Seven

"Mrs. Crindle, Physical and Test Medium, 681 Mission and Third. Correct information on stocks. Circles Friday, Sunday, Tuesday, 50c. Sittings, $1."
—*San Francisco Chronicle*, 1879

"Mrs. Fuller, so pleased to make your acquaintance. Do have a seat. May Albert pour you some tea, or perhaps some sherry, before he goes?"

Annie permitted Simon Frampton only a brief second to shake her hand before slipping free and turning towards the chair he had pointed out, saying, "No thank you, Mr. Frampton, that will not be necessary."

Albert, an imposingly broad-shouldered, middle-aged man dressed in the formal livery of an upper-class butler, bowed slightly to her and pulled the chair back so she could sit down. After nodding her thanks, Annie sat, placing her small beaded purse in her lap before looking up at Mr. Frampton, who stood smiling down at her from the other side of an imposing mahogany desk.

Simon Frampton was a surprise. As had been Albert. When Annie finished ringing the front doorbell, the last person she expected to greet her was a formal butler. She found herself wondering if they had brought Albert over from England with them and, if so, if he had any other special duties beyond that of butler. And who calls the butler by their first name?

Mr. Frampton, like Albert, revealed his origins in his British accent, but what surprised Annie was how his voice and demeanor quietly asserted that he was an upper-class English gentleman. She realized she had expected Simon Frampton to represent one or the other of the two kinds of Spiritualist impresarios she had encountered in Boston. There were the businessmen, whose waistcoats were always a little too flashy and a little too tight since shopping the afterlife clearly had provided the cash for sartorial and gastronomical over-indulgence. Then there were the purported ministers or professors, who seemed determined to prove their ready access to a "higher plane" through the emaciated nature of their physique and the seediness of their apparel.

Simon Frampton was entirely different. He was only of moderate height, and he was slim, yet conveyed an impression of strength. He wore a conservative but well-tailored black frock coat, with matching waistcoat and trousers, blindingly white starched collar and cuffs with heavy gold studs. The tasteful navy and burgundy paisley of his silk cravat offered the only hint of color.

There was a sprinkle of gray at his temples, yet his neatly trimmed mustache and beard were quite as black and glossy as the rest of the full head of hair that framed regular features. In fact, on the surface, there was nothing remarkable about Simon Frampton, except the cultured tone of his voice and the intensity of his gaze.

Annie held that gaze and then looked down again at her lap, her heart pounding. As Madam Sibyl, she made a living by her ability to judge men. Her disastrous marriage had taught her the danger of resting that judgment on what a man wore or what he said. She had learned to dig deeper, gleaning information about the true nature of a person from the tilt of the head, the nervous tap of a finger, the odd habits of phrase, and the slight shift of the eyes. What she had never before encountered was a stare that conveyed such assurance and power. For a split second, she had felt a physical pull so strong that she wasn't sure she hadn't actually leaned forward toward the man.

"Dear Mrs. Fuller, don't be nervous," Frampton said, sitting down at the desk. "This interview will be completely painless, I assure you. It is really for your benefit. The spirits are such sensitive creatures that they will not tolerate any sort of disharmony. Therefore, it is of the utmost importance that each circle be composed of like-minded souls."

Annie's heart rate slowed. *Good, he has misjudged my reaction as shyness. Of course that is how I should play this role, timid, easily flustered.*

"Oh, Mr. Frampton," Annie glanced up and back down again, letting her voice catch slightly on the first word, "I am afraid I am feeling very unsettled. I'm not even sure why I wrote you. I happened to see your advertisement. Normally I never look at such things, but for some reason it called out to me. I felt compelled to write, as if my dear departed father were whispering in my ear."

Annie took another artificially short breath and looked up at Frampton, who continued to smile at her encouragingly. "Do you think that is possible? I have been so lost since his death. There was my husband. But, you see, John never understood the bond that I had with my father, and then he died too." Annie paused, giving a small sigh.

"Mrs. Fuller, you must believe that the bonds we have on earth are not lightly broken, even by death itself. Do let me get you some sherry, and we will have a comfortable chat."

As Frampton got up from behind the desk and went over to the sideboard, Annie took advantage of his turned back to glance around. When the butler, Albert, had ushered her into the library, her first impression had been polished wood gleaming in soft lamplight. Now she also saw that a set of dark brown velvet curtains covered the windows, and all the rest of the walls were filled with floor to ceiling bookshelves. A striking oriental carpet of vibrant greens and browns covered almost the entire floor, and Annie could feel its soft deep pile under her feet.

I wonder if they brought the carpet with them from England as well? Annie had an absurd image of Albert walking off a ship's gangplank, the rolled carpet on his shoulder. *I can't imagine it came with the house. It certainly fits with the overall impression of wealth and good breeding that Mr. Frampton is cultivating.*

Since Annie had been careful to cultivate a similar image for the parlor in which Madam Sibyl met her clients, she fully appreciated Frampton's motives. She felt sure that a young woman like Sukie Vetch would have been suitably impressed.

Frampton placed the sherry, in a delicate cut-glass goblet, in Annie's hand, pulled a chair over, and sat across from her, their knees practically touching, saying, "Mrs. Fuller, you believe that it was your father, Mr. Edward Stewart, who guided you to us?"

Annie took a small sip of the sherry, sending a small apology to Miss Hamilton, her English Literature teacher under whose tutelage she had taken the "temperance pledge" at the age of sixteen. She then put down the glass on the small table Frampton had placed at her side, saying, "Yes, I feel quite sure it was he. However, I am unclear why he should want to communicate with me now. He has been gone for over six years."

"If all goes as we hope, he will be able to tell you himself," said Frampton, leaning over to take Annie's hand, giving it a warm squeeze. "Now, why don't you tell me a little bit about your father. Remember, I only want to determine if the Friday circle will be right for you. I find that a person's memories of the departed reveal a great deal about whether they will feel comfortable in the presence of the other spirits attending a particular circle."

Annie let Frampton continue to caress her hand, glad that she had decided to keep her gloves on for this meeting. Then she pulled away and opened her purse to take out a handkerchief, which she used to dab at imaginary tears as she began to talk about her father.

"Oh, my, I don't know. He was a very serious man, always reading the paper and rushing off to business meetings when I was little. Then my mother became ill, and we moved to Los Angeles. Well, a ranch outside of Los Angeles. We had been living here in San Francisco before that. Those years on the ranch were wonderful. Father took me riding. Percy was my horse's name, a bay. I had my own saddle, and Father even let me go on roundup in the fall. Once there was a stampede; I was very frightened. But the little calves were ever so cunning. Mother would be quite cross when I got back, said I was turning into a hoyden. She was a schoolteacher before she married Father, so she taught me my sums. I was good at math, not so good at spelling. Then she died."

Annie let her prattle stop at this point, again using her handkerchief to good effect. *That should give him enough information to work on*, she thought.

"I am so sorry, Mrs. Fuller. How old were you when your mother passed?"

"Twelve. I don't remember much about it; I was here visiting my Aunt Agatha and Uncle Timothy when she died." Annie paused, then pushed away that painful memory and continued to feed Frampton information, most of which he could easily verify if he had any sources among the San Francisco businessmen who knew her father. She hoped to keep him from feeling the need to dig any deeper in her past or present.

"Father took me back east after my mother died. On a large ship, all the way round Cape Horn. We moved to New York City and lived in this ever so grand townhouse. But I didn't get to see so much of him any more. I attended a very exclusive female academy. I hadn't had any girls to play with on the ranch, and now I had lots. There were classes, and debate society, and on Saturdays there were piano lessons, and in the afternoon, Cotillion."

She thought about how in reality that first year she had hated every moment she was at school. She missed her mother, and the girls treated her like some stupid country bumpkin, until she showed them up at exam time. Then they were even meaner. And every day she couldn't wait until after supper when it was just her father and herself, talking about his day, going through the business section of the paper, discussing what investments she thought he should make.

"And so, Mrs. Fuller, did you meet your former husband at one of those Cotillions? I suspect you turned heads, even at an early age."

Annie squirmed internally at the arch tone Frampton had decided to take with timid little Mrs. Fuller, but she tilted her head down to the side as if embarrassed and tittered. She then said, "Oh, Mr. Frampton. The truth is I didn't meet Mr. Fuller until after I had finished school, but once we met, it was just a whirlwind courtship. We were married in four months, and then we went to Europe on a lovely honeymoon. We traveled with John's parents. Father couldn't come, but he wrote to me every day I was away. I really didn't spend much time with him after I married, and he died just two years later. And then John died within the year, a terrible accident. Thank goodness I had my little . . . no, I don't want to talk about that. It is my father you asked about."

Annie paused and then gave Frampton what she hoped he would interpret as a brave smile. "You see, don't you, what a wonderful man my father was, how close we were. I can't believe that he would contact me unless it was important. Do you think I will be able to join the circle this Friday? I am so anxious to hear from him. My good friends, Mr. and Mrs. Herman Stein, thought that he might have something to tell me about my business investments. I may have been good at math, but I am ever so confused about bonds and assets and such."

Frampton again leaned forward and took one of Annie's hands, speaking so softly that she was forced to lean towards him to hear. "Mrs. Fuller, I cannot imagine a better presence to add to Friday's meeting. We have such a distinguished group. There is Judge Babcock, and Mr. Ruckner, he is a partner of the San Francisco Gold and Trust Bank, and I think you will find Mrs. Mott, a lovely motherly woman, to be such a comfort. And Mrs. William Larkson, perhaps you know her? No? Well, her husband is the owner of Larkson's Woolen Mills. Perhaps your friends the Steins know him?"

"Oh, my, Mr. Frampton. A judge and a banker, you say? That is splendid news. I was afraid that, if the people who attended were of the common sort, Father might be angry. I mean, you read in the papers about some of the people who get involved in fortunetelling and such, how gullible some of the more uneducated persons can be, and I . . ."

Annie stopped, irritated with herself for getting too carried away. What possessed her to bring up fortunetellers? If he connected her with Madam Sibyl, it could certainly ruin everything. But she was glad to have been given a little information about some of the other circle members. She must remember the names, Judge Babcock, and the banker was Ruckner. Perhaps Herman Stein would know him, and it was quite possible he would also know Mrs. Larkson's husband. She hadn't yet told either him or his wife, Esther, about her plan to help out Miss Pinehurst, but she was sure they would help out in any way they could.

Annie realized that she had missed the beginning of what Simon Frampton had been saying and refocused her attention, refraining from pulling away from him as he continued to clasp her hands in his own.

" . . . and so that is why I insist on these little interviews with those who profess to seek contact with the other side. I have to protect my dear wife, Arabella. Mrs. Frampton is, as you might imagine, very sensitive. She can't always control which spirits choose to communicate through her, but it helps if I can limit her contact to people that I believe are pure-minded and of a high sensibility. These sessions are a terrible strain. I sometimes fear for my wife's health."

"Oh, Mr. Frampton, then you yourself are not the one who communicates with the spirit world. I had thought . . ."

"No, Mrs. Fuller, I am not so blessed, or cursed as the matter may be. It is my responsibility, nay, my good fortune, to be able to assist Arabella in her work. Providentially, I have a small talent for discovering and fostering the abilities of those whom the spirits have chosen. For instance, there is a young girl, Evie May, whom my wife and I have taken under our wings. Extraordinarily talented for a child so young. Completely uneducated, but the wisdom that flows forth from her when the spirits speak through her is remarkable."

Annie interrupted, saying, "A child? What was her name again? Will I meet her on Friday?"

"Her name is Evie May. She is such a sweet soul, but it can be dangerous for one newly awakened to their gifts to be exposed to the throngs of the departed that sometimes gather at a circle. This is the reason I ask that if a spirit reaches out to someone through Evie May, that a private session be conducted in the cabinet I have had constructed for that purpose. The privacy this provides gives some protection to Evie May. However, I cannot predict who will be called into the cabinet."

The sincere enthusiasm in Frampton's voice as he spoke about this protégé startled Annie. Could this Evie May be the source of Sukie's belief she had contacted Charlie? How much easier it would be to believe that you were speaking to your dead son if you heard his words spoken through the voice of another child. Annie knew she must do everything possible to be invited to speak to Evie May in the mysterious cabinet.

Chapter Eight

"Mrs. Hubbard, Medium, 938 Mission Street. Sittings daily."
—*San Francisco Chronicle, 1879*

As the library door closed behind Mrs. Fuller, Kathleen took a deep breath and began to look around. She didn't want to move from the spot just inside the front door that the butler had pointed out to her, because she was sure he would be out again soon. Two of the houses she worked in when she first went out to service had butlers, and she had learned the hard way not to do anything that might get their backs up. Although this man struck her as a mighty odd choice for a butler. Wore the right getup, all black and formal, but he looked more like a prizefighter than a butler. And bald as a billiard ball! Maybe the English had different standards for butlers.

The house was the biggest she'd ever been in before; the hallway alone was the size of most of the rooms in Mrs. Fuller's place. Carved wainscoting went halfway up the walls, topped by fancy green and white striped wallpaper. Craning her neck upwards, Kathleen could see that even the ceiling was carved wood. *However do they keep that ceiling clean?* The door opened, and the butler came out and shut the door quietly behind him, turning to scowl at Kathleen, who felt guilty even though she hadn't done a thing.

"You, there. Sit yourself down. Your mistress will be awhile."

Ignoring her murmured, "Yes, sir," the butler moved silently down the hallway, disappearing through a door at the end that probably led to the kitchen and the butler's pantry.

He certainly wasn't interested in dragging any information out of me about Mrs. Fuller, Kathleen thought. *Maybe the mistress was wrong, and they don't care about the likes of me.* If this was true, at least she could snoop around a little while she waited. She was so proud of the faith Mrs.

Fuller had in her; she didn't want to disappoint. She and Mrs. O'Rourke's nephew, Patrick McGee, had helped Mrs. Fuller out a little this summer when she was looking into the death of Mr. Voss, but this was different. You could say she was Mrs. Fuller's assistant in investigating the Framptons. Like some sort of Pinkerton detective you read about in the newspapers!

Looking down to check there wasn't any dirt on her shoes that might give her away if she left her chair, Kathleen noticed that the black and white patterned floor was real marble, not the linoleum or printed oilcloth she had encountered before. *I sure wouldn't want to clean that floor every day.* On her left she saw the closed library door and a small settee, and a little way down the hall on that side was another doorway, probably to the dining room, its pocket doors closed. Across the hall from where she was sitting was an imposing wood hallstand, then the doorway to what she supposed was the front parlor, and the stairway. The hallstand itself had a mirror that must have been seven feet tall, surrounded by carved ornate curlicues that ran up the sides, topped by some sort of snarling cat, and resting on a shelf made of the same black marble as the hallway floor. *Whew, that must have cost a pretty penny. Telling people you can talk to their dead relatives must pay real handsome.*

There were a couple of umbrellas and a frilly blue parasol in the umbrella stands on either side of the marble shelf, and the wrap Mrs. Fuller had been wearing was one of two outer garments hanging from the hooks on either side of the mirror. A kerosene lamp, which accounted for the only light in the hallway, besides what came in through the fanlight over the front door, sat on the shelf, along with a card receiver. Kathleen moved quietly over to see if anyone had left their cards but was disappointed to find the silver dish empty. She then looked at her reflection in the mirror.

While she had a small looking glass in her room off the kitchen at Mrs. Fuller's, she had never seen a full reflection of herself wearing her wool tweed before. She twitched the collar straight and ran her hands along her sides, tugging the jacket down over her hips so it would lie flat.

Twisting so she could see the small stiff folds of material that fanned out from the small of her back, giving the suggestion of a bustle, she admired the way the jacket's construction showed off her figure. She still found it difficult to believe she had such a lovely outfit, and she thought warmly of how Patrick McGee had stared so when he first saw her in it. Stepping closer, Kathleen idly ran her gloved hand over one of the carvings around the mirror and was not surprised when the tip of her index finger came away with a thin film of dust.

She knew just how much work it would take to keep a house this large clean, and she also knew the butler wouldn't be doing any of the work. Just who else might be working here? Maybe when she accompanied Mrs. Fuller to the séance on Friday, Kathleen could wait in the kitchen. Then she would be able to meet some of the other servants the Framptons employed and pick up some important gossip that way. Maids and cooks were always the best sources of information for what was going on in any establishment. Mrs. Fuller certainly knew that from personal experience.

Not wanting to wipe the dust off on her own clothing, Kathleen had begun to blow on the tip of her glove when a sharp voice startled her.

"The competence of the staff here is shameful. I do apologize. I have complained and complained, but no one seems to listen. One maid-of-all-work is not sufficient, and the girl is, as far as I can determine, completely untrained. Please excuse me; I failed to introduce myself. My name is Miss Evelyn."

Kathleen twirled around and saw a young woman who had materialized in the hallway behind her. About her own height and slender, with piercing hazel eyes, this Miss Evelyn had a friendly smile on her face and was offering Kathleen her hand. The young woman's comment suggested she was a resident in the house, not a servant, so Kathleen curtsied while shaking the offered hand. She then backed away, saying, "Yes, Miss. I am Mrs. Fuller's maid, and she wouldn't put up with dust like this in her front hallway."

Kathleen quit speaking in confusion, realizing she had misjudged the young woman's age. The tone of voice and the comments had led her to believe she was being addressed by an adult in her twenties, but, on closer examination, Kathleen could see Miss Evelyn was barely in her teens. Her outfit added to the confusion. In the first house Kathleen had served, she had witnessed the young lady of the family going through the significant ritual of putting up her hair and lengthening her skirts when she turned twelve and became officially a "Miss." But while this Miss Evelyn spoke like a grown woman and wore her light brown hair up, the lack of any definition in the waist of her Basque top and the shortness of the matching skirt suggested she was still a girl under the age of twelve. And who was she? Did the Framptons have a daughter?

Before Kathleen could pursue this puzzle, an undoubtedly adult woman pushed through the door at the end of the hallway and bustled towards them, saying, "Child, there you are. You have your hat on, but where is your coat? Oh, never mind, we need to leave right now and it's such a warm day, you will be fine. Cook wants us to purchase another brace of quail for dinner; she thinks the last pair has gone off. Mr. Frampton works so hard, he deserves to have the best."

As soon as Kathleen saw that she was not the "child" being addressed, she slipped across the hallway and sat back down on the chair the butler had pointed out to her, sizing up this new arrival. Was she the housekeeper, or the girl's governess, or maybe another Frampton relative? What she definitely was, from Kathleen's point of view, was mutton dressed as lamb. Her printed silk dress was elegant but altogether too youthful for a woman well into middle age, and Kathleen pitied the poor maid who had the responsibility of squeezing the woman into her corset, because she looked like a sausage about to burst. *And speaking of sausage, the butcher's shop is a silly place to wear an outfit with that amount of lace trimming and multiple ruffles. And, if she thinks lathering on white face powder hides her wrinkles or that hennaed hair looks natural, or beautiful, she probably is losing her eyesight from old age.* Kathleen giggled to herself.

Oblivious to Kathleen's disparaging opinions, the woman pulled a light wrap over her shoulders, hiked up the handle of the basket, which was most likely destined to hold the quail, and pushed Miss Evelyn towards the front door, muttering about dinner and Simon Frampton and feckless children the whole time.

Kathleen watched the door close behind the older woman and the girl and was just congratulating herself on having something of interest to report to Mrs. Fuller, even if once again no one had expressed any interest in prying information out of her about her mistress, when she heard the slight rustle of skirts and looked up to see a graceful woman descending the staircase. What Kathleen noticed first was the tasteful severity of the woman's pale blue silk underskirt, with its single flounce and demi-train, and long tight overskirt in dark navy, with apricot trim. The severe cut, when carried through in the matching bodice, only served to accentuate the tiny waist and extraordinarily generous endowment nature had bestowed on her. Then, as the woman reached the bottom of the stairs, Kathleen nearly gasped when she saw the light of the hallway lamp strike sparks of fire in the woman's hair. This woman hadn't had to use artificial means to create the blazing red color of the curls that were gathered in an elaborate knot at the top of her head.

Lord have mercy, I hope Patrick never lays eyes on this woman. I wouldn't stand a chance.

"Hello, and who are you? Wait, of course, you must be Mrs. Fuller's maid." The woman addressed Kathleen in a deep, warm, but distinctly English-accented, voice. "I am Arabella Frampton, and I could feel a sympathetic presence in the house, so I came down to see who was causing it. I trust that Albert has offered you some refreshment? These interviews my husband conducts can take some time. No? Well let's remedy that error, shall we?"

To Kathleen's surprise, Mrs. Frampton walked over and pulled the tasseled end of a bell pull beside the front door and then came over and sat down on the chair beside her, indicating that Kathleen, who had stood up at her approach, should sit back down. She was even more striking close up, although Kathleen revised her first estimate of Mrs. Frampton's age upward to the mid-thirties, once she saw the faint telltale lines of crow's feet around her eyes, which were a fascinating shade of emerald.

Embarrassed to be found staring, Kathleen murmured, "Yes, ma'am," not quite sure to what she was agreeing, and looked down at her lap in confusion. While living and working in Mrs. Fuller's household had taught her that not every lady treated their servants with contempt, Mrs. Frampton's behavior was certainly unusual. Most ladies would have simply ignored a waiting maid's presence, much less offer them tea and come to sit down beside them.

"Now, child, what is your name? Kathleen? Ah, the 'pure of heart.' You do know that women with your Celtic heritage are prone to the 'second sight,' don't you? What do you foresee for your mistress? I hope that she is kind to you, such a sensitive soul that you are."

"Mrs. Fuller is the kindest mistress. She . . ." Kathleen stopped short, remembering that she had a role to play, and the woman across from her could also be playing a role as well. "I do hope that you all can help her. She has been so troubled as of late. She has been having bad dream, you see."

Kathleen felt a small surge of excitement. The bad dreams idea had just come to her, and she could see that Mrs. Frampton was interested because her emerald eyes widened.

"Bad dreams," Mrs. Frampton repeated. "How distressing. But often dreams are one of the first ways the departed use to reach out to their loved ones. Has your mistress confided in you about those dreams?"

Kathleen hesitated. She didn't want to appear too eager, so she said, "I don't know as it would be proper for me to say. I mean Mrs. Fuller wouldn't want me to be talking about such private things."

"My dear child, of course, I understand. I just thought that it might help me to help her. You see, from my experience, a woman's maid often has clearer insight into what is bothering her than the woman herself. And a young woman with such a pure heart as yours would never do anything to hurt her mistress, I am quite sure. But you must do what is right."

Kathleen pretended to consider this statement, biting her lower lip, then began hesitatingly, "If you think it would help, ma'am . . . I do want to do what is best. She has gotten to where she don't sleep at all well, and this past week I've had to sleep in her room, so I can wake her when she starts having one of her dreams. This makes her short with me the next day. Tiredness will do that. But I'm half asleep on my feet, myself. I dunno." Kathleen shook her head then rushed on, "It's the child, I think. I think she dreams about her child, Johnny."

Arabella Frampton frowned and then she said, "A child? But I understood that she was childless. Her letter to my husband mentioned her parents were gone, and her husband. So sad. Are you sure she dreams about a child? I do believe her husband's name was John."

Why ever did I call him Johnny? Mrs. Fuller never told me to do that, Kathleen thought, feeling slightly panicked. *As they say, in for a penny, in for a pound.* She continued, "But there was a son. Named for the father, I believe. She broke down and told me once when I found a picture hidden away under her pillow. Cutest little tyke. Mrs. Fuller said she was expecting when her husband died, and the boy was all that helped her keep her sanity. But then, two years later, the boy also died. Such a tragedy. She told me never to speak of it to anyone. She can't bear even to think about him. But when she cries out at night, she says, 'Johnny, Mother's here,' clear as day. And then she starts sobbing."

Chapter Nine
Thursday evening, October 16, 1879

"KALLOCH RECOVERING: It was reported at the headquarters of the
Workingmen's party yesterday afternoon that the ball in Kalloch's hip
wound had been extracted without surgical aid."
—*San Francisco Chronicle*, 1879

"I told you, Uncle Frank, just Judge Babcock. Don't know his Chris-
tian name, that's all Mrs. Fuller gave me. I checked the city directory,
didn't find anything. So you've never heard of a judge in town named
Babcock?"

Nate Dawson looked over at his uncle, who was putting on his coat
and hat in preparation to leave the office. The neat brass sign outside the
door said Hobbes, Haranahan, and Dawson, Attorneys-at-Law, but there
wasn't any Haranahan anymore; hadn't been for two years since his
uncle's long-time partner had finally succumbed to the inevitable effects of
a long life of cigars, whiskey, and energetic mistresses. Nate missed the
old reprobate. He had livened up the place considerably, as well as bringing some interesting cases to the firm. His uncle, Frank Hobbes, had
always concentrated on domestic law: wills, probate, property deeds and
such. Respectable, steady earners, boring.

"No, I am sorry; I can't say I can place him," his uncle said, pausing
as if to review the veracity of his own statement. "Just why does Mrs.
Fuller wish you to find out about this judge?"

Nate looked up from his desk at his uncle, biting back an irritated
reply. He had just told his uncle that Mrs. Fuller was trying to help out one
of her boarders, and to that end she needed to know any background he
could dig up on a Judge Babcock. Which was exactly all Annie had written
to him in the letter he had received from her this morning. As usual, his
uncle hadn't been attending.

Frank Hobbes then took his hat and placed it on a stack of tottering files on a table next to the door and walked back over to a shelf that held law journals and other periodicals, dragging out his reading glasses from his breast pocket. "Can't think of a single California judge, lawyer for that matter, with that name. However, if I remember, there was a Judge Babcock who sat on the Pennsylvania state bench back in the forties and fifties, an old Whig. Made his name in a number of cases regarding property rights. If I'm right, I should be able to find his name in one of these old University of Pennsylvania law reviews."

Nate's irritation slipped away as he watched his uncle pull off one book after the other, looking swiftly through their indexes. Despite the thought of re-shelving all the books since the one clerk they had was completely overworked, he couldn't help but marvel that his uncle, stooped from years of pouring over books and briefs, still had a mind like a steel trap. Nate had always admired that keen ability to concentrate, even when it meant he seemed deaf to his nephew's words.

Looking at his uncle, Nate noticed how white his hair had become and thought about the white that was dimming the gold in his father's hair and mustache. His brother Billy took after their father: short stature, tough sinewy body, fair hair and the sunny temper to go with it. Everyone said Nate took after his mother's side of the family, which meant his Uncle Frank: tall, thin, and dark in complexion and temper. Nate hated that age was beginning to weigh so heavily on both of the older men. Yet, his father seemed to be willing to hand over the reins to the next generation with much more grace than Uncle Frank.

"There he is," his uncle crowed, "Zebulon Babcock, who wrote the deciding opinion on an important case extending the right of eminent domain. He'd be at least in his seventies by now and probably retired from the bench. With a first name like that, it should be easy to determine if he is the same Judge Babcock that Mrs. Fuller is trying to locate."

"Yes, sir," Nate replied, getting up to look at the volume his uncle held. "You said he was a Whig, probably a Republican now? That reminds me, I stopped off at the *Chronicle* offices today. Appears the editor,

Charles de Young, is planning on coming back to town, now the election is over and Kalloch is alive and well and about to become mayor. Damned stupid move on de Young's part, shooting his candidate's opponent. Practically assured the Republicans would lose in this last election. Do you have any idea who he has retained for his defense team? Wouldn't I love to be working on a case like that?"

Nate's uncle handed the law review over to Nate, not deigning to respond, and he went over to take up his hat again. As he was about to close the door behind him, he addressed Nate, saying, "Anyone who would consider getting involved in what is surely going to be the legal circus of the century is a darn fool, and people don't entrust their business with our firm because we're fools; you just keep that in mind, young man."

Nate resisted the urge to hurl the book in his hand at the door as it closed behind his uncle. What was foolish was his uncle's refusal to take any cases that would give Nate any trial experience. While Haranahan had been alive, Nate had assisted him in a number of divorce and property dispute trials, but he had no experience on his own. Just one successful stint as a defense lawyer and Nate could begin to attract his own clients, which would increase the revenue to the firm and improve his own financial position. And improve his chances of marrying Annie.

Nate had been frustrated when Annie cut his visit so short on Monday, but he later admitted to himself that he had been fortunate that she had agreed to meet him at all, and he found her request that he find out information about Simon Frampton and his wife Arabella particularly hopeful. He knew she wouldn't have asked for this favor if she was planning on breaking off their relationship. *When I first met her, she wouldn't have even asked for my help at all, she's that independent, so this is a very good sign.*

Then Annie had written to ask him to find out about Judge Babcock and talk to Anthony Pierce, a newspaper reporter who had written a story about the Framptons some time back. Nate had visited the *Chronicle* offices today for that reason, since Pierce had written the story for that paper. Unfortunately, the harried clerk at the front desk had said Pierce was away on family business, due back in the next few days. He hoped he would be back before Saturday afternoon, which was when Annie had asked to meet. At least he might not have to come to their meeting empty-handed, thanks to his uncle's sharp memory. Surely a stop by the court-house tomorrow would yield someone who would know if a prominent Pennsylvania judge, named Zebulon Babcock, was in town.

Annie might be disappointed if all he had was a name, and nothing from Pierce, but from his perspective this would give him an excuse to see her again as soon as Pierce got back into town. Meanwhile, he looked forward to meeting her at Woodward's Gardens two days from now. *I wonder why she didn't want me to come to the house so we could go together? Hang it all, doesn't matter. I'll take seeing her in a public place, surrounded by strangers, over those old ladies and their lace, any day.*

*****

The girl opened her eyes and stretched. She stood up and tucked her shirt into her trousers, then straightened the canary yellow vest. She sauntered over to the tall oval mirror next to the northern window and began to tie a brown cravat, sticking the ends neatly into the top of the vest. She frowned at her image, and then she pulled a slouch hat on her head so the brim came down further, stood back, and nodded in satisfaction. She stroked the skin over her upper lip, looking puzzled, and then grimaced and shrugged. Walking over to the window, she pulled out a package of cigarettes and matches from her pocket. She tugged at the top window and, after some struggle, was able to pull it down a few inches. She lit the cigarette, inhaled, and then sent the smoke spiraling through the crack in the window.

Chapter Ten
Thursday evening, October 16, 1879

"SITUATION WANTED BY A GOOD COOK in a private family or
boardinghouse; no washing."
—*San Francisco Chronicle*, 1879

"So you see, Mrs. O'Rourke, I told Mrs. Frampton that the child's
name was 'Johnny.' Mrs. Fuller told me not to fret, that I hadn't done
wrong, but all day I haven't been able to get it out of my mind." Kathleen
stood twisting the dishtowel in her hands as she looked over at Annie.
"How could I have been so foolish as to give the boy your husband's
name? I wouldn't cause you pain for anything in the world, you know that,
ma'am!"

Annie walked over and put her hand on the young servant's shoulder.
"Now, Kathleen, don't worry yourself over this. My husband has been
gone nearly six years, and let me assure you I can handle hearing someone
use a variation of his name for a fictional boy. Fact is, using the name
Johnny was really quite clever. This way, if some spirit appears purporting
to be John, I can pretend to mishear and claim it is the spirit of my 'precious child.'"

She gave Kathleen's shoulder a squeeze, then walked over to the
rocking chair across from the stove and sat down. It was a little after seven
in the evening, and she had just finished with her last client, taken off
Madam Sibyl's wig, washed the powder and paint off her face, and come
down to the kitchen, as was her habit at the end of each day. The window
was fastened against the chill autumn night air. Beatrice O'Rourke stood
over the kitchen sink, washing up the dishes from supper while Kathleen
dried.

"I wonder if Mrs. Frampton usually gets involved in digging up
information on clients? Kathleen, tell us, what did you think of her?"

Kathleen turned, a wet dinner plate in her hands. "Oh, ma'am, I just don't know. First I couldn't get over how beautiful she is. Mrs. O'Rourke, you wouldn't believe her hair, like living flame, and eyes, I never in my life saw such a color, a kind of green that don't seem natural! I 'spect men go into a trance just looking at her. And she was so friendly. What did you think of her, Mrs. Fuller?"

Annie remembered her first impression of Arabella Frampton, but she wouldn't call her friendly. Hostile was more accurate. She had swept into the library after the most cursory knock, and it was Annie's distinct impression that Simon Frampton hadn't welcomed the interruption. He had been holding both of Annie's hands by that time and had been softly reassuring her of . . . what? She really didn't remember. His voice had been so soothing that she had found herself just listening to his tone, not the words. She did remember staring into his eyes, fascinated by the contrast between the deep black pupil, surrounded by cloudy gray iris, encircled by an odd black ring. Then the knock on the door had caused Simon to break off and utter an oath.

"Annie, love, are you alright?" Beatrice stood in front of her, using her apron to dry her soapy hands. "To be sure, we'd begun to think you'd gone to sleep on us. Would you like me to put on a pot of tea for you now?"

Annie sat up straighter and laughed. "Oh Bea, I think that might be a very good idea. I asked Esther Stein to come by when she gets in tonight, and I know she will want some of that chamomile. I would like some too. And as to Kathleen's question, I thought Arabella Frampton wasn't too pleased to see me. Which is strange, since clearly she knew her husband was interviewing me. She is quite beautiful; Kathleen was right about that. However, I found her very imperious, and there is a temper there to go along with those red curls. She announced, rather than asked, if I was ready to leave. Did anything happen to put her into a temper, Kathleen?"

"Well, ma'am, not really. We were sitting there, and she was asking me about you: how long you'd lived in San Francisco, who your friends were. Just like you said someone would. I made sure to tell her about Mr.

Stein and made it sound like there were all manner of rich people stopping by and dropping off cards, hoping for a visit with you. But when I mentioned how excited you were to join the circle on Friday, she seemed surprised. Said, 'What, this Friday?' That's when she stood up, knocked on the door, and went right in."

"That's interesting," Annie said. "She did say something to Simon about, 'promising not to fill the circle without consulting,' and then she made some excuse about Mr. Frampton having another appointment as she hustled me out. Did you see anyone else come in while you were waiting for me?"

"Just that strange girl and the woman who took her out to the butcher shop. But they seemed to live there. Who do you think they were, Mrs. Fuller?"

"I don't have any idea about the older woman, but I think that the girl might be Evie May, the young medium Simon Frampton told me about. I wonder if I will see her at Friday night's séance?"

Without warning, the back door to the kitchen banged open, startling the three women. A gust of cold October wind blew in a young boy and a small dog. The majestic black cat curled on the wicker chair next to the warm cast-iron stove hissed halfheartedly and settled back down to sleep.

"Mrs. Fuller, Mrs. O'Rourke, Miss Kathleen, you should have seen Dandy," said the boy. "There was this rat, down by Cooper's store, and Dandy killed it! I didn't even see it, dark like it is, but Dandy did. My friend Georgie says dogs can see ten times better than we can."

"Jamie, slow down," Annie interrupted the eight-year-old who had bent down to scratch behind the upstanding ears of a shorthaired black and white terrier. "How could Dandy kill a rat? He wasn't off his lead, was he? You have strict instructions from your mother never to let him go. Why, if one of the dog catchers found him loose, license or no, you'd be in for a fine."

Jamie's mother was Barbara Hewitt, who taught English Literature at Girls High. She and her young son lived up on the third floor attic of the boarding house. It wasn't entirely clear if there had ever been a Mr.

Hewitt, and Annie had never had the nerve to ask.

Jamie shook his head. "Oh no, ma'am. I never would. That's how dogs get killed. So easy to run under a carriage. I was just taking him for his last walk, and he was sniffing along the barrels in front of Cooper's, like he always does, when suddenly I heard him snarl and he lunged between two of the barrels. I heard this squeal, and then he backed out with this gigantic rat in his jaws. I had a terrific time getting him to let go of it. But it was dead as a doornail. Dandy must of broke his neck. Didn't ya, boy! What a clever dog!"

Annie looked down at Dandy, whose tiny crooked tail whirled around in pleasure at his master's kind words. The dog wasn't more than twelve pounds, no nose to speak of, and, although when he yawned his mouth opened as wide as a frog's, she just couldn't imagine him killing a rat. She didn't know whether to be appalled or impressed, but when the dog suddenly sat down and tried to scratch his ear with his back leg, almost falling over in the process, she decided to be amused and laughed.

"Mrs. Fuller, remember he is a Boston Terrier, and Georgie says terriers are bred to hunt rats and such." Jamie seemed to feel Annie wasn't taking Dandy's feat seriously.

Beatrice who had been busy scrubbing the last pan, sniffed at this statement. Both she and Annie had heard all about how Dandy was some special breed out of Boston. Beatrice, in fact, had been the one to name him when Jamie had rescued him and brought him home to the boarding house. The dog's neat black fur and white chest and white front feet, and most importantly, his air of supreme confidence, had made her think of a gentleman in evening clothes, hence the name Dandy.

"I guess, Mrs. O'Rourke, we should be glad to know if Queenie gets too lazy to keep mice and such out of the kitchen storeroom, she'll have an able lieutenant in Dandy," Annie said, nodding at the old cat, whose eyes opened briefly at the mention of her name. "But Jamie, you better skedaddle upstairs. Your mother will be waiting for you. It's getting near bedtime, and you will want to have time to tell her all about Dandy's exploits."

"Yes, ma'am. Oh, I'm so sorry, Mrs. Stein." Jamie had narrowly missed running into Esther Stein in his mad dash up the stairs.

Fortunately, chasing her own numerous grandchildren had kept Esther Stein nimble, and she lost neither the candle she carried nor her composure in the encounter. "Jamie, dear. We need to put a bell on you to alert us to your progress through the house. Mind your way going upstairs. Here, take my candle with you, and be quiet as a mouse; I believe Miss Minnie and Miss Millie have already retired for the night."

"Mrs. Stein, come sit down. I've just fixed a pot of tea," Beatrice said as she shooed Queenie reluctantly off the wicker chair.

Esther Stein, a wealthy merchant banker's wife, and Beatrice O'Rourke, a cook and housekeeper, could have been sisters; they were of such a similar build. Neither stood much taller than four and a half feet, and both had figures that once had been called "fine" but now reflected the spread that came with maturity and years of good food. Esther, in her mid-sixties and the older of the two, had hair that was pure white, while Beatrice's gray still permitted glimmers of the redheaded girl she had been. Esther's German heritage and Beatrice's Irish roots had produced blue eyes of a similar shade, and you would be hard-pressed to determine which woman's smile was more good-natured. Only their clothing and the tiredness in Beatrice's stance revealed their very different life experiences. Annie loved them both equally.

Oblivious to the comparisons Annie was making, Beatrice bustled back to the sink and Esther sank down in the chair with a sigh, saying, "Thank you, Beatrice, tea would be much appreciated. Now Annie, Miss Pinehurst confided in me this morning that you are helping her out with her poor sister. She said that you hoped by attending one of their séances to find out just how these awful people have gotten such a hold on Mrs. Vetch. She wasn't clear at all on the exact details. Tell me all."

"I wish I could say I had a well-developed plan," Annie said. "I thought that if I became a regular member of one of their 'circles,' as they call them, I could find out just what sort of tricks they were up to. Then I could use the information to convince Sukie, Miss Pinehurst's sister, that they are frauds. When I lived with John's Aunt Lottie, I read a number of articles in the Boston papers that exposed the methods of some of the most famous local mediums. Some are really quite simple. It is amazing what kind of shenanigans people can get up to in a darkened room. One article even showed how a famous trance medium joined together the hands of the two people on either side of her, so that she was free to lark around the room blowing on trumpets, whispering in people's ears, and generally making a ruckus while the people at the table swore she was sitting with them the whole time. She was exposed when one of the members of the circle pulled the same trick and turned up the gas-jet, so everyone could see the spirit was the medium herself."

"Do you think that is all that it will take?" Esther said.

"Probably not." Annie thought about how resistant Lottie had been when she had tried to point out some of the fraudulent tactics she'd read about.

"Ma'am, aren't you going to tell Mrs. Stein about tricking those Framptons with your made-up son?" Kathleen practically wriggled with the excitement of revealing her role in the plans.

"You tell her, Kathleen; it's really your story to tell," Annie said.

So, Kathleen told Mrs. Stein all about her conversation with Mrs. Frampton and how she had cleverly revealed the existence of a son called Johnny who had passed away, in order to trap the Framptons into creating a spirit of a child who had never existed. When she finished, Kathleen again looked to her for reassurance, so Annie smiled at her. She had been taken aback when Kathleen had first recounted the story to her on the trip home yesterday. But she was telling the truth when she said those six years had done much to ease the pain of her marriage. *Of course, Kathleen probably thinks that John's death would be the source of that pain, not the marriage itself.* Annie had talked to both Beatrice and Esther about the financial problems John had caused, and his suicide, but she hadn't revealed much to them about the actual marriage. Annie feared these two women, who had had the good fortune to find men who loved them, might not understand.

"I am sure you did just fine, Kathleen," said Esther. "I am also glad that Mrs. Fuller took you with her when she went. You have a good sensible head on your shoulders. Now, Annie, while I can quite understand your desire to help Miss Pinehurst, are you sure it is a good idea to try to fool people who are, at the very least, shady characters, and may be outright villains? You will be threatening their livelihoods if you are successful."

"Oh, Esther, I expected to hear something like that from Mr. Dawson when I explained to him what I am doing, but not from you! The most that will happen if I am successful in proving that the Framptons are frauds is that they will move on, which happens all the time with these sorts of people. I expect this is why they moved out of England in the first place and then moved out west."

Esther Stein frowned but changed the topic. "Beatrice said you asked Nate Dawson to help you."

"I asked him to look into the Framptons' backgrounds and bring me some information about one of the people who will be attending the séance with me tomorrow, a Judge Babcock. You haven't heard of him by any chance?"

"Babcock? Hmm. No, my dear. Do you know who else is going to attend the séance?"

"Actually, yes I do. Simon Frampton mentioned one or two others, and I thought you or your husband might know them. There is a Mrs. Larkson, who is married to a businessman, William Larkson, of the Larkson's Woolen Mills. A good old family-owned firm, I believe. Do you know anything about him or his wife?"

"I know William Larkson recently inherited the company from his father. Herman thinks he will do well. He married late in life, and his wife is a good deal younger than he is. They live in Pacific Heights, and I believe that Hetty, my youngest daughter, may know the wife; they are more of an age. I will ask her Sunday when I see her. Another birthday party. I swear, with thirteen grandchildren, there isn't a week that goes by without one or the other of them having a party."

Annie, who knew that Esther doted on every one of her

grandchildren, ignored this complaint and got right to the point. "That would be wonderful. I figure the more I know about who is sitting around the table with me, the more I will be able to judge how the Framptons keep their clients coming back. There is one other name I have, Mr. Ruckner, a banker, and I felt sure that Herman would know him."

"Abraham Ruckner, of course we know him! Oh dear, poor man, he lost his wife two months ago, left him with six children, all still at home. I hate to think of him getting involved with mediums. I wonder if Herman knows that? My goodness. He is a partner in the San Francisco Gold Bank and Trust, and, if I am not mistaken, that is the bank that Miss Pinehurst's brother-in-law works for as a clerk. You don't think there is a connection, do you?"

"There very well might be," Annie replied. "Although I am quite sure Mr. Vetch would not have gotten his employer involved with the Framptons. It may be that the Framptons are using Sukie in some fashion to gain information about him or the bank. In any event, this is very helpful."

"I can tell you, Herman has a good deal of affection for Abraham. If there is anything he can do to help you expose them and protect his friend, he will be more than willing to help. You know this really distresses me. To think of this couple preying on poor souls like Sukie Vetch and Abraham Ruckner. I think I will just go up now and tell Herman about this. Dear me, what is the world coming too, when the dead are used to hurt the living?"

Chapter Eleven
Friday evening, October 17, 1879

"J. J. Jackson, Medium. No 16 Stockton: circles Wednesday and Friday evenings; sittings daily."
—*San Francisco Chronicle*, 1879

Although the circle was not supposed to start until eight p.m., Simon Frampton had instructed her to arrive by seven-thirty at the latest. Annie now saw why, as a number of the occupants of the room were imbibing liberally of the brandy and sherry that stood on a sideboard. *Spirits to help prepare for the spirits*, she thought. Once an imposing formal parlor, the room's shoulder-high wainscoting and paneled wooden ceiling continued the decorative style of the hallway. The wallpaper, however, was a night-marish pattern of tiny gilt flowering vines against a dark green, and the marble from the hallway gave way to a parquet floor. A thick piled carpet covered the center of the floor, and there were matching dark green velvet curtains pulled over the windows. *The better to muffle the footsteps of any ghosties who might be running around.*

Annie found the color scheme of dark green and even darker wood, which had seemed elegant in the hallway, oddly oppressive in this room. The incongruous placement of a large oval table and chairs in the middle of the room added to her sense of discomfort. Parlors were supposed to have open floors, with the furniture in conversational groupings around the walls. Instead, this room was some strange hybrid, with dining room table and sideboard mingling uneasily with a brown velvet sofa, a pair of floral armchairs, and four ladder-backed chairs placed at the corners of the room.

Sitting stiffly in one of those chairs was a Mr. Hapgood, whom Frampton had pointed out to Annie as they entered the room. He had said, "Harold over there has been fortunate enough to contact his father and some of his brothers, who have been very helpful in offering suggestions in how to run the business. You may have heard of Hapgood and Sons, one of the first successful grocers in the city."

Annie had indeed heard of Hapgood's grocery store and even shopped there a few times as well, since it was only a few blocks from her boarding house. Mr. Harold Hapgood, a weedy sort of man, whose head looked too large for his thin neck, didn't seem all that excited about another evening of advice from his departed relatives. Another man stood staring down at the fire that blazed in a fireplace with an oversized green marble mantel that clashed with the wallpaper. Annie was beginning to suspect that the original owners of this mansion had more money than taste. According to Frampton, the somber gentleman decked out in evening dress was Judge Zebulon Babcock. Zebulon! She hadn't heard that old Puritan name for ages. She hoped that Nate had found out something about him, because he seemed an odd sort of person to be attending a séance. This thought was interrupted by a peal of laughter coming from the sideboard, where a young brunette in a gorgeous, dark bronze silk with brown velvet trimming stretched out her empty glass.

"Oh, Jack. Do pour me a drop more of that sherry. I declare that I can feel the chill of the graveyard already," the woman said, tilting her head quite charmingly.

Well, my goodness, this must be Mrs. Larkson, the wife of the new owner of the Larkson Woolen Mills, Annie concluded. *But the handsome young man pouring her more sherry is certainly too young to be Mr. Larkson.*

As if he had read her mind, Frampton leaned towards Annie and murmured, "Mrs. Larkson and Mr. Sweeter."

As Annie watched Mrs. Larkson tease Mr. Sweeter about his mustache, which framed very pink lips and nicely matched his mutton chop sideburns, she wondered if the two were long-standing acquaintances or had developed a flirtation as a result of attending a regular séance together. Maybe it was harmless; Annie knew that some women saw this sort of arch banter as the only way to communicate with someone of the opposite sex. Yet she was curious if Mr. Larkson ever attended these Friday night gatherings with his young and extremely beautiful wife.

Simon Frampton excused himself, saying that there were some preparations that needed to be attended to before he had finished introducing everyone to Annie. This left only one other unidentified male in the room, and Annie assumed he was the banker, Mr. Ruckner, who was having a very large brandy. Harried was the only word for him. He was formally dressed as befitted a man of his wealth and stature, but his collar looked wilted, and she could see that the cut of his suit coat was being ruined by something shaped suspiciously like a small doll stuffed into his pocket. If he had been consulting Madam Sibyl, she would in an instant have declared the problem domestic difficulties.

This left two unnamed women. One who was delicately sipping sherry, while the other was making her way over to stand and chat with Mr. Hapgood. The sherry sipper was rather overweight and tightly corseted, probably in her mid-to-late fifties if the gray in her hair was any indication. If Annie had to guess, she would say this must be Mrs. Daisy Mott since Frampton had described her as motherly. Her smile as Annie made her way across the room was certainly warm.

"Hello, I'm Mrs. Fuller," Annie said, holding her hand out. "I am the new member of your circle, and I can tell you I am feeling a little frightened. Have you been attending these meetings long?"

"Quite some months, actually. My name is Miss Herron. I find that my profession—I nurse the ill and dying, you see—brings me closer than most people to that frail boundary between the dead and the living. I was with Miss Barton on the battlefields during the war, and ever since then I have felt it is my duty to try to comfort my patients, even after death."

Not the motherly Mrs. Mott! This couldn't be the nurse who got Sukie Vetch involved with the Framptons, could it? No, I think her name was Hoskins. Annie nodded and smiled, trying to cover her surprise.

Miss Herron suddenly pointed, saying, "Mrs. Fuller, look, Mrs. Frampton has arrived! It must be time for us to form the circle." She then put her glass down on the sideboard and ran towards Arabella Frampton, uttering small cries, rather like an excited schoolgirl.

Tonight the medium was dressed in an exquisite outfit of pale green. The embroidered cuirass-style top was quite long, leaving room for only two deep flounces in the skirt, and its collar was lined with lace, dyed a darker hue, which drew the eye down to a rather daring décolletage, which revealed her quite substantial natural attributes. Annie fought off a stab of real jealousy at how beautifully the ensemble complimented Arabella's coloring and how dowdy her own refurbished brown striped camel's-hair suit with its single flounce and braiding was in comparison.

She then heard Mrs. Larkson, who had been abandoned by Mr. Sweeter as rapidly as Miss Herron had abandoned her, mutter under her breath, "Oh, goody. Our resident witch is here." For some reason, this made Annie feel much better.

"Mrs. Fuller, if you would please come and sit by me at this end of the table," said Simon Frampton, who had slipped up behind her while she had been eavesdropping on Mrs. Larkson. He took her arm, gently guided her past the fireplace, and pulled out a solid-looking chair for her near the end of the table. As she sat down, she saw that the arms of the chair pinned her in. *No running around in the dark to catch out their tricks for me!* She looked to her right and into the hallway, since the pocket doors had not yet been closed, and saw Kathleen sitting on a chair near the front door. Annie had the unexpected impulse to take out her handkerchief and wave at her, rather as someone who was standing on the bridge of a departing ship might do to a friend on shore who had come to see them off.

Simon Frampton sat down next to her at one end of the large oval table while his wife sat at the other end. *Just as if they were father and mother to this little gathering.* Sitting on Annie's left was the banker, Mr. Ruckner, then came Mrs. Larkson, followed by Mr. Sweeter, who seemed very pleased to be seated next to Arabella. Sitting with their backs to the hallway were Mr. Hapgood, then the nurse, Miss Herron, Judge Babcock, and finally on Simon's right, the woman who Annie had to assume was Mrs. Mott. This woman looked to be in her sixties, at least, with thin gray hair pulled back into a simple circled braid. Her face was long, with deep lines that pulled down the corners of her mouth. She had a square chin and a decidedly long nose, on which perched a pair of thin wire spectacles. Hatchet-faced was the term that came to mind. Two pink splotches on her cheeks and the faded blue of her eyes were the only color about her person, since she was wearing a severe black silk that, while of excellent material, hung loosely from her spare frame. The woman noticed Annie looking at her and used this as an invitation to reach across Simon to shake her hand, saying, "My dear, I don't believe we have met. I'm Daisy Mott."

Her smile transformed her plain features, and Annie, her hand being warmly shaken, now understood why Frampton had called Mrs. Mott motherly.

While everyone had been taking their chairs, Albert, the butler, had been moving around the room, extinguishing the lamps. He moved to the pocket doors that led to the hallway and pulled them shut, plunging the room into almost total darkness. There was only a faint glow around a screen that he placed in front of the fireplace. As Annie's eyes began to adjust, she heard a noise behind her. Twisting around, she saw that Albert had opened a set of doors that led to a smaller parlor behind her, which contained a tall cabinet. In that cabinet sat a girl, illuminated by a lamp sitting on the room's fireplace mantel. This young girl was all dressed in white, including some sort of gauzy scarf that was draped over her head and fell down almost to her waist. She appeared immobile, her eyes cast down. Annie was just thinking that this must be the young medium, Evie May, when the girl raised her baleful pale eyes and looked straight at her, causing Annie's heart to constrict in fear.

Chapter Twelve

"Carrie M. Sawyer. Materializing and physical medium. 115 Eddy.
Séances every evening except Saturday."
—*San Francisco Chronicle*, 1879

Albert extinguished the lamp on the small parlor mantel, plunging both rooms into semi-darkness. He then went into the hallway, causing a brief flash of light as the door from the smaller parlor to the hallway opened and closed.

No longer being able to see the girl or the cabinet, Annie turned back around, relieved when Simon Frampton claimed her attention by saying, "My dear Mrs. Fuller, it is now time for you to take my hand and join the circle."

Listening to the rustling of the other people around the table and the hiss of embers in the fireplace, she thought how effective séances were in establishing an atmosphere of anticipation. Annie had attended several in her days in Boston as Lottie's companion, and she realized now that she had copied a number of their elements when she set up Madam Sibyl's parlor. While she didn't turn out all the lights, she did keep the windows closed and curtains pulled, creating a profound silence in the room; and she placed the lamps around the room so their light left her, as Madam Sibyl, in shadow. This arrangement forced clients to focus on Madam Sibyl's hands, making it difficult for them to see the way that a wig and make-up obscured Annie's true features.

She had even, albeit briefly, fooled Nate Dawson in this way. She smiled at the memory, then had her thoughts wrenched back to the séance at hand when Mr. Ruckner spasmodically squeezed her left hand. She looked over and realized that all she could make out was a blurry sketch of his features within the pale oval of his face and his white shirtfront. This pattern was repeated around the table for each of the participants, except

Arabella Frampton, whose pale green gown glowed in the semi-darkness.

How odd, I felt sure she would wear black, Annie thought. *This must mean she has no intention of breaking away from the circle to skip around in the dark. And with Simon holding my hand, I should be able to determine if he is up to anything.*

Annie peered across the table at the silhouette of Arabella, who sat very still, head held high. The room was so quiet that Annie found herself aware of her own breathing. Ruckner sighed, and she thought a resulting sound was Mrs. Larkson fidgeting somewhere down the table. Annie knew they had been sitting only a few minutes, but it seemed much longer. Her arms were already tired from clasping hands with the men on either side, so she slowly lowered them to the cloth-covered table. Instantly, she became aware that the table surface was vibrating. She looked to her left to see if Ruckner was reacting to this phenomenon, but beyond the frown that seemed habitual with him, she couldn't see any expression of surprise.

Annie began to move her left foot, trying to find the table leg. She devoutly hoped she would hit the table leg before running into Mr. Ruckner's foot and silently gave thanks when she encountered a solid object, which with some slight maneuvering she determined was a table leg about two inches square. This felt too solid, as did the table top under her arms, to be shaken by the jiggling, accidental or intentional, of one of the circle members. However, Annie knew that rigging séance tables so that they would rise, tip, or spin, was one of the oldest tricks of the trade among fraudulent mediums, along with the raps made famous by the Fox sisters. She would just have to find a way to examine the table at some point to see how the movement was accomplished. Since no one else seemed to remark on the odd effect, she assumed it was a normal part of the séance.

A piano began to play, so faint that it appeared to come from far away. *Celestial music. What a nice touch. I wonder how they do that? The piano must be in another room, but then, who is the musician?* Annie glanced around the table again, counting, making sure that no one had slipped away from the circle. The idea of broad-shouldered Albert playing away rather tickled her, but she realized she was also feeling disappointed, thinking that all this seemed rather tame.

Then all hell broke loose.

Arabella Frampton suddenly raised her hands and began to utter deep guttural noises, so loud that they competed with the drum and tambourine that had joined the piano. Simultaneously, the table began to rock, painfully banging Annie's elbows.

Just as swiftly all noise and movement stopped, and, in the silence, Annie heard Sweeter say, "Sweet Jesus. You would think I would be used to this by now."

Mrs. Larkson nervously whispered, "Oh Jack, don't swear like that."

Annie stifled her own nervous desire to laugh at the interchange.

Arabella began to sway back and forth, making soft moaning sounds. Then she proclaimed, "Oh, spirits, come to us tonight. Bring your wisdom, shed your light on a dark world, and comfort those of us you have left behind. Tell us with whom you wish to speak."

Annie felt Ruckner jerk when Arabella began to speak in a high musical voice, entirely devoid of her English accent.

"Abraham, dearest, I am here. I miss you and the children so. Please tell me how they are."

Ruckner cried out in response, "Jennie! I don't know what to do. I've told them and told them you went to heaven, but they just don't understand. Little Susanna keeps crying, and that stupid girl I hired left without giving notice, and James got in a fight at school; he refuses to obey me, no matter what I try. I don't know how much longer I can go on. I need to have my wits about me as we go into the next quarter. The bank . . . well I don't need to tell you . . . oh Jennie, please tell me what to do."

Ruckner leaned forward, pulling her hand with his as he stretched towards Arabella, as if trying to touch her. The desperation in his voice twisted her heart, shaming her for her earlier lighthearted reactions to the séance.

The musical voice coming from Arabella answered, "Dearest Abe, you must have patience. The children will heal in time. Tell them to pray to me; I will hear them. Tell them I live in this lovely garden, and someday they will join me. And please write to Mama; ask her to come. I know you didn't get along with her, but she will know what to do for the children. She needs something to do with her grief, and she can run the house while you take care of the business. Please Abe, do as I ask, and come back and tell me what she said. I miss you all so."

There was a pause. Then Arabella slumped in her chair and the room became silent, except for Ruckner's soft sobbing. The raw emotion of the interchange left Annie wishing she could find a way to comfort the poor man. Before this thought went any further, the piano playing resumed, and Arabella sat up and in her own voice said, "Mr. Sweeter, I believe you also have a request of the spirit world."

Mrs. Larkson giggled and said, "Why Jack, who do you want to talk to who has died? Surely you don't want to talk to Great-grandpa Foster?"

Annie could barely hear Mr. Sweeter's response; although his tone made it clear he wasn't pleased with Mrs. Larkson's teasing. Sweeter and Mrs. Larkson were obviously related in some fashion. A common great-grandfather suggested they were second cousins. Perhaps Annie had mistaken the familiarity of a family connection for flirtation. This would explain why Mr. Larkson wouldn't feel the need to attend these séances since there was a male relative to keep his young wife out of trouble.

Arabella repeated Sweeter's last words more loudly, saying, "Oh, spirits, this young man wants to know when he is going to get his chance in life. He is troubled about his future. He has no job, no money, and no home of his own. He needs guidance from his ancestors. Will you help him?"

Mrs. Larkson broke out, saying, "Well, I never. Jack . . . I told you!" The thump of the drum and the jangle of tambourine drowned out her next words. Arabella again raised her hands, the music died down, and this time a large male voice boomed forth as the table resumed its violent shaking. Annie could see Arabella's mouth moving in the dim light, but the voice itself seemed to come from above, and it kept repeating the phrase, "Blood is thicker than water," over and over.

Annie was just trying to figure out how this was the answer to Jack Sweeter's question, when Mrs. Mott shouted out, "Uncle Zachary, is that you? Gracious me, don't I just remember you saying that when Petunia and I had an argument. My, that takes me back. Tell me, have you seen Petunia on the other side? And Aunty Grace, is she with you? Tell her how much I miss her rhubarb pie. Haven't had one as good in I don't know how long."

Annie had the impression that Daisy Mott's enthusiasm was not entirely welcomed by the spirit of Uncle Zachary, since the male voice continued in a quieter but monotonous tone to repeat the admonition about blood being thicker than water, even as Mrs. Mott peppered the supposed spirit with a stream of questions about various dead relatives. Annie thought she heard a whispered exchange between Mrs. Larkson and Mr. Sweeter, who seemed to be insisting that the repeated message was for him, not Mrs. Mott. Annie leaned forward, trying to hear better, finding the multiple voices confusing in the limited light.

"Mrs. Mott, I do believe you might consider leaving your uncle's spirit some time to answer your questions," said Simon Frampton, startling Annie, who had almost forgotten the man sitting on her right. So far, this had clearly been Arabella's show, but now Arabella's husband seemed to take the reins, continuing, "Better yet, why don't we give my wife a little time to gather her strength while we sing 'On the Other Side of Jordon.' The spirits enjoy it so."

On cue, the spirit of "Uncle Zachary" became silent, Arabella again slumped in her chair, eyes closed, and the piano music began to play a rollicking version of the old hymn. The ready acquiescence of Mrs. Mott, who immediately raised her voice in song, and the fact that she was joined by at least one or two of the other members of the circle, including the banker, told Annie that this was a common method of settling things down. She began to sing, not wanting to stand out, but she also looked around, trying to see which other members of the circle were singing. As she did so, she realized she was now able to see better, well enough, in fact, to see that Judge Babcock was looking at her with fierce concentration.

No, he isn't looking at me; he is looking over my shoulder at the girl in the cabinet, and that must be where the light is coming from. For some reason, the idea that the young medium might be still staring at her made Annie feel very uncomfortable, but she fought the desire to check, not wanting to alert Simon of her curiosity.

Just as the tension became unbearable, Simon himself looked behind them, letting go of Annie's hand to point at the girl sitting in the cabinet, saying, "Behold, the spirits have chosen to visit our young friend."

Annie, now released from Simon's grip, twisted around and was astonished to see that the source of the light behind her was not the lamp on the mantel but instead a faint beam, evidently emanating from somewhere above, that revealed the young girl still sitting, immobile, within the cabinet.

Simon continued, his voice deepening. "Departed ones, judge not our follies and our fears, but speak to us."

Annie watched as the young medium gave a start and stood up in the beam of light, which had strengthened. The girl then produced an exceedingly sweet smile, reaching out both of her hands in a form of supplication, saying, "Oh, Father, you're back. The nights are so long here. I was afraid you weren't coming. Do sit with me awhile."

The long moan that emanated from Judge Babcock left Annie in no doubt about whom "Father" was, and she watched in horror as the old man made an undignified scramble around the table and into the small parlor to clutch the girl to his breast. He then kissed the top of her head, dragged her into the cabinet, and pulled a set of curtains across to hide himself and the girl from sight.

Chapter Thirteen

"Miss Mayo, Medium. 327 O'Farrell-sittings daily 10 to 9 P.M."
—*San Francisco Chronicle, 1879*

Kathleen looked up at the hall clock, surprised that less than ten minutes had passed since the butler had closed the parlor doors. She had seen her mistress sitting next to that handsome man, Mr. Simon Frampton, but she hadn't seemed best pleased. Leastwise Kathleen guessed he was Mr. Frampton, since she hadn't seen him on Wednesday. Tonight he had welcomed Mrs. Fuller like they were old friends, so that's who he must be. Made sense that a beautiful woman like Arabella would have such a good-looking husband. *Although that's not always the way.* Many a poor specimen of manhood, if they had enough of the ready in their pockets, could catch a pretty girl.

But that certainly wasn't the case with Simon Frampton. He had that thick head of hair, and that voice, like rich plum pudding! As a general rule, she didn't respond well to Brit accents. In her experience, the people who had them tended to treat Irish girls like dirt. But Mr. Frampton had been ever so nice when they came in, asking her to wait in the hallway, saying he was sorry there wasn't a more comfortable place to sit.

Of course he wasn't as handsome as Mr. Dawson, so maybe that was why Mrs. Fuller didn't look very pleased. Truth be told, she looked sort of frightened sitting there, surrounded by all those strange people. Kathleen wasn't surprised. What kind of person went out on a Friday night to sit around in the dark and talk to dead people? Kathleen understood why people came to see Mrs. Fuller as Madam Sibyl. *Who wouldn't want a glimpse into the future? But talking to dead people just seemed against nature.*

Mrs. Fuller had been quite jolly in the horse car on the way over. Telling Kathleen about all the tricks that mediums got up to and what she would be looking for. She hadn't seemed scared then. But Kathleen knew what it was to whistle in the dark.

She remembered how terrified she was when she first went to work as a scullery maid. She'd just turned thirteen, her ma had been dead three years, and her pa had just been killed on the job, though it was the drink that had made him careless. He'd been pretty much soused round the clock since her ma had died. Within the week of his death, her uncles had divided up the boys and sent her, the only girl, to work in that grand kitchen, the cook yelling at her morning, noon, and night. It wasn't the work so much; it was being among strangers that she'd hated. She'd missed the boys so.

Course she didn't let on how scared she was, just cut up, the way she did with her brothers, got everyone to laughing, so it didn't feel so strange. Didn't go over at all well with the cook, which was why she lost that position so fast. From what Mrs. O'Rourke had said, Mrs. Fuller also had been forced to live with strangers after her pa and her husband died. Yes, Kathleen guessed both she and Mrs. Fuller knew what whistling in the dark felt like.

Kathleen cocked her head, sure that she had heard a door close upstairs, then she heard the faint sounds of a piano. Mrs. Fuller had a nice old upright in her parlor, and the sound reminded her of when Jamie's mother gave him lessons on it with the door closed. She wondered where the piano was and who was playing it. She didn't think she had seen one in the room where the séance was being held.

Kathleen got up and crept to the bottom of the stairs. She was certain the music was coming from the second floor. Since she was up, she decided to explore the hallway a bit. Soon after closing the front parlor doors, Albert had reappeared at the end of the hall and gone through the swinging door that led to the kitchen. She was curious to see if she could hear anything if she put her ear up to the door to what must be a back parlor. If anyone saw her, she could pretend she was looking for the way to the kitchen to get a spot of tea.

She wished she knew how many servants there were in the house; it was nerve-wracking not knowing who might pop up at any minute. Mrs. Frampton had mentioned a cook, and there was the butler, Albert. Certainly anyone who dressed as fancy as that Mrs. Frampton would need a lady's maid. Though Mrs. Fuller always said that Kathleen did a wonderful job on her hair, she knew that if Mrs. Fuller hadn't fallen on hard times she would have someone a great deal more experienced than a seventeen-year-old Irish maid to help her dress. And, even though the Framptons' house showed signs of neglect, someone was mopping the front hallway, so there would be a parlor maid in the house as well.

Walking silently, as over four years as a servant had taught her, Kathleen went cautiously down the hall. It was dark at this end, so it was easy to see that there was some light coming out from under the single door. It wasn't very bright but enough to discourage Kathleen from trying to open the door a crack. Instead, she just put her ear up to the door and listened. Nothing except that faint piano playing. She then thought she heard someone talking, but the voice was indistinct.

The sound of the front doorbell sent Kathleen scurrying back to her chair, and she had just settled herself when the strange older lady from Wednesday came barreling through from the back of the house to answer the door. This evening she was decked out in a badly made green gown, again with too many bows and fringes for a woman of her girth. She must be the housekeeper, even wearing that get-up, although by rights Albert should be answering the front door. What kind of mischief was old Albert up to?

The odd older woman opened the front door to a younger woman, saying, "Mrs. Hapgood. How nice to see you this evening. It's been some time since I saw you last. They have been at it for nearly a half hour. Would you like to have a cup of tea while you wait for your husband?"

Mrs. Hapgood was a petite blonde, in her mid-thirties, who seemed taken aback by the warm welcome she was being given. Kathleen noted that, although Mrs. Hapgood's outfit was neat and well made, her shoulders were a little wider than was fashionable, and she looked like she had known hard work. Her eyes were of a striking dark blue but appeared too large for her face. This, plus the rather limp nature of the fringe of bangs over her forehead, gave the impression of a woman who had been quite pretty but was worn down by work or some illness. Those dark blue eyes turned towards Kathleen with an implied question, and the other woman seemed to notice Kathleen for the first time.

Taking Mrs. Hapgood's outer wrap, she said, "That girl must be Mrs. Fuller's maid. Mrs. Fuller has just joined the Friday circle, replacing old Mrs. Donnelly. I understand she is a widow, like myself. So you see, Mrs. Hapgood, we will not be the only ones kept waiting while others commune with the spirit world. Do come here and take a seat on the sofa, and we will have a nice chat. I will ring for tea."

"You are very kind, Mrs. Nickerson," Mrs. Hapgood replied, looking to Kathleen as if the last thing she wanted was a cozy chat with . . . had she said Mrs. Nickerson?

After Mrs. Nickerson gave the pull next to the front door a sharp tug, she ushered Mrs. Hapgood to the settee across from the stairs and sat down next to her. Mrs. Hapgood sat, played a little with her purse, and then said politely, "I assume your daughter Evie May must be participating in the séance tonight. How is she getting along? If I remember, when I saw you several weeks ago, she had been slightly discomposed, a chest complaint, I believe?"

Kathleen was so surprised by the news that Mrs. Nickerson was the young medium's mother that she missed the first part of Mrs. Nickerson's response.

" . . .felt so strongly Mrs. Frampton was not taking Evie May's illness seriously enough. That woman doesn't have a motherly bone in her body. I told Simon, such a wonderful man, that I might just have to take my dear girl right out of this dreadful city, with its awful fogs, if he didn't take better care of her. Of course he complied *immediately*. He really wants what is best for us both. I was terribly sorry I had had to get so sharp with him; it's not his fault his wife doesn't know a thing about running a household. Just the other day, the cook discovered she hadn't ordered enough . . ."

Kathleen let the steady stream of Mrs. Nickerson's comments run over her as she examined this new information. If this was Evie May's mother, then the girl she met in the hallway, the one who talked like a grown woman but dressed like a child, must be Evie May. *What do you know about that? No wonder the girl is so odd, probably doesn't know which way is up, speaking to the dead like that. Poor mite!* The heavy tread of a large older woman coming down the hallway, bearing a tea tray, caught Kathleen's attention.

"Thank you, Cook. Oh, good, you brought enough cups. You, girl, come be useful and bring that little table over here." Mrs. Nickerson was pointing to a small table next to her chair, so Kathleen, who hated being called "girl" as much at the woman bearing the tray most likely hated being called "Cook," pretended for a second not to hear the command. Then, remembering Mrs. Fuller's instructions to learn all she could from the household staff, she got up and brought over the table, giving the cook a warm smile and helping her lower the large tray onto the table surface.

"Danke schön," said the cook to Kathleen, wiping her hands on her rather dirty apron. Turning her back with obvious disdain on Mrs. Nickerson, she lumbered back down the hall.

"My word, the nerve of that woman," said Mrs. Nickerson, once the cook was out of earshot. "And her English is just awful; I don't know why Mrs. Frampton hired her. She does make a good roast, but half the time you don't know what she puts in the sauces, and she doesn't know her place at all. Since the parlor maid doesn't live in, such an inconvenience, don't you know, we are left with the cook's gruff German ways in the evening. Of course that irritating lady's maid of Mrs. Frampton's wouldn't sully her hands to wait on her betters. Shall I be mother and pour? You, girl, take a cup and go back to your place."

Kathleen took the cup that was being thrust at her and lingered while she helped herself to the cream and sugar on the tray. When neither of the women seemed to object, she also picked up a pastry and returned to her seat by the front door. So, the cook was German, and it didn't sound like she would get much out of any conversation with her, although she did make wonderful pastries, and the lady's maid didn't sound like someone who would chat with an Irish serving girl. Such a shame that the parlor maid, who would be the most likely prospect among the staff for gossip, wasn't here in the evenings, which in itself was very unusual.

The thin voice of Mrs. Hapgood caught her attention as she said, "Mrs. Nickerson, do you think they will be much longer?"

"Now, my dear, you know the circle stays together as long as the spirits are willing," replied Mrs. Nickerson. "Won't you call me Rowena? I confess I miss my friends from back in Brooklyn. But I just had to come when Simon, Mr. Frampton, asked me to let Evie May accompany him to the west coast. He says that without his guidance, her talent could put her in real danger. I couldn't let my little girl go all this way without her mother."

Kathleen continued to listen to Mrs. Nickerson's steady stream of confidences with fierce concentration, wanting to be able to report to Mrs. Fuller exactly what she had said, when she was startled to hear a muffled, masculine voice coming from the top of the stairs. She couldn't see anything except a brief glimpse of trousers on the stairs right above the landing. It couldn't have been Albert, since the trousers were brown, and the voice definitely didn't sound English. A few minutes later, Albert came through the door at the end of the hallway, stopping when he got to Mrs. Nickerson and whispering in her ear.

Kathleen was interested to notice the way the older woman leaned away from him with obvious disgust. Albert sneered and jerked his head in what was clearly a command. Mrs. Nickerson got up slowly, giving her regrets to Mrs. Hapgood, and mounted the stairs, followed by the butler.

Kathleen looked at Mrs. Hapgood, who returned her gaze with a small shrug and went back to nervously picking at her purse. If no one had left the séance room, and all the servants besides the butler were female, who was the man at the top of the stairs?

Chapter Fourteen

"Madame Jacquemieu, Spirit Medium. Communications given from 10
A.M. to 8 P.M."

—*San Francisco Chronicle*, 1879

Annie's frustration increased as she tried to hear what Judge Babcock
and Evie May were saying and keep up with the increasingly active spirit
manifestations around the séance table. The light focused on the cabinet
had dimmed, so Annie once again found it difficult to see, but the noise
level had gone up considerably. *As if designed to mask what was going on
in the cabinet*, thought Annie.

The piano, drum, and tambourine competed with Arabella, who had
returned to the guttural sounds of earlier. Meanwhile, Miss Herron and
Mrs. Mott, who had joined hands once the Judge had broken from the
circle, were both swaying as if in trances of their own. Mrs. Larkson had
moved her chair closer to Mr. Sweeter when the Judge left the circle, and
Annie could hear furious whispering going on from their direction in the
dark.

She now felt a slight cool breeze against her left cheek, as if a window had been opened. *Or a spirit was hovering at her side,* Annie thought
with a self-conscious shiver. Mr. Ruckner and Mr. Hapgood were mercifully silent. As was Simon, until he started murmuring something in her ear
about it being her turn next to speak to the spirits.

While Annie knew that the whole point of attending these séances
was to catch the Framptons using the false information Kathleen had fed
them about a deceased son, she hoped the spirits would pass her by this
evening. Therefore, she was relieved when Arabella's nonsense syllables
were replaced by yet another "spirit" voice, this time that of an old
woman.

"My lovely things, oh, my pretty treasures, where are they, who has stolen them?" asked this new voice, quavering with age and indignation.

"They have all stopped dancing, never to dance again, and it is all your fault. Ha . . ."

"That's for me," the nurse cried out joyfully. "She said Herron, so she must be speaking to me! The spirit must be Mrs. Jones; it sounds just like her. Please, Mrs. Jones, I am here. Don't be sad. Your dancing days may be over, but you have gone to a better place; you are dancing with the angels now."

Then, in a sort of stage whisper, Miss Herron continued, "You see, I had this patient last spring, Mrs. Artimus Jones, quite respectable, married a man who made his fortune in iron manufacturing. But there were rumors she had been a dance hall girl in her youth. Married up, you see. Poor woman, her mind wandered near the end, and she kept trying to get up out of bed to dance."

"No, no, you don't understand. It's my boy, it's my boy I need to speak with," the aged voice rang out.

"Miss Herron, you got it all wrong," said Mrs. Mott, triumphantly. "The spirit is my Aunty Grace, and she wants to talk to her son, Harry. Remember when I asked Uncle Zachary about Aunty Grace? He must have gotten her for me. Her son Harry still lives in Topeka; I must write to him and tell him his mother wishes to speak with him."

While Miss Herron and Mrs. Mott argued over whom the spirit was addressing, Annie ruminated over how effective Arabella was at changing characters. Although she knew that the medium was responsible for the voice of this spirit, in addition to that of Uncle Zachary and Mr. Ruckner's Jennie, Annie still found herself picturing an elderly woman, dressed all in black, with the wide hoopskirts of the sixties, jet beads around her neck, lace gloves on her hands, and a querulous expression on her face. Whoever this spirit was, she was getting irritated trying to be heard above the voices of the two earthly combatants vying to claim her.

Annie heard Simon sigh and was not surprised when he again interceded to bring the séance back to order, his voice ringing out. "Let us welcome the Judge back home with a song. Please, Mrs. Mott, could you lead us in 'Heavenly Pastures?'"

Mrs. Mott dutifully began to sing a song Annie was unfamiliar with, so Annie looked around the table again, noticing that since Simon's mention of Judge Babcock, the light coming from the smaller parlor had increased, making it easier to see. Arabella sat upright, her eyes closed. Mrs. Larkson and Mr. Sweeter seemed to have made up, and Annie noticed that, rather than holding hands, Mr. Sweeter had his arm around Mrs. Larkson's shoulder. Annie found herself revising her opinion about their relationship once again.

She also noticed that the grocer, Mr. Hapgood, seemed distressed. He was sitting very still, eyes wide, staring straight ahead as if he had indeed seen a ghost, and he was making no effort to sing. Miss Herron was singing, in what seemed an attempt to overpower Mrs. Mott, and the two women dropped hands with noticeable alacrity when Judge Babcock reappeared between them. Annie could see that the Judge was in the grips of great emotion. His breathing seemed rapid, and he kept licking his lips. Before rejoining hands with the two women on either side of him, he took out a large white handkerchief and wiped his brow.

"Welcome back, Judge. I hope that your session with your daughter brought you both peace," said Simon.

The Judge nodded grimly. The piano music had died down again. A weak stream of light emanated from the next room, throwing grotesque shadows across the table. Annie could still feel the breeze and was just turning her head to see if the curtains hanging on either side of the fireplace seemed to be moving when Simon continued.

"Please give my lovely wife your full attention. As you all know, we have a new member to our circle, Mrs. Fuller; a sympathetic addition you will all agree, for the spirits have come out in force in her presence. Let us sit in quiet prayer, welcoming the spirits to our circle."

Arabella began to sway again, emitting a low hum. Mr. Ruckner began to sit up straighter, and Annie wondered if a spirit ever returned in any given night. For once, Mrs. Larkson and Mr. Sweeter seemed to be taking things seriously, as they both sat with their eyes closed. Mr. Hapgood continued to stare at some point outside the circle.

"Behold, departed ones," Simon louder this time, startling Annie. "Mrs. Fuller craves your help. Mothers and daughters, fathers and sons, come give us your wisdom and guidance."

Annie noticed the Judge was once again looking past her shoulder, but then he shook his head, as if in disappointment. She willed herself not to turn around. She really didn't want to know if Evie May was still visible and if she was staring at the back of her head. Annie was concentrating so hard, it took a second to register that a new voice was speaking, from behind, but not the voice of a young girl. This voice sounded older, more mature.

"Annie, my love. My sweet darling, I am here, your very own mother. Annie, come sit with me a spell. You are all grown up. How I have missed you."

*****

Annie was never sure how she got into the cabinet, but there she was, sitting on a narrow bench next to Evie May, with the curtain cutting off the sight of the rest of the members of the circle in the next room. She took a deep breath and tried to regain her calm. She did remember that, when she first turned around in response to her name, she had been momentarily at a loss because it seemed that the young medium had been replaced by a grown woman. Now she realized Evie May had looked taller because she was standing on the upraised floor of the cabinet. The girl had also pulled up her hair into a knot and brought down the headscarf, turning it into a shawl, which transformed the way she looked from girl to woman. In the close confines of the cabinet, it was easier to see the girl behind the illusion, despite the fact that she continued to speak in adult tones and kept referring to Annie as her daughter.

Oh, my, she really got to you, didn't she? Annie scolded herself. *No wonder Simon is cultivating this one's "talent," and I thought Arabella was a good actress.* When she closed her eyes, the spell rewove itself, and, for a moment, she could imagine again that it was her mother talking to her, after all these years. But it was just nonsense. Evie May kept repeating

meaningless phrases any mother might say to any daughter she hadn't seen
in some time, interspersed with more concrete details about the ranch
Annie grew up on, her father, Edward, and her favorite horse. Not a single
fact that Annie herself hadn't let drop in the interview with Simon.

When she opened up her eyes, what she saw was a young girl, maybe
as young as thirteen or fourteen, doing a very effective imitation of an
adult woman. The erect carriage, the furrowed brow, the mature voice, all
reinforced the vision, as did the graceful use of her hands as she reached
out to caress Annie's face.

Annie pulled back, repulsed, and said, "Stop this. Evie May, this is
wrong."

The girl ceased speaking for an instant, then resumed, saying in
sorrowful tones, "Oh Annie, you are angry. You have every right to be
angry with me, leaving you when you were just a little girl. But you had
your father to guide you, and I watched over you from Summerland.
Please, you must believe me. My time on this earthly plane is limited;
don't let's waste it. Tell me all about your life, all the things I missed."

Annie shuddered, realizing how incredibly seductive this girl/woman
was, with her sad, pale eyes and her soft voice. How easy it would be for
someone to embrace the idea that she was the embodiment of a loved one
who had died.

But she was here to expose Evie May and Arabella and Simon for the
frauds they were, so that women like Sukie didn't spend the rest of their
lives under that seductive spell. To do that, she had a role to play, so she
took another deep breath and said, "Dearest Mother, I am sorry, this is all
so strange. What do you want to know?"

Evie May smiled and seemed to relax, saying, "Tell me all about your
lovely husband, John. I had so wanted to be with you on your wedding
day; I was there in spirit. I was so distressed for you when I learned you
had lost him after such a short time. Your life has been a sad one. Shall I
try to find him? In Summerland there are many gardens, you know, and I
feel sure I would be able to find him, if you wished. This circle has such
strength, I am certain that they can coax him to come and visit you."

Oh, my heavens, that would be a miracle! Annie thought. *If John is anywhere it's not heaven, but hell. But his appearance could help me convince Sukie that the spiritual manifestations produced by the Framptons are a lie.*

She found that Evie May's inaccurate representation of Annie's husband actually steadied her. Embarrassed that she had lost her objectivity for a few moments, she focused her attention on observing Evie May, trying to determine if she was following some sort of memorized script. Arabella obviously had years of experience convincing gullible people, but Evie May was another matter.

She could see the girl pretty clearly, noticing for the first time that the back of the cabinet was made of a curtain, not wood. This curtain was of some sort of rough cloth that created an eerie glow within the cabinet, obscuring more than it illuminated. In the half-light, she couldn't tell if Evie May's hair was blond or just a light brown, nor could she determine what color her eyes were, except that her pupils were huge. There was also a distinct odor of lavender in the cabinet, and Annie wondered if that was a scent that had special meaning to the Judge.

Evie May had gone silent, looking expectantly at her. Annie knew she was supposed to unburden herself to this false mother, which would in turn give Simon and his two mediums more information to feed back in subsequent séances. Not knowing how much time she had left in the cabinet, she needed to figure out a way to prompt Evie May to bring up Annie's fictional son. She started with a general statement, saying, "Oh, Mother. I needed you so, when I lost Father, then John, and then my precious treasure."

When Evie May just smiled sweetly at her and patted her on the shoulder, Annie became more direct, saying, "Mother, in those gardens, have you seen my Johnny? He was just walking when he was taken from me. Such a sweet baby."

Evie May seemed to hesitate, her face froze for a moment, and then she closed her eyes as if she had a sudden headache. Annie, speculating that this might be a form of diversion while the girl tried to remember her lines, felt a pang of guilt. Such a young girl, and who knew what kind of compulsion she was under to act in this charade.

Just as Annie was about to say something more, Evie May opened her eyes, gave her a shy smile, and said in a small lisping voice, "I'm baby. Can I sit in your lap?"

Annie had barely registered this request, when Evie May, who gave the impression that she had shrunk in size, scrunched up close to Annie, throwing her legs over her lap and snaking one arm around her waist. Then, with her head snuggled onto Annie's shoulder, she popped her thumb into her mouth and began sucking. The transformation from woman to young child was so rapid and complete Annie had trouble believing it wasn't real. In fact, she noticed she had put her right arm around Evie May and was cuddling her. Almost afraid to break this new spell, Annie whispered, "Evie May, who are you now?"

Evie May reared back, pulled out her thumb, and said with a childish pout, "Not Evie! Don't be silly, Maybelle's my name."

"Maybelle, what a pretty name," Annie said. "Can you tell me how old you are?" Annie thought perhaps Evie May had shifted back to the child who visited with Judge Babcock.

"I'm six," said Evie May proudly, holding up first one hand, her fingers spread, and then the index finger of the other. "I'm a big girl now. Been with the angels for ever so long, bet I 'prised you something good, mother."

Annie couldn't breathe. *Mother, she called me mother, and she is six. Just the age . . . if she had lived . . .*

*****

The memories rushed in as Annie was thrust back in time to the hallway of her and John's house in New York City, feeling the sharp pains that had shot through her abdomen that awful day. She had stood doubled over, rereading and rereading the telegram from her husband telling her that her father was dead.

John hadn't permitted her to come with him to Maine, saying only that he had gotten a letter from her father instructing him to come north to discuss some business matters. John had insisted that she needed to stay and prepare for a dinner party they were having that weekend. He must have known her father was ill and kept the knowledge from her until it was too late.

The telegram said that all the funeral arrangements had been made and her father was to be buried that afternoon at three. Annie had stupidly looked up at the hall clock, as if it would tell her there was time for her to get all the way from New York City to the small New England town cemetery in which her father was already interred.

The next thing she remembered she was lying on the floor of that same hallway, in the gathering shadows of evening, the pains dulled to a fierce ache, her nostrils filled with the strong smell of fresh blood. Susan, her young maid, was sitting next to her on the floor, holding a tiny bundle and crying. Annie finally understood that she was saying, "It was a girl, poor mite, a girl, but she's gone to sleep with the angels."

Somehow, Susan had gotten her upstairs and cleaned up, and she had forced her to drink cup after cup of some strong-tasting tea. She had also washed all of Annie's clothes, although Annie never saw that particular outfit again, never having the nerve to ask the young maid what happened to it. She lay on her bed, riding wave after wave of cramping agony while in the dead of night the young servant went out and buried the poor mite who was sleeping with the angels. Later, Annie had planted forget-me-knots in the small patch in the far end of the back garden. *Just one more grave in my life that I will never see again.*

Annie felt chilled when she thought about how competently that sixteen-year-old servant had handled everything and what it revealed about Susan's own experiences before she came to work for Annie. But she had handled everything, and Annie had only to play the role of grieving daughter, because John never knew he had lost a child. He had never even known she was pregnant, never registered her physical changes; he was that uninterested in her.

Already in despair about her loveless marriage, Annie had wanted to save this precious news until she could tell the one man in her life she knew would truly rejoice, her father. Consequently, although she was nearly four months along, she hadn't told anyone, not even her doctor, waiting for her father to come home from that long business trip. But her father never came home, and Annie never told anyone, not even Beatrice O'Rourke, that she had miscarried a child six years ago, a girl who had gone to sleep with the angels.

Chapter Fifteen
Saturday afternoon, October 18, 1879

"The many friends of the late "Charley" Williams…killed in the balloon accident last Sunday, have decided to tender his family a benefit on next Sunday afternoon at Woodward's Gardens."—*San Francisco Chronicle*, 1879

As Nate walked towards the imposing entrance to Woodward's Gardens, with its classical figures and California Grizzlies looking down at him, he checked his pocket watch again, as if this would change the fact that he was ten minutes late. He had started to leave the law offices early enough, but his uncle had delayed him with some damn fool question just as he was putting on his coat, so he missed the #14 car that would have gotten him there with time to spare. In her letter, Annie had said she would meet him at the bottom of the long flight of stairs that led to the main museum, which had originally been R. B. Woodward's residence. He had hoped that if he got there early he would be able to pay her admission, but his uncle had foiled that plan as well. As he paid his own twenty-five cents and was going through the turnstile, he could see Annie across the small plaza, sitting on a bench.

When she saw him, she stood up and waved, and he felt relieved that she didn't seem upset with his lateness. As he strode over to her, Nate couldn't help but notice with approval that Annie was wearing a navy wool coat that fit snuggly over the soft curves of her body and that the cool air had left her cheeks pink and her eyes sparkling. Monday night her eyes were so dark he could barely distinguish the iris from the pupil, but today they were the shade of autumn leaves. As he apologized for his lateness, he observed she seemed distracted, so he dispensed with further niceties and asked if she wanted to enter the main grounds.

She agreed and, taking his arm as they made their way up the stairs, she said, "Shall we go on through to the conservatories? I had thought to stroll the gardens, but it is too cold today."

"Whatever you wish," Nate replied and guided her to the left where he knew the entrance to the first conservatory lay. "I believe that there is a quiet alcove in the fern conservatory."

Annie's light laughter was her answer, but as they came to the small cast iron bench between two gigantic specimens of *polystichum setiferum* and sat down, she looked more serious and said, "Much as I would like to pursue just how you know about this little hideaway, we really must get to the business at hand. Were you able to meet with Mr. Pierce, the *Chronicle* reporter, and have you been able to find out anything about Judge Babcock?"

Nate, taken aback by her abruptness, said, "Unfortunately, Anthony Pierce was out of town when I checked on Thursday, but I left a message at the new *Chronicle* offices. Evidently, he is back in town now because I got a note from him this morning arranging to meet for lunch on Monday. But Annie, it would help if you were to give me a better idea about what you hope I will learn from him."

Annie explained in some detail the basis for Miss Pinehurst's concerns and her own hope that, if she could discover the tricks behind the séances, this would disillusion Sukie Vetch and convince her that they were frauds. Nate noticed, as he listened to her, that all of her light-heartedness had disappeared, replaced by clear signs of distress. He had seen those signs before, the hunched shoulders, the slight frown, the way her eyes darkened, and he began to worry that she was becoming too involved with solving Miss Pinehurst's problem. From experience, however, he knew any opposition from him would only spur her on.

Annie continued, "Last evening, I attended my first séance. Arabella Frampton is the main medium, and she is an exceptionally fine actress. She was able to throw her voice so convincingly it didn't seem to be coming from her, and she spoke first as a refined wife of a banker, then a gruff older man, and finally as an old woman, all in various regional American accents. Quite remarkable. I suspect she must have had some sort of training in theater. The article Pierce wrote about them was vague about her background."

"So you want me to ask Pierce if he knows any more details about her training?"

"In part. I am hoping he knows something more concrete about their methods or any scandal attached to them back in England that he didn't put in his article for the *Chronicle*. Compared to most of the other mediums in town he reported on, the Framptons got off lightly. However, there may be rumors he heard and didn't follow up on or didn't feel were safe to print. I must say they put on a pretty sophisticated show last night. Someone, and I don't think it was either Arabella or her husband, did an amazing job of setting up the proper atmosphere."

In spite of himself, Nate found his interest stirring. He'd never attended a séance, but from her description, this one seemed particularly well produced. "You make it sound like a stage act," he said.

"I guess that is what it felt like," Annie replied. "There was a piano, drum, and what was probably a tambourine, that would play softly, or loudly, or not at all, depending what was going on around the séance table. Kathleen, who was sitting out in the hall, said that the music was coming from the second floor, and it seemed to me to be coming from above. But the timing was so perfect that either the Framptons had some way of signaling whoever was making the music or that person or persons had a way of observing and hearing what was going on down below, and they played with the lights and sound accordingly. Oh, and the table moved."

"What! You aren't serious. The table turned? I always thought that was a joke when I read about Spiritualism in the papers," Nate exclaimed. He was glad to see that Annie seemed less distressed than she had been at the beginning of this discussion.

"Rocked was more like it. What I wouldn't give to have a chance to examine that room. I expect we would find that the table legs are controlled in some fashion. I have read about mediums using iron rods attached to their knees to lift up tables that look heavy but are actually made from very light materials. I wondered if there were holes in the ceiling, and even wires, like the sort used to connect the upper rooms to the kitchen to call servants. Only these would connect the séance room to the room above."

"You want me to find out what sorts of tricks they were up to in England, if there was any scandal, and what kind of training Arabella had, perhaps as an actress," Nate summarized.

Annie nodded and then added, "Also ask Pierce about Simon Frampton's background. He doesn't claim to be a medium, but Pierce described him as a mesmerist, and that intrigues me. He has a commanding presence."

Just then, a troop of women turned onto the path in front of them, arguing over which of three species of ferns were most nearly related. Nate looked a question at Annie as he rose and doffed his hat to the women. She nodded in response and rose in turn so they could make their way down the path and into the rest of the grounds. The cool air was a shock after the humid warmth of the conservatory, and while some of the clouds had begun to break up, letting the sun break through here and there, the wind still was quite brisk. They found themselves overlooking two ponds holding a number of sea gulls and pelicans, in addition to a dozen or more sea lions and seals, raucously barking. The air smelled strongly of fish.

"My goodness, they are noisy, but it is fun to see them up close like this. Is that a seal pup?" Annie raised her voice. "Look, there are two. How cunning, see how they splash each other."

Without thinking, Nate said, "Do you remember our picnic at the Cliff House?"

Annie's demeanor changed, and she seemed to hunch up as she said flatly, "Oh, yes. The seals . . . I . . . well, that was certainly a warmer day than this." She tugged at the top buttons of her coat, which she had opened while they were inside.

What an idiot I am, Nate thought, remembering how that day last summer had ended. Trying to change the subject, he replied, "See here, you must be cold. Let's move on. Is there any particular place on the grounds you want to see? We could go through the tunnel to the zoo, or stop at the pavilion . . ."

Annie didn't reply right away as they walked around the ponds. They had just entered a path surrounded by tall hedges, with a sign that said Marine Aquarium, when she shook her head and said, "I haven't been to the Aquarium yet; I hear it is very impressive. I have only managed to make it to the Gardens a few times this past year. Did you go all the time when you were in the city for high school?"

Conscious of the continued stress in her voice, he tried to lighten her mood, saying, "Yes, it was one of my favorite treats when my parents came to town to visit me while I was boarding with Uncle Frank. I have been here a few times since then with my sister Laura, and that is why I knew about that alcove, I might add. Surely you went here when you were a child?"

"Actually, it had just opened the last summer I came up from the ranch to visit my aunt and uncle. We were scheduled to go the day we received the telegram . . . I . . . it came just as we were leaving the house. I remember we were in the hallway . . . I had a new dress for the occasion. The servant answered the door . . . gave the telegram to my uncle. He . . ."

Nate, who had been listening with puzzlement to Annie's increasingly disjointed words, saw the start of her tears and instinctively pulled her close to his chest. At the same time he turned his back, so she would be screened from the prying eyes of anyone who might pass them on the path. He leaned his head down close to hers, wishing her hat wasn't in the way, and said, "Annie, love, what is it, what telegram?"

"My mother . . . it said . . . it said she had died."

"Annie, I am so sorry." Nate pulled her tighter. "I never would have asked . . . do you want to leave?" Noticing that she was struggling to free her purse, which had lodged between them, Nate leaned away from her far enough to fetch his own handkerchief from his inside coat pocket and gave it to her. She made delicate use of it and then turned back into his arms, where he could feel her taking deep breaths, trying to stop crying.

From his perspective, in all too short a time, Annie had regained enough composure to pull away from him. He tucked her arm in his, and they began to walk silently down the path to the Marine Aquarium, both absorbed in their own thoughts.

Chapter Sixteen

"A feature of great interest to the visitor is the Marine Aquarium. This is not as complete as a few of the more magnificent European ones, but, nevertheless, is noted as being, at the present time, the largest aquarium in this country."
—*California Notes*, 1876

That was embarrassing, Annie thought as she walked beside Nate. *It's been thirteen years since mother died; you would think I would be reconciled by now. That wretched séance stirred up my emotions. Yet it's not like I really thought I was speaking with my mother when I was in the cabinet with Evie May last night.*

Evie May's performance as her mother wasn't what had shaken Annie to her core. It was Evie May climbing into her lap and announcing that she was her daughter that had upset her so. Annie had expected the Framptons to produce a small two-year-old boy named Johnny, not a six-year-old girl, a girl the age her own daughter would have been if she hadn't miscarried. A girl who seemed so real that Annie had momentarily accepted her as the spirit of her own lost child. She must have cried out, because the next thing she knew the curtain was being thrown open, and Simon Frampton stood there, looking decidedly angry. She remembered him saying something sharp to Evie May, who then scooted away from Annie. He then helped Annie to her feet and brought her back to the circle. The séance must have been about to end because, after a short hymn, the door to the parlor was thrown open by Albert, and the lights were turned on.

Annie had immediately left the room, rebuffing an attempt by Simon to engage her in conversation by saying something about a letter she needed to get home and write. She had put on her coat, and she and Kathleen were on the way to the horse car seconds later. Thank goodness Kathleen had been willing to do most of the talking, telling her about the music from upstairs, Albert's coming and going, and a strange conversation between Evie May's mother and Mrs. Hapgood. When Kathleen had asked Annie about the séance, she had fobbed her off by saying that she knew Beatrice would want to hear everything, so it would be better to tell her tale later to both of them, which she had done this morning. Only she hadn't told them about Maybelle.

Maybelle. It was that name that had eventually brought Annie to her senses. Sitting in her room alone, late last night, she'd found herself imagining what her life might have been like if she hadn't miscarried and her daughter had lived, wondering if a living child would have saved the marriage or kept John from committing suicide. Most of all, she struggled with what it would mean if Maybelle was the spirit of her daughter. However, every time she'd said the name Maybelle in her mind, she'd thought, *No child of mine would be called Maybelle*!

And, of course, she couldn't dismiss the unlikely coincidence of Maybelle being a variant of Evie May's middle name. Gradually, Annie's good sense had returned. Remembering how Mrs. Mott and Miss Herron each claimed the spirit of the old woman as their own, she had even been able to laugh at herself for being so taken in. But today's waterworks told her she was still unsettled by the whole experience.

Nate must think me a ninny, falling apart like that over a simple question about where I wanted to go in the Gardens. But, oh, it was good to feel his arms around me again.

These thoughts were interrupted when they reached the entrance to the aquarium, and Nate indicated that she should precede him down a short flight of stairs. She felt like she was entering a cave, deep underground. The light, dim and dancing from the large glass tanks set in rock walls, and the artificial stalactites hanging from the roof, added to this impression.

"Nate, look, sea turtles. And what is that frightening fish, such teeth. Look here, there are little notices that help identify each species." Annie ran up to the glass wall and peered in, enchanted when a school of tiny yellow fish flashed by, inches from her nose. She looked back at Nate and saw he was smiling at her. She said, "Now, don't you laugh at me. I didn't know what to expect, but this is wonderful. See, this tank is sea water and the tank over there has freshwater fish."

Nate followed her over, but as he stood next to her, watching two large trout swim majestically past, she got up her nerve and said, "I must apologize for that outburst. I guess I have been thinking more about my mother than usual this past week. As I told you, Simon Frampton interviewed me on Wednesday, and of course he wanted to know details about her. Then, last night, it was the supposed spirit of my mother that the Framptons produced for me. I guess it has stirred up . . ."

"Do you mean to tell me Arabella Frampton pretended to be your mother? That is outrageous. No wonder you were upset." Nate glowered at her.

"Actually it wasn't Arabella, but a second medium, a young girl, Evie May Nickerson. Quite extraordinary . . . but unsettling. She sits in this cabinet, and you go in and sit beside her." Annie found her voice beginning to shake and realized she wasn't ready to tell him about her experiences with Evie May, and so she said, "Nate, do you mind if we don't talk about this any more just now? I would like to enjoy the aquarium and forget about Miss Pinehurst and her sister's problems for a bit."

Nate took her by the arm, giving it a squeeze, and said, "Good idea. These fellows deserve our full attention. My sister Laura told me the last time we visited there are at least fifty varieties of freshwater fish in these tanks. Unfortunately, she felt the need to read off the name of every single one, in Latin, just to annoy me."

For the next three-quarters of an hour, Annie and Nate walked slowly through the exhibit, peering into all of its sixteen tanks. Annie noticed that Nate was taking full advantage of the limited light and cool temperatures in the building to keep his arm around her shoulders. As he regaled her with stories about his sister, who had just graduated from San Jose Normal School and was teaching for the first time, she realized that one of the reasons she was attracted to Nate was his obvious affection for and pride in his sister.

When they eventually made their way out of the aquarium, Annie asked Nate the time, surprised when he said it was just past five. She suggested they have dinner at the Gardens restaurant before heading home, and he agreed with flattering alacrity.

Annie noticed as Nate took off his overcoat at the restaurant that his suit jacket seemed a bit tight about his shoulders, and she imagined him digging postholes and wrangling steers all fall. This prompted her to inquire after his visit with his parents.

Nate seemed to hesitate, then he said, "I always enjoy the time spent outdoors, a good break from my usual desk work. However, the visit was . . . less satisfying than usual." He then told her about how his father had handed over the running of the ranch to his younger brother, Billy.

"Is he to inherit the ranch?" Annie asked, then she said, "I'm sorry, that was none of my business."

"No, that's quite all right. Yes, it has always been understood Billy would get the ranch. My inheritance was the money to go to college and law school, and I have never minded that. It's just . . . well, growing up, Billy always felt the need to challenge me. He had to ride farther, faster, harder than me, be the better man with the rope . . . lift a bale of hay by himself, that sort of thing. Stupid really. Seemed like every time I came home, first from boarding with Uncle Frank while I was in high school, then after getting my bachelor's from Western Reserve, and the last time when I returned from Harvard, we would get into a fist fight." Nate sighed.

"Does that still happen?" Annie asked, fascinated by this new insight into Nate.

"No, Pa put an end to it a good few years back. He could see that I was having more and more difficulty. I mean when we were young, I would let Billy win. What else could I do? He is four years younger than me, my little brother. But by the time he was sixteen, I could either really hurt him or let myself get beat up pretty badly. Fool boy doesn't know his own strength."

"So what was the problem this year? Did you fight again?"

"No, on the surface everything was fine. It was me. I didn't mind working side by side with Billy, when Pa was giving the orders. Just didn't like Billy bossing me around. He enjoyed it too much. Don't get me wrong, Billy's a fine man, and he's doing a great job with the ranch. He's been working to shift the operations from cattle to orchards and truck farming, which seems to be the future for the Santa Clara valley. I just didn't like being his hired hand."

Nate paused for a second, then continued. "I guess I felt like I had gone from the frying pan into the fire. First Uncle Frank bossing me around, treating me like a first year law clerk, then my pipsqueak little brother telling me how to throw a rope." Nate sighed again, and Annie fought a desire to lean over and pat him on the shoulder.

The waiter came with their orders, and Annie thought it might be a good time to change the subject, so she asked after Nate's mother and laughed as he described Billy's very pregnant wife Violet following his mother around like a puppy.

Wiping his mouth with his napkin, Nate leaned back when they had both finished eating and said, "Well, Annie, I think it is time you told me a little more about what got you so upset at that séance last night. I hope you noticed I didn't say a word about your decision to start investigating again, which shows remarkable restraint on my part, given what happened last time. But you need to tell me exactly what your plans are. I will be glad to help, but not if you leave me in the dark."

Annie felt her temper flare, but then she took a deep breath and let the anger go. She had asked him for help, and it was reasonable for him to want more information. When she looked up and saw how anxiously he was examining her face, she chuckled. "Oh, Nate, I suppose I should thank you for not lecturing me about minding my own business. As you might guess, I have already gotten a variation on that theme from Beatrice and Esther. Kathleen, on the other hand, is quite excited, and I do believe she is reading that series of short stories about the Pinkertons that came out last year, looking for tips on undercover investigations."

"Heaven help us, I am not sure the Framptons know what they're facing," Nate said. "But back to my point, what upset you last night and who is this young girl you mentioned?"

Annie told him everything she had learned about Evie May, her extraordinary talents, and her odd mother. "She is some sort of chameleon. Kathleen said when she met her she acted like a young woman in her twenties. On Friday, I saw her transform, in front of my eyes, from a young girl, supposedly Judge Babcock's daughter, to an older woman, who said she was my mother."

And then she turned into a six-year-old girl, but I'm not ready to tell him about Maybelle or that I thought she might be the spirit of my own daughter.

"Judge Babcock? Judge Zebulon Babcock?" said Nate.

"Yes, he is a permanent member of the Friday séance. That's why I asked you about him. Do you know him?"

"No, I don't. He's not from San Francisco. But Uncle Frank remembered there was a Pennsylvania Supreme Court Justice Zebulon Babcock in the forties and fifties, and I was able to find a few old-timers who knew of him. There's this saloon that is frequented by members of the legal profession, and round about lunchtime you can find four or five retired lawyers and judges who play checkers there and tell stories about the good old days. I stopped by and asked if anyone had heard of Judge Babcock being in town. Two of them spoke up and said he had arrived a few months ago. Staying at the Baldwin Hotel."

"Did they know why he was in town?" Annie asked.

"It did sound strange at the time, but now it makes more sense. Judge Fullerton said he had heard rumors Babcock had decided that some girl was the reincarnation of his daughter and had followed her to San Francisco. Fullerton seemed to think Babcock had gone senile and was reluctant to say anything else. All of the men sitting around the table were at least eighty, so I guess this was a subject that made them pretty uncomfortable. Does this help?"

"Gracious me, that poor man. Nate, don't you see? This is just what happened to Sukie Vetch. They have used this poor man's grief to . . . you should have seen the Judge! He ran and held onto Evie May like a man drowning, and when he came back from his session in the cabinet . . . it was downright disturbing. He acted like he had just been with a lover, not the spirit of his dead daughter. Do you think we could talk to him, try to convince him of how he is being defrauded?"

"Whoa, Annie, I don't think so. You don't know men like Babcock. Judges, especially someone who has been a Supreme Court justice, they're like gods. They don't want to hear someone tell them they're wrong about anything. Believe me, if he has picked up and moved out west because he has decided this girl is his daughter brought back from the dead, he isn't going to listen to any evidence from you or me. Besides, you are operating on the assumption he is sane about this issue, which, from your description and what Fullerton intimated, is debatable."

Annie sat and thought for a moment, picturing Judge Babcock as she saw him last night, and sighed. "You may be right. Frankly, I don't have any confidence that proving Arabella is a fake, or exposing the way the table moves or where the music is coming from, is going to be enough to convince Sukie Vetch, either."

"How do you think you are going to convince her?"

"I told you about Kathleen telling Arabella Frampton that I had had a son who died at about age two. I hoped that at the séance last night the Framptons would produce the spirit of that young son, and then I could tell Sukie it was a lie, as proof they were making everything up. Instead, Evie May portrayed the spirit of my mother. This doesn't mean they won't come up with the boy in subsequent séances, but it does mean I am going to have to keep attending until this happens. I also would like to see if there are any other people who attend these séances who would be amenable to helping expose the Framptons, even if the Judge isn't a good prospect."

"Do you think there is anyone who might be upset enough to support you if you were able to show them how the tricks worked?" Nate leaned forward towards her.

"I don't know. I am planning going to the Monday night circle, and I will go early enough to get more acquainted with the people who are attending. Surely one of the regulars would be upset if they discovered that they had spent all that money on a group of confidence tricksters. Just think, someone like Sukie, who attends two circles a week at $2 a night and several private 'sittings' a week, which are more expensive, is spending as much as $10 a week. That would mean Sukie is handing over as much as fifty percent of her husband's salary to the Framptons. No wonder her poor husband is frantic."

Nate whistled and then said, "The Framptons must be making a lot of money."

"Yes, but they also have a lot of expenses. Renting that house can't be cheap. Kathleen thinks there are at least four servants, and the Framptons seem to be living quite well. I can't help but wonder if they aren't using the power over their clients to make money from them in other ways than just the fees they are charging."

"What do you mean?"

Annie shook her head. "I'm not sure, but I have heard of mediums getting clients to will their fortunes to them or getting them to invest in risky stock schemes. I just had a thought. Even though the newspaperman, Pierce, wrote favorably about the Framptons in his article, he was skeptical about Spiritualism in general. When you meet with him, you might see if he would be interested in writing another article, if you could get him details about the tricks they use but also about how they are exploiting poor people like the Judge and Sukie."

"That's a great idea. I assume you want to keep your own name out of this when I talk to Pierce. I thought I would do the 'friend of a friend' angle. But you need to think about how to handle this if he agrees to write up a story. Maybe I need to start attending some of the séances, then I could keep you right out of it."

"Wouldn't your attendance at a séance hurt your reputation as a lawyer in town? I can't imagine your uncle would permit it."

"Hang what Uncle Frank says. I've been thinking about leaving the firm and striking out on my own. Anyway, if it ever came out, I would just let it be known that I was 'helping the police with an investigation.' Now that I think about it, I might just stop by Detective Jackson's office tomorrow, see what the police think of the Framptons, if they have any dirt on them."

"Beatrice would support that idea. As soon as I told her about my plans, she said I should leave it up to the police. We could get her nephew Patrick involved. It wouldn't do his career with the police any harm if he participated in the exposure of some swindlers."

Annie realized that Nate's willingness to share in her investigation of the Framptons had buoyed her spirits. She found the idea of him attending one of the séances with her particularly attractive. She would ask Simon on Monday if there were any chance of extending the circle's membership on Friday. She thought they would be glad to add a lawyer to their list of clients. If not, maybe she could figure out a way to get one of the regular members to drop out. Mrs. Larkson didn't seem to be taking the séance seriously.

"So, Annie," Nate broke into her thoughts. "Shall I escort you home? I don't want to get into Mrs. O'Rourke's bad graces by bringing you back too late." As he helped Annie into her coat, he continued. "Perhaps I should meet you at the Framptons Monday night. Escort you and Kathleen home. I could ask Simon Frampton about attending a séance myself, and then I could tell you what I learned from my meeting with Anthony Pierce earlier in the day. I must confess I have developed a hankering to meet this Evie May."

Annie shivered and buttoned her coat all the way up as they left the warmth and lights of the restaurant. Much as she talked about finding out how the ghostly effects of the séance were created, or tricking the Framptons into producing a son that never existed, Annie knew that the only way to convince Sukie Vetch she wasn't meeting her son, Charlie, was to get to the bottom of Evie May's strange abilities. And that meant getting back into that cabinet herself and confronting both Evie May and the spirit of Maybelle, which Annie knew with a certainty she didn't want to do at all.

Chapter Seventeen
Monday afternoon, October 20, 1879

"On Saturday, J. C. Ainsworth, President of the Oregon Steam Navigation Company and the Managing Director of the Northern Pacific Railroad… arrived in San Francisco and was interviewed by a reporter of the *Chronicle*, at his rooms at the Baldwin."
—*San Francisco Chronicle*, 1879

As Nate walked down the short flight of steps into the entrance of the Elite, a restaurant that lived up to its name with dark wood paneling, crisp white table linen, and French cuisine, he realized he didn't have any idea what Anthony Pierce looked like. He may have run across him a few times when he stopped by the old *Chronicle* offices to see his friend Tim Newsome, and he'd certainly read a number of his articles. Pierce was known for his biting political satire, but Nate had never been introduced to him.

He was surprised Pierce had named the Elite as their meeting place, since its prices were pretty steep, and from Tim's frequent complaints he'd understood that reporters made even less money than junior law partners. Nate only dined here when a client was paying. He supposed, since he was asking Pierce for a favor, he would have to foot the bill. But it would be worth it if he enlisted his help in exposing the Framptons. Annie would be so pleased.

When the maître d' came up and Nate murmured that he was meeting Pierce, the man nodded and led the way to a small table tucked into the far back corner of the restaurant. *Good, this will give us some privacy.* He walked up to the table where a spectacularly ugly man was sitting. Pierce, who rose and shook his hand, was quite short, and only his powerfully muscled neck and shoulders kept his large head from appearing ridiculous. Disheveled black hair failed to hide a pair of jug ears, and his nose, which had clearly been broken at some time, reigned over a straggling mustache;

yet his wide grin and fine dark brown eyes turned the disaster of his other features into a pleasing whole. Nate found himself grinning back at Pierce, attracted by his air of extreme confidence.

"Well, well, Mr. Nate Dawson, what a pleasure. Tim speaks highly of you, which must mean he owes you, because in my experience, old Tim Newsome doesn't throw around praise lightly. What'ya do for him? Give him a tip on the harness races? Provide an alibi for him to his wife?" Pierce laughed heartedly.

"Why, Mr. Pierce, Mrs. Newsome would box my ears if she thought I was in cahoots with Tim," Nate said. "No, I met him when I was a boy. He was a senior at Boys High when I was a freshman, and I am afraid he was instrumental in leading me astray. Been trying to make it up to me ever since."

After their meals were ordered and Nate and Pierce had mined the fertile subject of local politics and what the recent election of Isaac Kalloch, the Workingmen's Party candidate for mayor, was going to mean to the city, Pierce finally introduced the topic of the Framptons.

"So, Nate. Don't mind if I call you Nate, do ya? What's your interest in Simon and Arabella Frampton? Your message was pretty cryptic."

"One of my clients, you understand I can't say who, has a relative who has become a frequent participant of the Frampton séances. My client is worried that he might be getting involved in something unsavory and dishonest. Undue influence and all that. I remembered that you had written some articles about local mediums, and I thought you might be able to give me a little background on them." Nate stopped, hoping that Pierce wouldn't press him on the identity of the client or their relative.

"You want to know if they're honest?" Pierce rubbed his head vigorously, further encouraging a wayward cowlick. "Guess it depends on whether or not you believe in the ability to talk to spirits. Now, for myself, it seems like a lot of claptrap. After fighting in the Union army for four years, don't know I would want ready access to the dead. Haunt me enough in my dreams, so I don't have any desire to pay good money to have them chatter at me in the daytime. But, if you do believe in such things, the Framptons, as far as I could see, give good value for the fees they charge."

"Good value. What do you mean?"

"You see, I attended a couple of their séances, and they put on quite a show. Lights, music, spirit voices, and a strange girl in a cabinet. Now, are you asking me if all of it was real? Don't know. Probably not, but I didn't see any tricks. No strings or fake hands on sticks or mediums slipping out of the circle to prance around as ghosts. And the folks sitting around the table seemed satisfied with the little talks they were having with their dearly departed. Not like some of the other mediums and fortunetellers in town."

Pierce again indulged in one of his full-throated laughs and then said, "Lord almighty, there was one woman who promised if you would let her connect you up to a battery then the electric current would rearrange your magnetic fluids and reacquaint you with your past lives! I tell you, after the hours I spent sitting in dark rooms, having some old gypsy fondle my hands and give me bad advice, or peering at the indecipherable scribbling on slates by so-called professors, the Framptons' séances were a treat. And that Arabella, have you met her? Easy on the eyes, I've got to tell you. I didn't mind letting her hold my hand at all!"

Nate smiled, as he knew he was supposed to, but he didn't like the coarse sort of humor at which Pierce obviously excelled, particularly when it was directed at women. He remembered that he'd heard rumors that Pierce had expensive tastes in the female sex, not just restaurants. He'd also had a sudden shock when Pierce had mentioned a gypsy fortuneteller, and he wondered if Pierce had been to see Madam Sibyl when he did his investigation for his article. Surely Annie would have mentioned this to him if it were true.

Nate decided he'd better get right to the point. He didn't want any more reminiscences about fortunetellers, so he said, "I can see you were impressed by the Framptons, but I do have to gather as much background information as I can, if only to reassure my client. If you could let me know if there was any information you learned about them that you didn't put in your article. For example, what kind of training did Mrs. Frampton have before she became a medium, and what exactly does it mean that Simon Frampton was a mesmerist?" Nate took out a small notebook and pen that he carried around in his coat pocket to signal he was ready for more serious business.

Anthony Pierce smiled at him, took a sip of his coffee, leaned back, and began to spell out in detail the background story he had gotten on the Framptons. As Nate wrote down the spew of facts, he recognized with increased admiration that Pierce was one of those men whose mind was like a steel-trap. It caught and held every bit of minutia that came his way. According to Pierce, Simon Frampton was born in England in 1834, the younger son of a wealthy Southampton wine merchant. He was expelled from a good public school, and, in defiance of his family, he apprenticed at age eighteen with a touring magician. By the age of twenty-three, he had his own show, and he took on Arabella, whose family had a tumbling act, as his assistant when she was only fourteen. In 1860, when she was sixteen and he was twenty-six, they married, and at some point in the next ten years he added mesmerism to his magic act.

"Simon showed me a bunch of clippings; he was billed as 'Simon the Seer,' and evidently this part of the act was such a hit that for several years they even toured the cities of Europe," Pierce said.

"What role did his wife play with his mesmerism act?"

"Now, that wasn't clear to me. I suspect by that time, she'd have been in her twenties, and contorting herself so she could 'disappear' into various trunks and boxes wasn't as easy. She may still be small, but her endowments are, let's say, substantial. I can imagine just by standing on stage and striking pretty poses that Arabella would have been an asset to any act."

Pierce went on to tell Nate that sometime in the early seventies, the couple settled down in London, and Arabella began her career as a medium, with Simon acting as her business manager. "I don't know why they decided to come to the States when they did. Simon said they'd heard good things about the support of Spiritualism over here. I suspect it might have had something to do with the big scandal that year in England, when some famous British medium was caught running around in the dark wearing white sheets. Simon probably thought it was a good time to get out of town."

Nate looked up from his notebook and said, "Did you hear of any scandal associated with the Framptons themselves?"

"No, not a whiff. I even wrote a friend of mine in New York to see if maybe they came to the west coast because of some difficulty with the good citizens of that fair city. He wrote back that the good citizens were sorry to see them go, especially the lovely Arabella!"

Nate confessed to himself he was beginning to develop a strong curiosity about Mrs. Frampton. But it didn't look like he had dug up anything useful for Annie. He thought he would take one more stab at it, saying to Pierce, "I was wondering if you might be interested in doing a follow-up article on the Framptons, if I did find out anything new. For example, if I found out how the 'show,' as you called it, was carried off or, maybe, evidence that the people attending the séances are being unduly influenced. You know, like the rumors about how Mrs. Lincoln was being manipulated by those mediums she invited into the White House to contact her son Willie during the war."

Pierce sat up straighter and leaned towards Nate, who felt that for once he had fully engaged the journalist's attention.

"Well, Nate," he said, "I can't say my editors would feel another article revealing the secrets of the séance would have much to offer our readers. They weren't all that pleased with the last set of pieces I wrote. Didn't feel the subject was worthy of my 'keen political mind,' I think is how Charles de Young put it. That was before he went off and shot old Kalloch, which wasn't particularly worthy of his keen political mind, was it? But if there was some real scandal, maybe some wealthy businessman was . . . say, this doesn't have anything to do with that whole Voss affair this summer? I believe Newsome said you were mixed up in that somehow."

"No, not at all. My uncle's firm does represent the Voss family, but this is an entirely different matter." *And Annie certainly wouldn't thank me if I somehow got you interested in opening up that whole mess,* Nate thought to himself.

"Right, then," said Pierce. "Let me tell you what I will do. You just sit tight; last thing you want to do is put a scare into the Framptons by nosing around. I will shake the trees a little, see if anything falls out, and if I think there's something worth writing about, I will try to sell my editors on it. I'll get back to you as soon as I can, but since I've been out of town, I am behind on a number of stories. You tell that client of yours to hold their horses. Some good people in this city support Spiritualism and might get their noses out of joint if you aren't careful. Now me, I make my living upsetting people, but I expect with a respectable firm like yours, a low profile is what sells."

"You sound like my uncle," Nate replied. "Truth is, I'm getting a little tired of being respectable and maintaining a low profile."

"God, don't I know what you mean," exclaimed Pierce. "I had an uncle who actually refused to ever have anything to do with my ma because she married a man he didn't think was respectable enough. What an ass. His wife was even worse, treated my mother like dirt."

Pierce frowned and thought for a moment. "You know what, Nate my boy, when Kalloch takes office in December, there's going to be some real shake-ups happening in town, Republicans thrown out, Workingmen's Party and Democrats coming in. You wouldn't happen to be a registered Democrat, would you?"

Nate shook his head. "Actually I'm not officially affiliated with any party. Uncle Frank likes the firm to be seen as independent, although I'm a staunch supporter of the national Republicans."

"Of course you are. Let me think on it. City attorney's office could use a good man like you. Then there's the state level. We may have lost the city, but danged if the Workingmen's Party didn't siphon off enough Democratic votes to give the governorship to a Republican. Going to be even bigger changes in Sacramento."

Standing up abruptly, Pierce crammed on his hat and shot out his hand to give Nate a hearty shake. "Got to run, deadline and all. Thanks for the fine meal and some mighty fine conversation. I'll get back to you as soon as I can, but you stay away from the Framptons until I do."

Chapter Eighteen
Monday evening, October 20, 1879

"Mrs. Upham Kendee. Electrician and medium. 207 Kearny St. Sittings
daily. Circles Tuesday and Friday evenings.
—*San Francisco Chronicle*, 1879

Annie hadn't really understood how nervous she was about being
called to sit in the cabinet again with the disturbing Evie May until the
point in the séance on Monday night when the lights behind her brightened
and she heard the words, "Father, come to me," issue forth from the young
medium. Relief washed over her as she watched Judge Babcock push
away from the table. This time, at least, she was safe. *But safe from what?
Safe from Maybelle? Just one more of Evie May's inventions. What harm
can she do me?*

Annie still hadn't mentioned the disturbing encounter with Maybelle
to anyone, telling herself that this would just bring up unnecessary questions and emotions about a past she wanted to stay buried. Yet she knew
she would need to enter that cabinet again if she had any hope of the
Framptons producing the fictional Johnny, still her best plan for convincing Sukie Vetch of the Framptons' perfidy. And that meant risking another
meeting with Maybelle. Hearing the agitated voice of the Judge behind
her, apparently unhappy with what the spirit of his precious daughter was
telling him, Annie thought again about what Nate had said. If he was right
and the Judge was invested in his belief that Evie May was his daughter,
nothing would persuade him she wasn't. Was there any reason to believe
Sukie would be any different?

Annie sighed and felt Simon Frampton squeeze her hand, as if to
comfort her. This brought her attention back to what was going on around
the table. So far, the Monday night séance had followed pretty much the
same routine as Friday's. There were some changes. Miss Herron was

absent, which made sense. Few live-in workers, even nurses, got more than one evening off a week. In her place was a bland but pleasant woman, a friend of Mrs. Mott's, and the two women had chatted animatedly during the half-hour Annie spent in the parlor with them before the séance began. This had prohibited her from talking to them, which was a nuisance, since she had come early for the purpose of getting to know her fellow circle members better.

Mrs. Larkson and Mr. Sweeter were also absent, and she had wondered if the discord she had witnessed between them on Friday was the reason, but then Simon had introduced Mrs. Henderson and Miss Reynolds as Monday night regulars. Mrs. Henderson was a widow, here to communicate with her departed husband, a pharmacist. Miss Reynolds was her sister. She had evidently developed a lovely relationship with a minor Greek philosopher who spoke to her through Arabella.

This Greek had, in fact, been throwing out pithy sayings for a good ten minutes, to the delighted exclamations of Miss Reynolds, when Simon intervened and sent him on his way, giving the Judge his chance with Evie May. Annie had to admire the erudition that Arabella had displayed in this example of trance mediumship. To have memorized all those quotes was a prodigious feat, and Annie would have been even more impressed if she hadn't had to memorize the exact same sequence from her classics text at the academy. Once more she wondered at Arabella's background and hoped that Nate had gotten some useful information from Pierce.

Ruckner, the banker, sat again on her left, looking more disheveled than ever. Annie's attempt at engaging him in conversation when they first sat down at the table had failed. She reminded herself to ask Miss Pinehurst to arrange a meeting with Sukie's husband, Arnold Vetch, because she believed there was something too coincidental in Sukie's husband working for Ruckner's bank. Harold Hapgood from the Friday circle was also in attendance, but Annie had been tied up talking to Mrs. Henderson and Miss Reynolds when he made his appearance right before the séance was to begin, so she hadn't learned anything more about him.

So far, in addition to the usual piano music, Arabella had entertained them with assorted groans, advice from Mr. Ruckner's wife, a visit from Mrs. Henderson's departed husband, and another of Mrs. Mott's relatives, this time her oldest sister, who had died and taken a secret recipe for plum sauce with her. As Arabella, doing an excellent imitation of a uneducated Midwesterner, mumbled out various ingredients, Mrs. Mott was obliging enough to call out suggestions, saying things like, "Myrtle, did you mean to say citron?" and, "Speak up, dear, remember how Mother taught us to enunciate." Then had come the Greek. All in all, while amusing, the séance hadn't yet produced anything that forwarded her plan to expose the Framptons.

"Annie, it's me, your father. Pay attention, child. I don't have long."

Disconcerted, Annie looked to her right, to the door, from which the male voice seemed to emanate. Then, recalling Arabella's ability to throw her voice, she looked back to see with relief that it was indeed Arabella's mouth that was moving.

"Annie, you must pay attention. I know you want some advice about your financial affairs. I will try to help you, but you must concentrate. What do you want to ask?"

For an interminable few seconds, all Annie could think of is how unlike her father this spirit sounded, despite a credible attempt on Arabella's part to duplicate a New York accent. Simon leaned close and whispered, "Mrs. Fuller, this is your chance. You asked to speak to your father, here he is. Don't be shy."

Gathering her wits, Annie said, "Father, is that you?" Then, taking a deep breath, she continued, trying to sound as plaintive as possible. "Father, why did you have to die? I feel so lost without you." *There, that's better. Now is the time to do my own bit of acting.* "Please, I know you always said not to touch the trust, to live on the interest. But San Francisco can be so expensive. I need you to tell me what to do. You promised I would be well taken care of after you died!"

The spirit of her father replied, "Daughter, perhaps if you tried to economize, you wouldn't be in such difficulty."

That sounded more like John! Annie remembered how her husband had berated her when she asked for additional money to pay the house-keeping bills. Of course, it didn't enter his mind that his insistence on buying the best wines and inviting his drunkard friends to dine most every night caused her financial difficulties. The spirit certainly didn't sound like her father, which Simon may have realized, because she could feel him stir beside her. She had the impression that he was about to speak when the spirit continued, this time less harshly.

"Dear Annie, don't worry. I will guide you through this difficulty. If you just put your worries in my hands, I will use all my powers to keep you on the path to financial happiness. Perhaps when next we speak, you can have specific questions prepared. Tell me where your money is invest-ed, and I will divine what actions you should take to ensure a beautiful future."

"Oh, Father, that is wonderful," Annie cried, trying to sound as enthusiastic as she could. "But don't go yet, please. Mother left before she could tell me; have either of you seen my sweet boy?"

Arabella suddenly slumped and began to moan, most piteously. Simon again whispered in Annie's ear, saying, "Please be patient, Mrs. Fuller. Our visitors from the other side often have difficulty staying long when they first communicate with us."

Annie was nevertheless frustrated. Perhaps it was the intention of the Framptons to postpone her encounter with her son for as long as possible. She suspected that face-to-face chats with Evie May were the most effec-tive method they had of hooking a person, but the risks were high as well. There was a big difference between what Arabella was doing, producing a disembodied voice, and what Evie May did, which was to create a flesh-and-blood illusion of the departed loved one. As had happened to Annie on Friday, the illusion could go wrong, and the Framptons might be reluctant to schedule another meeting right away. *I will just have to convince them that they have to give me a chance to sit and talk and hold my little boy.*

Arabella's groans grew louder, the light from the back room dimmed further, and the music died away. The table began a terrific rocking, the first occurrence of this phenomenon that evening. A cold wind brushed so strongly against Annie's face that she felt the lace at her throat flutter. A hollow-sounding male voice began to speak. Annie could swear it came from above their heads, but the darkness in the room was now so profound that she couldn't see Arabella's face clearly enough to determine if she was the source. *How impressive!*

"Harold! Harold, my son, account for yourself! I left you in charge, and yet all has gone awry!"

Annie heard a soft anguished moan coming from the end of the table where the non-descript Mr. Hapgood sat, and she thought that this surely wasn't what you wanted to hear from your dead father. *Poor man!*

"Harold, how many times must I tell you, be a man, not a boy? That wife of yours has more backbone than you."

"F-Father, please, let me explain. I don't know what happened. I . . ."

"Don't snivel!" the spirit barked, prompting another moan from Hapgood. "How can you say you don't know what happened? Your brothers are furious. They told me to tell you, 'You know what happens to little brothers who don't behave.'"

"No, Father, please . . ." whispered Hapgood.

Suddenly, Arabella slipped into the swaying and humming portion of the night's entertainment, the music swelled, and Simon made one of his pronouncements, saying, "Beloved spirits, answer our heartfelt calls. Let us welcome the Judge back with the hymn 'Heavenly Pastures.'"

As the hymn ended, the doors from the hallway rolled open, and Annie was bedazzled by the increase in light. Albert moved to turn up the lamps throughout the room, revealing Mr. Hapgood being patted consolingly on the shoulder by Mrs. Mott's friend. Annie noticed he didn't seem to appreciate the good woman's ministrations. The Judge was looking quite serene and pleased with himself, much to Annie's disappointment. Whatever the disagreement with his daughter, it looked like it had been resolved. *What am I going to tell Miss Pinehurst when I see her tomorrow? I can't keep attending these séances forever, but I don't seem any nearer to finding a way to extricate Sukie from the Framptons.*

*****

The girl, dressed in a white wool suit, put down the lamp on the floor and knelt in front of the large, battered trunk, staring motionless into its depths. She reached in and picked up a faded pink hair ribbon and brought it to her face. Standing up, she hurled the ribbon back into the trunk, looked down, and swore. Struggling with the buttons at the back of her skirt, she successfully unfastened the top ones and pulled the skirt and petticoat down, kicking them away from her when they reached the floor. Then she took the jacket off, revealing a plain white chemise. Diving into the trunk, she pulled out a brown and yellow sweater and a pair of boy's brown knickers, which she shimmied up over her white wool stockings, taking the time to button the pant cuffs below her knees. She then pulled on the sweater. She searched in the trunk again, finally finding a brown cap large enough so that she could cram her hair, with its white bow, into it. She stood still for a second, stuffing her hands into the pants pockets, started and then smiled widely. Pulling out a chunk of sarsaparilla gum, she unwrapped it and popped it into her mouth. Chewing slowly, she walked over to one of the windows facing the street and looked out. She stepped back hastily, then sidled up next to the window and peeked out again. She stood so still, only the slightest rise and fall of her shoulders revealed she was breathing at all.

Chapter Nineteen
Monday, October 20, 1879, late evening

"Patrick Carroll, while drunk last night, entered the dining room of J.N. Schneider's boarding house, and proceeded to demolish the furniture."
—*San Francisco Chronicle*, 1879

Kathleen squirmed on the hard wooden seat of the horse car, made more uncomfortable because her toes barely touched the floor. She was tired, it was well past nine-thirty, and normally by this time in the evening the dishes would be done, Mrs. O'Rourke would have put the dough for the morning rolls onto the windowsill for their slow rise, and the two of them would be having a last cup of tea before turning in for the night. Since it was Monday, she had been up at four-thirty this morning. Washday. Even though Mrs. Fuller had recently hired a laundress, Kathleen still had to get up early to start heating the large kettles of water, and she had refused to give up responsibility for the men's collars and cuffs and the women's clothing. Mrs. Kantor might be a good soul and did a splendid job on the bed linens and tablecloths, but Kathleen shuddered to think what her rough, chapped hands might do to the ladies' delicate underthings.

Mr. Dawson had shown up at the Framptons just as the séance ended to escort them home. Exhausted though Kathleen was, she wouldn't have missed this evening and the chance to see him and Mrs. Fuller together. She knew Mrs. O'Rourke would want a full report. The light cast by the passing gas lamps was strong enough to give Kathleen a clear picture of the couple sitting across the aisle from her. Mr. Dawson was turned towards Mrs. Fuller, a smile on his face. Mrs. Fuller, forced by her bustle to sit almost sideways on the bench, vigorously stabbed the air to make some point, then looked up into his face and laughed.

Kathleen sighed. After all the time Mrs. Fuller and Mr. Dawson spent together in August, Mrs. O'Rourke and Mrs. Stein had been sure the two of them would be hitched by Thanksgiving. But then everything had fallen apart.

Kathleen was convinced something had gone wrong the last time Mr. Dawson visited the boarding house before going to visit his folks. When he'd left the house, he'd looked like he'd bit into a sour persimmon, and he didn't have his usual kind word for Kathleen. As for Mrs. Fuller, it was plain as the nose on her face that she'd been out of sorts the whole time he'd been away.

"Like she'd gone back to sleep," she'd said to Patrick, Mrs. O'Rourke's nephew, one morning several weeks ago. "When I started work here I saw how sad she looked when she was alone. She's always kind and good humored to me, and she isn't above laughing at a joke when we're all sitting around in the kitchen, but when no one is around, she'd look tired and sad. Like someone took all the stuffing out of her. But when Mr. Dawson came into the picture, he sort of woke her up, like one of those princes in the fairy tales. Then he went away, and it's like the curse of the bad witch has got her all over again."

At that point, Patrick had got all cheeky and said he'd be glad to wake Kathleen up with a kiss if she wanted him to, and she'd slapped his face, ever so gently, to put him in his place. Then he tried to put his arm around her, and, well . . . about that time his aunt had come in from the garden to find out what he'd done to make Kathleen screech and she hadn't thought any more about it.

Now, however, it seemed to Kathleen that Mrs. Fuller had woken up again, ever since Mr. Dawson got back in town, and it did Kathleen's heart good to see the change.

Oh, dear, what's gone wrong now? Kathleen thought when she heard Mrs. Fuller utter a sharp exclamation, which wiped the smile from Mr. Dawson's face.

"Nate, you aren't saying I should stop attending, are you?"

"No, that's not what I said. I said that Anthony Pierce advised against *me* poking into the Framptons' affairs until he had had a chance to check them out further. He doesn't know a thing about you, and we need to keep it that way. Pierce warned that if a lawyer like me started to ask questions, Simon Frampton might get the wind up. That is why I didn't go ahead tonight and ask to attend a séance. Maybe I shouldn't have come at all, but I wanted to at least check out the place, see the Framptons in person."

"But Pierce did say he would look further into whether or not there was any scandal associated with them?" asked Mrs. Fuller.

"Yes, although he didn't seem to feel there was much chance of finding out more than he had. Pierce seemed a good enough sort of fellow. Even offered to . . . well, that's neither here nor there. What's important is that he will ask around to see if there is anything he missed. I'm sorry that he didn't seem to know much more about Arabella Frampton's background."

"But what you learned does answer some of my questions," Mrs. Fuller replied. "For example, where Simon got his upper-class accent. And tonight Arabella quoted from a classics textbook I had as a student. Clearly, she didn't have that sort of schooling, but her husband did. She has got to have a terrific memory to do what she does. Keep all those characters straight. He must have had her memorize all those passages, just for Miss Reynolds."

"Was Miss Reynolds the tall, formidable lady?"

"My, no." Mrs. Fuller laughed. "That was Mrs. Mott, who is really much sweeter than she looks. She appears to view Arabella as some sort of telegraph operator connecting her with her Kansas relatives, alive and dead. Miss Reynolds was that small woman, rather nearsighted, who bumped into you. She comes to the Monday circle with her sister, replacing Mrs. Larkson and Mr. Sweeter. That was a disappointment. I did want another chance to observe them after what Esther Stein told me."

Kathleen leaned forward to hear better, since the rattle of the car wheels on the track had gotten louder as they crossed Market Street. She had been in the kitchen this morning when Mrs. Stein started to tell Mrs. Fuller what she had learned about Mrs. Larkson, but she'd had to leave to help Mrs. Kantor drain the first tub of wash water, missing the whole story.

Mrs. Fuller continued. "It turns out Esther's youngest daughter, Hetty, knows Isobel Larkson quite well. She says the mothers of Jack Sweeter and Isobel Larkson were cousins, and the two of them grew up just living down the street from each other in Portland. That's where Mr. Larkson met Isobel, on a business trip. When Mr. Sweeter came to San Francisco to look for a position four months ago, of course Mr. Larkson invited him to stay with them. Hetty told her mother that initially she thought this was a good idea, because Isobel, who is so much younger than her husband, seemed very homesick. She thought having a relative from back home staying with them would help. But now she's not so sure. Mr. Sweeter hasn't found work yet, and Hetty feels he hasn't been a good influence on Isobel. 'Encouraging her to gad about, neglecting her wifely duties,' were Hetty's exact words. Esther said Hetty is a firm believer in 'wifely duties.'"

"In what way do you think this couple can help you expose the Framptons?" Mr. Dawson said, which was what Kathleen had been thinking.

"If there is anything untoward about the relationship between Mrs. Larkson and Jack Sweeter, and I must say the term 'kissing cousins' seemed quite fitting, given the way they behaved, then they would be prime candidates for blackmail, if that were the Framptons' game."

"Blackmail?" Kathleen blurted out. "Oh, ma'am, sir, I'm sorry, I didn't mean to interrupt. I was just so surprised."

"Miss Kathleen," said Mr. Dawson, "don't apologize! You took the words right out of my mouth. So, Mrs. Fuller, are you going to tell us why you think the Framptons are engaged in blackmail?"

"I don't know anything for a fact, but sitting there tonight, listening to Mr. Ruckner and some of the others spilling out intimate details about their own lives, thinking about what Judge Babcock might be saying to his supposed daughter in the cabinet, I couldn't help but wonder how easy it would be for the Framptons to use this information to their advantage. You know successful mediums depend on good intelligence gathering. I am sure they discover secrets that clients might pay to keep hidden."

"That's real interesting, and you could be on the right track," Mr. Dawson said. "Anthony Pierce might not have been much help, but after lunch I stopped by to see our old friend Chief Detective Jackson, see if he had heard anything about the Framptons. He said they keep files on any complaints made against the mediums, fortunetellers and such that work in the city."

"Heavens, do you think they have a file on Madam Sibyl?"

"Well, they might, but I wouldn't worry. I doubt there is anything in it, and from what Jackson said, usually the police don't even follow up on the complaints, since speaking with ghosts or telling people their future isn't against the law. Interestingly, while the file on the Framptons was slim, there was one long letter written by a lawyer on behalf of Judge Babcock's sister and heir, asking the San Francisco police to forward any information of wrongdoing by the Framptons, to be used in a suit the sister was filing to have the Judge declared incompetent.

"The Chief Detective said, 'Unfortunately, being a damn fool doesn't make you incompetent,' so he didn't think the sister was going to have any luck. But we might think about contacting her anyway."

"Nate, this is good news. Was there anything else in the file?"

"Three other letters, all anonymous but, according to Jackson, all from different women. One woman wrote that her husband had lost all their money investing in a business his dead brother recommended. She blamed the Framptons, saying they had benefited from the investment, so they had committed fraud. Jackson told me that the police had looked into the complaint but couldn't find any relationship between the Framptons and the company. The second letter complained that the Framptons and their spirits were driving her husband to drink, and the third, which is what I found most interesting, was from a woman who had made the mistake of telling the ghost of her dead mother a secret, and now the Frampton's were pressuring her to do something 'awful' and couldn't the police shut them down."

"Oh my, what did the police do about that complaint?" Mrs. Fuller asked.

"There wasn't anything they could do because there wasn't any return address or name given and no description of what the letter writer was being asked to do, so no evidence of a crime. But if there is any truth to the letter, it sure does suggest the Framptons aren't above blackmail."

Kathleen, who had been startled by something Mr. Dawson had said, used a brief pause in the conversation to ask a question. She leaned into the aisle that ran down the center of the car and said, "Mr. Dawson, sir, did you say one of the letters talked about driving a man to drink? Cause I think I might know who sent that letter."

Mrs. Fuller responded quickly, saying, "Kathleen, whatever can you mean? Who . . ."

Just then, Mr. Dawson stood up and yanked on the cord that rang the bell by the driver, who pulled on the reins, bringing the car to a slow stop.

"Ladies, I do believe this is O'Farrell. Time for us to get off," he said, leading the way to the front of the car. He then stepped down and offered Mrs. Fuller his hand, helping her down on to the street. As Kathleen was about to disembark, he reached up and helped her down as well. *Such a gentleman,* she thought. *Patrick could learn a thing or two from him.*

Once they all reached the sidewalk and began the short block and a half up O'Farrell to the boarding house, Mrs. Fuller again asked Kathleen to explain what she had meant.

Kathleen, rather embarrassed that she had said anything, hesitated a moment.

"I'm probably wrong. It's just that Mrs. Nickerson, Evie May's mother, came and sat and talked to me tonight. I think that that Mrs. Frampton told her to keep an eye on me. I saw her whisper something and point over at me, just before she went into the room with all of you. As a result, Mrs. Nickerson and I were together the whole time, and she was quite chatty. I learned all about where she grew up, her husband who died, her older children and how they all abandoned her, except Evie May, and how she felt that Mrs. Frampton didn't take proper care of Mr. Frampton. But at one point she mentioned that Mrs. Hapgood, the lady who sat with her on Friday, couldn't make it on Mondays because she had to close up the store she and her husband run. She said Mrs. Hapgood worried that he might be tempted to stop off somewhere on the way home if the séance upset him too much."

Kathleen flashed on the memory of her mother sending her out as a little girl to whatever job site her father was on, hoping she could convince him to come straight home. Sometimes that had worked. But after her mother died, Kathleen had had to stay home with the little ones, and her father never came straight home again. *Off drunk in some dive is where I thought he was the night he didn't come home at all, ever again. Never thought he was dead from falling headfirst from a crossbeam on the job. Drink killed him all the same. Never would have slipped if he hadn't started drinking first thing in the morning. Never would have died if Ma had been there to josh him out of one of his black moods.*

"How interesting. Harold Hapgood has a problem with alcohol," said Mrs. Fuller, pulling her away from these dark thoughts.

"That makes some sense. I noticed tonight that when he first came in, he went straight for the sideboard where Albert was pouring drinks. He just stood there for a moment, then turned away and went and sat down at his place at the table. I can imagine he might want a little sip of courage if he had any idea of how nasty the spirit of his father was going to be. Simon Frampton said that Hapgood comes to get advice about running the business, but what he got tonight was an earful of recriminations.

"What I don't understand is why he would keep coming back, if that is what most of his communications were like. I could certainly see his wife trying to stop him from coming and, if she couldn't, writing the police in desperation. I think that a little chat with Mrs. Hapgood might be very useful."

They had just arrived at the front of the boarding house, and Mrs. Fuller stopped and gave Kathleen a little hug, saying, "Thank you, Kathleen. I think this might be the most important piece of information we've gotten yet. I just knew bringing you along with me was a good idea."

Kathleen felt her chest expand, like her heart had somehow grown, and she was searching for the right words to express how glad she was to have been of service, when Mrs. Fuller turned and said rather stiffly, "Mr. Dawson, I would invite you in, but I am afraid it is late, and both Kathleen and I have early morning duties tomorrow. But I do thank you for escorting us home."

Kathleen wished she could excuse herself and slip down the sidewalk to the back entrance to the kitchen, so that Mr. Dawson would have a moment alone with her mistress. But she knew Mrs. Fuller had strictly forbidden Mrs. O'Rourke from waiting up for them, so the back door would be locked. Instead, she moved forward and up the steps to the front porch, where the light from the oil lamps sitting in both parlor windows created bars of light. *How nice of Mrs. O'Rourke to leave them both burning, but I will need to remember to refill the lamps in the morning*, she was thinking when she was startled by a cry from Mrs. Fuller, who had mounted the stairs behind her.

Turning, she saw that her mistress was staring at a slip of paper in her hands. Mr. Dawson was taking the stairs up to the porch two at a time, saying, "Annie, whatever is the matter? What do you have there? Here, let me see it."

Mrs. Fuller shook her head, letting Mr. Dawson take the paper. "I found this in my coat pocket when I was looking for the front door key. Someone must have slipped it in while I was at the séance. It must be a joke, Nate."

Kathleen looked at the piece of paper that Mr. Dawson now held out to catch the light from the windows and saw, written in thick black ink, three simple, chilling sentences.

YOU MAKE A GRAVE MISTAKE. CANT FOOL THE DEAD. STAY AWAY IF YOU KNOW WHATS GOOD FOR YOU.

Chapter Twenty
Tuesday afternoon, October 21, 1879

"STREET CAR ACCIDENT. On Monday afternoon as Mrs. Fay was stepping from one of the dummy-cars on Larkin street, with a child in her arms, she was thrown to the ground by a sudden jolt and severely bruised. The child escaped injury."
—San Francisco Chronicle, 1879

Walking briskly down O'Farrell, Annie felt the steady push of wind on her back. She knew once she turned onto Market that the taller buildings along this main thoroughfare would offer her some protection. For now, she wished she had taken the time to change out of the refurbished black silk she wore during the day as Madam Sibyl, but she had more clients to see this evening. Late afternoon, however, was the only time Miss Pinehurst had free in her job as head cashier at the restaurant Montaigne's Steak House.

The chill, damp October air at least woke her up. The discussion last night between Nate, Kathleen, and herself, following the discovery of the threatening note in her coat, had gone on for some time. It had been midnight before she made it to bed and more like two in the morning before she fell asleep. She had almost dozed off waiting for Madam Sibyl's last afternoon client.

She felt wretched about keeping Kathleen up so late, knowing she would be up again by five to get breakfast for the boarders and start on the ironing. Thank goodness the laundress, Mrs. Kantor, was here again today to help. If this investigation into the Framptons went on much longer, Annie would have to either stop bringing Kathleen with her, which would break the girl's heart, or hire some additional help. She certainly couldn't foist any additional work on Beatrice.

This morning, Annie had felt guilty when she saw the dark circles under Kathleen's eyes, but the truth was she had been afraid to be left alone with Nate for any length of time last night. She'd felt too shaken and vulnerable, and she knew from experience that in that frame of mind she would either throw herself into his arms in tears or pick a fight with him. With Kathleen present, she had reasoned, neither would happen.

At the time, she hadn't taken Kathleen's suggestion that the note was from a jealous Arabella very seriously. She had merely been glad of an excuse to deflect Nate from his argument that the note proved that the Framptons had discovered the connection between Mrs. Fuller and Madam Sibyl, a line of thinking that led inevitably to him insisting that Annie shouldn't attend any more séances.

However, as she thought about the note again this morning, she wondered if there was any truth to Kathleen's reading of the situation. She wasn't vain enough to think that she offered any real competition to Arabella. The look on Nate's face last evening when Mrs. Frampton came into the hallway confirmed what Annie already knew: no man was immune to the medium's beauty. Nevertheless, Annie had enough experience with human nature to recognize that insecurity can strike anybody, particularly a woman in her thirties facing the inevitable effects of time. Annie was younger and more similar in background to Simon than was his wife, and that might indeed explain the hostility she had felt from Arabella from the start.

Having turned onto Market, Annie saw she was almost to the entrance of the restaurant, and she began to wonder what she was going to say to Miss Pinehurst. Nate wanted her to say that she was giving up the investigation, and once Kathleen told Esther and Beatrice about the note, they would probably concur. On the other hand, despite the note and her dismal lack of progress, Annie just didn't feel she could give up yet.

Montaigne's, with its prime location across from the Palace Hotel at the corner of Kearney and Market, catered to a lunch crowd of local businessmen from the Montgomery Street financial district and women taking a break from shopping at the City of Paris department store. In the evening, it attracted the theater-going audience. Conversely, at four in the afternoon, the restaurant was practically deserted. Annie had never been here before; its prices, even for a midday meal, were far above her financial resources; and she was curious to see what 'all the fuss was about,' as Beatrice would say.

The dark, paneled ceilings and crystal chandeliers, soft Brussels carpeting, tables featuring white linen and gleaming silverware, upholstered chairs, and silent waiters in black, formal attire all whispered elegance, and Annie was swept back to a time when her father took her to Delmonico's on 14th Street in New York for her birthday lunches. Montaigne's headwaiter interrupted this reverie. He smiled warmly when she murmured, "Miss Pinehurst," and escorted her to a small dining room off the main room, which in the evening would be for special parties.

At this time of day, the room seemed the exclusive domain of her boarder. Walking over to where Miss Pinehurst sat, she noticed that the exquisite tailoring of the older woman's dark-burgundy silk and the stunning, black-onyx brooch pinned to the lace at her throat perfectly matched the elegance and good taste of the restaurant. As the waiter removed her coat, Annie thought how fortunate she hadn't worn the brown polonaise; the black silk, no matter how old, was much more appropriate to her surroundings.

Miss Pinehurst measured out a tiny smile, then nodded to the large, leather-bound menu on the table, saying, "I hope you don't mind if I have my dinner while we talk. This is the only time I have to eat until the restaurant closes at midnight. Do feel free to order for yourself, as my guest."

"Miss Pinehurst, thank you, but I dined earlier. A pot of tea and perhaps some bread and cheese would be lovely."

When Annie saw the rich strips of sirloin on Miss Pinehurst's plate and tasted her own aged Camembert, she understood why Miss Pinehurst seldom ate at the boarding house. Beatrice was an excellent cook, but Annie couldn't afford to serve this quality of food and keep her boarding charges at a reasonable rate.

Miss Pinehurst cut up a small piece of meat, then looked over at

Annie and said, "So, Mrs. Fuller, what have you learned? Is there anything I can use to convince my sister the Framptons are frauds?"

"I am sorry, Miss Pinehurst. I don't have anything definite. However, I do have a few avenues I would like to pursue further," said Annie.

She went on to tell Miss Pinehurst about getting the reporter, Pierce, to do some more background checks, the possibility of contacting Judge Babcock's sister, and her suspicions about the coordinated use of music and lights from the room above the séance.

"I am trying to find out if there is any time when the Framptons are out of the house when I might get access to the séance room to figure out how some of the tricks are played. I still believe our best chance of success rests with getting the Framptons to conjure up the ghost of my alleged son, Johnny. So far, they have produced the spirits of my mother and my father. I have asked for a special sitting with the young medium, Evie May, tomorrow afternoon, when I hope that Johnny will appear."

Miss Pinehurst, who had been steadily eating throughout this recital, put down her fork, neatly wiped her mouth, and gave Annie a hard stare. "So you do agree that this Arabella is just a trickster?"

"I do, Miss Pinehurst. She is a clever actress, with a broad range of accents, but I heard her say nothing that demonstrated any supernatural knowledge. She merely parroted back to me what she had learned from me about my father, and, in fact, she completely misread my father's character when she tried to speak for him."

"What of the girl? The one that Sukie sits with in that infernal cabinet? The one she says turns into our Charlie?" Miss Pinehurst's voice cracked with emotion.

Annie hesitated, taking a sip of her tea to buy time.

"Evie May is another matter; she actually seems to change her physical appearance. I have seen her shift from a young woman, who Judge Babcock believes is the reincarnation of the daughter who died twenty-five years ago, to a woman the age my mother was when she died, and again to a six-year old girl." Annie stopped speaking, discomforted anew by her memory of Maybelle.

Miss Pinehurst burst forth. "Mrs. Fuller, you aren't saying you believe that child is possessed?"

"No, I believe that Simon Frampton has discovered a young girl with remarkable natural acting talent, and he is shaping her into a lucrative source of income, just as he did twenty years ago with his own wife. However, if I did believe that the dead could take possession of the living, Evie May would be terribly convincing."

"Such wickedness to use a young child like that." Miss Pinehurst shifted angrily in her chair.

"I agree, and I would very much like to know how Simon Frampton is doing it. I suspect his abilities as a mesmerist might play a role. I have read about people being put into a trance and acting as if they were younger or older. Perhaps this is what he does to Evie May. In any event, if tomorrow he has her play the role of Johnny, I still believe this might be enough to convince your sister. If they will risk it. You see, there is a possibility that the Framptons have developed some suspicions about my motives."

Annie then told her about the note and Nate's concern that it might mean that the Framptons had found out about her living in the same house as Madam Sibyl or, worse, being Madam Sibyl herself. She said, "I knew that was a risk, but it might just as well be someone else in the household or in the séance circle who sees me as some sort of a threat. I will know better if they let me have the planned sitting with Evie May."

Seeing the droop in Miss Pinehurst's usually stiff shoulders, Annie tried to offer the older woman some hope, saying, "Listen, even if I should be denied access to the séances or Evie May, that doesn't mean the end of it. There is still the Judge's sister. And there are several others, relatives of members of the circle, who might have similar concerns and would be amenable to joining forces. It would help if we could find out who wrote the letter to the police saying that the Framptons were blackmailing her. Then we could get a criminal investigation going."

"Blackmail? You think that the Framptons might be blackmailers? I didn't want to believe . . ." Here Miss Pinehurst stopped and put the napkin to her lips as if to stifle further comment."

"Miss Pinehurst, what do you mean? You must be honest with me if I am to help you."

Miss Pinehurst closed her eyes as if in prayer and began to describe a conversation she had Sunday night with her sister's husband. He had taken her aside after dinner to tell her that Sukie was expecting, but he feared for his unborn child's life. "He said that when the doctor informed them of the good news, instead of rejoicing as he had hoped she would, Sukie had appeared distressed. She told her husband that when she had first confided to Charlie that she might be going to have another child, he had seemed very happy. But then he said this would mean that someday soon he would have a new little brother or sister as his very own playmate in Summerland. Sukie has interpreted that to mean that this new child won't live very long either."

"Good heavens, Miss Pinehurst, that is awful. Why ever would the Framptons suggest that to her?"

"I don't know if it is the Framptons' doing. Sukie is so angry with her husband for refusing to come with her to the séances that she has decided Charlie is lonely and that is why he wants the new baby to join him. It's sinful. God has blessed her with another chance at a child, and she has turned her back on that child. But that is Sukie. From the day she was born, all she has ever thought of is herself. She would mope around and refuse to eat if she didn't get her own way. Mother indulged her, and when she died, Father was even worse. I suppose I was no better. I felt so sorry for her losing our mother at such a young age. I was working full time, first in the store to help out Father and then as a waitress, trying to put food on the table after Father died. As a result, I had little time for her."

Miss Pinehurst paused, then continued. "When she met Arnold Vetch, she was only seventeen. I was against the match because he didn't seem strong-willed enough to handle her tantrums. But there was nothing I could do. She wanted Arnold Vetch, so she got Arnold Vetch.

"Then Charlie was born, and for a while everything was all right. Sukie was happy, and she was even able to share her happiness with me. I know I will never have a home, a husband, or a child of my own, but every

Sunday night, sitting with Charlie in my lap, reading to him, it was somehow enough."

Annie watched as a tear slid down Miss Pinehurst's cheek, and she had to fight to hold back her own tears in response. Shaking her head to regain control, she said, "Miss Pinehurst, I am so sorry. For you and your sister and brother-in-law. But I don't understand how this relates to blackmail."

The waiter came into the room just at this point to remove Miss Pinehurst's dishes and pour her another cup of coffee. Annie turned down another pot of tea and watched as the interlude gave Miss Pinehurst the chance to pull herself together.

"Mrs. Fuller," Miss Pinehurst began calmly, once the waiter was gone, "my brother-in-law was so disturbed by what Sukie had told him that he went to see Simon Frampton last Saturday afternoon, to plead with him to refuse to let Sukie attend any more séances, for her sake and the sake of her unborn child."

"What did Frampton say? I assume he refused?"

"Mr. Vetch told me that Frampton pretended to show great concern, but he said there was nothing he could do, that he had no control over the spirits or Sukie. He said if he denied Sukie access to Evie May, the spirits would simply find some other way to speak to her. Then, and this is the important part, Frampton said he believed that Mr. Vetch was making a great mistake in not meeting with Charlie himself. He said that perhaps if he met with Charlie alone and was willing to answer every question the spirit asked of him, maybe Charlie could be convinced to help his mother come to terms with his death and welcome the new child."

Annie repeated the phrase "answer every question the spirit asked of him" and said, "What did Mr. Vetch think Simon meant by that? What do *you* think he meant?"

"I asked my brother-in-law that same question. He professed to have no idea, but I couldn't shake the feeling he wasn't being honest with me, or maybe himself," Miss Pinehurst replied. "I have already told you of my concerns regarding the financial burden Sukie has put on him by her reckless expenditure of money. I am also worried that if anyone learned of his wife's involvement with the Framptons, it might damage his reputation at his place of employment, the San Francisco Gold Bank and Trust."

Annie nodded and said, "I've always thought it couldn't be a coincidence that one of the owners of that bank, Mr. Ruckner, also attends the Frampton séances. I thought at first that maybe Sukie had been involved with getting him there. But now I wonder if the connection isn't more sinister. What if Simon Frampton hopes to get Mr. Vetch to reveal privileged information about the Bank or Mr. Ruckner?"

Miss Pinehurst leaned forward, her face grim. "My brother-in-law told me he flatly refused Frampton's suggestion to visit Charlie, that he threatened him with the police if he didn't stop his pernicious influence over Sukie. But I saw in his eyes the real truth. My brother-in-law is a good man, an honorable man. But he is weak, and his greatest weakness is Sukie. I fear something terrible is going to happen if these evil persons aren't stopped."

Annie and Miss Pinehurst talked a little longer about what Simon Frampton's motives might be and decided that it was imperative for Annie to meet with Sukie's husband as soon as possible. Then Mr. LeFrey, the proprietor of Montaigne's, entered the room and graciously inquired after Annie's small meal. He encouraged her to come to Montaigne's again when she could enjoy the delicacies of the full menu, saying that any friend of Miss Pinehurst would be an honored guest. Miss Pinehurst gave LeFrey the first genuine smile Annie had ever witnessed from her, then said it was time for her to return to her responsibilities. Annie, looking at the watch pinned at her waist, realized that she needed to hurry if she didn't want to be late for Madam Sibyl's six o'clock client.

When she got ready to leave the restaurant, she discovered to her dismay that it was raining quite hard. Miss Pinehurst pressed her own umbrella on Annie, saying that Mr. LeFrey always called a cab to take her home if the weather was inclement. Fortunately, one the frequent horse cars that plied Market had just stopped at Kearney when Annie left the restaurant. Even though it was so crowded that she was forced to stand on the open platform at the back of the car, there was a roof over her head, and the crowd of people around her blocked most of the wind and rain.

Remembering how everyone at Montaigne's Steak House had been so kind and thoughtful with Miss Pinehurst, Annie realized that until today she had felt sorry for this woman, whose life seemed narrow and confined. Yet, despite the tragedy of her nephew's death, she did have family. And she had a family of sorts at Montaigne, where she had worked for over ten years, where people treated her with respect and cared enough to order a cab to take her home. Thinking fondly about the people she had gathered around her at the boarding house, Annie recognized for the first time the similarities between her life and Miss Pinehurst's.

But would I be content ten years in the future to say, as Miss Pine-hurst has said, that I was reconciled to having no husband, no child? This thought led to thoughts of Nate, and then she noticed the horse car was slowing to let people off at Fourth and Market. Annie began to squeeze through the platform to the steps leading down to the street. Just as she got to the top of the steps, several men in front of her hopped down, opening the way for her. People pressed up behind her, no doubt trying to get off before the car began to move forward, so she hurried to open the umbrella, which had an unfamiliar kind of catch. She had just managed to get it open when she found herself leaping into space, the umbrella torn from her hands by a ferocious gust of wind. Hands miraculously now free, she was able to break her fall enough so she only went down on one knee.

"Lady, are you hurt?" said an older man who rushed up to her from the sidewalk and leaned down to help her to her feet. "I never seen anything like it, that brolly almost had you airborne!"

"Thank you so much, sir, I'm fine," Annie said, embarrassed by the crowd that had gathered, despite the continued downpour. "I'll just be on my way; we all need to get out of this rain."

"Oh, there's a good lad, he's caught your umbrella for you. That will help keep some of the wet off, if it don't decide to go flying again," the man said with a chuckle as he raised it over her head.

Annie wiped a sopping strand of hair out of her eyes, opened her purse, and found a penny to give the young boy, who grinned and ran off. Walking over to the sidewalk, she thanked her protector, who tipped his hat and also went on his way. As she turned to walk up Stockton, she realized that, with each step, pain blossomed in her left knee. She wondered if the wetness running down her leg was blood or just her soaked skirt. Her left wrist was also hurting, and when she turned her hand over she saw a trickle of blood seeping from under the top of her glove. She took a deep breath. *It was just a fall. There's nothing wrong that a little arnica won't cure.* Then a wave of dizziness rolled over her as she remembered the distinct feel of a hand shoving her in the small of her back, right before she and the umbrella took flight.

Chapter Twenty-one
Wednesday afternoon, October 22, 1879

"Lena Moroney, Spirit Medium, Private Sittings, 1023 Stockton Street."
— *San Francisco Chronicle*, 1879

Twenty-four hours had done much to bring down the swelling in her knee, so Annie was able to walk without much discomfort as she and Kathleen made their way to the Framptons, where Annie was scheduled to have a "private" sitting with Evie May. On Monday, before the séance had begun, Simon had offered her this chance to meet alone with Evie May. Later that evening, when arguing with Nate about whether she should return to the Framptons, Annie brought this up as proof that Simon didn't know about her connection to Madam Sibyl. After yesterday's accident getting off the horse car, she wasn't so sure.

While the storm had rumbled its way out of the city sometime late last night, yesterday afternoon it had been throwing its full force at Annie as she hobbled up the hill from Market. She was a sorry mess when she finally arrived home: hair soaked, coat muddy, gloves ruined, and limping so badly she had trouble making it up the stairs to her room. She'd had some faint hope of repairing most of the damage before encountering anyone else in the household, but, as luck would have it, just as she was about to creep into her second floor room, the Steins' sitting room door opened and Kathleen came out, followed by Esther Stein.

Annie thought Kathleen had actually shrieked, so she must have looked awful, but Esther had made no comment, just ordered Kathleen to go down to the kitchen and bring up the hip bath and as much water as she could get from the hot water reservoir on the stove. She then told Annie to strip while she got a pile of towels from the hallway linen closet. In a short time, Annie was sitting in steaming hot water, having her hair washed by Kathleen and her knee looked to by Esther. Her story of an errant gust of wind, unwieldy umbrella, slippery horse car steps, and a fall seemed to satisfy both women, who were more concerned about making sure Annie didn't catch cold and unsuccessfully arguing that she cancel Madam Sibyl's evening clients. What she didn't reveal to the two women, or later to Beatrice, was the role a sharp shove had played in her accident, nor her discovery of another note in her coat pocket. Written in black ink like the first note, the message was short and sour: STAY AWAY OR ELSE.

She hadn't stayed away since here she was, once again at the Framptons' door. Ringing the door pull, she reassured herself that there wasn't anything to fear. It was a sunny afternoon, Kathleen was with her, and the worst that could happen was that the Framptons might turn her away and refuse to let her have her private sitting with Evie May.

On reflection, she couldn't even take the shove too seriously since whoever did it couldn't even be sure Annie would fall, much less be hurt. Unbidden, Annie had an image of Arabella, wearing some long hooded cloak as a disguise, following her to the restaurant, maybe expecting to catch her in a secret tryst with Simon, and using the confusion of the rain and the crowded horse car to slip the note in Annie's pocket. She then imagined Arabella so overcome by jealousy that she had shoved Annie in a fit of anger.

Rather amused by the scene she had just conjured up, Annie's fear dissipated, permitting her to address Albert with equanimity when he opened the door and stood glaring at her. "If you will be so good as to summon Mr. Frampton," Annie said, stepping forward, forcing the butler to give way. "I have an appointment with Evie May at three. I will wait for him in the parlor. Kathleen, you wait for me here, and I am sure that Albert will see that you are given a cup of tea."

Annie walked over to the parlor door. She had hoped to have a few moments in the séance room alone to explore its secrets, but when Albert opened the door, she was disappointed to see Simon standing in front of the fireplace, waiting for her. The curtains were pulled open, revealing two sets of French doors leading to the side garden, a dark tangle of shrubs whose rain-washed green contrasted favorably with the artificial leaves of the room's wallpaper. Overall, this room did not fare well in natural light, which exposed the worn edges of carpet, the sheen of an inexpensive velvet tablecloth, and a chip in the marble mantel.

Simon moved to her side, shaking her hand, and commanding her attention with his extraordinary gray eyes as if, she thought, he feared letting her spend any more time in observation. "Mrs. Fuller, how good it is to see you. Please let me take your coat. Albert will hang it in the hallway for you."

"No thank you, Mr. Frampton. I believe I will keep it on. I got a little chill yesterday from the rain," Annie said. She stepped neatly around Simon and moved towards the fireplace. She thought for a moment that leaving her coat in the hallway might give Kathleen a chance to see if someone deposited another note. She decided, however, to keep her coat on. She was once again wearing one of her older black silks, not only for convenience since this evening she again had appointments as Madam Sibyl but also because Annie had only a limited number of outfits appropriate for the role she was playing as a wealthy young widow.

"I am so sorry, Mrs. Fuller," Simon Frampton said. "Please, why don't you have some sherry before we commence the sitting? It will warm you nicely." He walked over to the drinks table and, without waiting for her response, poured out a very generous helping.

Annie had no intention of dulling her faculties in preparation for her sitting with Evie May, so she said something about it being too early in the afternoon, walked over to the second set of windows, and looked out to see if there was a path that would provide access to the room from outside. The strong breeze she had felt at each séance prompted this curiosity. Despite the overgrown nature of the side garden, the patch of ground right next to the house was cut back, and she could see a narrow opening in the bushes that would lead to the rear of the house. Albert, or the yet unseen lady's maid, could easily slip into the room and stand behind the curtains until one of the sections of the séance when the room was in complete darkness. *To do what? Fool around with the lights? Play the tambourine?*

Not wanting Simon to note her interest in the side yard, Annie turned and began to burble out a series of questions designed to establish further her credentials as a naïve, unthreatening woman. She asked how the spirits knew to come, did his wife have a way of calling them, and did they come to Arabella when she wasn't holding a séance. She then asked if someone could communicate on their own . . . because she felt sure that last night as she lay in bed, she heard her mother's voice, "clear as a bell."

Simon got a word in edgewise when Annie paused. "Please, Mrs. Fuller, do have a seat, and I will try to answer your questions." He then indicated the small sofa in the corner. When she sat down, trying not to react to the sharp twinge in her knee, he sat beside her and reached out to take both of her hands in his, his thumbs resting on her wrists in uncomfortable intimacy.

Annie resisted her impulse to pull away, reasoning that his move would not have been unwelcome by most women, Mrs. Larkson, for example. However, she also knew from her experience as Madam Sibyl that Simon could use the beat of her pulse under his thumbs to determine how agitated she might be.

So, she sighed and said, "Oh Mr. Frampton. You are such a comfort," while at the same time she pulled her hands from his grip and swiftly clasped his right hand in her own, squeezing tightly. "I am glad that I have you here to advise me. Father seemed extremely upset with me on Monday. He sometimes hid my dollies away when he wanted me to study my sums more diligently. I don't know that I will listen to him if he persists in being so mean."

Annie pretended to pout, glancing upwards through her eyelashes to gauge Simon's reaction.

Simon smiled at her and used his free hand to pat her on the shoulder. "Mrs. Fuller, I can assure you that your father is just looking out for your interests. I am confident that he will have some very good suggestions on how to invest your money. But tell me, why aren't you asking Madam Sibyl for this sort of advice?"

Her first thought was, *Blast you, Nate Dawson. Did you have to be right?* Her second was, *I should have been prepared for this. I have*

seriously underestimated Simon, but he hasn't indicated that he knows
Madam Sibyl and I are the same person, thank goodness.

Fortunately, several years of working as Madam Sibyl had taught
Annie how to think quickly while stalling verbally, so she let her mouth
continue to rattle on in the same vein as before.

"Why, Mr. Frampton, do you know Madam Sibyl? Of course, I don't
know what would make me think you wouldn't, seeing as you are in the
same business. Is there some sort of organization? A secret society? My
father was a member of the Masons. Oh dear, he told me over and over
again that I should never reveal that. Well, he's dead, so I can't see that it
would hurt him. You don't think they have such groups in the afterlife? Oh
my, that could be awkward. Please promise you won't mention it, I mean
to your wife. I wouldn't want it to slip out the next time she communicates
with him. He already seems so unhappy with me."

Annie, pleased to see a small, puzzled frown on Simon's brow, judged
it was time to answer his original question. "But at least I get a chance to
see him, or at least hear him, when I attend one of your séances. Madam
Sibyl just reads palms or talks about the stars. Silly business. I admit I did
think at first that she could help me. I mean, how convenient, right there in
the house, and I got a discount on her fees. It was one of the reasons I
agreed to rent out the downstairs parlor to her. It would help pay my
expenses, and she would be able to advise me in my investments. But it
was all a sham. I tried investing money as she suggested, but my income
didn't increase at all, and when I wanted to sell shares to purchase a new
gown, she got quite cross.

"That's when I decided to try to talk to my father. Maybe he is angry
with me because he knows I have gone to a fortuneteller. He always said
they were charlatans, and now I am inclined to agree. If I didn't need the
income, I would ask her to leave. But Mr. Stein said I shouldn't do anything so hasty."

"My dear Mrs. Fuller, I do hope you will find better success with your
father," Simon interrupted her. "But I do believe that financial advice is
not your only motivation in contacting the spirits. I was under the impres-

sion that you had a request of a deeply personal nature. Which is why I suggested this sitting with Evie May, she has such an extraordinary way of channeling the spirit world."

Feeling as if she had passed some sort of test, the knot in Annie's stomach began to ease. *What would have happened if I hadn't reassured him of my lack of complicity with Madam Sibyl? Probably Evie May would have then turned out to be indisposed.* She would have to be very careful from now on not to deviate from the role she had created for herself. She was sure Simon had not spent a lifetime fooling people with his magic, mesmerism, and mediums without developing a well-honed ability to detect when other persons were trying to pull the wool over his eyes.

Pushing that unsettling thought aside, Annie replied, infusing her voice with nervousness she didn't have to pretend. "Mr. Frampton, I am so uneasy. I know I asked for a chance to speak with my little boy, but now I am afraid. He was so young when he went. What if he doesn't remember me?"

Simon pulled Annie to her feet while telling her not to worry. "If your boy comes, as I am sure he will, you may find his spirit will seem older than when he left you. I don't understand it myself, but my wife tells me that some spirits, particularly those of children, continue to grow and mature in the afterlife."

What a convenient way to cover any discrepancies, thought Annie. He had just told her not to be concerned if the child he produced isn't anything like her dead son. What inconsistencies about Charlie had he explained away to Sukie? At least he couldn't explain away the manifestation of a child who never existed. The sudden memory of her own real lost daughter intruded, and Annie shivered.

Simon had moved over and opened the pocket doors to the small adjoining parlor where the cabinet sat. In this room the curtains remained closed so the only light came from the larger parlor and that mysterious shaft of light coming from the room above. Sitting in the cabinet, in that shaft of light, was Evie May. Today she was again dressed all in white, but this time in a very young fashion, with a linen sailor top, pleated skirt, and white stockings. Her hair was pulled back into a braid, with the front bangs prominently displayed. Annie was startled to realize that if she hadn't known Evie May was a girl, she could have passed in this outfit as a very young boy. Someone had spent a good deal of time dressing her for this particular sitting. She speculated that this was what the girl wore when she was "Charlie" and had her private chats with Sukie. *Did they ever just dress her as a boy?*

As they walked up to Evie May, she seemed to be staring right through them, which was disconcerting. There was no recognition of Annie, no hint, thank goodness, of Maybelle, no expression at all on her face.

"Please, Mrs. Fuller, come join Evie May in the cabinet, and I will pull this curtain to give you privacy. I will be in the next room if you need me," Simon said, giving Annie's shoulder a reassuring pat. She sat down, and the girl didn't move a muscle. As the curtain closed, the light in the cabinet dimmed considerably. Annie knew her eyes would adjust quickly, but for an instant she could neither see nor hear Evie May, although she could feel the girl's knees touching one of her own, which ached in response.

Outside, Simon intoned as he did in the séances, "Oh, departed ones, call the spirit of this woman's child, let Annie Fuller speak with him and find comfort." Evie May stirred.

Annie, aware that Simon could hear everything that went on in the cabinet, admonished herself to stay in character. "Oh, it's so dark," she said, making her voice tremble. "Johnny, are you there? Can you hear mama?" Her eyes becoming accustomed to the dim light, she could see that Evie May was now sitting cross-legged, doing something with her hands. Annie almost laughed out loud when she realized the girl was pretending to stack objects, probably blocks, one on top of the other. Of course, since they only knew that her son had died when small, they had Evie May play the one game every child by the age of three knew. *How clever!*

Annie went along with the charade and said, "Johnny, is that you?

What are you doing? Are you playing with your blocks? Darling, do you remember? They were painted such pretty colors."

Evie May looked up at her and said in a child's lisp, "Mama, course it's me. Do you want to play with me?"

"Certainly I will play with you, my sweet," Annie replied, and she proceeded to pretend to build a tower of blocks, laughing when Evie May pretended to knock them all down. Annie was surprised at how at ease she felt with this pretend Johnny, doing pretend things. Then she thought about how this would feel if, like Sukie, she believed she was playing with the spirit of a real child, and her mood darkened.

She lowered her voice and began to ask Evie May a series of questions about where Johnny had been ... if he had seen his father, his grandfather, grandmother. Finally she said sharply, "How do I know you really are my son Johnny?"

Annie stopped, aghast when she saw that Evie May had started to cry. Instinctively, she put her arms around the girl, who snuggled closely and started to suck her thumb. Fighting to keep her voice no more than a whisper, Annie said, "Please, child, tell me who you are. Are you my son, Johnny?"

Evie May reared back and said, "No, I'm not! The bad man told me to make-believe, but I don't want to, cause I'm not a boy." Then the girl smiled and said, "You know who I am. I'm Maybelle. Why didn't you come the other day? I saw you, sitting right in that other room. I tried to tell that old man I didn't want to see him; I wanted to see you. But you came today, I'm glad. I didn't want to be that Johnny."

Frantic thoughts cascaded through Annie's mind. Could this really be her child? Could Simon have been telling the truth, that children aged in the afterlife? And if Johnny was made-up, but Maybelle was real, was the spirit of Charlie real or not?

As the girl again popped her thumb in her mouth and put her head on Annie's shoulder, Annie whispered urgently in her ear. "Maybelle, tell me, who are you? Where did you come from?"

The girl sniffed and said, "I'm Maybelle. You said so yourself. I dunno where I come from; I just am. Aren't you my mother? I thought you might be. I guess I wished you. You will take care of me, won't you?"

"Maybelle, who is the bad man? Tell me who is he? Does he hurt you?"

Annie felt the girl go rigid in her arms, and then she was pushed away as Evie May sat up and glared at her. Before Annie could say another word, the girl spoke, this time in a different, much rougher voice. "Lay off, she's just a kid. She don't know. Can't remember. Silly girl, always looking for her ma; she don't need a ma. She's got me to protect her."

With this, Evie May turned around and started to scrabble down behind the bench in the cabinet, coming up with what looked like a boy's cap, which she jerked on her head, stuffing her braid up and under it in the back. She then leaned back and crossed her arms and glared at Annie, who said in bewilderment, "And just who are you?"

"Lady, don't be stupid. I'm Maybelle's brother, Eddie."

Annie was absolutely speechless for a few seconds. She then pulled herself together and started asking this new person questions. First, she asked him what his last name was and how old he was.

"Nickerson, watcha think? I'm no baby, that's for sure. Think I'm nine. But no one's ever given me any birthday parties or presents, so you might say I'm a little fuzzy on that," the boy answered. Then, again reaching behind the bench, he pulled out a small cup and ball toy. He began to count under his breath while he flipped the ball into the cup.

Annie was surprised at how much this "Eddie" seemed like a real boy, playing with a real toy, unlike the imaginary Johnny playing with his imaginary blocks.

Annie watched him play the game for awhile and then said, "Did Mr. Frampton ask you to visit me, or Maybelle?"

Eddie stopped his game and glared at her, saying, "I got no truck with that man, and he'd better not try to mess with Maybelle. It's Maybelle who wanted to talk to you."

"Why?" Annie asked.

Eddie just shrugged, so she continued, "Maybelle told me she 'slept with the angels.' How long ago did she die?"

Eddie guffawed and said, "Hell's gate, Lady, where'd you get the idea she's dead! That's a good one. She's just talking about the prayer. When she gets all riled up, I repeat the angel prayer Miss Evelyn taught us and tell her to go to sleep, so she says she sleeps with the angels. She's no more dead than I am! Watcha think, I'm some kind a haunt! Can't no dead person do this," he said, leaning over and pinching Annie on the arm.

Chapter Twenty-two

"COMPETENT GIRL WISHES A SITUATION to do housework; can give references."

—*San Francisco Chronicle*, 1879

Kathleen sat on what she had begun to think of as her chair near the front door and watched the butler, Albert, walk down the hallway and through the door to the back of the house. For such a solidly built man, he was unusually silent on his feet. He also didn't seem to like her mistress very much if the scowl he gave Mrs. Fuller meant anything. She wondered if it was Albert who had put the note in Mrs. Fuller's coat on Monday, maybe on Arabella's behalf. Since he met all the members of the séance at the door and deposited their wraps on the hallstand hooks, he had plenty of opportunity.

The hallway was cool, so Kathleen was glad of her shawl since she had no expectation that Albert would comply with Mrs. Fuller's request to bring her a cup of tea. Too bad, she could do with a cup and some of the German cook's pastries. Given how uncomfortable the wooden chair was, she wondered if anyone would complain if she moved over to the small sofa where Evie May's mother and Mrs. Hapgood had sat on Monday evening. She wished she were brave enough to go back to the kitchen on her own to look for the parlor maid.

To be honest, she wasn't used to doing nothing. Couldn't remember when she had sat so often in her life before this past week. Not that she wasn't proud to help her mistress, but she worried about leaving Mrs. O'Rourke to manage the house by herself. She had tried to get all the ironing done yesterday, but then Mrs. Fuller had come home, looking like something the cat dragged in. Of course, she had to help with the bath, and that put her behind. Then this morning, between the breakfast and lunch dishes, dusting the downstairs room, and refilling all the lamps, she hadn't been able to finish. She had told Mrs. O'Rourke not to touch the last pile. Ironing was not her business. She would get to it this evening after dinner, but she had no faith the older woman would pay her any mind.

Mrs. Fuller, bless her, had tried to get Kathleen to stay behind this afternoon, saying that there wasn't any need for her to have a maid with her during the day. Mrs. O'Rourke would have none of it. She'd said, "Annie, if you think I'm going to let you go into that house alone, after you got that note! I would have thought that this summer's adventures had taught you the danger of going off alone and sticking your nose into other people's business."

That had been that. Nobody crossed Mrs. O'Rourke when she put her foot down. Kathleen thought that secretly Mrs. Fuller was glad not to come alone. To be certain, something had been bothering her today. Didn't say hardly a word on the way here. And she tried not to show it, but Kathleen could tell her knee was bothering her. Funny business, her fall. Those crowded horse cars could be dangerous, but generally Mrs. Fuller was so graceful. The sound of the library door opening and a woman's voice interrupted Kathleen's thoughts.

"Thank you for coming, Mr. Sweeter. I believe we are in agreement. I look forward to seeing you this Friday," said Arabella Frampton, ushering out a very handsome young man.

Well, well, who's this? Kathleen asked herself. *Mr. Sweeter! Wonder what he's doing here, all on his own, without his cousin that Mrs. Stein was telling us about.*

She watched as the young man preened under Arabella's attentions, smoothing his very considerable mustache before putting on his bowler. Dressed pretty fancy for a man without a job. When Kathleen saw how Sweeter frowned when he realized that he and Mrs. Frampton weren't alone and hurriedly exited the house, she decided he was up to no good. *Looks like Mrs. Frampton isn't too pleased by me being here either. Well, too bad.* Kathleen smiled cheekily at the medium, who looked like she was going to say something, then glanced over at the closed door to the séance room, frowned, shrugged, and then went rapidly down the hallway, disappearing through the door to the kitchen area. *There's another who isn't happy about my mistress visiting today. I'd bet my blue satin ribbon she's the one who wrote the note.*

A soft noise from down the hallway drew her attention. A young woman, wearing the white apron and cap of a parlor maid and carrying a bucket, crept out of the dining room, tip-toed to the doorway at the back end of the hall, and stood for a second, listening. She then turned and began to move towards the front of the house. She had just reached the door to the library when she first noticed Kathleen, who had been watching her with curiosity.

"Sakes alive, where'd you come from?" the girl snapped, dropping her bucket with a thump.

"Biddy? Biddy O'Malley! Don't you recognize me? Whatever are you doing here?" cried Kathleen, getting up and moving over to where the girl stood, her mouth hanging open.

"Kathleen Hennessey, as I live and breathe. I work here, going on three months. Better question is, what are you doing here? Are you here about a position? Drat it, I knew that old bat was going to get me in trouble," the young girl said with disgust.

"No, no, Biddy, I'm here with my mistress, Mrs. Fuller. She's in there," Kathleen pointed to the séance room, "with Mr. Frampton, having a 'sitting' or whatever you call it with that girl, Evie May. This is beyond wonderful, to find you here. I have so much to tell you."

Biddy looked over her shoulder, brought her voice down to a whisper, and said, "Did you see a lady, red hair, temper to match, come out of this room?"

Kathleen nodded. "Yes, Mrs. Frampton. She let a man out the front door and then went to the back part of the house. What's up and who's the old bat? Not Mrs. Frampton, she's a stunner!"

Biddy sighed. "Good. The master told me at lunch to dust the library, but just as I was getting my rags together, didn't the Mrs. nip in with some gentleman caller. I hid in the dining room. If I went back to the kitchen, Mrs. Bloody Nickerson would've just found something else for me to do.

She's the old bat."

"Oh, Evie May's mother. What's it to her what you do? She the housekeeper?"

"No, thank heavens. What she thinks she is, is the next Mrs. Frampton. Lord, makes me laugh. And that girl of hers. She's just odd. Talks like a baby one moment, next she walks around like she's the mistress of the house. Then I'll come into her room to clean, and there she sits, staring at nothing. Acts like she can't even hear me. Gives me the creeps something awful. But I can't be found out here talking to you. Tell you what. I'll go into the library, start dusting; you can stand at the door, be lookout. We can talk, but you give me a shout if someone comes."

Kathleen agreed to this plan, leaning up against the doorframe so that she could see if any of the doors leading into the hallway opened but where she could also see if someone was coming down the stairs. She couldn't wait to tell Mrs. Fuller about their good luck. Biddy was a few years younger than Kathleen, but when they were both very young they had lived in the same cramped lodging house and became the best of friends. They'd kept up, even after Kathleen went into service, meeting occasionally at mass or at one of St. Jo's parish dances. Biddy, a tall, strong, dark-haired girl, had been working off and on since she was eleven. But as the oldest of thirteen children—her ma ran to twins—she usually did sewing work so she could help take care of her brothers and sisters while her mother went out to work.

"What'cha doing working out days?" Kathleen asked.

"Ma got a good job at St Mary's Hospital. The Sisters got it for her. Pays well, but she's got to work nights. Mary Margaret can take care of the little ones, now she's ten, but I need to be home at night to keep the boys in hand. Speaking of boys, how's your bunch of ruffians doing?"

While Biddy climbed up on a stool to begin dusting the library bookcases, Kathleen told her about her younger brothers, Colin, Aiden, and Ian. Colin at sixteen was apprenticed out as a carpenter's assistant, Aiden and Ian were still in school, although despite Kathleen's protests, Aiden worked when school was out and would probably drop out to go to work full time when he turned fifteen this spring. She told Biddy of her hopes that Ian, the youngest, would stay in school long enough to make something of himself. After Biddy had caught her up on her own family, Kathleen turned the conversation back to the Framptons.

"Biddy, Mrs. Fuller, my mistress, is sort of looking into the Framptons, seeing if they are on the up-and-up. Do you know how the Framptons work their tricks? Do they let you clean over there in the room where they hold the séances?"

"My goodness, no. Only places I'm allowed to mess with alone are the library, dining room, hallways, and the old bat and Evie May's room. Albert takes care of the rooms across the hall, and his wife takes care of the master and mistress's rooms upstairs."

"The butler's got a wife?" Kathleen forgot her job as lookout and came into the room to make sure she'd heard right.

Biddy laughed and moved over to work on the shelves near the door, so Kathleen could go back to her post. "Butler, my foot. You tell me, Kathleen Hennessey, have you ever seen a butler like him? And who calls their butler by their first name? No, I've heard Mrs. Frampton call him Uncle Albert when she thought no one was listening. Since her maid sleeps in the same bed with old Albert, sort of stands to reason she's his wife, though Mrs. Frampton calls her just by her first name, Delia, so maybe I've gone and jumped to conclusions. I do that if you remember."

Kathleen giggled. She had nearly forgotten how much fun Biddy could be. Then she thought she heard a noise from the hall. She whispered, "Biddy, I think someone's coming. I just know my mistress will want to talk to you. What time do you get off evenings?"

"I'm off by seven. They eat early cause of the séances. Sunday night is cook's night out, so everyone goes out to dinner. Since Ma doesn't work Sunday nights, I stay until about ten, to watch the house while they are away."

"Any chance you could stop by Mrs. Fuller's, maybe tomorrow night, when you get off? I know she would pay for you to take a cab home."

Biddy looked at her for a moment, then nodded. "Hey, the boys can't get into too much trouble if I'm a little late, and we have a cousin staying with us who'll help out. Sometimes the Framptons keep me past seven anyway. What's the address?"

"436 O'Farrell. The Central car going up Sixth takes you right to O'Farrell; here's a nickel." Kathleen proudly pulled out her change purse, pleased she had saved some of her last week's earnings.

Biddy took the coin and said with a smile, "Kathleen Hennessey, look at you! Change in your pocket. Well, I have some stories to tell you and that mistress of yours, might just be worth cab fare home. Strange goings on in this house, and that's a fact."

Chapter Twenty-three
Thursday evening, October 23, 1879

"WANTED BY A YOUNG GIRL, 15 YEARS old, a situation; city or country."
—*San Francisco Chronicle*, 1879

Annie settled Queenie, the old black cat, on her lap and began to rock gently, noticing the slight twinge of pain in her knee. Silence, a tangible contrast to the earlier excited chatter of Kathleen and her young friend, Biddy, filled the nighttime kitchen. Beatrice had gone with Kathleen to see Biddy safely into the hansom cab that was waiting out front, to pay the cabbie and impress upon him the necessity of taking the young girl straight to her home south of Market. Annie used the oasis of quiet to reach into the jumbled heap of worries she had been accumulating over the past few days, trying to create some sort of order.

She still had to prepare for Mr. Andrew's appointment tomorrow morning at nine, but her eight o'clock client was out of town, so she could use that time to search through today's papers for an investment tip. The rest of Friday's appointments were routine; all she needed to do was listen and repeat the advice she had given before. Thank goodness there were no new crises among Sibyl's clients; Mrs. Crenshaw was even looking better as she made preparations for her daughter and grandson's visit in a few weeks. Beatrice had said she would go over the weekend menus with her when she brought up her breakfast in the morning, and at lunch she should have time to finish going through the household accounts.

She needed to make sure there was enough extra money for the next few weeks to pay for Biddy's cousin to help out in the kitchen while Kathleen was accompanying her to the Frampton house. This would solve the problem of keeping the household running while she continued to investigate the Framptons. She wished she had confidence that she was making progress. She could almost feel Miss Pinehurst's eyes on her in the morning since their rooms were next to each other. But as usual, their paths didn't cross in the house. She still hoped to speak to Sukie's husband, Arnold, to ensure he wasn't planning to give into Simon's veiled threats. Annie wasn't certain how much longer she could carry on with this investigation. Attendance at two séances a week, plus a private sitting with Evie May, was taking a toll on her time and her financial resources. She had a little extra money put by, but she'd planned on investing it, not spending it.

Then there was the conundrum of Eddie. When Evie May made the switch from Maybelle to Eddie, who was clearly older and wiser than Annie's fictitious son, Johnny, Annie had been strangely relieved. A cocky street urchin was much easier to deal with than the clingy little girl, Maybelle, and Annie found it refreshingly easy to converse with him. Eddie was very straightforward, and Annie had rather liked the boy and found his insistence that he wasn't dead very comforting.

His loud laughter at her question must have caught Simon's attention because, without warning, Simon's voice came from right on the other side of the curtain. He'd said something about Johnny saying good-bye to his mother and returning to the everlasting gardens, and then he had opened up the curtain. He evidently had not expected to see Eddie because he had let out an oath, snatched off the cap, grabbed the toy, and said, "Evie May, what are you doing?" When Annie had looked back at Evie May, Eddie was gone, and the girl was sitting with her eyes closed, slumped like some broken doll.

Annie was disturbed at this memory. While her conversation with Eddie had done much to reassure her that Maybelle wasn't some reincarnation of her own lost child, it hadn't answered the question of who or what Maybelle or her brother Eddie were. Maybe they were versions of Evie May's real sister and brother; Eddie had said his last name was Nickerson. She should be able to find out if Rowena Nickerson had two children by those names. But who was Miss Evelyn? For some reason, that name had sounded familiar.

"Mrs. Fuller, see who we ran into out front." Kathleen burst in through the back door of the kitchen, bringing in crisp air, crimson cheeks, and an air of suppressed excitement.

Annie looked up and saw Nate Dawson ushering Beatrice through the door, his hat off and his manner deferential. She wished that her heart didn't thump quite so decidedly whenever she saw him. She kept hoping that familiarity would breed, not contempt, but at least composure, on her part.

"I trust I have not come too late?" Nate walked over and stood looking down at Annie, who remained sitting in the rocking chair, the cat still in her lap.

Nate had asked her Monday night if he could stop by later in the week, and she had put him off until tonight, telling him that there wouldn't be anything to discuss until after her sitting with Evie May. She had rather hoped he had forgotten since she hadn't decided what information she wanted to share with him, and she longed to retire, just this once, at a reasonable hour.

Before she could respond, Kathleen finished hanging up her shawl and came skipping over to Annie and Nate, saying, "Mrs. Fuller, have you told Mr. Dawson what we've planned for Sunday?"

Annie's heart sank. She needed to take control of this conversation before Kathleen spilled everything. She stood up, dumped poor Queenie unceremoniously on the floor, and gave the girl a gentle push towards the stove. "Kathleen, if you please, go help Mrs. O'Rourke fix us all some tea and give Mr. Dawson a chance to catch his breath. Mr. Dawson, do have a seat. I believe a few of Mrs. O'Rourke's cookies are left."

Nate smiled, removed his topcoat, placed it and his hat on the kitchen table, and pulled out a chair. Of course, he wouldn't sit until she did, so when she saw that Beatrice was already piling a plate with some of her oatmeal cookies, she returned to the rocking chair and sat down.

"Mrs. Fuller, do tell me, what are these grand plans that have Miss Kathleen so excited, and just who was the young girl Mrs. O'Rourke was putting into a cab? I gather she was visiting you, but I didn't catch who she was and why she was here," Nate said as he pulled his chair closer to Annie.

Annie chose to focus on the last and less dangerous question, replying, "Biddy is Miss Bridget O'Malley, an old friend of Kathleen's, who, by sheer coincidence, is the parlor maid who works days at the Framptons. Kathleen met her Wednesday while I was having my session with Evie May, and she invited her to stop by after work tonight. She was able to provide invaluable insight into the household. Do you remember me telling you Arabella Frampton had a lady's maid? Turns out this maid is married to the butler, Albert, and Albert is Arabella's uncle."

"That is certainly interesting information." Nate paused. "You know, that makes some sense. A confidence man like Simon Frampton couldn't afford to have a close servant who wouldn't be entirely loyal. Pierce said Arabella came from a theatrical family. I think he said they were tumblers, maybe even circus folk. Albert and his wife may have always been part of Simon and Arabella's act. Wouldn't be surprised if they had a large role to play behind the scenes during the séances. Maybe Albert is the one causing the table to shake. His wife could be working the lights and sound effects you described." Nate stopped to take the cup of tea Kathleen handed him and snagged a cookie from the plate.

"Thank you, Kathleen," Annie said, taking tea but refusing a cookie. She had eaten her fill during Biddy's visit. "That would explain why neither Kathleen nor I ever saw hide nor hair of the lady's maid during any of our visits." *She also could be the one who slipped me the second note and shoved me off the horse car. Since I never have seen her, she could have stood right next to me. I'd never have known,* Annie thought to herself.

"What else did you learn from Kathleen's friend? Did you say her name is Biddy?"

Annie laughed. "Yes, Biddy, short for Bridget. She has only been working there three months. It was her impression from the cook, who does speak just a little English, that she was the third servant they have had since they arrived in town."

Kathleen was hovering near Nate and Annie, and she said, "Biddy thought the Framptons might not want a local servant to stay for very long. Might learn too much about them and their shenanigans. That's why she's willing to risk letting us in Sunday night. Figures she probably is going to get the sack sooner or later."

Good heavens, she isn't going to let this rest, thought Annie. "Bridget might be right, but I'm not entirely sure that I feel comfortable about asking her to risk her position. Which is why I haven't decided whether or not to take her up on her offer. Now, Kathleen, it's late. If you would, make a quick run through the parlors, make sure the fires are out and the lamps turned off, and it will be time for you to retire."

"But, Ma'am, I don't see the problem about Sunday. I will visit with Biddy, and the two of us can keep a lookout while you snoop around the parlor, maybe even get into the upstairs room. Biddy says no one ever gets back before nine, so there would be plenty of time. You might never get as good a chance to find out what tricks Mrs. Frampton and her relatives are playing. You said yourself it might be the only way to get the goods on them to convince Miss Pinehurst's sister."

Beatrice O'Rourke came up behind Kathleen, put her hands on the girl's shoulders, and scolded her. "Now, me girl, you pipe down. It's not for the likes of you to be telling your mistress what to do. Mrs. Fuller will do what's best, and I for one am not so sure this harebrained scheme you two girls thought up is such a good idea. Now you go and do as you were told, then off to bed with you."

Kathleen's lower lip trembled as she looked at Annie in confusion. Then she turned and started towards the back stairs, looking so distressed that Annie couldn't stand it. She stood up and followed the girl to the back stairs, where she gave her a quick hug and whispered, "Dear, don't despair, we'll still be going on Sunday. It's just I'm not sure Mr. Dawson is going to think it's such a good idea either, and I hadn't decided yet how much to tell him."

Kathleen gasped and whispered back, "Ma'am, I hadn't thought!"

Annie gave her another quick hug. "Never you mind. Better to tell him ahead of time. He'll no doubt ring a peal over me either way, and at least he can't blame me for keeping secrets."

Annie then turned back and came over to where Beatrice stood talking to Nate, who had risen as soon as Annie got up from her chair. "Dear Beatrice, you need to turn in too. I can tell that Mr. Dawson is not going to leave until I have told him what Kathleen was talking about, but I will be brief, and I am sure he won't stay too long. Isn't that so, Mr. Dawson?"

"Mrs. Fuller, I promise not to overstay my welcome. Mrs. O'Rourke, thank you so much for the cookies. I hope you won't mind if I stuff a few in my pockets to take home with me. I am afraid Mrs. Randall, the cook in my boarding house, doesn't hold with sweets of any kind." Nate then shook Beatrice's hand, a reminder to Annie of what lovely manners he had.

As Beatrice went up the back stairs, Nate waited until she had regained her seat to sit down, and then he took her hand, looking into her eyes. "Annie, I really won't stay long. You look tired. It was good of you to let me come. I know how long your days are. But please, what was Miss Kathleen talking about?"

Annie, wishing to postpone the inevitable, if only for a moment, ignored Nate's request and said, "Before I get into that, what of you? Have you heard anything more from Anthony Pierce?"

"No, but I have an appointment with him tomorrow afternoon. I gather you did have your meeting with the young medium, Evie May. You weren't turned away? No more threats?"

Annie felt her cheeks go hot but answered quickly, again ignoring the questions she didn't want to answer. "No, I wasn't turned away. Right off, Simon asked me why I hadn't gotten my investment advice from Madam Sibyl. I told him she hadn't been at all helpful. He seemed quite willing to accept my explanation and didn't show any sign that he thought that Mrs. Fuller and Madam Sibyl were one and the same. I told him that I didn't believe in fortunetelling—not as reliable as ghosts!" When Nate chuckled, she felt she had successfully slid through one difficult spot in the conversation. Perhaps she could get away with not telling him about the second threatening note or the push.

She continued. "I also had my meeting with Miss Pinehurst. Oh, Nate, it was quite distressing. Her sister is expecting, again, and instead of this helping her get over her son's death and end her obsession with attending the séances, she seems to believe that the new baby will die."

"Good heavens, what do you mean?"

When Annie repeated what Miss Pinehurst had told her about Sukie and her fears about her unborn child and Simon's veiled threat to Arnold Vetch, Nate said, "Annie, this is outrageous. Don't you see? This might be of use to Pierce, at least convince him to investigate Simon further."

"Please don't tell him. At least not yet. I want to get a chance to talk to Mr. Vetch, maybe even Sukie. I wouldn't want to get them into any trouble. Can we trust Mr. Pierce not to run off with this story, maybe get Mr. Vetch fired? Miss Pinehurst said she would try to arrange a meeting for me on Saturday afternoon. If it seems appropriate, I will mention to Mr. Vetch the possibility of enlisting Mr. Pierce's help. See how he reacts."

"That makes sense. I will just let Pierce know that I have some reason to believe that the Framptons are engaged in blackmail, but I won't use any names or particulars. Now, tell me, what happened in your private meeting with Evie May? Did she produce your fictitious son?"

"Indeed she did. But I am afraid I may have inadvertently limited my time with him. Evie May really is an extraordinary actress, and she was quite convincing as a very young boy, playing with imaginary blocks, babbling to his mama. But when I thought of how she might be using those same acting talents as Charlie, I let my anger show. And Johnny disappeared."

"Disappeared? Whatever do you mean?" Nate said. Then, noticing that Kathleen had just come down the stairs, he leaned in and lowered his voice. "Are you saying he vanished from your sight?"

Annie, amused by the look of astonishment on Nate's face, laughed and said, "Good heavens, no." Then turning to Kathleen, who was trying to tiptoe past them, she continued, "Good night, Kathleen. Don't forget that Tilly will be over first thing. I appreciate your willingness to help train her."

When Kathleen had disappeared down the hallway that led to the laundry room and her private quarters, Annie explained to Nate. "Bridget has a cousin living with her who is fresh off the train from New York, and before that, the boat from Ireland. The poor girl's thick accent and her lack of experience have meant she hasn't been able to find a job, even in domestic service. Bridget says she's bright, and if she could just get some training and a little polish she should do fine. Beatrice, saint that she is, offered to give the girl a chance. For the next week or two, she will help out in the kitchen when Kathleen is accompanying me to the Framptons. Later, if she works out, I will hire her to work on Kathleen's regular nights out. I just hope that she isn't more trouble than she is worth."

Nate, uninterested in these domestic details, again raised the subject of Johnny's disappearing act. Annie described how Johnny had been replaced first by Maybelle, then by her nine-year-old brother, Eddie.

She said, "I know it sounds impossible, but somehow she alters her voice and facial expressions, even her body, to such an extent you feel you are talking to someone quite distinct from Evie May herself. And I am not sure that Simon understands what is happening. He seemed quite surprised, and even angry, when he opened up the curtains to the cabinet and found me talking to Eddie, not Johnny."

"How odd. Could these be roles the girl plays for other clients, and she has gotten mixed up somehow?"

"I thought of that, but Eddie swore he wasn't a spirit and laughed at the idea. I've begun to realize I just don't know enough about the principles behind Spiritualism. Arabella is obviously a fraud, but I have begun to wonder about Evie May. What if she is able to communicate with the spirits of those who have died? Might it then be possible for those spirits to not realize they were dead? There is a woman who lives in San Francisco, a Flora Hunt, who was a very famous trance medium in the sixties and early seventies. I read that while she has given up mediumship she is still a strong leader in the Spiritualist movement, dedicated to rooting out fraudulent mediums. Don't you see? She might be able to help us. Tell me what to look for at the séances."

"That sounds like a very good idea," Nate said. "But I don't see how this relates to these mysterious plans you may or may not carry out on Sunday."

Annie thought that Nate had a distressing habit of getting back to the main point, no matter how much she had tried to distract him. She sighed and then began to relate how Biddy had told them that on Sunday evenings, the German cook's night out, everyone in the Frampton household was absent, finding dinner accommodations elsewhere.

"She said that it is her impression that Mr. and Mrs. Frampton and Albert and his wife all go out together to someplace outside of town where they aren't known. Said the Framptons dress very inconspicuously, for them, and that all four leave and return in the same enclosed hackney. Mrs. Nickerson and Evie May normally eat together at a local family restaurant, whose proprietress comes to séances at the Framptons'. She gets free meals, although Biddy said she complains a lot about not being invited to eat with the Framptons."

"Yes, but I still don't get the point."

"You see, Kathleen and Biddy decided that, since the Framptons leave Biddy in charge of the house from seven to about ten in the evening on Sundays, she can let Kathleen and me in the back door to look around. See if I can figure out how the music and lights are operated, how the table shakes. I confess the idea is attractive. But as I mentioned, I haven't quite made up my mind since I am afraid that if for some reason one of the household comes back early, not only will Biddy lose her job, but it will certainly ruin my ability to continue to play the role of the naive Mrs. Fuller."

Annie looked up at Nate, expecting to tell her why she shouldn't, under any circumstance, go to the Framptons' on Sunday. He sat looking at her for a moment, then rose and walked quickly across the room, looking out the back kitchen window. Annie was impressed by his self-control. This summer in similar circumstances he had gone on forever about how dangerous her plans were and how inappropriate it would be for a woman to act in such a fashion. It occurred to her that, except for when he expressed his reasonable concerns about the meaning of the first threatening note, Nate had been uncharacteristically reticent about stating his opinions. As if he were preoccupied by something more important than her plans to expose the Framptons. *Or maybe he just doesn't care as much as he did this summer.* She had just begun to worry at this distressing thought when Nate returned and sat down again, retaking her hands in his.

"Listen, Annie. Don't bother to pretend you haven't made up your mind. I know you better than that. But would you make a deal with me? I won't try to stop you if you at least try and resolve this issue with Miss Pinehurst's sister before Sunday. Get this Flora Hunt to help. Tell Mrs. Vetch everything you have learned so far. Tell her about the note. Maybe that will convince her the Framptons are up to no good. There is no reason to risk Biddy's position, your safety, Kathleen's, unless you get nowhere with Mrs. Vetch. And if you have no success and still plan on trying to ferret out the Frampton's secrets while they are out of the house on Sunday, I will come with you."

Annie was stunned. She opened her mouth to protest, but then she admitted she couldn't think of a single reason why he shouldn't accompany her. In fact, she realized she couldn't think of anything that would make her happier.

Chapter Twenty-four
Friday afternoon, October 24, 1879

"Yesterday General Grant returned from Sacramento and spent the morning at the Palace Hotel. At 2 o'clock in the afternoon he was tendered a reception by the California Pioneers at their hall."
—*San Francisco Chronicle*, 1879

Pierce was already ten minutes late, and Nate wondered if this meant he wasn't coming. Six o'clock was a deuced early time for dining. Nate was uncomfortable sitting at one of the only occupied tables in the Palace Hotel's Gentleman's Grille, but it had been Pierce who had chosen the time and the place to meet. He just hoped the reporter showed since he couldn't justify staying and ordering dinner for himself. He had been rather looking forward to a nicely grilled steak, knowing cold leftovers would be all he got if he went home to his boarding house.

The Palace Hotel was only four years old and still impressed Nate each time he came through the arch into the Grand Court and looked up at the seven stories of marble balconies. He wondered what it would be like to stay in one of the upstairs suites. Maybe for a honeymoon. For a moment he unleashed his imagination and pictured Annie lying beside him on silk sheets, her hair set loose in fiery gold curls, her dark brown eyes half asleep, her full lips parted.

God, there was little chance of that happening, at least anytime soon. Nate ran a finger along his too-tight collar, picked up the whiskey he had ordered, and took a long swallow. Not unless he got his Uncle Frank to budge on taking on a new partner or at least look for some more lucrative clients. He'd had another one of those frustrating conversations just this morning, where he would make his case and his uncle would smile and nod and say that Nate shouldn't be so impatient, and "everything in good time." *What the hell does he know about it, finicky old bachelor? I'll be damned if I let him dictate my future and end up like him, with no wife, no children, no home. At this point, I probably couldn't even afford to rent a room in Annie's boarding house, much less support her so she doesn't have to work.*

At least he hadn't bungled his conversation with her last night, or for that matter on Monday night when she'd found the threatening note and he'd come so close to forbidding her to ever go back to the Framptons'. But he wasn't stupid. She had been asked to help out Miss Pinehurst, and she was going to see it through to the end. That was just her nature. Interference from him was only going to make her start shutting him out.

He had learned that lesson the hard way when he first met her. He also had come to terms with the fact that her fierce passion, her sharp, uncompromising intelligence, and her stubbornness were some of the very reasons he found her so attractive. He'd just never met any woman like her, ever. If only he made enough to support her, and they got married; then she could quit work and spend her time do-gooding as much as she wanted without wearing herself out.

She had looked so drained last night. Her skin was almost translucent against the stark black of her dress, and for some reason she was limping. He had refrained from asking her why. The glare she gave him when he mentioned how tired she looked had been warning enough. He'd remembered his little sister once telling him that women found any reference to their health insulting because it suggested that they didn't look their best.

Nate smiled at the thought of Laura in charge of her first school. He was so proud of her. Thirty students, of all ages. Hard to imagine. He was sorry he hadn't seen her when he was at the ranch, but he knew she'd be home over the winter holidays. He hoped he could convince Annie to come with him to visit the ranch in December when Laura would be home. But that wouldn't happen if he couldn't figure out a way to help her without getting her back up. He really didn't want her going to the Framptons' on Sunday. Maybe if Pierce had any new information, combined with what she had learned already, that would provide enough evidence to convince Mrs. Vetch to give up going to the séances. But if not, and Annie still planned to go to the Framptons' on Sunday night, he was glad she'd agreed to let him come with her.

He had nearly laughed out loud at how surprised she'd been when he'd said he would join her. He'd expected her to resist the suggestion and argue she didn't need his help. But that was Annie. She might be damned independent, but she didn't let this get in the way of achieving her goals. She had accepted his reasoning that having two of them searching the Frampton house would increase the chance of success. Yes, overall, he was quite pleased at how he had handled what could have been a very difficult conversation. And he couldn't have asked for a better reward. When he stood at the back door and wished her good night, she had permitted him to kiss her. *God, what I wouldn't do to get a kiss like that every night.*

"Sorry I'm late. Got held up. Busy day. Had to cover President Grant's reception at the Pioneer Hall this afternoon, then there's the banquet tonight, and I'm working on a big story, have to write it all up before tomorrow. Going to be a long night. But a fella's got to eat, and since the press weren't invited to the dinner the Mayor's having for Grant, I thought I'd have an even better meal here! Lord, won't the city feel dull once Grant starts his trip back east this weekend."

Pierce waved Nate back in his seat after shaking his hand and, as he sat down, barked at the waiter for "his usual." Turning to Nate, he said, "So, still looking into Simon Frampton? Find out anything?"

Nate didn't reply, distracted by the implications of Pierce having "a usual" drink at a restaurant as expensive as the Palace Grille. Pierce didn't wait for an answer; instead, he opened up the menu, scanned it quickly, and threw it down.

The waiter appeared with what looked and smelled like bourbon, and Pierce said, "I'll have the steak, grilled, medium, liver and onions, piece of your pie. Dawson, what's your pleasure?"

Nate ordered a salad and a steak and, thinking about Beatrice's oatmeal cookies that were waiting for him at home, declined dessert. He asked about the "big story." Pierce kept him entertained with some convoluted yarn about a bribe, a new bride, and a barroom brawl. The man did have a way with a tale, but Nate wondered if any of it was true. After their meals were served and each of them had made respectable inroads into their steaks, Nate brought the conversation back to the subject at hand. "To answer your earlier question, yes, I am still interested in finding out more about the Framptons, but more to the point, have you come up with anything?"

Pierce took a swallow of his bourbon then said, "Well, now, I did ask around. Sounds like they are doing a pretty brisk business. My sources say they actually turn people away, and they have upped their prices since they first arrived in town. Become one of the popular forms of entertainment for the smart young set. But nothing sticks out as suspicious. Lots of old ladies who aren't going to stop nagging their poor husbands, even after their death. A few of our more successful businessmen, who should know better. And, as I mentioned, some young people looking for an excuse to sit and hold hands in the dark."

Nate hid his disappointment by turning back to his meal and thought about how he could bring up what Annie had learned without giving her away. "I suppose you may be right about the majority of the people who attend, but I did a little asking around myself, including at police head-quarters. There have been a number of complaints filed, including from a relative of a judge who believes he is being defrauded. And from my own contacts, it looks to me like the Framptons could be using information they get from some of their clients to blackmail others."

Nate could swear this last comment caused a flicker of interest in Pierce, but the man continued to stuff his mouth with the last of his steak, washing it down with the end of his drink.

Pierce then signaled the waiter, asked for his pie and a cup of coffee, and leaned back in his seat. "Well, now, young Dawson, you have been busy. Of course I checked with police myself, and my source said there wasn't anything prosecutable in the complaints. I can tell you, my editors get one whiff that a judge is involved, and they smell lawsuit. Makes them downright timid. Besides the police, where'd you get your information?"

Nate hesitated. "I'm sorry, I can't really give you any names, at least not without getting their permission."

Pierce nodded, not saying anything while the waiter delivered his pie and coffee. Nate thanked the waiter for his coffee and sat back, satisfied at least with the meal, if not with Pierce's lack of enthusiasm for exposing the Framptons.

He tried again. "Pierce, I can understand that it might seem foolhardy to take after people like the Framptons who have the support of some of the better-connected members of society. And Simon Frampton, with his upper class accent, beautiful wife, and his butler and all, seems very respectable. But I know for a fact that people are being hurt."

"You've been to one of their séances, have you? What'ya think of Arabella, something out of the ordinary, isn't she?" Pierce grinned.

"I didn't go to a séance. I took your recommendation not to do any-thing that would get Frampton's wind up." Nate paused, looking for a way to describe his visit that wouldn't give Annie away. He chose his next words. "But I did discover some acquaintances who attend, and I offered to meet them and escort them home. That's when I met the Framptons."

"These acquaintances the ones you think are being hurt? If so, if you could get them to talk to me, I might be able to do something. Otherwise, far as I see it, there just isn't much there. At least not enough to interest my editors."

Nate wondered if Annie could convince either Miss Pinehurst or Mr. Vetch to talk to Pierce. It was worth a try, so he said, "I will see what I can do. I will let you know if I can get anyone to talk to you directly."

"Good, good," Pierce said, taking out his watch and checking the time. "Now, I've got to run. Wish I'd more time. I've been thinking about your future, young man. Augustus Hart, our next state attorney general, is in town next week. A little victory tour of the state before he takes office. I have an interview scheduled. 'What the new constitution means to the attorney general's office.' That sort of thing. But I can guarantee he's looking for a few good lawyers who aren't corrupt to work for him up in Sacramento. I'll be sure to put in a good word for you." Pierce rose, threw down some bills on the table, stuck out his hand to Nate, and gave him another of his wide smiles. "I assume you wouldn't mind relocating up river, if necessary?"

Nate rose as well and shook Pierce's hand vigorously. "Pierce, that's damned good of you. Of course I would be interested. Just let me know if there is anything I can do. If there was a chance to arrange a meeting, take Hart out for a meal. Whatever you think best."

"Good man. I'll let you know. But I have to run. I think I left enough, but you will settle the bill, won't ya? Good talking to you."

Nate sat back down, watching as Pierce wound his way through the tables, which were beginning to fill up, shaking hands, slapping backs, and leaving a ripple of laughter in his wake. He then took up the bills Pierce had left and counted them. When he had consulted the tab, he wasn't surprised to see he was going to have to fork out more than two-thirds of the total. But if Pierce got him an interview with Hart, it would be well worth it. Sacramento! Probably wouldn't have to be there full time, except when the legislature was in session. Even then, only about a six-hour steamboat ride away. He could come home some weekends. Wouldn't have to do it forever, but the salary had to be better than he was making working with his uncle. And the connections he would make!

With prospects like that, he might even propose to Annie and have a chance of her saying yes. *I wish I could tell her about this. It would help take her mind off the fact that Pierce didn't have anything we can use against the Framptons. But I'd better not, in case nothing pans out.*

Chapter Twenty-five
Friday evening, October 24, 1879

"Mrs. Lennett, Medium and Independent Slate Writer, has resumed her private sittings. Office hours from 11-6 pm, 817 Bush St."—*San Francisco Chronicle*, 1879

Doesn't look like there is going to be any Evie May tonight, Annie thought. Simon hadn't opened the doors to the small back parlor, and he had whispered something to Judge Babcock that had clearly upset him. Annie was disappointed, not only because she was increasingly curious about whom she would meet if she entered the cabinet again, but because she had hoped to test her theory that Simon triggered Evie May in some fashion by the words he spoke at the beginning of each sitting.

Annie remembered Simon said something like "dear departed ones" when it was time for someone to go to the cabinet, and she was pretty sure he also quoted a phrase that had the word judge in it when it was time for Judge Babcock to go and meet his daughter. In her own case, she thought the key word was mother, combined again with the phrase "dear departed ones." What she wasn't so sure about was whether there was some phrase used to end the sessions. Tonight, she had hoped to test her theory.

Instead, she was battling to keep awake. This was only her third séance with Arabella, and already she was growing jaded. The only thing that had happened of any interest was the sudden attention Jack Sweeter paid to her at the beginning of the evening. When she had first arrived at the séance room, he'd given her a charming smile, introduced himself and his cousin, and neatly maneuvered her and Mrs. Larkson into a corner by the drinks table. He'd then begun a series of twenty questions that were clearly designed to figure out precisely where Mrs. Fuller fit into the social strata of San Francisco society. Mrs. Larkson had at first looked bored and then irritated, and Annie had gotten very tired of trying to find new ways to appear to know people she had only heard about.

She'd felt relieved, therefore, when Arabella had arrived, and the séance had begun, following a now familiar routine. They had moved into the moaning stage, the lights and music had risen and fallen, the table shook, Mr. Ruckner had discussed the impending arrival of his mother-in-law with his dead wife, and now Mrs. Mott was again conversing with one of her deceased Kansas relatives, this time about their special cure for bunions. Annie didn't know how Arabella had the patience to conduct this sort of charade night after night.

What am I thinking? I know just what it is like. Spouting out nonsense about the heart line and Mercury to convince a sweet woman she is too ill to travel or telling a merchant he should invest in timber shares because he was born under the sign of the lion. Am I really any better than she is?

Annie pushed this thought away, leaned over to Simon on her right, and whispered, "Am I going to be able to have a session with Evie May tonight?"

Simon leaned close to her ear and replied, "No, I am sorry, the girl is indisposed. Communing with the afterworld can be a difficult enterprise."

As he pulled away, Annie realized he had been so close to her that his beard had touched her cheek, leaving her with a terrible itchy feeling, which she couldn't scratch without letting go of the hands of the men on either side of her. *Bother! Thank goodness Nate is clean shaven*, she thought, shaking her head gently to dispel the feeling. Annie's husband had sported the usual mustache and beard, even some ridiculous straggly sideburns. As their marriage disintegrated, she had begun to loathe the feel of a man's hair on her face.

A sudden shriek from the other end of the table distracted Annie from that distasteful memory. She peered into the dim light to determine the source, which seemed to be Isobel Larkson, who was still uttering little squeals of distress. Arabella, just a vague white blur, was speaking in an odd whine, her words at first incomprehensible to Annie. Then she began to make some sense of what was being said, over and over.

"Izzie girl. Don't you leave me. Izzie girl, you promised. Don't leave, not tonight. Izzie, a promise is a promise. Don't you leave, not tonight, not ever. Izzie girl."

The light in the room brightened. *How did they do that?* Annie could see that Mrs. Larkson had broken away from Mr. Ruckner on her right and had buried her head in her cousin Jack's shoulder. He appeared to be trying to calm her down, but Annie, thinking about his private meeting with Arabella on Wednesday, couldn't help but believe this little scene was all his doing. *What he's getting at?* She also wondered about the identity of the spirit who was speaking. Obviously it was someone from Mrs. Larkson's past, someone who had passed on, someone whom she had disappointed. Who better to know her secrets than her childhood friend and relative, Jack Sweeter? *I wonder if she is clever enough to figure that out?*

Annie heard Mrs. Larkson say, "Jack, I don't want to stay. Please, let's go."

"Isobel, my dear," he replied. "We must stay. Don't you see? If you go now, you may anger her even more. Listen, she's gone for now. Be a good girl, take Mr. Ruckner's hand and just see what happens next. After all, if we leave this instant, we will be unfashionably early for the Reingolds' party."

Arabella suddenly switched to a new voice, this one that of a young child, who was crying out, "Nurse, Nurse, please help me. Nurse, Nurse, I am thirsty, why don't you answer? Mama said she would come, but she hasn't. I'm hot."

Not unexpectedly, Miss Herron sang out, "It's Vincent. Vincent, I am here. Don't you worry. I will get your mother for you. She will come next time; I am sure. Please don't be frightened. You are in a special place, where your heavenly father and mother will take care of you."

Annie felt ill. Miss Herron sounded sincere. Nevertheless, she was trying to drag another poor bereaved mother into the Framptons' net. Annie wondered if Miss Herron had replaced the nurse who had lured Sukie to the Framptons or if they had several nurses working for them at the same time. They had to be stopped, at all costs. If only Nate could convince Pierce this was a story worth telling. He was supposed to have met with the reporter earlier today; maybe he would have good news. When Nate had left the boarding house last night, she had meant to ask if he was planning on coming by the Framptons' tonight, to escort Kathleen and her home from the séance. For some reason, when he had kissed her, the question had slipped her mind. He had been very considerate, asking permission, and the kiss had been so gentle. John had never been gentle, ever.

"Mrs. Fuller, are you all right? Your father's spirit is calling." Simon's voice in her ear brought her back to the present.

The light once again had dimmed, and the piano had shifted to a soft hymn. Annie realized that the same male voice Arabella had used on Monday was again addressing her. She had to force herself to treat the supposed spirit of her father seriously. The accent was not bad for a typical New Yorker, but her father had never been typical of anything. He had also never treated her like an imbecile; instead, he had instructed her in the intricacies of the financial world, trusting her to make her own investments by the time she was sixteen. *Yet at the end, he didn't trust me with his fortune. Left it all in John's hands as my trustee.*

Wishing to end these painful thoughts, Annie broke into Arabella's monologue. "Father, you are confusing me. Can't you just write down what my investments should be, with spirit slate writing? That would be ever so easier." Nate had suggested this plan to her last night. If they could get the Framptons to commit to writing down the investments they were recommending, and it turned out that they had a financial stake in those companies, this evidence would be so much more incriminating than just oral testimony. Beside her, Simon stiffened, and Arabella chose to respond by going into one of her moaning spells again. Annie thought she had better show some distress at the abrupt ending of her conversation with her father, so she uttered a few disjointed phrases asking him to please come back and not be angry. Then she let her head drop, as if in great disappointment.

Just as she began to wonder if this was the end of the evening's entertainment, Arabella began to breathe heavily, and an eerie bluish light began to illuminate her face. This was a brand new effect, and Annie was impressed. She hoped that if she and Nate were able to explore the house Sunday night, they might at least unravel the mystery of the lights and sound. Perhaps the former medium, Flora Hunt, who had agreed to meet with Annie tomorrow, would have some ideas. If Annie remembered correctly, the one time she had seen Mrs. Hunt on stage back in New York, she had seemed to be bathed in a very similar glow.

"Harold, Harold, this here's Buddy speaking. Do ya hear me, you little good-for-nothing?" Arabella's voice had taken on a rough masculine quality, infused with anger.

"Harold, why aren't you answering? Speak when you're spoken to, got to be polite. That's all you were good for, mister manners."

"What do you want?" Harold Hapgood's voice slid up to a higher register.

"What do I want? It's what Pa wants. He wants to know why you did it? You got everything. All you had to do was do your duty. That's all. You can go to the devil for all I care."

Annie looked to see how Mr. Hapgood was reacting, again wondering why he would keep attending the séance if all he ever got was abuse, last week from his father, now from a brother? However, it was hard to read Hapgood's expression since he leaned as far away from Arabella as he could, putting his face in shadow as he spoke.

"I tried, I really tried. Nothing I could do was enough. You were her favorite. You're the one broke her heart."

Annie heard a loud crash, and the curtains billowed out into the room, accompanied by a blast of cold air on her face. She noticed that a chair in the corner of the room now lay on its side.

"You worm," Arabella's voice thundered. "You can't blame me for your failures. You'd better hope she didn't hear you. She will make your life a living hell."

Harold Hapgood slumped in his chair, in what looked to Annie like a dead faint.

Chapter Twenty-six
Friday evening, October 24, 1879

"Perfect German Cook wants a situation in a first-class family; no washing."
—*San Francisco Chronicle*, 1879

The day had flown by as if it had wings, and Kathleen leaned her head on the back of the chair in the Framptons' front hall, sighing contentedly. Tilly, Biddy's cousin, had shown up first thing this morning, her cheeks pink, her hair a mass of black corkscrew curls, and her mouth filled with the soft sounds of Gaelic, which reminded Kathleen so much of her own mother's voice. While teaching Tilly meant every task took twice as long, it had been ever so much fun to be working with someone. Making the beds, dusting the parlor, beating the rugs, washing the dishes, every task had felt more like a game, borne along by Tilly's shy giggle.

The Framptons' front doorbell pealed again, and Kathleen turned to see who was coming. The double doors to the séance room were still open, and Kathleen could see that the judge, the banker, the two old ladies, and that sorrowful looking storeowner, Hapgood, were already gathered. Oddly, neither Mr. Frampton nor Mrs. Frampton had made an appearance yet, and Albert had been busy shuttling between the drinks table in the séance room and the front door.

Here he was, bowing slightly and almost grabbing the top hat and cane from that handsome Mr. Sweeter, who had just come in with Mrs. Larkson. Tonight, Mrs. Larkson was wearing a luscious, fur-trimmed pelisse. When she took it off, Kathleen saw that she was in a dark-green silk evening dress, with a low-cut neckline and a long train of light-green brocaded satin. Kathleen whistled silently, thinking, *What a get-up, must have cost a fortune! Dressed like that, they must be going to some shindig after. Sweeter sure looks the part of a gentleman in his fancy dress. Wonder if the lady's husband is meeting them later?*

Kathleen thought about the little changes her mistress had been making to her good navy and her best black silk to hide the fact that she only had two fashionable dresses to choose from for evening wear. The men at the séance wouldn't notice; Mr. Dawson, heaven knows, wouldn't care if Mrs. Fuller was wearing a sack, he was that besotted. Kathleen would bet that Mrs. Frampton and Mrs. Larkson had observed that the supposedly well-to-do Mrs. Fuller was recirculating the same two gowns. Maybe they would just take this as confirmation of the story her mistress had told Mr. Frampton, that she needed to speak to her father because her income wasn't enough to make ends meet.

Arabella Frampton came down the stairs and waited until Mr. Sweeter and Mrs. Larkson had moved into the parlor, then came and put her hand on the butler's arm.

"Albert, please tell our guests that the start of the circle will be slightly delayed. Then, after everyone's drinks have been taken care of, you are needed in the kitchen. Oh, and please close the door to the hallway when you go in; I believe everyone is assembled."

While Mrs. Frampton was dressed, as usual, in an elegant silk gown, this one a dark lilac that somehow managed to complement not clash with her bright auburn hair, she didn't look quite as collected as usual. A strand of hair was slipping loose from the spray of flowers that held up the curls at the top of her head, as if she had been interrupted in the midst of getting dressed.

Albert nodded and went into the séance parlor, closing the doors behind him. Mrs. Frampton then climbed the stairs and was soon out of sight, although Kathleen thought she heard voices in the upstairs hall. A few moments later, Simon Frampton came down the stairs, accompanied by Mrs. Nickerson, who was clinging to his arm and whispering urgently. Kathleen was amused to see Mr. Frampton replace a sour expression with a fixed smile when he noticed Kathleen sitting on the chair by the front door.

Once he made it to the first floor, a task made more difficult by Mrs.

Nickerson's attempt to lean her head on his shoulder, he said, "Mrs. Nickerson, please, I must leave you now. I have a room full of anxious men and women waiting for me. But here is Mrs. Fuller's maid, Miss Kathleen, I believe her name is, and I am sure she will be so good as to escort you to the kitchen. You wouldn't mind helping us out in this fashion, would you, Miss Kathleen? Mrs. Nickerson is indisposed, and I do believe a nice cup of hot tea is very much in order."

Kathleen had risen as soon as Mr. Frampton had addressed her, and she gave a little curtsy in acknowledgement. She was thrilled to be given license to go on to the back of the house and finally see the kitchen. She would also get a chance to find out what had upset Evie May's mother. She moved forward and let Mr. Frampton ruthlessly transfer a now weeping Mrs. Nickerson from his arm to her own. He then opened the doors to the parlor and disappeared.

"Now, Ma'am, let's get you that cup of tea, and maybe one of Cook's pastries," Kathleen cajoled. When Mrs. Nickerson ignored her and turned to follow Mr. Frampton, Kathleen held onto to her and said sharply, "Mrs. Nickerson, you don't want to be going there, not at leastways until you have had a chance to refresh yourself. Tears can age a woman so."

That got her attention, Kathleen thought, beginning to herd the older woman down the hallway.

"Oh, dear me, I hadn't thought . . . I just was so upset. I must look a fright. I do believe a cup of tea . . . a cool cloth to my eyes . . . Simon has his work to do; I realize that. What must he think of me? Such a gentleman."

"That's all right," Kathleen said, patting Mrs. Nickerson on the shoulder.

Then she pushed through the door to the short, narrow back hallway, where the wood floor and wainscoting of the front hallway were replaced by dark, scuffed oilcloth and dingy plaster. Straight ahead she could see the kitchen, well lighted by kerosene lamps, and the German cook standing over a breadboard next to the sink, vigorously kneading. Kathleen pulled out a chair from the kitchen table and urged Mrs. Nickerson to sit.

Biddy had told her the cook's name, so she addressed her directly. "Please, Mrs. Schmitt, Mr. Frampton asked that you fix Mrs. Nickerson some tea. But I can see you are busy. If you wouldn't mind, I will just put on the kettle. If you point the way, I am sure I can assemble tea for the lady."

The cook, who had glared at them when they first entered the kitchen, now smiled. Wiping her floury hands on her apron, she pointed to a steaming kettle and then to a tea service that was already set up on a table underneath a back window. Kathleen thanked her, went over and picked up a towel hanging over the oven door handle, and lifted the kettle off the stovetop. Seeing that the tea was already in the pot, she then went and poured the water into the teapot. Mrs. Fuller had taught her to heat the pot first and put in the tea next, but who was she to argue with how the Germans did it?

While she waited for the tea to brew, she turned and looked around. Mrs. Nickerson was sitting with her elbows on the table and her head in her hands. Now that she no longer had a male audience, she looked exhausted and very much her age. Mrs. Schmitt had gone back to her kneading. The kitchen seemed well stocked. Plates and glasses filled a glass-fronted cabinet, different sized bowls nested together on a counter, and a series of ceramic crocks, which probably held flour and grains, stood on a shelf. Kathleen, looking back at the entrance to the kitchen, noted there was a closed door that must lead down to the cellar. On the other side, a second door stood open. It appeared to lead to the pantry and perhaps the cook's quarters. She remembered Biddy said the laundry was located down in the cellar.

Pouring the tea into two cups, Kathleen said to Mrs. Nickerson, "Would you like some cream and sugar in your tea, ma'am?" She interpreted the moan that came from the older woman as an affirmative and liberally added both. Noting that Mrs. Schmitt had slapped the ball of dough into a bowl, she raised the second cup and inquired, "Mrs. Schmitt, would you like me to pour you a cup? And I wondered if there might be any of those wonderful pastries you served last Friday?"

The cook shook her head but again smiled and walked over to take off a dishtowel that lay over a plate, revealing a stack of lovely yellow cakes topped with sugar and sliced almonds. Kathleen practically swooned. Mrs. O'Rourke was a wonderful cook, but everyone knew the Germans were the best bakers.

"Mrs. Schmitt, those look so wonderful! Now, Mrs. Nickerson, do drink up. You will feel much better."

Kathleen poured a cup for herself and, bringing over the plate of cakes, sat across from Mrs. Nickerson. "Ma'am, can you tell me what's upsetting you? I can see you're that troubled. Maybe I can help."

Mrs. Nickerson, who had gulped down half a cup of tea and now had her mouth stuffed with cake, seemed to find Kathleen's question insulting because she drew herself up and tried to look down her nose. If she meant to be intimidating, the thick black smudges under her eyes from the burnt cork she had used on her eyelashes, the raw red of her nose, and the liberal dusting of powdered sugar on her chin simply made Kathleen want to laugh.

"Girl, you have been kind enough, but it is none of your business what has caused me such distress. No, I must trust in Simon. Mr. Frampton, that is. He won't let anything happen to . . . no, mustn't say. He said I should just wait. Albert . . ." Mrs. Nickerson, who clearly wanted to talk, popped the rest of the cake in her mouth as if this was the only way to stop herself.

Just then, as if summoned by Mrs. Nickerson's words, Albert appeared at the entranceway to the kitchen. He gave a grim nod of satisfaction when he saw Mrs. Nickerson with her back to him, and he silently retreated, disappearing up the back stairs.

Kathleen shivered. That man was altogether too quiet on his feet. Biddy said it was as if he could magically appear and then reappear from one room to the other, and he always seemed to materialize just when she was taking a break from work. Kathleen tried several more times to engage Mrs. Nickerson in conversation, but to no avail. Finally, she decided that there wasn't anything more to be gained from her or the silent cook, who was fiddling with something on the stove that smelled like beef broth. She finished her tea, had one more pastry, stood up, and said, "Excuse me. I believe I need to use the privy. Can I assume it is out back?"

Biddy had told her that the Framptons didn't permit her to use the toilet installed in the upstairs bathroom, so Kathleen knew the answer to her own question. She thought a trip to the back yard would give her a chance to nose around a bit before Sunday night. Mrs. Nickerson just stared at her, but Mrs. Schmitt said something that sounded like "ya" and pointed to a lantern that sat on the counter next to the back door.

After lighting the candle in the lantern, Kathleen opened the back door, which was unlocked, and went out into the dark. The light from the kitchen window only spilled out a short distance. The cloudy night sky held no moon or stars, and it took a second for her eyes to adjust. Looking down and swinging the lantern, she saw a gravel path leading straight back to a shed surrounded by bushes. As her vision improved, she saw that behind the privy bulked what was most likely the old carriage house, which Biddy said was abandoned. Off the path to the privy, the remnants of a gravel drive were overgrown by grass. She first walked over to the privy, in case she was being watched, then turned around to see if Mrs. Schmitt, whom she could see in the kitchen window, was looking her way. The cook seemed to be looking down, and then she moved away from the window. Kathleen used this opportunity to look for a path that would lead around the side of the house.

Last night, when Mrs. Fuller talked to Biddy about her plan to search the Frampton house, she had said she was especially interested in trying to get into the rooms underneath the two connected séance parlors. Biddy had told her that the door to the cellar remained locked, unless Biddy was doing wash. Even then, the door from the washroom to the next room, which held the wine and the cask of beer, stayed locked; she had tried it each time she did the laundry, just out of curiosity.

Once, Albert had let Biddy into the wine cellar to help him fetch several bottles, and she saw that from the wine cellar there was another door that most likely led to the rooms underneath the upstairs parlors. She had assumed this door was locked as well.

Biddy had mentioned there was another entrance to the cellar on the side of the house, which Kathleen wanted to explore. Evidently, there was a little-used track that went from the alley, passed the old abandoned carriage house, and ended at the woodpile on the side of the house. Biddy said that between the woodpile and the French windows to the small back parlor there was a kind of trap door that she assumed led to stairs or a ramp for delivering goods into the cellar. Mrs. Fuller had said most grand old houses had such things so that when there was a big party, with lots of deliveries, the tradesmen wouldn't have to track through the kitchen.

What Kathleen hoped to check out was if this trap door was locked and, if so, what kind of tool they might use to pry it open. She hadn't mentioned this idea to Mrs. Fuller because she thought her mistress wouldn't be comfortable with the idea of a little breaking and entering. But Kathleen thought it would be good to have a plan in mind, just in case.

She could see by the light of the lantern that she had reached the edge of the house and that there was indeed a partially overgrown track. She shifted the lantern to her left hand and put out her right to touch the side of the house, using this to guide her passage, watching her feet to make sure she didn't trip over anything. Without warning, someone grabbed her around the waist and, after she let out a yelp, cupped a hand over her mouth. She tried to get free, but she was hampered by the fact she still held the lantern in her left hand. She was afraid to let it loose, in case it might set her skirts on fire. She then realized the man was whispering in her ear.

"Settle down, darling. I'm not going to hurt you. If you promise not to screech, I will let you go. You startled me. I was just having a smoke. Want one? There, that's better."

Kathleen stilled, and the man removed his hand from her mouth, but his arm stayed firmly around her waist. The strong smell of tobacco showed he was telling the truth, at least that far. Her heart began to slow, and her mind turned over quickly. Kathleen had had her share of experiences with amorous young men, usually drunk. To her mind, whoever this was, he wasn't drunk and didn't seem to be a great physical threat. She judged that he must be pretty young if the short stature and the higher register of his voice were any indication. He took the lantern from her hand and let it shine in her face. Blinded for a moment, Kathleen put up her hand, tried to get a look at her captor, and whispered, "Stop that. I can't see a thing. Who do you think you are? Scaring a poor girl half out of her wits."

He abruptly released her and set the lantern down on what Kathleen saw was a waist-high pile of wood. She could now see him. He was no more than half a foot taller than she was and was clean-shaven, with a slouch hat crammed down low over his forehead. He had a loose suit jacket over some sort of light-colored vest, and he was looking at his hands where he had a box of matches and a cigarette. After lighting the cigarette, he took a deep pull and looked up, extending the cigarette in an unspoken invitation as he exhaled. Kathleen started to shake her head, and then she froze as she stared into the pale, unforgettable eyes of Evie May.

Chapter Twenty-seven
Friday evening, October 24, 1879

"Shortly before 12 o'clock last Friday night officer Waite…was set upon…by a crowd of Barbary Coast hoodlums, who struck him several times over the head and face with a billet of wood."
—*San Francisco Chronicle*, 1879

"Ma'am, it was Evie May, dressed up like a young tough."

From the moment that Annie left the séance room and was scooped up by Kathleen and practically dragged out of the house, she knew the young maid had something of great import to tell her. She'd barely had time to get her coat on before Kathleen grabbed her hand and began to pull her out the front door. When they'd had to wait for a moment while Mrs. Larkson and Mr. Sweeter preceded them down the front steps, Kathleen had vibrated with impatience. Once they reached the sidewalk, she set such a rapid pace that they were soon several yards ahead of Mr. Ruckner, who was the only member of the circle who took the same horse car home as they did. Now safe from prying ears, Kathleen began to spill out the whole story of her evening, ending with the young man who had grabbed her and whom she swore was Evie May.

Annie was flabbergasted. "Evie May? How can you be sure?"

"Her eyes. Remember when I ran into her that first day we visited, when she said she was Miss Evelyn? I noticed her eyes. Such an odd, pale color. Afterwards, I thought to myself that I wasn't sure if they were a green or gray. They might even be a light brown. Strange. Piercing. You've noticed them, haven't you, ma'am?"

"Yes, yes, Evie May does have very distinctive eyes. Changeable, just like the rest of her. But mightn't the young man be a brother or young male cousin? Maybe she even has a twin?"

"I thought about that, but you see, it was Evie May who was missing.

That's what all the fuss was about. She wasn't in the cabinet, was she?"

Annie said, "No, she wasn't. But when the séance was over, Albert came in and whispered something to Simon, who then told Judge Babcock that he thought Evie May would be able to give him a sitting tonight if he was willing to wait until everyone was gone."

"But don't you see, ma'am, that just proves it. I learned later from the cook that Mrs. Nickerson had been so upset because when it came time for the séance no one could find Evie May. I don't know what the girl was up to, but for some reason she slipped out of the house dressed like a young man. Then, right after she slipped back into the house, suddenly Evie May was available for a sitting."

By this time they had reached Sixth and Harrison. Since there were several people standing at the car stop, Annie slowed down so they wouldn't be overheard. "What do you mean, she slipped back into the house?"

"I had just whispered her name when we both heard the back door to the kitchen slam open and Albert give a shout. I guess someone in the house must have heard me yell. Anyway, Evie May looked at me, said, 'Sorry, Miss, but you can call me Edmund.' Then he winked, pinched my cheek, and climbed up the woodpile. Then he, I mean she, grabbed a rope hanging down the side of the house, and darned if she didn't clamber right up to an open window on the second floor and disappear."

"My goodness! How unexpected. She must have gotten out that way as well. From your description of where the woodpile is, the room above it on the second floor would be at the back of the house. When we see Biddy on Sunday, she will be able to tell us if that is Evie May's room." Annie then noticed that their car was approaching, and she said, "Wait to tell me until we get on the car. Here comes Mr. Ruckner. Let's make sure we sit as far away from him as we can, so we can continue to talk."

Once Annie and Kathleen had made their way to the far end of the car, and Mr. Ruckner, who probably had no desire to associate with a fellow member of Framptons' circle, took a seat right near the front, they resumed their whispered conversation. Kathleen told her how she snatched up the lantern and blew out the candle, then crept down the track that led to the alley, so as to miss Albert. When she saw him go back into the kitchen, she cut across to the privy so that when she returned to the house she would be coming from the right direction. When she re-entered the kitchen, she told him some tale about the candle in the lantern blowing out, which had caused her such a fright she had screeched.

"Albert started to question me, but just then a woman I have never seen before, she must be the lady's maid who is his wife, came running into the kitchen, saying, 'She's back.' Albert and Mrs. Nickerson hotfooted it up the stairs, leaving Mrs. Schmitt and me just standing there."

Annie thought for a moment and said, "I must say, Kathleen, that does all seem to fit with the young man you saw being Evie May. She said her name was Edmund? Are you sure he, I mean she, wasn't pretending to be a younger boy? I told you about Eddie who I met on Wednesday."

"Well, ma'am, she wasn't dressed like a boy, not with that slouch hat on, and long pants, and she didn't act like a young boy. She acted like a young man on the prowl."

"Remarkable." Annie sat for a moment, trying to take it all in. "I must say, your night was more exciting than mine, except for the very end."

"What happened then, ma'am?" Kathleen leaned closer, eager to hear Mrs. Fuller's adventures.

"Most of the séance was pretty much the same as the other two I have attended," said Annie, "except of course for there being no Evie May. Mrs. Larkson was visited by a spirit that upset her a good deal. The spirit seemed to be accusing her of breaking a promise of some sort. Given her cousin Jack's little visit to Arabella on Wednesday, I think we can assume that those two are in it together, whatever it is. I wonder if Mrs. Stein's daughter could have a talk with Isobel Larkson, to get her to confide in her.

"But the real excitement came when the spirit of Mr. Hapgood's brother appeared. He was a very angry spirit, abused poor Mr. Hapgood terribly, called him names, and accused him of not doing his duty. Then everything got very noisy. Wind whipped through the room, knocking over a chair, and Arabella, in this extraordinary voice of doom, said something about hell fire. Mr. Hapgood fainted."

"What!" Kathleen's voice rose, and then she put her hand over her mouth.

"He fainted, or at least he looked like he fainted. Miss Herron, the nurse, went into action, taking his pulse and chaffing his wrists or something. About then, the lights went up, Albert came into the room, and Simon ushered us all out, saying that Mr. Hapgood would be fine."

"Hilda will be so upset. She was very worried."

Annie looked at Kathleen strangely. "Hilda? Who is Hilda? Is that Mrs. Schmitt's first name? Why would she be upset?"

Kathleen giggled. "Oh, no, I meant Mrs. Hapgood. She asked me to call her by her first name. Albert eventually came back to the kitchen and told me to return to the front hallway but to take Mrs. Hapgood some tea. We had ever such a nice chat. Turns out Hilda goes to St. Boniface, near us. Course you know I go there some times for mass when there isn't time to go to St. Mary's. Mostly Germans at St. Boniface, but it doesn't matter, Latin is Latin, no matter the accent."

Annie smiled to herself, thinking about how good Kathleen was at putting someone at ease. "In your nice chat with Mrs. Hapgood, did she confirm what Mrs. Nickerson told you, that Harold Hapgood has a problem with alcohol? Remember, I had wanted to follow through on the possibility that Mrs. Hapgood was the one who wrote the anonymous letter to the police."

"She didn't talk about writing any letter, but she did talk a little about her husband's struggles with the drink. First she told me how she met Mr. Hapgood. Her father runs a dairy farm in Happy Valley. Harold used to come out to pick up cheeses for his pa's store, and he fell head over heels in love. Hilda said there was a terrible row. Mr. Hapgood's folks felt she was beneath them. Real snooty about anyone who didn't come to America with the pilgrims. But she said Harold stood up to his pa and told him he didn't care. He said his pa could disinherit him if need be, but he was marrying his Hilda. Wasn't that romantic?"

Annie smiled and said, "Yes, very. So what happened? Since Mr. Hapgood is running the store, I guess his father didn't disinherit him?"

"Not in the end. Hilda said that at first Harold did have to go out and find another job, and they were pretty hard up. Her folks helped out as best they could. But then Mr. Hapgood's remaining brother died or got killed or something, and his pa got real sick and he had nowhere else to turn. So back Harold came."

"Like the prodigal son," Annie murmured.

"But Hilda said she wishes it never happened. Her in-laws just sucked all the life out of him. 'Nothing were ever good enough,' were her exact words. From what she said, that's when she found out her husband had always had problems with drinking. I'd told her about my pa, so she felt comfortable confiding in me. She said Mr. Hapgood had even been under a doctor's care when he was younger, before he met Hilda. She said he didn't drink at all when they met; it was a real disappointment to her when he started up again."

Annie said, "But, Kathleen, did she explain why he would come to these séances? You would think he would be glad to be free of them if they were such wretched people. They certainly aren't very pleasant ghosts."

"Hilda told me that Simon Frampton wrote her husband a letter, said he had a message from his departed father. She wanted Harold to ignore it, but he couldn't stay away. She says he keeps hoping to get their approval. He tries to tell them how splendidly the store is doing, but they won't listen. Oh, ma'am, she sounded so sad. She said, 'They never let him live when they were alive, and they won't be content until he is as dead as they are.'"

Chapter Twenty-eight
Saturday afternoon, October 25, 1879

"Spiritualism. Mrs. Ada Foye 126 Kearny st Sittings daily. Meetings
Wednesday evenings at 8."
—*San Francisco Chronicle*, 1879

As Annie followed the maid up a narrow flight of stairs, she experienced an odd sense of familiarity. While this lovely, Italianate-style house on Octavia Street in Pacific Heights had probably been built within the last decade and was, therefore, more modern and elegant than her own, Annie recognized the telltale signs that Mrs. Flora Hunt, the famous trance medium, now lived in a San Francisco boarding house. The first clue had been the two young men who passed her on the front steps without a single glance. Next came the unusual number of coats and umbrellas hanging from the coat rack in the front hallway. Finally, the maid had led her up the stairs to what should have been the private section of a single-family home. She was now standing in front of the door to a suite of rooms like the ones Esther and Herman Stein occupied in her own boarding house.

Annie's nervousness abated somewhat. She realized she had been approaching this meeting with Mrs. Hunt as if she was still the schoolgirl who had gone with her father to see the medium perform in New York City, nearly fourteen years earlier. Flora Stockwell Trainor had been her name then, and in her twenties she had been at the peak of her popularity, filling the three thousand-seat theater on Broadway every night for weeks on end. While her father saw Mrs. Hunt as no more than a clever performer, Annie, thirteen and still reeling from the death of her mother, had been quite taken by the idea that this young woman was able to communicate with the dead. She remembered looking up at the tiny, beautiful, doll-like figure on stage, hearing her deep voice spin magical visions of eternal gardens, and thinking that surely this woman, her pale blond hair glowing in the darkened theater, cornflower blue eyes lifted upward, was touched by the angels. When Flora Hunt had wakened from her trance and began to field the series of questions asked by a group of ministers, Annie had been impressed by her calm, reasonable answers and had felt angry with the men for expecting this heavenly creature to bandy words with mere mortals.

The evening had made such an impression on her that, even when she was much older and had come to her father's conclusion that it had all been a sham, she was still thrilled when she discovered *Shadows and Light*, Mrs. Hunt's memoir. Annie lived with her husband's aunt Lottie at the time, and she was searching for ideas to help create Madam Sibyl. While Mrs. Hunt hadn't repudiated her Spiritualist beliefs in her book, she did have a very detailed chapter on the fraudulent practices of those mediums she dubbed "false prophets," which Annie found very helpful. As she stood waiting to meet Mrs. Hunt, Annie thought it somehow fitting that once again she was turning to her childhood idol for advice.

The maid opened the door to a pleasantly appointed sitting room, bathed in late afternoon light from a set of spacious bay windows. A man and a woman were sitting in two armchairs grouped in front of the fireplace, where a small blaze competed with the sunlight. They rose as Annie entered the room. Annie would have recognized the woman anywhere. Flora Hunt was still petite: her dark gray silk emphasized her tiny waist. While her blond hair now showed some gray and tiny lines surrounded her blue eyes, she still gave the overall impression of ethereal youthfulness.

Moving forward, her hand outstretched in welcome, Mrs. Hunt said, "Dear Mrs. Fuller, how nice to meet you. I must say I was very intrigued by your note, and I do hope that I will be of service to you. Please, let me introduce my husband, Mr. Hunt."

Mr. Hunt, who came to stand behind his wife and rested one large hand on her shoulder, nodded and gave a reserved smile. Annie marveled at the contrast between the two. Mr. Hunt, while not much taller than his wife, was solidly built; his sun-roughened skin, sandy brown hair, wide shoulders, and short legs suggested he was a man who was rooted in the earth. She then remembered from Mrs. Hunt's memoir that she had met her second husband in a tiny town in Nebraska and that, in addition to being a Universalist minister, he had been a farmer. A man who, with his spinster sister, had taken in Flora, whose health and spirit were broken, and healed her.

"Won't you please have a seat by the fire? The afternoon has turned chilly." Mrs. Hunt pointed to the chair she had just vacated and turned to the servant. "Maureen, if you would please bring the tea set over by our chairs. I will ring if we need you further." She and her husband then sat on the other two chairs grouped around the fire.

Annie sat down and said, "Thank you so much for seeing me. As I explained in my letter, I have been asked by an acquaintance, actually a woman who lives in my boarding house, to help convince her sister to stop attending the séances held by a couple, Simon and Arabella Frampton. From reading your memoir and the articles you wrote for the *San Francisco Morning Call*, it was my understanding that you sometimes helped expose those mediums you felt were using fraudulent methods. I hoped you might be able to help me."

"The Framptons, yes, I have heard of them," Mrs. Hunt responded. "I believe they arrived in San Francisco this past spring. I haven't heard any particular complaints about them from among the Spiritualist community. May I ask why your friend wishes to stop her sister from attending these séances?"

Annie recounted Miss Pinehurst's fears that Sukie's obsession with her dead son was damaging her health and her marriage, if not, in fact, her future salvation. Mrs. Hunt replied, "Well, I can understand why, if Miss Pinehurst doesn't believe in universal salvation or the tenets of Spiritualism, she would find her sister's behavior distressing. However, as you have read my memoir, you must realize I do accept the possibility of communicating with those who have died. It is only those unscrupulous individuals who use tricks to feign communications with the spirit world that I have any interest in exposing. Do you have evidence that the Framptons are insincere?"

Mrs. Hunt's direct gaze unsettled Annie. Her cheeks grew hot at the embarrassing thought that Madam Sibyl might fall under Mrs. Hunt's definition of unscrupulous individuals. Trying not to sound defensive, she explained why she believed the Framptons were frauds. "First of all, I have learned that Simon Frampton previously had a career as a magician, with his wife as his assistant, and the séances I have attended seem to be heavily dependent on the use of manufactured lights and sounds, carefully orchestrated for effect. From my reading about Spiritualism, it was my impression that the use of piano music, drums, trumpets, and tambourines are commonly associated with mediums who were later discovered to be frauds."

Mrs. Hunt smiled and said, "Yes, despite the Scripture's frequent reference to musical instruments and heavenly choirs, it is those mortals who wish to fool the unsuspecting who pipe music in from the next room, not the celestial spheres."

Charmed by Mrs. Hunt's sense of humor, Annie continued. "It isn't just the theatrical nature of the séances that concerns me. It is the content of the communications. While my own experience has been fairly benign —for example, Mrs. Frampton's attempt to reproduce my father's voice was laughably inaccurate—nevertheless, some of the spirits she conjures up appear quite malevolent. One threatened a poor young man with hell-fire. Even more disturbing, Miss Pinehurst's sister has been told by the purported spirit of her son that he is going to be playing soon in Summer-land with her unborn child. She has interpreted this to mean her pregnancy will either not carry to term or that she will lose this child in infancy as well."

Mrs. Hunt drew in her breath sharply, and her husband reached over and took her hand as she began to speak. "Mrs. Fuller, no wonder you and Miss Pinehurst are concerned. While communication with the spirit world is difficult and can produce inexplicable and incomprehensible results, what you have described is wicked and not true mediumship. Now tell me how you believe I can help."

Annie asked Mrs. Hunt for suggestions on what to look for if and when she and Nate got a chance to examine the séance room Sunday night. Mrs. Hunt described the different ways tables could be made to shake and how a medium might use her unencumbered feet to press levers and push buttons attached to wires to make noises.

"From what you have told me," said Mrs. Hunt, "the Framptons haven't gone in for some of the newer uses of photography or material manifestations, and you do seem confident that neither Mrs. Frampton nor her husband moves around during the séance. Could they have confederates?"

"Most certainly," Annie replied. "We have discovered that the butler and the lady's maid employed in the house are Arabella's uncle and his wife. I assume they must be working the lights and music in some fashion."

"That makes sense," said Mrs. Hunt. "I wouldn't be surprised if they weren't responsible for the events you described happening at the end of Friday's séance. The butler or maid could have entered the room from the outside window and gone over and quietly pulled the chair over. Then, as they left, they could open the window wide and slam it shut. This would produce the blast of cold air and loud noise you described, and when the lights went up and you noticed the chair turned over, it would be easy to make the assumption that the phenomena were connected. A magician would be very familiar with these sorts of tactics of misdirection."

Annie, picturing the events in her mind, nodded. She then said, "All this is very helpful, but I worry it will not be enough to convince Miss Pinehurst's sister it isn't her son Charlie she meets when she goes into the cabinet with Evie May."

When Mrs. Hunt looked puzzled, Annie went on to tell her about the young medium and the role she played during the séances and in private sittings. She continued, "Arabella Frampton is quite skilled. I am sure that she is an important reason the Framptons have been so successful. However, I am equally confident that she is not a true medium, and I hope, with the help you have given me, I will be able to demonstrate this to Sukie Vetch. What concerns me is that she won't care, because it is the talents of

Evie May that produce her son for her."

Mrs. Hunt asked, "You mentioned her talents. What did you mean?"

"Mrs. Frampton is a good actress. She can throw her voice in such a way that it seems to be coming from somewhere else in the room, but when you look at her, what you see is Arabella Frampton, with her eyes closed, rocking back and forth and pretending to be in a trance. When Evie May speaks, she isn't pretending to be someone else. She *becomes* someone else, like a human chameleon. She changes her voice, her mannerisms, her facial expressions; even her body seems to change from that of an old woman, to a young girl, then a small boy."

Mrs. Hunt leaned forward, her voice sharp. "And how do you think she does this?"

"I don't know," Annie replied. "When I learned that Simon Frampton had been a successful mesmerist for a number of years in England, it occurred to me that perhaps he puts her into some kind of trance, which would explain why I don't feel any sense of artifice. I read once that when people have been put into a trance, they can be asked to behave in a certain fashion and that they will do so, with every sign of sincerity.

"I noticed that Simon always disappears for about ten minutes before a séance begins. I can't help but think he is with Evie May, mesmerizing her. Whatever that entails. I also noticed that he uses the same phrases at the beginning and at the end of each session she holds in the cabinet, and it seems like these are a kind of trigger. She will be sitting in the cabinet, as if asleep, and he will say the phrase, and her whole being changes. Later he will say the other phrase, and she will seem to go asleep again."

Mrs. Hunt again looked meaningfully at her husband and then turned back to Annie. "I don't know how much you remember of my history from my memoir, but what you are describing is exactly what my first husband, who like Simon Frampton was also my manager and a skilled mesmerist, did with me on occasion. When I spoke in public, I entered the trance state on my own, something I started to do as early as age eight. But Mr. Trainor, who became my manager when I was thirteen and married me two years later, would invoke the trance when I had a private sitting with a special client. As I grew older and wiser, I began to understand how reprehensible this was. He was abusing my talents for his own financial gain, and in the process he was exposing me to unspeakable, immoral acts."

Mrs. Hunt paused, taking a sip of tea, and Annie could see how much the subject distressed her. She remembered reading in *Shadows and Light* that Flora Hunt, as a child, had undergone some awful trauma at the hands of a family friend. This, combined with the unexpected death of her father, explained how she came under the domination of Mr. Trainor, who was thirty years her senior. Annie, who was reading the book when she was still raw from the abuses of her own failed marriage, had been profoundly moved by the story of how Flora's love and adoration of this man had turned to bitterness and despair. Annie then had a terrible thought. *What must it be like for Evie May to sit in that closed cabinet with a man like Judge Babcock, who was caught in the delusion that when he caressed her, he was caressing his own beloved daughter?*

Mrs. Hunt put her cup down and took Annie's hands in hers, her penetrating gaze holding her own. "Mrs. Fuller, you are upset. Tell me, what are you thinking?"

"Mrs. Hunt, I can't help but be struck by the parallel between your experiences and Evie May's. From what I understand, she lost her father at a young age, and now Simon, this much older man, has complete control over her. It is bad enough that she may be an instrument of manipulation in the Framptons' quest for money, but how dreadful it must be for her to sit hour after hour, confined in that cabinet with adult men who impose their own desires upon her. And her mother is no protection; she is completely infatuated with Simon Frampton."

"Ah, her mother," said Flora Hunt, looking at her husband. "Yes, I understand. My mother also was infatuated with my tormentor. She tried to be a good mother, but she suffered lifelong pain from neuralgia and became quite dependent on an elixir that Mr. Trainor manufactured. That was how he first came into our life. He had moved on from mesmerism to selling patent medicine when he met my mother and me. I guess he saw more profit in me than his magical elixir. She died when I was but fifteen, and from then until the day I met Mr. Hunt and his wonderful sister, I had no human protectors. Yes, you are right to be concerned about Evie May. Please tell me more about what you know of her."

Annie hesitated. She was still uncomfortable when she talked about Maybelle, and she still hadn't told anyone about how she had at first thought Maybelle might be the spirit of her miscarried daughter. However, Mrs. Hunt might be able to shed some light on Maybelle, Eddie, and the others she and Kathleen had encountered.

So she said, "One odd aspect of Evie May's performance is that sometimes she seems to deviate from the path that Simon Frampton has laid down for her. Once, when Evie May was speaking in the character of my mother and then again when she was speaking as my dead son Johnny, whose existence was a complete fabrication on my part, she changed into a young six-year-old girl named Maybelle. Then, while I was speaking to Maybelle, she was replaced by a slightly older boy who called himself Eddie and who said he was Maybelle's brother. He seemed to feel that he protected Maybelle.

"Even more oddly, my maid Kathleen twice ran into Evie May outside the séance room, and each time she seemed to be someone completely different. Once she was a young woman calling herself Miss Evelyn, a name Eddie mentioned when he was talking to me. Then last night, Kathleen was accosted outside the Framptons' house by Evie May, who was dressed as a young street hoodlum calling himself Edmund. None of these people, or whatever you would call them, seem to have anything to do with the Framptons. In fact, it was my impression that Simon was upset when he found me talking to Eddie in my private sitting with Evie May on Wednesday."

Annie was startled to see Mrs. Hunt smiling sadly.

Mr. Hunt looked over at his wife and said, "Flora dear, you need to tell her. This young girl needs our help, and Mrs. Fuller has to understand if we are to work together."

Annie, who was still thinking about Evie May and what Mr. Hunt meant, was taken off guard when Mrs. Hunt leaned forward again and asked, "Mrs. Fuller, why did Miss Pinehurst ask *you* to help her?"

Annie looked down at her hands, searching for some sort of inspiration. She found nothing beyond the truth, which the woman across from her deserved. So she told Mrs. Hunt about Madam Sibyl. She explained how she had first created this alter ego to protect Lottie, a silly but kind woman, from being bilked out of her inheritance by local mediums. Finally, she told her of Mr. Stein's suggestion that she use Madam Sibyl as a way to supplement her income when it became clear the proceeds from the boarding house were insufficient to pay Beatrice and Kathleen decent wages and provide a little savings for Annie herself.

Annie concluded, saying, "Miss Pinehurst felt that my experience as Madam Sibyl made me particularly qualified to figure out how Simon and Arabella Frampton were tricking the people who attended their séances."

Mrs. Hunt then said, "I am curious, Mrs. Fuller. Is that how you see yourself? As someone who has something in common with the Framptons?"

"No, I don't," Annie replied, surprised at the anger she felt when she heard someone else ask the very question she had been asking herself. She continued, "But then I wouldn't, would I? I tell myself that what I do is different because my intentions are honorable. If I were a man, I wouldn't have to use such artifice, so I tell myself it is society's fault that people would rather get their financial advice from a fake clairvoyant than a well-trained and experienced business woman. But the more involved I have been in trying to expose the Framptons, the more I have begun to question my own actions."

"Do you believe in the astrology and palmistry you use as Madam Sibyl?" Mrs. Hunt asked.

"No," said Annie, pausing. "I guess I accept the possibility that a body of knowledge or set beliefs that have developed over thousands of years might have some basis in truth. Maybe honest practitioners of these so-called sciences do receive some wisdom from studying the arrangement of the stars or the lines in a person's palms. But I am not one of those honest practitioners because, although I do believe in the advice I give, I don't get that advice from the stars or my clients' palms."

Annie paused again, thinking about what she had just said, then continued. "I also don't know if there is life after death or if the spirits of the departed speak to the living. But I am willing to believe this might be true, and I do believe that honest Spiritualists, such as you, believe it to be true. Yet I am convinced that the Framptons are not Spiritualists and that the spirits are not speaking through them. Evie May, I am not so certain about."

"Mrs. Fuller, I commend you for your frankness," said Mrs. Hunt. "Honest self-doubt and a willingness to accept that other people's beliefs have validity are rare commodities in today's world. I don't believe you have anything in common with the Framptons, but I do think you need to consider the damage you are doing to yourself if you continue to spend your days lying to the very people you are trying to help. The ends seldom justify the means.

"However, that is between you and your conscience." Mrs. Hunt smiled over her shoulder at her husband, who smiled in return. "What we must figure out now is how to help you expose the Framptons. You have quite convinced me that they must be stopped, for the sake of people like your Miss Pinehurst's sister, as well as for the good name of true Spiritualists. But even more importantly, we must consider how to help Evie May. I believe Maybelle, Eddie, and the other spirits you have described are her protectors, but from my own experience I can tell you that they are going to need our help if the girl isn't going to be destroyed by what is being done to her."

*****

The girl was neatly dressed in a dark, royal-blue walking suit, tailored to suggest the beginning of a woman's curves, with blinding white lace at collar and cuffs. Her hair, parted in the center, was pulled into a topknot of intricate curls. Polished, black, high-button shoes peeked out from her long skirt. She stared straight into space, the china doll held loosely in her lap. The faint chimes of church bells seemed to awaken her. She stood up, looked puzzled for a moment at the doll, and dropped it onto the chair. She then glided over to the tall mirror, which was illuminated by a shaft of afternoon sun. She stared, then tilted her head, touched her hair, and smiled. Noticing a film of dust on the mirror, she frowned and looked around. Seeing a worn and ragged jersey lying on top of a trunk, she walked over to pick it up, but in doing so her long skirts stirred up clumps of mud on the floor. Making a small sound of disgust, she lifted up her skirts, moved rapidly to the opening in the floor that led down to the set of steps, and began to descend.

Chapter Twenty-Nine
Sunday evening, October 26, 1879

"REV. MR. GRAVES ON SPIRITUALISM. The speaker said that angels are superior to men, but inferior to man redeemed."—*San Francisco Chronicle*, 1879

As Annie sat between Kathleen and Nate in the close confines of a hansom cab, exquisitely aware of Nate's arm pressed up against her own, she labored to keep from fidgeting by clasping her hands tightly together in her lap. She feared that the slightest sign of nervousness on her part would give Nate an excuse to abort this evening's plans to search the Framptons' house. Biddy had told them that the cook, Mrs. Schmitt, left at five, and the rest of the household left to partake of their dinners by seven; consequently, if they arrived at seven-thirty, they should find the house empty.

The plan was for Biddy to keep an eye on the front door and Kathleen on the back while Annie and Nate searched the séance rooms and as many of the other rooms in the house as they could in the allotted time. They needed to be gone by eight-thirty, nine at the latest, if they wanted to be sure to miss the return of the house's occupants. She hoped that an hour would be time enough.

As the cab made its way down Taylor, she distracted herself from worrying about the risks they were taking by turning her thoughts back to the strange story Flora Hunt had recounted the day before about what she called her spirit protectors. Mrs. Hunt had explained that, throughout her life, she would go into a trance state and these protectors would appear. The first came when she was eight and lost in the woods. An old woman took over her body and led her home. Mrs. Hunt later identified the woman as her grandmother, who had died before she was born.

She had said to Annie, "My childhood was relatively happy until the age of eleven. My father, a carpenter and radical reformer, had been my closest companion, but then something happened to him. He changed. His mood darkened, and he began to spend more and more time at the local tavern, becoming irritated when I tried to talk to him. The greatest betrayal came one evening when he lay in a drunken stupor in the parlor while one of his friends took me on his lap and put his hands on me. That was when Zachariah, my second protector, first appeared. He is the spirit of a young schoolmaster, and he explained the fundamentals of geometry during my ordeal."

Mrs. Hunt had gone on to say she had experienced ten different spirits during her lifetime. She said, "I believe they are angels sent by God to protect me. They comforted me, spoke through me when I performed, and kept me sane. Without them, I would never have survived my life with Mr. Trainor. When I was on stage and these protectors came to me, that was the only time I felt completely safe."

Touched by angels, Annie had thought as a child when she saw Mrs. Hunt perform. *And Maybelle sleeps with the angels. Could there possibly be a connection?*

Mrs. Hunt then told Annie that she was convinced these spirit protectors had led her to the small Nebraska town where she had met Mr. Hunt. She said that after Mr. Hunt and his sister had nursed her back to health and helped her obtain a divorce from Mr. Trainor, she had ended her career as a trance medium.

"I didn't feel it was right to use my protectors for financial gain. I no longer needed them to give me courage to speak in public, and I have turned my energies to speak on behalf of other women caught in the snares of godless and abusive marriages. These spirits visit me infrequently now, some I haven't heard from in years."

At this point, Mrs. Hunt had again smiled at her husband and said, "Today I have my own human protector, but I know that if I need them, they are with me always, sent by God."

When Annie had described the work Evie May did for the Framptons, Mrs. Hunt asserted that Maybelle, Eddie, Miss Evelyn, and even the young man Edmund, who Kathleen had met, were probably Evie May's own protective spirits.

She had said, "Mrs. Fuller, I don't believe it is an accident that Maybelle and Eddie showed themselves to you. They knew that you would work to save Evie May from the life of degradation that faces her if she stays with Simon Frampton."

Yesterday, Annie had demurred when Mrs. Hunt said this, but now she remembered how Maybelle clung to her, and she wondered if what Mrs. Hunt said was true. She had, in any event, promised to try and arrange a meeting between Mrs. Hunt and Mrs. Nickerson and Evie May.

As if he could read her thoughts, Nate broke the silence in the cab, saying, "Annie, you never finished telling me about your visit to Mrs. Hunt. Did you find her helpful?"

"Yes, she not only gave me some useful suggestions about what to look for when we search the séance room, but she also will make inquiries among her Spiritualist friends to see if anyone knows something about the Framptons that could be of help."

Annie paused. She hadn't yet mentioned what Flora Hunt had told her about her past, her spirit protectors, or her ideas about Evie May, and she didn't feel this was the time or place to bring up this subject. Instead, she said, "What might be most helpful is Mrs. Hunt's willingness to meet with Sukie Vetch, because I got nowhere with Miss Pinehurst's sister when I saw her this afternoon. Miss Pinehurst had arranged to meet me at the Vetchs' around three, and Sukie's husband agreed. However, when the maid showed me into the parlor, Sukie and Miss Pinehurst were in the midst of a heated battle."

Annie had never met Mrs. Vetch before, and she doubted she would have guessed that this was Lucy Pinehurst's little sister. Unlike the tall, slim, dark-haired, plain-faced Miss Pinehurst, Sukie Vetch was short and blond with a full figure, a pertly turned-up nose, and a rosebud mouth, which was screwed up at that time into a definite pout. The only things the two sisters had in common were their dark-brown eyes, which were flashing in an identical fashion.

Annie continued, "Unfortunately, Miss Pinehurst hadn't been able to refrain from telling Sukie about how Evie May pretended to be the spirit of my son Johnny, a child who never existed, and how this proved that the Framptons were frauds. As I entered the room, Sukie was shouting that Miss Pinehurst was just a jealous, dried-up spinster who couldn't stand that, even in death, Charlie preferred his mother to his aunt."

Kathleen, who had been listening closely to Annie and Nate's conversation, said, "Oh, ma'am. What a wicked thing to say to Miss Lucy. Sukie Vetch sounds like a spoiled brat."

Annie smiled at Kathleen's outburst and said, "Miss Pinehurst had intimated that since childhood Sukie tended to throw a tantrum when she didn't get her way. Yet, when I walked up to Sukie and saw what a sad state she was in, I confess I felt real pity for her. Her eyes were red-rimmed, as if she hadn't slept in a month. Her skin was dry and splotchy and pulled too tightly over her cheekbones, and her hair looked unwashed. And her hands, which she had clasped over her stomach, as if she was protecting her unborn child, visibly trembled. No wonder Miss Pinehurst is so worried about her health."

Nate spoke up. "Did you get to talk to her at all?"

"No," Annie said. "As soon as she noticed I had entered the room, she stalked out without speaking to me. Her husband did stay, and he said that he had decided to meet with the spirit of Charlie. This, of course, means he would meet with Evie May but only with Sukie present. He reasoned that since Sukie called him a liar when he told her about Simon putting pressure on him, if Evie May does ask him questions about Mr. Ruckner or the bank, this might open up Sukie's eyes. If that didn't work, he was seriously considering having Sukie committed to a health sanitarium, for her own and her baby's well being. Then the poor man began to cry."

Nate uttered an oath and then said, "You did tell me Mrs. Hunt offered to speak to Mrs. Vetch. What good do you think that will do?"

"Mrs. Hunt thought that Mrs. Vetch might be willing to listen to someone who was a true Spiritualist, who wouldn't try to persuade her that contact with her dead son was impossible. She put it this way, 'Her family is asking her to give up this one connection with her son, without giving her any hope of another way of keeping him part of her life. I can give her that hope.' It is worth a try. I gave Mr. Vetch her address and told him to contact her."

"Ma'am, sir. We are here," said Kathleen as the cab came to a halt next to the alley behind Harrison Street.

Nate tapped the hatch on the roof. When it opened, he reached up and said, "Here's your fare, and I will double it if you promise to return within the hour and wait for us here."

Annie heard the cab driver reply, "Yes, sir. Be glad to." Then Nate opened the doors at the front of the carriage and stepped down to the road. He turned and helped Annie, then Kathleen, alight.

Kathleen lifted the lantern they had brought with them, having lit the candle within, and began to lead the way down the dark alley. The first block wasn't too bad, since the houses were all occupied and the alley had been kept clear of debris. However, when they crossed Fifth and entered the alley behind the Framptons' house, the general neglect of this block became evident. They had to pick their way past leaning fences, half-dried patches of mud, and piles of odiferous refuse. Annie silently thanked Kathleen for the foresight in bringing the lantern.

"This is the entrance to the back yard," Kathleen whispered, swinging the lantern around.

Annie stopped and saw that she was pointing to an overgrown path that led from the alley toward the house, silhouetted against the night sky. A three-quarter moon had started its climb upwards, not yet erased by the nightly creep of fog from the west. Looking up, Annie didn't see any lights in the upstairs, and she was transported to a night this past summer when she looked up at the darkened windows of a house full of danger and death. A wave of fear raised the hairs on the back of her neck. Nate came up behind her, putting his warm hand on her shoulder, and the spell was broken.

Chapter Thirty
Sunday evening, October 26, 1879

"Mrs. C. H. Sawyer will hold Materializing Séances in the light, without a cabinet, every evening except Saturday. Honest investigators can call and see for themselves."
—*San Francisco Chronicle*, 1879

"I am so glad you made it," Biddy said. "Everyone's gone, and Mrs. Nickerson asked me this afternoon if I would mind staying past ten since she and Evie May are attending a party. They are the ones most likely to return early, so this should give you at least until nine. Kathleen will stay here in the kitchen, and, if Albert or anyone else should come in the back way, she can just say I asked her to come visit. What can they do to me, 'cept fire me, and I plan on giving my notice the end of next week, anyway. Larkson's Woolen Mills are hiring, and I've already been promised a job." Biddy positively beamed.

Annie stood blinking in the blaze of lights from multiple lamps placed around the kitchen, a large but comfortable room that smelled strongly of cinnamon. She was rather overwhelmed by Biddy's enthusiasm.

Biddy continued, "Mr. Dawson, Mrs. Fuller, please let me take your coats and hat. And take these candles, if'n you please. Not as heavy as an oil lamp and easier to snuff out quick if someone comes." She pointed to three candlestick holders with lighted candles that sat on the kitchen table, taking up one herself. "I figured you would want to start with the séance rooms. Such luck, Albert was in a hurry this afternoon and let me into the back room to take care of the fireplace. I was able to put a bit of sticking plaster over the lock on the back parlor door as I left, so you shouldn't have any trouble getting in."

Annie, content to let the young servant girl lead the way, smiled over at Nate and picked up a candle. As they left the kitchen, Biddy pointed to the door on the left and said, "That's the door down to the cellars, but I am afraid it's locked. I did bring a crowbar from home today and stashed it in the woodpile. So if you have time, you might try and break the lock on the trap door on the side of the house."

Annie muttered to Nate, who had come up beside her, "Biddy's thought of everything. You don't think she is really a housebreaker in her spare time, do you?"

Biddy held the door to the front hallway open for them, and they could see a lamp burning on the hallstand near the front door. She handed her candle to Annie, turned towards the door to the smaller back parlor where Evie May's cabinet sat, jiggled the doorknob a little, and then slowly pushed the door open.

"See, the plaster worked just as I hoped. It kept the little tongue from sticking in all the way when Albert turned the key in the lock. He was in such a rush, he didn't notice. Evie May had been in the room all afternoon with those 'private sittings,' poor girl, and I needed to clean out the fireplace and lay the logs for a new fire, as well as dust. He never lets me in those rooms by myself, and I could tell he was anxious for me to finish up so he could go up and get dressed for his night on the town. Sunday nights he replaces his butler togs with a flashy get-up. Shows his real colors, you might say." Biddy giggled and moved aside to let Annie and Nate into the room.

She darted to the windows and made sure the curtains were pulled completely tight; then she opened the doors to the bigger front parlor and checked the curtains there. Going over to an oil lamp that sat on the mantel, she lighted it, turning the flame to a medium height. Since the lamp was up against a mirror, the reflection increased the visibility in the room enough so that Annie and Nate could move around freely.

"Ma'am, I will just go out to the front hall now. I'll shout out if I see anyone coming up the walk, but I think you should have at least an hour before anyone could possibly return. If you want, when you are done with these rooms, I will take you for a quick tour upstairs." With this statement,

Biddy sketched a curtsy and left the parlor.

Annie sprang into action. Crossing to the side of the table where Arabella always sat, she pulled up her skirts and knelt down onto the carpet, saying, "Nate, please come over here and try to lift this end of the table." Placing her candleholder on the floor, she ran her hand down the table leg under the velvet tablecloth that draped almost to the floor, and Nate came to stand near her and began to lift the edge of the table.

"Damn, I thought these tables were supposed to be light as a feather, easy for the medium to levitate upwards," said Nate. "Annie, what are you doing?"

As she slipped her hand under the leg of the table, Annie replied, "Don't let go, or you will smash my hand. There is some sort of metal rod that comes out of the bottom and goes down through a hole in the carpet. I think it goes all the way through the floor. Here, let's trade places. You take a look."

Annie sat back, showing him her hands were now safe, and Nate put the table down and leaned over and helped her up. Annie straightened her skirts and petticoats, which had gotten hung up nearly to her knees, showing an immodest amount of silk encased calves and ankles. She hoped Nate hadn't noticed, congratulating herself for choosing one of her older outfits with the unfashionable but wider skirts. At least she had been able to get down and up without falling over.

Noticing that Nate was now bending down to look under the table, she said, "You know, it might not be that the table is that heavy but that the rod has added weight to it. How difficult would it be to make the table shake and rock if someone down below was pushing upward on one of the rods?" Straining to lift up the table edge, Annie said, "Do you see what I mean?"

Nate knelt down and pulled his candle back so that its light reached where the table leg met the floor. Then he lifted up the tablecloth and put his head all the way down on the floor where he could see the small space Annie had created. He said, "Well, what do you know. There is a rod." He scrambled up and went to one of the other table legs, kneeling down and pulling the leg up enough to feel under it. "There's one here too. What do you bet that Albert is the one who goes down during the séances and works whatever mechanism these rods are attached to? Guess we might want to take a look at those cellars after all."

Meanwhile, Annie had knelt down to run her fingers over the carpet where Arabella's feet would be during a séance. She sat back on her heels for a moment, not finding what she had been looking for. "Mrs. Hunt said we should find some sort of lever or button here, but I can't feel anything. Wait, what if it is Simon who does the signaling?"

Annie scrambled up and went to the opposite end of the table and, kneeling down, exclaimed, "Nate, it's just as Mrs. Hunt said it would be. There is some sort of metal lever, almost flush with the carpet. If it is connected by wire, either to the cellars or the room upstairs, it could be a way for Simon to signal, for example, when it's time to start the music or rock the table. In fact, it might be his way of letting Arabella know what he thinks should happen next. He signals for piano music, and she shifts out of one spirit and into another."

Annie pulled herself up, using the chair and table, and then snatched up her candle and went to the fireplace where the servant's bell pull was located. She bent down to look at the wood that edged the fireplace and pointed out a wire to Nate who had come up beside her. "Look, this comes up from the floor, right along the edge of the wood and the wall paneling. The wire parallels the bell pull but goes right up to the ceiling."

Nate looked to where she was pointing and said, "I think it would be useful to see what that wire connects to in the room above. You mentioned that there must be holes in the ceiling to help direct the light and sounds downward. If we can get into the rooms upstairs, we might have a better idea how that would work. The ceiling is too high in this room to see from here."

Turning off the lamp on the mantel and then going back into the hallway, they found Biddy standing on a chair, looking out the fanlight over the door. She hopped down and relit her candle, taking them up the stairs to the second floor while they told her what they were looking for.

"I don't know that we will be able to get into those rooms," said Biddy. "Albert's wife takes care of the Framptons' rooms; the only places I am allowed to clean upstairs are the hallway, Mrs. Nickerson and Evie May's room, and the bathroom."

Going over and trying the doors to the Framptons' two rooms above the séance parlors and then Albert and his wife's room, Biddy found all of them locked. Shrugging, she said, "Do you want to see the Nickersons' room? It isn't usually locked," showing them a door at the end of the hallway.

Annie, squashing her disappointment, replied, "I guess so. I wanted to check out Evie May's room anyway, to see how she was able to get out of the house on Friday. Did Kathleen have a chance to tell you about all the excitement when she went missing and Kathleen running into her dressed like a young man?"

"Yes, ma'am," said Biddy. "Kathleen came to St. Boniface this morning for mass. She wanted to check to see if everything was still on for tonight. She told me then. I must say that girl is a strange one. Here's the room she shares with her mother. That would be the window she got in by."

Evie May's bed was up under the window while her mother's was across the room. By candlelight, Annie couldn't make out much beyond how crowded the room was. It contained two beds, two large wardrobes, and a dressing table cluttered with small bottles, powder puffs, tangled jewelry, scarves, combs and brushes. She went over to Evie May's bed and looked closely at the windowsill.

"Nate, I can see where something has scored the wood on the sill." She felt down between the mattress and the wall. "Oh, my, look what is stuffed under the mattress." Annie pulled out a long sturdy hemp rope. "I wonder what she attaches it too. Would the bed be heavy enough?"

Nate, who had gone over to a door that was in the back wall, said, "Miss Bridget, where does this door lead to? It seems locked."

Biddy said, "That opens on a set of stairs that go up to that square tower on the roof. I don't know why it's locked. Evie May often plays up there. Just some old furniture and trunks. Here, I remember seeing a key on her mother's dresser."

Biddy moved several strands of glass beads, revealed a small china saucer, and triumphantly brandished an old-fashioned iron key on a long cord. Before she could hand the key to Nate, Annie slipped off the bed and took it from her, saying, "Let me look at it. I just had a thought. The same key opened all the interior doors in Aunt Agatha's house when I first inherited it. I had to pay to have new locks installed in all the rooms when I turned it into a boarding house. Maybe this key opens up one of the Framptons' rooms."

"Let's go see," Nate said. "It's more important for us to get into those rooms than check out an attic playroom, and we don't have that much time left."

Annie found her heart beating rapidly as she stuck the key into the lock of the room that was directly over the front parlor. Nate and Biddy pressed in close behind her. The key went in easily, but it wouldn't turn at first. She jiggled it a little and tried again. Suddenly it turned; she heard an audible click, and the doorknob began to turn.

"We're in!" Biddy cried.

Annie stopped with the door partially opened. Handing the key back to Biddy, she said, "Bridget, I am starting to get nervous about the time that has passed. If you stand in the window at the end of the hallway, you should be able to see to the street. Let us know if anyone comes down the street or pulls up in a carriage. But blow out your candle. Mr. Dawson and I will search the room."

Annie and Nate then went into the room, which appeared to be a sitting room. Before looking around, Annie checked to make sure that the curtains were closed. "I think we better risk lighting one of these," she said, moving over to a lamp on a nearby table. She pulled up the glass chimney so she could touch the wick with her candle flame as she turned the crank. She then blew out her candle to conserve it.

Nate exclaimed, "This is where the mischief is done, that's for sure. No wonder they never let Biddy into this room."

In addition to the usual chairs and tables found in any woman's sitting room, there was an old upright piano. On a shelf next to it sat a tambourine, a set of small drums, and a mandolin. Annie walked over and picked up a brightly painted gourd that gave off a shushing sound.

"I wondered what made that sound," said Annie. "Listen to this! Just imagine hearing it while you sat in the dark." Annie had picked up a thin piece of metal that made an eerie, warbling sound when she shook it up and down.

Nate lifted a long, twisted, funnel-shaped metal object off the shelf. "Annie, what do you think this is?" He put the narrow end to his mouth and blew into it, but it didn't make any distinctive noise.

Annie laughed, took it from him, and carefully placed the narrow end over his ear as she talked into the wide end of the funnel.

Nate jumped back, startled, and then he said, "Oh, I understand now. It's an ear trumpet for someone hard of hearing. If it was placed in a hole in the floor while the musical instruments were being played, it would amplify the sound."

Annie looked down at the floor, noticing for the first time that there was a rug in the middle of the floor that was too small for the size of the room. When she bent and flipped it over, she saw several holes drilled into the wood floor. The small end of the speaking trumpet fit perfectly into the holes.

Nate stood looking down at the holes very thoughtfully, and then he took the device from Annie and flipped it over, putting the wider end over the hole and said, "You know, if you used it the other way around, it would make it easier to hear what was going on down below."

"Albert's wife must be a very talented lady, a virtual one-man-band, to play all these instruments," Annie said. "Albert probably comes up to help her when he isn't running down to the cellars to shake the table. Now that I think about it, on Friday the table didn't shake but once or twice, and the musical interludes were pretty tepid. He must have been busy looking for Evie May throughout most of the séance."

As she had been speaking, Annie had gone over to the wall that held the room's fireplace. "Nate, there is a wire coming up from the floor, just like we thought we would find. If you look behind this table, you can see it is attached to a little bell, like you find in kitchens. Simon would just have to step on the lever at his feet and this bell would chime. They might even have a code of sorts, probably worked out in their earlier magic and mesmerism acts. What are you doing?"

Annie had noticed that Nate had picked up the oil lamp and was setting it down on the floor, near one of the holes.

"I just wondered what would happen if you shone a light over these holes," Nate replied. "Would you have noticed?"

"I think so. It would have looked like a spot of light on the table, you know, the way moonlight will come in if there is a hole in the shade. They must keep the lights turned down very low during the séances. There were shafts of light, however, in the next room, the one with the cabinet. And sitting at the table you wouldn't be able to see the ceiling; the door frame would be in the way. Let's see what is next door."

Nate walked over, opened the door that connected the sitting room to Simon and Arabella's bedroom, and walked in. Since he took both his candle and the oil lamp with him, Annie found herself plunged into darkness. While her eyes adjusted to the dim glow coming from the next room, she couldn't help but think about how frightening all this would have been if she had been exploring the house without Nate. Even know-ing that Kathleen was downstairs and Biddy was outside in the hallway didn't bring her the comfort of having Nate close at hand.

Once she could see clearly enough to maneuver, she located her candle and followed Nate into the bedroom. He stood in the center of the floor, the oil lamp held high, giving her a good look at the whole room. At first glance, it appeared pretty innocuous. There was a substantial double bed, a wardrobe, and a dressing table that, while neater than Mrs. Nicker-son's, held even more objects designed to maintain a woman's beauty. Then Annie noticed that the bed was oddly placed, crammed up along the outside wall, its end at right angles to the room's fireplace.

A bed simply wasn't put up against an outside wall and under a window unless there wasn't an alternative. She had unconsciously thought how selfish Mrs. Nickerson had been to take the inside wall of their bedroom, leaving Evie May to sleep on the colder end of the room. But there wasn't any reason for Simon and Arabella's bed to be where it was, subjecting their bodies to the cold drafts from the window and their feet to the scorching heat from the fireplace. There wasn't any reason, unless they wanted to leave the floor in the center of the room clear of furniture.

Nate must have come to the same conclusion because he had put the lamp down on the dresser and was now rolling the rug back. Annie walked over and saw there were three metal plates set into the floor, two set about four feet apart about a third of the way in the room, the third set about two feet further in the room, equidistant between the other two. If the plates were connected, they would form a triangle.

"What in heaven's name are those for?" she asked Nate, who had knelt down and was doing something with the plate farthest away from her.

"Why those clever bastards. Annie, pardon me. But come look what they have done." As Annie came closer, Nate pulled at a small ring that she now saw was bolted to the plate. As he did so, the plate and a chunk of flooring that was attached to it pulled free, exposing a opening about four inches square that looked right down into the room with the cabinet. As she leaned forward, he touched his candle flame to her wick. With both candles producing light, they could look down and actually see the pattern of the carpet on the floor below.

Annie pointed. "See, there is the edge of the top of the cabinet. This is why it was so easy to see Evie May when she stands in front of the cabinet, which she usually does at the beginning of a session." She took the plate and chunk of wood Nate had removed and turned it over. "The wood is the same as the paneled wood of the room's ceiling. I bet if you glanced up, given all the carving, you wouldn't even see the slight line where the block and the ceiling joined. Where do you suppose the light I saw shining through the back of the cabinet came from?"

Annie put the chunk of wood down and walked over to the side of the bed, noticing that there was another small rug over the floor here. When she kicked it back, she wasn't in the least surprised to see another plate. She said, "This one must be open throughout most of the séance since there was always a glow emanating from the back of the room. When they want to feature Evie May or cast more light into the front room, they just have to open up more of the plates." Annie saw that Nate was looking in the drawer of the table that was placed next to the head of the bed, and she asked him what he was looking for.

"I wondered about the odd shape of this table, with this narrow drawer. Didn't seem right for a bedside table. And what do you know, I found these." Nate held up what appeared to Annie to be several pieces of stiff colored paper. When he brought them closer, she saw they were actually several pieces of thick glass, each of a different color. He bent down and put one over the hole they had opened in the floor.

"How clever, Nate. No wonder I thought the lights felt 'otherworldly.' I can't wait to see what it looks like from below." Annie went to the door to the hallway and opened it, calling for Biddy to come.

When Biddy entered the room, Annie told her to watch her step and pointed out the plates and the open hole with the pane of glass over it.

"Sakes alive. What's that? Oooh. You can see right down to the room below, like a nasty spy hole. Do you think they have these all over the house? It makes me feel so odd, just to think of that Albert's eyes on me while I do my work. I will be glad to be shut of this place."

"Yes, Bridget, I think it's an excellent idea for you to move on. But what I would like is for you to take the lamp and shine it over this hole. Mr. Dawson and I will go downstairs and see what it looks like from below. We will be just a moment. Then when we give a shout, I think you had better put everything back as we found it and come downstairs. This glass plate goes into that drawer there with the others, and the metal plate and chunk of wood fit back into the hole. Then you can smooth down the rugs and take the lamp back to the sitting room. The rug in that room also needs to be put right. When all this is done, lock the doors to both of these rooms as you leave. Can you do that for us, please?"

Biddy assured them she would do all that was asked, looking excited to have a little time to explore a room that had been forbidden to her. Annie and Nate took up their candles and made their way carefully downstairs. Annie whispered to Nate as they descended, "Can you tell what time it is? I worry that Kathleen is going to get impatient and come searching for us. Do I have time to go and assure her everything is all right?"

Nate took out his pocket watch, opened it up, and held it up to the candle. "Good Lord, it's already eight-thirty. We need to finish up. Better that we look at the lights and then be on our way. I don't think we will have time to go down to the cellars, but I think we have discovered enough of their tricks."

Annie led the way into the back room with the cabinet. As soon as she walked in, she noticed a difference. She blew out her candle and asked Nate to do so as well. Then she closed the hallway door to block out the light, taking off the sticky plaster so she wouldn't forget when it was time to leave.

"Nate, see how eerie the glow is with that red glass over the hole. I have this image of Albert and his wife scurrying back and forth, playing instruments, opening up the holes and then closing them, putting different colored glass in at different times. It must be exhausting."

"Yes, but if they are theater folks, this all must be just like any nightly performance. Since the séances don't last but an hour, it's not a particularly difficult performance at that. Probably pays a lot better," Nate replied. As he talked, he opened up the curtain to the cabinet and stepped in and sat down. "Annie, this is really quite substantial. And I see what you mean about the back being made of burlap. This certainly would let in a lot of light if the hole were open."

Without warning, Nate grabbed Annie and pulled her into the cabinet with him. Putting his hand over her mouth, he whispered in her ear to please be quiet. When she stilled, she heard the voice of Arabella Frampton raised in anger. Simultaneously, the reddish light in the room disappeared, plunging them into complete darkness.

Chapter Thirty-one
Sunday evening, October 26, 1879

"The Rev. Dr. Graves lectured to a fair audience…on the "Mental and Physical Phenomenon of Modern Spiritualism," beginning by saying that he should not notice the cabinet séance and other legerdemain tricks which had so often imposed upon the credulity of the people."—*San Francisco Chronicle*, 1879

Nate was acutely aware that Annie sat snugly on his lap, a distraction he couldn't afford and, as a gentleman, shouldn't permit. Reassured by Annie's silence, he again put his mouth up to her ear, trying to ignore her intoxicating fragrance, and whispered, "I'm going to shift you. Can you lean forward as I do so and close the curtain?" He felt her nod. As she reached out to pull the curtain, he put his hands at her waist and lifted her, twisting to place her on the bench beside him. He then heard her put something down on the floor. *Ah, her candle. Where the devil is mine?* Nate wondered, until he remembered placing it on the bench next to him before grabbing Annie.

As Annie straightened, Nate slid his left arm tightly around her, noticing her stiff stays and the quick rise and fall of her breath. Anchored by her warm body, he began to try and distinguish who was speaking out in the hallway. Shockingly, the voices became much louder, and Nate concluded they must have entered the larger parlor.

" . . . saw a light, I swear to you. From this room," said a female.

"Look, Arabella, there is no one here and the door was locked. Who do you think it was, one of your spirits?" The man, clearly Simon Frampton, laughed softly.

A thin bar of light appeared at the bottom of the curtain. Either Simon or Arabella must have turned on one of the lamps in the next room. Nate wondered if this light was enough to expose their own presence in the cabinet.

"What I *thought*," said Arabella, "is that Evie May was in here play-ing one of her stupid tricks. She is going to be the ruin of us, slipping off as she does when she is needed and messing up her lines when she is working. I tell you, clients like Judge Babcock aren't going to put up with it, not at the rate they've been paying."

"Old Judge Babcock would continue to contribute to our coffers if we put a wooden doll on his lap and told him it was his darling daughter, my love," Simon replied with a nasty laugh.

Nate had a strong desire to wipe what he was sure was a sneer off Frampton's lips. It made him sick to think that the former Pennsylvania Supreme Court justice his uncle had so admired was the object of ridicule by a confidence man like Simon Frampton.

Arabella responded, "Don't be so sure. He was pretty upset when she didn't show Friday at the séance, and you said it took you forever to get her into the trance state so she could give him his private sitting."

"You let me worry about Evie May, Arabella. Just stay away from her. Don't think I don't know it was you who got her all upset Friday afternoon. She told me what you said. No wonder she slipped away."

"What I said! The little bitch. She'd snuck into my room while Delia was cleaning the sitting room, and she'd put on my new blue silk wrapper and played around with my cosmetics. When I told her to take it all off and never put her filthy paws on my stuff again, she told me the blue made me look old. So I told her it made her look like a tart."

Arabella sounded to Nate as if she found the memory satisfying.

"Don't be so petty, Arabella. The girl was just playing dress-up. Perfectly natural, she is, after all, only thirteen."

"So her mother says and you want to believe. But then, that is just about the age I was when you first saw me, wasn't it, Simon, dear?"

Arabella's question sent a chill down Nate's back. Pierce had said that Simon had met Arabella when she was in her early teens and married her at sixteen. From Annie's description, the girl, Evie May, could act a lot older than her years and did so routinely when she sat in the cabinet.

Perhaps Arabella had a reason to be jealous.

It's beyond me why any man would look at a skinny girl when he is married to a gorgeous woman like Arabella, he thought, *but there is no accounting for taste.* Nate felt Annie draw in her breath and realized he had unconsciously tightened his arm, pressing her even more closely to his side. He relaxed his grip, but he was gratified when she moved closer of her own volition. He then felt the weight of her hand on his leg. For a moment, Arabella and Simon's voices faded away, and all he could hear was the thrumming of his blood in his ears.

Arabella's voice rose to a higher pitch, bringing Nate back to his senses.

"We have had a good thing going here in San Francisco if you don't ruin it. You heard him. If we don't start to be more careful, he might not be able to keep helping us, and the information he's given us so far is worth it's weight in gold."

Simon replied, "He worries too much. So what if the man who came to escort Mrs. Fuller home on Monday happens to be a lawyer. I expect that half of our clients know lawyers; that doesn't mean that they are all out to expose us."

Annie turned her head towards his, and Nate swiftly touched his finger to her lips to ensure her continued silence.

Arabella spoke next, sounding exasperated. "Don't pretend to be stupid. The problem is you should never have accepted her into the circle without checking with him first. Then, when he told you of her connection with the fortuneteller, you should have come up with an excuse to keep her from returning. He told you explicitly to get rid of her, and you didn't.

"Even if all she is doing is trying to gather information for the competition, she is a threat. I really wonder if that is all that is going on. I left her a few little presents this week, and, by rights, she should have decided that our séances aren't for her. I think there is a lot more to this poor little widow woman than meets the eye. But then you never could see past a pretty face. No wonder he was so angry tonight. If you don't take care of her, I promise you, I will."

"You leave Mrs. Fuller to me. He was angry because your last séance didn't produce the effect he wanted, despite your special coaching session on Wednesday. That's why he now wants us to use Evie May for this job."

"Evie May, she's always the solution for you. I have half a mind to leave you to her and that harridan of a mother. What a sweet little family you would be."

Arabella's voice then became so soft that Nate couldn't hear her words, but Simon's voice rose, and he said, "Arabella, don't be a little fool." Nate heard a sharp intake of breath, and then all was silent, except the rustle of a woman's skirts.

He'd begun to wonder what was happening when Simon spoke again and said, "Let's go upstairs; Delia should be done. You go on ahead. I need a last word with Albert about our schedule tomorrow."

There was a soft murmur from Arabella, and Simon replied, "No, the girl said she would wait up for Mrs. Nickerson and Evie May. I'll lock up here, be up in a moment."

The bar of light under the curtain disappeared, and Nate thought he heard a door close. A second later, he heard the door to the room they were in rattle. Then silence.

Annie whispered, "Nate, what are we going to do?"

"Let's sit tight. Biddy should have made it down to the kitchen by now. You heard Simon. They expect her to wait for Mrs. Nickerson. She'll come and get us when the coast is clear. But we should keep quiet, in case Albert or his wife should pass by."

Nate felt rather than saw Annie nod in agreement, because they were again sitting in complete darkness. He closed his eyes against the blackness and concentrated on his other senses. Their mingled sounds of breathing filled his ears. He inhaled deeply, registering Annie's scent: a combination of sunshine, roses, and the faint whiff of cedar. She wasn't wearing a hat, thank goodness, so he could feel the tickle of her fine hair when she turned her head. The material of her dress was soft and silky, sliding under the arm he had clasped around her waist each time she took a breath. With his free hand, he reached out to her face, finding first her left ear, the shape of a small, delicate seashell. Then he slowly ran his hand along her jaw, drew his thumb along the small dimple in her chin, and touched the edge of her lips.

Annie pulled away, and Nate froze, fearing he had gone too far. With a rush, she slipped her right arm around his waist and with her left hand began to trace a similar path on his face. First, he felt her fingers run along the hair at the nape of his neck, then up to his ear. Next, she ran her thumb along the upper curve of his ear, then down along his jaw, rubbing back and forth along the beginning of stubble that was always there by this time of night. Finally, she cupped the side of his face and drew it to hers.

They had kissed before, but never like this.

"Mrs. Babbit, Medium. 104 Powell. Circles Sun. Wed evenings, Thursday night."

— *San Francisco Chronicle*, 1879

A soft knock on the door woke Annie. As she pulled herself upright in the old mahogany bed and rubbed her eyes, she saw Kathleen enter the room. After placing a pitcher of hot water under the washstand, the young maid lit the oil lamp sitting on the round table by the window since, at half past five, sunrise was at least an hour away.

As quickly and silently as she had come, Kathleen left, and Annie knew she had gone to get the breakfast tray. This left her a few minutes of solitude to remember last evening, and her mind went immediately to the time she and Nate had spent in the cabinet, waiting to be rescued by Biddy. The complete absence of light in the cabinet had created a feeling of such intimacy that Annie had felt all rules of proper conduct just slip away. As she had turned into Nate's arms, their bodies had become so entwined she hadn't been able to distinguish between the beat of his heart and her own. The kiss that had started out so softly, so sweetly, became so intense it awakened a hunger she had never experienced before, not even in the brief few weeks of her marriage when she had thought she had loved John.

The door to her room opened again, and she wrenched her thoughts away from this disconcerting memory. Kathleen entered the room, saying cheerfully, "Did you sleep well, ma'am?" Then she began to remove from the tray the tea pot, cup and saucer, and a covered dish, which would hold scrambled eggs, a freshly baked biscuit, and a sliced orange.

Annie had tasted her first orange on the Los Angeles ranch where she had spent her childhood. To her mind, the accessibility of fresh, inexpensive oranges was one of the many advantages of returning to live in

California. She took the robe draped over the end of her bed and put it on, tying the belt tightly while her feet sought out her slippers. "Yes, thank you. I am surprised after all our excitement last night that I slept a wink. But I don't remember a thing after my head hit the pillow. And you?"

Kathleen, who was moving swiftly through the room and pulling out the clothes Annie would wear as Madam Sibyl, said, "Me too! Mrs. O'Rourke said she could hear me snoring before she went upstairs to bed. Ma'am, she's joshing, isn't she? I don't snore!"

Annie laughed. "I'm quite sure you don't. But I am glad you got some sleep. I know how long and hard wash day can be."

"Oh, Mrs. Fuller, with Mrs. Kantor doing most of the heavy white wash and you hiring Biddy's cousin, Tilly, to help out with the noon and evening meals, my day's going to be a breeze!"

Annie knew from personal experience that, even with a laundress and a second maid, Kathleen's day was going to be one of unremitting, hard physical labor. However, if the recent additions Annie had made to the boarding house staff had relieved Kathleen of some of her burdens, she was glad.

As Kathleen left to bring water and wake-up calls to several of the other early risers in the house, Annie's thoughts returned to the night before. As she sat down at the table and began to pour out her tea, she imagined a future morning, just like this one, with Nate across the table from her discussing his plans for the day or the news in the *Morning Call*. With his income from the law firm combined with the continued income from the boarding house, they might even be able to afford to hire some-one like Tilly full time to help Beatrice and Kathleen. Maybe Annie could cut back on the number of clients she saw as Madam Sibyl so that, when Nate came home in the evening, they could have dinner together, right at this table.

I might even be able to risk dropping the fiction of Madam Sibyl altogether and try to build a business as Annie Fuller, financial and domestic advisor, she thought, smiling happily as she slathered butter and jam on her biscuit. *No, I'd be Mrs. Nate Dawson,* came the unexpected realization.

Annie had never played the game, familiar to most girls, of thinking about what her new name would be when she married. Yet, when she had married John, a prince charming who had rapidly turned into an evil prince, she had begun to associate her new name, Mrs. John Fuller, with the complete loss of her own identity. On their honeymoon, a two-month trip to Italy they took with her new in-laws, John had begun the irritating habit of calling her "the wife" in public, and in private she had rapidly gone from "darling" to just "you." She remembered bursting into tears the day they finally arrived back in the States, and her father met them at the boat and called her Annie. She had felt he had given her a piece of herself back.

Annie wondered how Nate would react if she used her maiden name, Annie Edwards, just for business purposes. Would he see it as an insult, or would he be relieved not to have his name associated with a woman working in such an unusual occupation?

Sitting for a moment, thinking about past arguments with Nate, Annie suddenly chuckled to herself. It would be a lively discussion, no doubt about that! She then chided herself for letting her past mar her present. *Which isn't fair to Nate or myself. Besides, why do I assume he even wants to marry me?*

She resolutely shelved both the speculation about her future and her anger at her past and thought about what she should do with the information she and Nate had gained from their search of the Framptons' house. Their romantic interlude last night had been rudely interrupted when Biddy scratched on the door to the small parlor and called their names. When they opened the door and met her in the hallway, she put her finger to her lips and pulled them rapidly through the empty kitchen to the back door, whispering that Kathleen was out in the alley waiting for them.

They handed over their candles, picked up their coats, and slipped out to the alley. Kathleen later told them Biddy had been able to do everything they had asked her to do. She had wiped away any sign of intrusion and nipped down the back stairs to the kitchen just before Albert and Delia had come in the back door. Kathleen, having heard voices, had the presence of mind to gather up their coats and Nate's top hat and hide in the pantry until Albert and his wife had gone upstairs. Then she had scared Biddy half to death when she re-emerged in the kitchen.

Once Annie and Nate had reunited with Kathleen, they went down the alley, glad there was enough moonlight to make their way. The cabbie was waiting, as promised, but this also meant they really didn't have time to talk about the night's events before the ride home. When they got to the boarding house, Annie had insisted that Nate have the cab drive him on home. She told Beatrice and Esther, who were in the kitchen anxiously waiting for their return, that she would give them a full accounting the next day and sent Kathleen off to bed.

But now, before she had to get dressed and prepare for Madam Sibyl's morning clients, she wanted to think about what the conversation she had overheard between Arabella and Simon meant. For one thing, given how upset Arabella was with Simon's refusal to deny Annie access to the séances, she felt it was even more likely that Arabella had been the author of the two threatening notes, the so-called "little presents." She also wondered if there was any truth to Arabella's accusations about Simon's intentions with Evie May. The truth, or the ravings of a jealous wife, either way, Annie believed it was imperative to find a way to remove the young medium from the Framptons' pernicious influence.

She speculated on the identity of the man Simon and Arabella kept mentioning. The man who told them about the connection between her and Nate and that she lived at the same address as Madam Sibyl. He certainly sounded like someone who had been giving the Framptons information that helped them bilk their clients. Any of the men who had attended Monday's séance and seen Nate might have recognized him. She had trouble, however, seeing Judge Babcock or the banker, Mr. Ruckner, or even the hapless Mr. Hapgood, as masterminds behind the Framptons' success. They seemed so much like victims rather than conspirators.

But Mr. Sweeter, that was a very different matter. Simon had said something about a coaching session on Wednesday, which was when

Kathleen had seen Mr. Sweeter and Arabella together. Sweeter could have run some sort of confidence racket back in his hometown. Maybe, when he moved to San Francisco, he had joined in partnership with the Framptons, using his cousin's society connections to gather information and steer clients to the séances. Annie really needed to talk to Esther after dinner and find out if she had learned anything more about Sweeter and the Larksons from her daughter yesterday. If she skipped tonight's séance, she could also catch Hilda Hapgood alone at their store and try to find out if it was her who sent the police that anonymous letter accusing the Framptons of "driving her husband to drink."

If she didn't go to the séance, this would at least postpone the inevitable argument she was going to have with Nate. The minute she heard Arabella Frampton tell her husband about how he had better stop Annie from coming or she would, Annie knew what Nate was going to say. Sure enough, just as she was about to get out of the carriage last night, he'd detained her for a moment, saying, "Annie, you will not be attending any more séances or private sittings at the Framptons. It is clearly too dangerous."

She had smiled and nodded. But she hadn't agreed.

Chapter Thirty-three
Monday evening, October 27, 1879

"Robbed of $25 by Insidious Confidence men. Charles Hilton, the complainant, and a person evidently not at all familiar with the tricks of confidence swindlers, told his story on the stand with apparent great relish."

—*San Francisco Chronicle*, 1879

"My dear, I must say from your description of events that you and Mr. Dawson certainly had an exciting time of it last night," said Esther Stein tartly. "However, when Mrs. O'Rourke confided to me about your scheme, I was quite upset. The scandal if you had been discovered! The Framptons could have called in the police, charged you both with breaking and entering." Mrs. Stein put down her crocheting and waved a finger. "No, Annie, not a word until I've finished having my say."

Annie swallowed the defensive retort she had been about to make. She owed Esther Stein and her husband Herman so much that the least she could do was hear her out. Without the Steins, her Uncle Timothy and Aunt Agatha's oldest friends, Annie would probably still be living back east off the reluctant charity of her husband's relatives. Herman Stein, as the executor of her aunt's will, had tracked her down in Boston and sent her the money she needed to make her way to San Francisco by train. He had also authorized her use of the small amount of capital she had inherited to outfit the O'Farrell Street house as a boarding house. He had then moved, with his wife, into the second floor two-room suite, becoming Annie's best paying boarders.

Along the way, the Steins had become like parents to her, and she shouldn't have been surprised to discover that Mrs. Stein wasn't happy about the turn her investigation into the Framptons had taken. She knew something was up when Kathleen had given her the message this afternoon that Mrs. Stein would like Annie to come to her sitting room when she was done with her last client. Most evenings, when her husband Herman was away on business, Mrs. Stein joined Annie downstairs in the kitchen for the pleasant end-of-the-day conversations she had with Beatrice and Kathleen. Tonight, she had clearly wanted to spare Annie the embarrassment of being dressed down in front of the other two women.

Mrs. Stein continued. "I know that I tacitly gave my agreement to your plans on behalf of Miss Pinehurst when I said I would ask my daughter about Mrs. Larkson and her cousin, Mr. Sweeter. But that was when I thought your goal was to attend the séances, using your powers of observation to discover how they carried out their fraudulent practices and turn that information over to Miss Pinehurst. But I would never have condoned your decision to enter that house, at night, when the occupants were out. Let me tell you, Mrs. O'Rourke and I were worried sick waiting for your safe return."

Feeling guilty that she had caused her friend unnecessary worry, Annie said, "Dear Mrs. Stein, I am sorry. I had no idea you would be so upset. I had quite determined that if we were discovered, I would pretend that I had come to see the Framptons because I had had a communication with the spirit of my father and that Biddy had kindly let me in to wait for their arrival. Even if the Framptons didn't believe me, they wouldn't have dared to take the matter up with the police. The most that would have happened is that I would suffer a little embarrassment, and I might have lost any chance of returning to the séances for further observation."

Mrs. Stein shook her head sharply, her features rearranged in what Annie recognized as her "stern grandmother" expression. "A little embarrassment? Annie, just because your investigation this summer had a positive outcome, don't be so sure that meddling with someone like Simon Frampton and threatening his livelihood won't have very dangerous consequences."

She paused, continuing to frown. "I know that you think that the unfortunate circumstances of your past, and the necessity of maintaining the pretense of Madam Sibyl, have already put you beyond the confines of normal societal rules. But that isn't true. To the eyes of the world, you are a beautiful young widow who runs a respectable boarding house. Don't throw that reputation away lightly. And, my dear, if you aren't concerned about your own reputation, think of the damage to poor Mr. Dawson's future prospects if you had been caught and the Framptons had decided to make an issue of it. You know he would never have done such a foolish thing if he wasn't so besotted with you."

Annie opened her mouth, ready to explain that what Nate Dawson did was his own business, not hers, when she stopped, realizing that this wasn't completely true. All last night, she'd been thinking how comforting it had been to have him with her as she snooped around the Frampton house, how wonderful to have met a man who respected her enough to be her partner in what was, she had to admit, a risky enterprise. Then, this morning, she had even gone on to imagine how agreeable it would be to be married to such a man.

Yet she had stubbornly refused to consider how a relationship with someone who truly cared about her entailed responsibilities on her part in turn. She remembered the reporter, Pierce, had even warned Nate that the Framptons had influential friends and it might be dangerous if it came out that he was investigating them. Unbidden came an image of Judge Babcock using his legal connections to punish Nate for daring to threaten his contact with his daughter's spirit.

"Mrs. Stein, I hadn't realized . . ."

"That he is in love with you?"

"No, I didn't mean . . . of course I know he cares about me. But he hasn't said anything to me . . . about the future. I don't really know his intentions."

"Well, my dear, he is probably waiting until he feels he is financially secure enough to offer you a future. Or he is simply unsure about your feelings towards him."

It's hard to believe after last night that he has any doubts, Annie found herself thinking.

Mrs. Stein continued. "And are you unsure about your feelings for

Mr. Dawson?"

"No, I mean, yes. Oh, Esther, before I met Mr. Dawson this summer, I would have sworn to you that I would never remarry. I promised myself that I would never again become dependent on a man, who by law could do as he wished with my property or my person. But Nate is so different from John. I just don't know. Do I care about him? Absolutely, and you are quite right, I need to be more careful. But do I trust him enough to marry him? I don't know. I don't know if I will ever trust any man that much again."

"Annie, dear. Don't say that. To think that you would deny yourself a future as a wife, a mother."

Annie's heart constricted. She thought of the daughter who had been born too soon, a victim of her loveless marriage to a man who had betrayed her trust, over and over. Would she ever risk that kind of pain again? Yet when Evie May had wrapped her arms about her and Annie had believed, even for a short time, that Maybelle was that lost daughter, she had recognized she wasn't ready to give up the sweet promise of children forever. A tear, unexpectedly, slid down her cheek.

Mrs. Stein gave a little cry and leaned forward in her chair, taking Annie's hands in hers. "My darling girl. Please forgive me. I should never have said a thing. Now you know why my children get so furious with me and my meddling. But you are like a daughter to me, and I let my affection take me too far."

"Mrs. Stein, you have no need to apologize, and your daughters, who adore you, would be quite as sad as I would be if you stopped caring enough to meddle. Oh, I meant to say, stopped giving us the benefit of your wisdom!"

Annie saw her last statement had returned a smile to the older woman's face, as she knew it would, and she continued. "And you are quite right. I shouldn't let my past experience with John ruin my faith in all men. Good heavens, I have the daily reminder of what a good marriage looks like when I see you and Mr. Stein together, so I shouldn't despair."

Mrs. Stein laughed again, and, giving Annie's hands one more quick squeeze, she leaned back and picked up her crocheting. "Speaking of marriages, if you are still interested, I have a strange tale to tell about the marriage of Isobel and William Larkson and the mysterious Mr. Sweeter."

*****

An hour later, Annie thought about what Mrs. Stein had told her as she walked with Kathleen up Hyde towards Hapgood's Grocery Store. The evening was mild, although a light mist haloed the gas lamps along their way. It was a little after eight, and Annie's plan was to visit Harold Hapgood's wife at their store during the hour he would be attending the Monday night séance. She had sent a letter by the morning post to Simon Frampton, telling him that she would not be able to make the séance that night but hoped for another private sitting with Evie May on Wednesday.

Nate had sent a note to her at lunchtime by one of the scores of errand boys that trolled the financial district for work, asking if he could come by this evening. She had sent an answer back with the same boy, saying that she would not be attending the séance this evening but was otherwise engaged. She asked if they could meet on Wednesday evening instead. She knew it was cowardly to put off seeing him until after she saw Evie May, because she was sure he would interpret the fact that she was skipping tonight's séance to mean she would stop going to the Framptons' altogether. But she would rather have that fight after the fact.

"So, ma'am," said Kathleen, interrupting this thought, "what exactly did Mrs. Stein tell you?"

"She had dinner with her daughter, Hetty, yesterday and it turns out Hetty had done a little investigating herself," Annie replied. "She invited an acquaintance over to lunch this week, a Mrs. Frankle, who had gone to school with Isobel Larkson back in Portland and was quite willing to talk about her. Hetty told her mother she was actually a little shocked at how much this woman revealed, but the woman's excuse was how worried she was about their friend."

Annie then went on to recount what Hetty had learned. Isobel Larkson had been raised primarily by her maternal grandparents in Portland, Oregon, her father having died at Gettysburg, and her mother dying shortly after of the usual cause of heartbreak. Her grandfather eventually died as well, as old men do, leaving his wife a substantial fortune, which kept Isobel in private schools, dancing lessons, and silk frocks.

Life, however, was not a complete bed of roses for Isobel, since by the time she was in her late teens her grandmother was completely bedridden with arthritis, and Isobel was the only one of her descendants (she had five living children and fourteen grandchildren) who could successfully alleviate her pain, which she did by brewing special teas and reading and rereading the entire works of Charles Dickens out loud to her.

Then, when she was twenty-three, Isobel met William Larkson, a man thirty years her senior, who was in Portland for a week on business. At the end of that week, she and Mr. Larkson were married and off on a honeymoon. While they were away, Isobel's grandmother, who by this time was paralyzed by a stroke, died, leaving all her money to Isobel.

"Mrs. Fuller, what about all the other relatives? Didn't they get anything from the old lady?" interjected Kathleen at this point, as the two of them stood at the corner of Hyde and Geary, waiting for a heavily laden wagon to pass by. "I mean, isn't Mr. Sweeter one of those other fourteen grandchildren, and mightn't he be upset that Isobel ended up with it all?"

Annie smiled broadly. "Kathleen Hennessey, you are a clever girl. Hetty said Mrs. Frankle specifically mentioned a rumor that the rest of the family was going to challenge the grandmother's will. Evidently, nothing ever came of it. However, according to Mrs. Frankle, Isobel had a rude awakening when she arrived in San Francisco from that honeymoon. Turns out it wasn't just her pretty face and possible inheritance that had attracted Mr. Larkson. His mother, in her eighties and crippled with rheumatism, lived with him, and he believed that Isobel's experience with her grandmother would make her the perfect daughter-in-law to look after his mother."

"Oh my," said Kathleen. "Mrs. Larkson must've thought she had jumped from the frying pan into the fire."

"Exactly. Hetty told her mother that Isobel's friends all agreed she had a hard time of it in her marriage, adjusting to an older man who was set in his ways and catering to his cranky mother. That's why they were all happy for her when Jack Sweeter came to town, which happened just a few weeks after her mother-in-law finally passed on. Everyone thought it would make a nice change for her to spend some time with someone more her own age, everyone but Mrs. Frankle. Having grown up in Portland, she actually knew Jack Sweeter. In fact, her older sister had been courted by him at one time."

Annie paused to catch her breath. The last two blocks up Hyde to where the Hapgood's store sat on the corner of Hyde and Sutter were fairly steep, and she wanted to finish her story before they got to their destination.

"Mrs. Frankle had a lot to say about Mr. Sweeter. Most of it was about how he had led her sister on, practically leaving her at the altar; however, there were two very important pieces of information that are relevant to our inquiries. Mrs. Frankle told Hetty that Mr. Sweeter had been fired from his position in a stock brokerage firm for selling inside information. And, when he moved to San Francisco, he expected Mr. Larkson to give him a position in his company. Something that Mr. Larkson, clever man, has so far refused to do. So you see, Mr. Sweeter might very well be the kind of man who would go into partnership with the Framptons."

Chapter Thirty-four
Monday evening, October 27, 1879

"A BOLD DAYLIGHT ROBBERY. Two thieves enter a Grocery Store and
Steal $400."

—*San Francisco Chronicle,* 1879

By the early sixties, Hapgood's Grocery Store had made a name for
itself for stocking a wide range of canned goods as well as high quality,
fresh produce. At that time, the store was located on Sutter and Kearney,
putting it equidistant to the financial district, the docks, and the upper class
suburbs of Rincon Hill. When Annie came back to San Francisco a year
and a half ago, she had discovered that ten years earlier Hapgood's had
followed the western path of the Sutter Street Railroad. The store was now
located at the southwestern corner of Sutter and Hyde.

The founder, Jezidiah Hapgood, had certainly been a visionary,
because the store was now within easy reach of the occupants of both the
Nob Hill mansions to the north and the miles of new homes for the pros-
perous business classes west of Van Ness. In fact, the one time Annie had
walked the five blocks from her home to the store, she had found it too
crowded and the prices too dear, so she did her shopping at a smaller store
on Taylor.

Given the nasty comments made by the spirits who had addressed
poor Mr. Harold Hapgood, the current owner, Annie half expected to find
the store had undergone some terrible financial disaster in the year since
she had been there. However, as she and Kathleen crossed the street to get
to the gas-lit front entrance to the store on Sutter, the number of people
coming and going suggested that the store was doing just fine. The sign
over the door still said, in gilded letters, Hapgood and Sons. Annie wondered if Harold had kept the sign when he inherited in the hope that some
day there would be a new generation of little Hapgoods to carry on the

family business. Maybe that was the failure in doing his duty that his dead relatives were pointing out during the séances. He wasn't being fruitful and multiplying.

"Ma'am, I don't see Mrs. Hapgood. Do you think we've missed her?" Kathleen asked as they wove through the press of people lined up to pay a harried young male clerk at the front counter.

"I don't imagine we have. If the store is usually this busy this time of night, the Hapgoods wouldn't leave a single clerk. She is probably somewhere else in the store. However, I'm not sure if we do find her that she will feel free to talk."

"I see her, ma'am; she is in the corner talking to that lady."

"Let's get the things Mrs. O'Rourke asked us to pick up. Maybe, once we've paid, she will be free," Annie said as she walked over to slanted boxes by the front window of the store where apples, oranges, figs, and grapes basked in the harsh glare of the gaslights mounted on all the walls. She knew that her local store didn't yet have figs in, so she added a few of these oval fruits, plus some lovely purple grapes, to the basket she carried. Moving to the next row of boxes, she was surprised to see that there were actually fresh peas, which must have been grown in greenhouses to the south, since her local store hadn't carried any in a month. They were too expensive to buy, but she did pick out carrots and acorn squash.

"Kathleen, look, the first of the walnuts have come in; would you get about two pounds?" Annie asked, pointing out a barrel off to the side. Really, Hapgood's did have a great selection. Perhaps she should think about coming at least once a week to pick up some of the items she just couldn't get at her local store. She then finished off Beatrice's list, getting half a dozen eggs, blocks of aged cheddar and Swiss, a pound of rye flour, and a packet of sea salt. By the time she was done and made her way to the counter, she saw that the store had thinned out and there was only one woman in line ahead of her. Just then, Mrs. Hapgood came up beside the clerk and motioned Annie forward.

Kathleen, who stood beside Annie, took the initiative as they moved up to the counter, and she said, "Mrs. Hapgood, I had hoped I would see you. You have such a beautiful store. I'd never been here before. Please, I don't believe you have met my mistress, Mrs. Fuller. She asked me to introduce her to you and wondered if there is any way you could spare some time this evening to talk with her."

Mrs. Hilda Hapgood looked to be of Scandinavian stock, dark-blue eyes, silvery blond hair, pale skin that stretched over broad, flat cheekbones. Cheekbones along which a thin raspberry stain of embarrassment spread as Kathleen spoke to her. The woman, older than Annie but probably no more than her mid-thirties, was certainly attractive. Annie could imagine Harold Hapgood, such a thin, ungainly sort of man, would have found a fresh-faced young farm girl, ten years younger than he, pretty irresistible. Mrs. Hapgood's dark-blue cashmere dress and the tasteful gold brooch at her throat suggested her marriage had brought with it some degree of town polish. This should have enhanced those original good looks even further.

Yet the gray smudges under those blue eyes, which darted back and forth nervously, and the loose tailoring of her outfit, reflecting a recent loss of weight, did the opposite. Annie was reminded of the faded looks of another blonde she had met recently, Sukie Vetch, and she realized that in front of her stood another one of the Framptons' victims.

Mrs. Hapgood briefly shook the hand that Annie had extended, saying, "Very pleased to meet you. I hope you found everything you were looking for. Are you ready to pay for your purchases?"

"Thank you, Mrs. Hapgood. I think I have found everything I need. But I wanted to thank you for keeping Miss Kathleen company on Friday while I was attending the séance. I know it must be boring for her to sit in that hallway with nothing to do."

Hilda Hapgood murmured something about it being her pleasure, and then she concentrated on picking through Annie's basket, weighing the fruit, nuts, and cheeses, wrapping them in paper, and adding up the total, which Annie then paid.

Looking around and seeing that the store now had only one other customer, Annie said as she put the change into her purse and handed the basket of goods to Kathleen, "Please, Mrs. Hapgood. If you could spare a moment, I have only been attending the Monday and Friday séances at the Framptons for a short time, but I have begun to worry that they are not as honest as I had first thought. When Kathleen mentioned that your husband had been attending their séances for several months but that you didn't seem entirely pleased by the results, I thought you might be just the person to talk to, to help me decide whether or not to return."

"I'm not sure I can be of help, Mrs. Fuller, and I must . . ."

"Please, Mrs. Hapgood," broke in Kathleen. "My mistress is really concerned about the Framptons and making sure they aren't hurting anyone with their spirits and such. Do speak with her."

Annie reached out and touched the woman's arm lightly. "I can promise you that I will be discreet. No one will know that I have spoken to you. We can just pretend to be discussing this year's walnut crop. No one need be the wiser. Let me start by telling you what I am worried about."

Mrs. Hapgood stood motionless for a minute, then she turned to the young clerk, who had just come back to the counter from ushering out the last customer, and said, "Karl, after putting away the fresh stock in the cellar, would you please lock up and turn off the gaslights in the front of the store? Oh, and bring in the last box of canned goods that was delivered this evening. You can shelve them tomorrow. Let me know when you need to be let out. I will be in back. These good women and I have some business to discuss. Don't worry about your cash drawer. I will add up the receipts tonight while I am waiting for Mr. Hapgood to stop by and walk me home. Be here on time tomorrow."

Mrs. Hapgood then led Annie and Kathleen to a deep alcove at the back of the store, partially hidden by tall shelves of canned goods. It was crammed with a desk, two wooden chairs, a file cabinet, a dolly, and, in the corner, a cast iron safe. She shifted a stack of papers from one of the chairs and indicated that Annie sit there. Kathleen had already squeezed her small self into the space between the safe and the filing cabinet, so Mrs. Hapgood sat down on the chair behind the desk. As Annie sat, she realized that the shelf that was now at eye height was empty of cans, which gave anyone sitting down at the desk a clear view of the rest of the store.

Clever, she thought. *I wonder if that was Hapgood Senior's plan or an innovation by Harold or Hilda.*

"Karl is my younger brother. You don't need to worry about him overhearing us. He's a good boy, and I hope that he will make something of this chance to leave the farm and work in a store. Right now he's too busy thinking about getting his chores done so he can meet his chums," said Mrs. Hapgood, who then sat still, her shoulders drooping, as if the last few minutes of action had taken everything out of her.

"Mrs. Hapgood, I really do appreciate your willingness to talk," said Annie, who had discussed with Kathleen about how best to approach Harold's wife. She didn't want to tell her, at least not yet, about the real reason for her investigation since she must keep Sukie and her husband's identities secret. However, if she wanted Hilda Hapgood to confide in her, a little sharing of information was in order.

Annie continued, "I came to the Framptons initially because I thought it might be useful to contact my father for some financial advice. However, I have become suspicious of their methods and was hoping that your husband's experience, from your point of view, might help me better evaluate those suspicions. For example, I don't really believe that all the lights and music and such are really caused by spirits from beyond. I think somehow they are being manufactured by the Framptons."

Mrs. Hapgood stirred and looked up at her and said softly, "Yes, I'm sure you're right. I couldn't help but notice that music seemed to be coming from upstairs and asked Mrs. Nickerson about it. She actually laughed. Thought it all quite the joke. She swears her daughter really communicates with spirits, but she has told me that much of what goes on in that room is all hokum 'to create the right atmosphere,' she said."

"Is that what your husband thinks, Mrs. Hapgood? Because he seemed to take everything very seriously and seemed quite alarmed last Friday when the music became so loud."

Mrs. Hapgood looked down and shrugged slightly before answering. "I just don't know what he believes. He no longer talks to me about what

goes on. He did at first. You know he got a letter from Mr. Simon Frampton, inviting him to come to the first séance? I didn't want him to go. But
when someone we trust said they had a good reputation in town, he
decided he had to give it a try. I determined to go with him, but that Mr.
Frampton said my inner spirit weren't, I mean, wasn't compatible. So I
haven't been let in that room once. It's awful to feel so helpless. Can you
tell me what is going on?"

Annie now understood why this woman had made up her mind to talk
to her; she was starved for information of her own. "Mrs. Hapgood, I will
try to explain what I have been seeing. Everyone sits around in the dark,
then Arabella Frampton goes into some sort of trance, although I am not
sure if she is just pretending, and at various times there are lights, the
sound of a drum, piano, and so forth. Mostly she talks in various voices
purporting to be different relatives of the people around the table. Her
rendition of my father wasn't very good, which was one of the reasons I
began to suspect them of not being completely honest. Then, of course,
there is the cabinet, which not everyone goes into. Has your husband had
any sessions with the young medium, Evie May?"

"No, he hasn't. It is my impression it is always that Arabella woman
who speaks to him. Mrs. Nickerson hasn't come right out and said as such,
but she keeps hinting that Mrs. Frampton doesn't really have the 'power'
to communicate with the dead or at least that her power is weaker. She
wants me to pressure Harold to ask for a session with her daughter; she
feels he would have more luck. I just want him to stop going altogether."

Mrs. Hapgood stopped speaking, and Annie had the impression she
was fighting back tears. The lights at the front of the store blinked out
suddenly, and Kathleen and Annie jumped. Karl came around the shelves,
and Mrs. Hapgood stood up and excused herself while she let him out the
back of the store. She wasn't gone but a minute, but she seemed more
composed when she returned.

"Please, Mrs. Fuller, it would help if you could tell me what the so-
called spirits are saying to Harold. I just know he seems more upset each
time he attends one of these gatherings."

Annie thought back to the three séances she had attended and then answered. "I think there have only been two times when he was spoken to. The first time the spirit identified itself as his father. On this past Friday, I was under the impression that it was an older brother; I think he called himself Buddy."

Annie heard a sharp intake of breath at the last name, and then she said, "These two spirits didn't talk long, but both of them sounded quite angry. They seemed to be accusing your husband of failing in his duty or something. Does that make any sense?"

Mrs. Hapgood sighed. "His father passed on in 1873, five years after Harold and I got married. He did talk a lot about duty. It was Harold's duty to marry some banker's daughter, not me, to add to the family's fortune. It was his duty to move back into the house he had been thrown out of when we married to take care of the business when his father had a stroke. It was his duty to take care of his mother, no matter how difficult she was. It was his duty to have an heir to carry on the family name."

Mrs. Hapgood stopped, and Annie felt the pain that laced through that last statement. She wondered why there were no children after ten years of marriage. When it looked like Mrs. Hapgood wasn't going to say anything further, Annie prompted her. "And Buddy? Who might he be?"

"That was the nickname for his older brother who died in a stupid drunken brawl. I don't see where Buddy would have any cause to lecture Harold about duty."

"What I don't understand, Mrs. Hapgood, is why your husband would continue to attend these séances if all that happens is members of his family berate him. Most of the other people I have met at the séances seem to get something positive from coming there, a chance to reconnect to a cherished relative, good advice from the spirit world, or just entertaining theatrics."

"Mrs. Fuller, I wish it made sense. He says he needs to prove himself to them. They always made him feel like he wasn't strong or clever enough to be successful, to make something of himself or the business. When he was young, before I met him, he had some sort of breakdown when he was away at college. He was studying business back east. Had to come home in disgrace. His older brothers never let him forget it. So now he works day and night, pushing himself. Then he goes to that wretched house to tell them what he has done and comes home crushed and feeling guilty."

"Why guilty? From what I can see, the two of you are doing a splendid job with the store. He should feel proud."

Annie again heard the sharp intake of breath and was startled to see the raspberry stain had reappeared. Mrs. Hapgood wouldn't look at her, and Annie wondered if perhaps the store wasn't doing as well as she thought.

Mrs. Hapgood rose and stuck out her hand, saying, "Thank you for coming. I wish I could be of more help. But I can only say I would trust your instincts about the Framptons. They have brought to my husband's life, and consequently mine, nothing but misery. Now if you will be so kind as to follow me, I will let you out of the front of the store. I really must get to work on counting up the money before my husband comes. His cousin has thankfully offered to meet him at the Framptons, so it is my hope he will be here soon."

And be sober, Annie thought, swept back unwillingly to those nights when she sat waiting for John to return home, knowing he would be drunk and consumed by guilt for whatever new financial disaster he had created that day. *Is that why she mentioned guilt? Has her husband's drinking created some financial disaster for them, and is he asking the spirits for redemption? Or are the spirits the ones driving him to drink?*

*****

The girl stood in the shadows of the old carriage house. She was wearing a slouch hat, pulled down low, and a short dark sack coat above tightly fitting black pants. A yellow handkerchief around the neck was the only spot of color to catch the moonlight. A small dot of red glowed brightly in the dark, then disappeared, as she tossed the cigarette down and crushed it under her boot. A man came down the path that led from the front of the house to the servants' back entrance to the kitchen. The man stopped and knocked lightly on the kitchen door, which was opened and then closed swiftly behind him. The girl moved silently to an open window and leaned against the wall, out of sight, listening intently. Then she shook her head and disappeared into the night.

Chapter Thirty-five
Tuesday evening, October 28, 1879

"No Fun for the rats. A ratting match for $200 took place the other evening in a well-known sporting resort…The dogs were the imported bull-terriers 'Crib'…and 'Flow.'"—*San Francisco Chronicle,* 1879

"Jamie, hold tight to Dandy's leash. I don't want any rat-catching tonight," said his mother, Barbara Hewitt, who then glanced over the boy's head at Annie and smiled.

Jamie's mother, a statuesque brunette who taught English literature at Girls High, had moved into Annie's boarding house with her young son last January. Most evenings and weekends, she was either working on grading the mountains of papers her students seemed to produce or supervising Jamie in his own homework. She did try, however, to spend a little time each evening with her son, walking Dandy. Tonight, when Annie ran into them coming down the stairs to the kitchen, Barbara had asked Annie if she would join them on their walk.

Annie had been very pleased. A brisk walk was precisely what she needed. Today had been a difficult one for Madam Sibyl. Not only had she seen seven of her regular Tuesday clients but two others who had canceled last week had asked her to fit them in today at lunch time. Since they were two of her favorite clients, Annie had obliged. This had meant she had skipped lunch and had only time for a hasty dinner on a tray in Sibyl's parlor so that she wouldn't have to take off the wig before the first evening client came.

In addition, the time she had been spending investigating the Framptons had been cutting into her ability to get through all the local and national newspapers, which is where she garnered most of her financial information. Thank goodness her clients themselves provided a good deal of expert opinion on San Francisco business trends, so that she had been able to do an adequate job. In her opinion, however, adequate wasn't good enough. She found herself resenting the time it took to cast horoscopes for those clients who insisted her advice be presented in this form. Faking the use of palmistry was easier but still increasingly distasteful. She just didn't know what to do since she had no reason to expect that most of her clients would stay with her if she suddenly forswore Madam Sibyl.

"How are your students progressing?" Annie asked, trying to distract herself from that gloomy thought. The warmth of the sunny day had begun to drain away with the setting of the sun, and they had decided to head down Taylor to Turk, then west to Leavenworth, and back up to O'Farrell, an easy ten-block circuit.

"They are quite excited because we are having a contest for the best poem written on the theme of All Hallow's Eve. We have been studying Robert Burns' poem. Do you know it?"

"My, that brings back my days at the academy," said Annie, who began to disclaim in her best Scottish brogue, "'Amang the bonie winding banks, where Doon rins, wimplin, clear; where Bruce ance ruled the martial ranks, an' shook his Carrick spear; some merry, friendly, country-folks together did convene, to burn their nits, an' pou their stocks, an' haud their Hallowe'en fu' blythe that night.'"

"That was splendidly done, Mrs. Fuller," exclaimed Barbara.

Annie laughed. "I guess I've always had a theatrical streak. The drama club was my favorite extracurricular activity in school. But, please, I asked you to call me Annie."

"Yes, I'm sorry," replied Jamie's mother softly. "There is such formality among the teachers at Girls High that I have quite gotten out of the habit of using someone's given name. Of course, I would be so pleased if you would call me . . . Barbara."

Annie, struck by the way Barbara had paused before giving her first name, wondered if this had any significance. Since she and Jamie's mother were both widowed, of a similar age, and both working to support themselves, there should be a natural affinity between them, but Annie really knew very little about Barbara Hewitt's past. She never spoke about where she grew up, if she had any living relatives, or where she had taught before coming to San Francisco.

She certainly never mentioned her marriage or what had happened to her husband. This reticence was so familiar to Annie that she couldn't help speculating that the deceased Mr. Hewitt, like her own husband, hadn't been the best of helpmeets. A distressing incident with a neighbor last month had finally forced Jamie's mother to reach out to Annie. Since then, Annie had welcomed any opportunity, like the offer tonight, to become better acquainted.

They had just turned into Turk Street, which was lined with a variety of small businesses, when Jamie ran up to them and said with excitement, "Mother, look at that pile of pumpkins! Can we buy one? Mr. Chapman said he would help me carve a jack-o'-lantern for Halloween. Mrs. O'Rourke said there's going to be a party!"

Barbara looked a question at Annie, who said, "I think that is an excellent idea. In fact, get two smaller ones as well; we can put them on the front porch for decoration. I forgot that the two of you weren't here last year when we had our first ever All Hallow's Eve party at the boarding house. Mrs. O'Rourke invited a number of her young relatives, and Kathleen's brothers all came, in addition to a couple of her friends. And of course the boarders were welcome."

Annie realized that she had been so preoccupied with her investigation of the Framptons that she had neglected to discuss the upcoming festivities with Beatrice, and she was glad to hear that plans were moving forward anyway. When she was young, she had been fascinated by the ranch hands' celebration of the Day of the Dead. And the girls at the female academy she had attended in New York had duly memorized Burns' poem and giggled about the ghosts who rose from their graves on the last night of October.

But it wasn't until last year's party that she realized how many of the rituals associated with that night came from Ireland. No wonder Beatrice had been so pleased when she dropped off the walnuts they had bought at Hapgood's yesterday. Annie's mouth began to water when she thought of some of the tasty treats Beatrice had produced last year. She would have to think about whether she would still go to the séance on Friday since it would interfere with the party and Kathleen would be too busy to come with her that night. Perhaps, if she asked Nate to accompany her in Kathleen's place, he would be less likely to object to her making one last attempt to conclude her investigation.

Annie noticed that Barbara was taking money from her purse to pay for the pumpkins Jamie had picked out, and she moved forward, saying, "Let me at least pay for the two smaller ones. Jamie, can you manage Dandy and carry this very impressive specimen you have chosen? We still have several blocks to go." The boy had picked out a plump pumpkin, twice the size of his own head, and Dandy was twisting around his ankles, threatening to up-end him.

After making her contribution to the purchases, Barbara took the large pumpkin from her son and asked Annie if she would mind taking Dandy for the rest of the walk while Jamie carried the two smaller, future jack-o'-lanterns.

Taking the leash, Annie said, "I would be delighted. Dandy always makes me feel quite the lady when I walk with him." The small black and white dog cocked his head and looked up at her, as if he understood every word, and then trotted smartly beside her as they continued on Turk towards Leavenworth.

This early in the evening, all the shops were still open. There was a good deal of foot traffic and delivery carts, whose ends jutted over the wooden sidewalk while their goods were off-loaded. As a result, their conversation halted as Annie carefully monitored Dandy, impressed by the way the diminutive dog wove neatly around every obstacle, his white front feet flashing in the light from the gas lamps. When they were almost to Leavenworth, Jamie again ran back to his mother, asking her if they could step into a used clothing shop.

"I thought if I could use some of my spending money I'd get an old hat to put on my pumpkin. Mr. Jack would look more true-to-life and scary and all," he said, pointing at the stack of hats piled up on a cart outside the store.

Annie smiled at his enthusiasm. When his mother agreed to his request, she said to her, "Barbara, you go ahead with him. Put that big old pumpkin down, and Dandy and I will guard it with our lives while you help him pick out a suitable hat."

Dandy seemed very interested in the large pumpkin that was now at her feet, snuffling lustily at it with his squashed-in nose. Annie had a sudden vision of him deciding to anoint it, so she bent over and scooped him up. He delightedly started licking her face.

"Oh, Dandy, that is quite enough. You are no gentleman, to give a lady such kisses on the public street," Annie scolded and tried to hold him away from her. Although he didn't weigh more than ten or twelve pounds, she feared his excited wiggling could cause her to drop him, so she bent over and placed him on the ground again, tightening her hold on the leash and hoping he had lost interest in the pumpkin.

He sat down and looked up at her, as if to say, now what game are we to play? Then, without warning, he began to bark frantically and pull her down the sidewalk. Despite his bantam size, she had no choice but to follow him because it was either that or jerk the poor fellow off his feet. After about a yard or so, she dug in her heels and successfully stopped him by scooping him back into her arms. Then a noise like rolling claps of thunder caused her to whip around, just in time to see the large wooden barrels piled high on a cart tumble down, crashing onto the sidewalk where she had just been standing. Crushing the pumpkin to smithereens.

Chapter Thirty-six
Wednesday afternoon, October 29, 1879

"It would be so nice if something made sense for a change."
— Lewis Carroll, *Alice in Wonderland,* 1865

"When Mrs. O'Rourke told Mrs. Stein about the barrels, she was very upset. Mrs. O'Rourke said Mrs. Stein felt quite strongly there was more to what happened than meets the eye. Mrs. O'Rourke said . . ."

"Kathleen, I have heard quite enough about what Mrs. O'Rourke said for one day. I would really prefer if you would change the subject," snapped Annie.

Not surprisingly, the accident with the barrels had been the sole topic of conversation in the kitchen ever since last evening when they got back and Jamie had excitedly told Beatrice and Kathleen all about the unfortunate demise of the pumpkin and how Dandy had saved Annie from a similar fate. On the walk home, Annie and his mother had encouraged Jamie to view the incident as just one more example of Dandy's extraordinary powers, right up there with rat-catching. However, the worried frown and warm hug Barbara had given her before ushering her excited offspring upstairs to bed gave a hint of the seriousness with which she really viewed the incident.

Beatrice and Kathleen, also having refrained from expressing anything but loud praises for Dandy's prowess while Jamie was still in the kitchen, swiftly bombarded Annie with a series of questions as soon as he was upstairs and out of earshot. She felt like the questions and speculations about the event had never stopped since then. As a result, when Kathleen had brought the topic up as soon as they boarded the horse car, she had finally had enough.

Seeing the stricken look in Kathleen's eyes, Annie regretted her ill-tempered words. Patting one of the young servant's hands, she said, "I am sorry; that was uncalled for. I just hoped for a moment of quiet reflection while we were on the way to the Framptons. This may be the last chance I will get to meet with Evie May alone in the cabinet, and I need to decide how to approach her."

Kathleen smiled tentatively and then reached up and made the motion of twisting a key in a lock in the center of her mouth. This made Annie laugh and loosened the knot of tension that had been in her chest ever since she had stared down at the destruction several tons of beer barrels could do when they crashed from a height. Only one of the barrels had actually split apart, a testament to the cooper who made the rest. Even so, fifty gallons of beer mingled with pulped pumpkin and broken staves made an unholy mess.

Thank heavens she and Dandy had been standing at a slight incline from the accident, so the other barrels had rolled away from them, three of them fetching up against the side of the building next door to the saloon where they were being delivered. One errant barrel rolled on down the sidewalk, slowly gathering speed, while several men worked to stop its momentum.

Annie was not sure she would ever get the image of that ponderously turning barrel out of her head, or that of the squashed pumpkin. Jamie and his mother had been standing outside the store when the rumble of cascading barrels had arrested their attention, and they had run over to Annie almost instantly. Fortunately, between calming Dandy, who was trembling in her arms, keeping Jamie from running through the mess to join in the exciting sport of stopping a runaway barrel, and assuring Barbara that she was indeed fine, Annie hadn't had time to take in how close to death, or at least a severe injury, she had come. Then, as an excited crowd began to gather, rather like ones that showed up at the scene of a carriage accident, Annie and Barbara concentrated on herding Jamie around the corner and up Leavenworth toward home as quickly as they could.

Only after Jamie and his mother had left the kitchen and she had a second to assimilate Jamie's claim that he had seen a man run away from the back of the cart did the full implication hit her. Her near death may not have been an accident.

The shock of this idea must have shown on her face, because Beatrice, who had been urging Annie to tell them "the real story," pulled her across the kitchen and pressed her into the rocking chair while directing Kathleen to pour her mistress a strong a cup of tea, well-sugared. "Now dearie, you just sit and get warm. Feel those hands, cold as ice. It's the shock, you know. It was the same with me in '56 when my Peter came in all bloodied during the vigilante riots," she'd said, chafing Annie's hands.

As Annie had sipped at the hot tea, listening to Beatrice and Kathleen speculate about how the barrels could have gotten loose, she thought about the man Jamie saw running away. The cart had been the typical two-wheeled brewer's dray with slatted sides and an open back, where the barrels could be easily rolled down the ramp that would be formed when the cart was tipped. Whether by accident or on purpose, the ropes holding the stacked barrels in place must have given way. Yet that alone shouldn't have caused all the barrels to come crashing down. The cart itself must have been tipped up, or the barrels pushed as they sprung free, or both simultaneously.

The Framptons' butler and his powerful shoulders had suddenly popped into Annie's mind. As did the two threatening notes, the push off the horse car, and Arabella's overheard statement that if Simon didn't discourage Annie from continuing to come to the séances, she would.

Unfortunately, about the same time, Kathleen had come to a similar conclusion, and she had blurted out, "Oh, ma'am, what if it weren't an accident? What if the person who wrote that terrible note you found in your pocket Monday last was behind it? The note said you were to stay away, and you haven't, have you?"

That had put the fat in the fire. Beatrice shook a spoon at Annie while begging her to promise she wouldn't "go near those dreadful people again." Kathleen had suggested they ought to send for the police, in the form of her beau, Patrick McGee, "this instant." At least the effort it took to calm these two worried women had diverted Annie from her own fears.

However, once she had repeated her assurances that she wouldn't do anything rash and that she would take their concerns under advisement, she was forced to flee to the sanctuary of her bedroom and a sleepless night. This morning, she'd delayed leaving her room until it was time to meet with her first client as Madam Sibyl, thereby avoiding any further argument with Beatrice. With Mrs. Stein now in the picture, Annie did not look forward to this evening. No wonder she had been short with Kathleen.

The one bright spot had been a note she had gotten from Nate canceling his plans to visit the boarding house this evening because of an emergency meeting with a client. This gave her some breathing room before he found out about the barrels. Thinking of the discussion she'd had with Mrs. Stein about Nate's feelings towards her and her ambivalence about her own feelings, Annie worried at a niggling kernel of guilt. She hadn't told Nate about the second note and the push off of the horse car.

She hadn't told anyone, convincing herself that both notes and the push were simply the act of a jealous Arabella, and, therefore, she wasn't really in any danger. Last evening's events suggested otherwise, and she knew Nate would be angry that she was going ahead with her plan to visit Evie May one more time. And could Annie blame him? Wouldn't she be upset if he did something she thought threatened his safety?

"Ma'am, we're at Harrison. We need to get off." Kathleen had gently touched her arm to get her attention.

Annie took a deep breath, shaking her thoughts free of this conundrum, and got up, leading the way to the front of the car.

"Thanks, Kathleen. Now, when we get there, can you please see that Mrs. Nickerson gets this letter from me? Obviously, it would be best if you can hand it over to her in person. If not, could you slip down to see Biddy and ask her if she would deliver it?"

Annie handed over the letter she had written asking Evie May's mother if she would join her, with her daughter, for tea tomorrow morning at Woodward's Gardens. Flora Hunt had written her yesterday, asking if she could arrange this meeting and suggesting the venue because it would provide more opportunities for Flora to take Evie May aside to speak with her. Meanwhile, Annie could entertain Mrs. Nickerson and possibly learn more about Evie May's childhood.

"Should I make sure no one else is around when I give the letter to Mrs. Nickerson?" Kathleen asked.

"Good question. Yes, we can't trust anyone else in the house but Biddy. I am hoping that Mrs. Nickerson will keep the contents of the letter to herself. If you are able to give the letter to her directly, you could tell her you would be glad to convey her answer to me."

Standing at the Framptons' front door, Annie reflected that it had been two weeks since her first visit. She knew she couldn't pursue this investigation much longer. If the details Nate and she had learned on Sunday about how the séance effects were handled weren't enough to persuade Miss Pinehurst's sister that the Framptons were frauds, she wasn't sure there was anything else she could do for Sukie Vetch. If Annie were successful in getting Flora Hunt and the Nickersons together, she would have done all she could for Evie May, too.

She would ask Nate to accompany her to the séance this Friday and promise to send Simon a note telling him she would no longer be availing herself of Arabella's or Evie May's services. That should allay Nate's concerns and end any possible threat against her from Arabella.

Annie hadn't realized how nervous she had been about confronting Albert, who very well might have tried to kill her last night, until the front door opened and she felt a wave of relief when she saw it was Biddy who was standing there, ushering them in.

"Oh, Mrs. Fuller, I didn't know you were the girl's next client." Biddy then lowered her voice. "Something's going on. There's a man in the library with Mr. Frampton and Albert. I didn't see who it was, but the master told me to answer the door and . . ." Biddy stopped abruptly, then in a louder voice she said, "Please, Mrs. Fuller, the master asked if you would be so kind as to step into the parlor. He will be with you straightaway." Sketching a brief curtsy, Biddy winked at Annie.

Biddy then turned and acknowledged Mrs. Nickerson, who was

coming down the front stairs, saying, "Ma'am, I told Mr. Simon that you wished to speak with him, but he is otherwise engaged. He said to tell you he would see you at dinner."

Mrs. Nickerson did not appear pleased, saying querulously, "Such a bother. I had postponed going out in the expectation of being able to speak with him."

Annie made a split-second decision and walked swiftly over to Evie May's mother, her hand outstretched. "Please, Mrs. Nickerson, I am so glad to have this chance to meet you. My name is Mrs. Fuller, and I am about to have a private sitting with your wonderfully talented daughter. How very proud you must be. I had begun to despair of ever contacting my loved ones, sitting night after night in Arabella's circle . . . I know she is supposed to be quite in tune with the spirit world . . . but I haven't seen, well, that is neither here nor there . . . but your daughter. Oh my, the power she has . . . the feeling you are speaking directly to the dearly departed. Mrs. Nickerson, I shouldn't delay you, but I was wondering if you would oblige me . . . my servant has a communication to you that explains everything. If you would just read my little note and let Kathleen here know if you would be willing . . . oh, I must not keep your daughter waiting. I so hope you will look upon my request favorably. It would mean the world to me."

Annie finally released the speechless Mrs. Nickerson's hand and practically ran to the door to the parlor. As Annie passed by, Biddy grinned and then closed the door behind her. Annie hoped she had read Mrs. Nickerson's character correctly and that she would be amenable to Annie's proposed meeting. If Simon would just delay coming out of the library long enough for Kathleen to do her part. Who was the man meeting with Simon and Albert? Could it be the same man Simon and Arabella talked about on Sunday?

She then noticed that the door to the small parlor was open and saw that Evie May was sitting in the cabinet. She was dressed all in white, but, unlike last Wednesday, today her outfit was clearly feminine. She didn't appear to see Annie. Instead she looked down where her arms cradled the air. She hummed a monotonous tune, faintly reminiscent of a nursery rhyme. Annie went over to the girl but, not wanting to frighten her, stood for a moment, hoping to get a sign of recognition.

Evie May slowly raised her face and stared blankly up at Annie, her eyes an odd light amber shade today. She then went through one of her amazing transformations. She pulled up her knees, scrunched down, and tilted her head, all of which seemed to shrink her overall size. With one hand twirling her hair and the other tugging at Annie's sleeve, she smiled beatifically, lisping, "Have you come to put me to bed? I was a naughty girl, the bad man says, 'cause I won't play with him. Bad girls have to go to bed without their suppers and they get scared all alone. I don't like being all alone."

Annie responded to the insistent tugging and sat down on the cabinet bench next to Evie May, who immediately sidled closer to her and put her arms around her neck.

"Maybelle, is that you?" asked Annie.

"Course it's me. Silly. Can you sing me a bedtime song?"

Annie stroked Evie May's hair and said softly, "Maybelle, who is the bad man? The one who sends you to bed without your supper?"

"He says he's papa. He's not my papa. My papa loves me. I'm the bestest girl in all the wide world." Evie May pulled away from Annie and glared, her voice rising. "I am his beautiful girl, and he loves me best, better'n anybody."

Flora Hunt had suggested that Annie try to contact Evie May's "Miss Evelyn," the young woman Kathleen had met in the hallway two weeks ago, because as an older spirit she might be able to provide more information about Evie May and her past. With this in mind, Annie said, "Yes, Maybelle, you are a very good girl, and I am sure your papa loves you. But it's time for you to go to sleep. Could you ask Miss Evelyn if she would be willing to visit with me awhile?"

"I love Miss Evelyn. She sings me a bedtime song, and I fall right to sleep." Evie May yawned hugely and put her head back down on Annie's shoulder, becoming a dead weight.

Annie tightened her arms around the girl, thinking about the horrors that Flora had hinted at from her own childhood and wondering if Evie May had a similar past. She also wondered if Flora was correct and that the personalities Evie May experienced when she was in a trance were "protective" spirits.

How could this sweet child, Maybelle, provide any protection for Evie May? Or, for that matter, what good could the nine-year-old boy, Eddie, do? How could the spirits of such young children protect a girl who was actually older than they?

"Oh, Evie May, what has happened to you? And where was your mother?" Annie whispered, rocking the girl in her arms.

"Get your hands off of me. Who do you think you are?" Evie May had metamorphosed into an outraged young woman who was now sitting as far away from Annie on the cabinet bench as she could get. Sitting ramrod straight, she appeared tall, and the soft wool dress now revealed the modest, but definitely promising, shape of a womanly figure. The deft way she was rearranging the soft curls that had been cascading down her back into a fashionable topknot suggested she was not without vanity.

Annie said tentatively, "Miss Evelyn?"

"Yes, and who might you be?"

"I'm Mrs. Fuller. Mrs. Annie Fuller. I actually was hoping I might meet you. I've been worried about Evie May. She, rather Maybelle, has mentioned a man who sounds like he might be frightening her. Can you tell me who he is?"

"That is really none of your business. I appreciate your concern, but no one is ever going to hurt any of us again, I can assure you. Edmund will make sure of that."

"Edmund?"

"Yes, he may be a regular hoodlum, but, for all that, he's learned a thing or two on the streets."

Annie made another try. "Please, Miss Evelyn. There is a woman, Mrs. Flora Hunt, who feels that she might be able to help you . . . all. I have asked your mother to meet with Mrs. Hunt tomorrow, and I think it may be helpful if you were to encourage this meeting."

"Well," sniffed the young woman. "I'm going to be pretty busy. Thursday's market day. But Eddie might want to come, and he's a sensible little chap. He looks after Maybelle when I'm not around. Now, if you'll excuse me, I can see that our time together must be ending."

Annie heard a sound from the adjoining room, and, without thinking, she shook the hand that had been graciously offered her. Feeling quite like Alice down the rabbit hole, she watched as Miss Evelyn disappeared, to be replaced by Evie May, slumped in the corner of the cabinet.

Chapter Thirty-seven
Thursday morning, October 30, 1879

"M.H de Young, one of the proprietors…explained all the modern conveniences connected with this confessedly most perfect and thorough journal office…from the business office, on the first floor, to the mailing room, on the upper floor, there is combined elegance and convenience…"—*San Francisco Chronicle*, 1879

As Nate approached the new five-story *Chronicle* building on the corner of Bush and Kearny, he tried to put a damper on the excitement he had been feeling ever since yesterday when he got a brief note from Anthony Pierce, setting up a meeting for this morning because he had an "interesting proposition" to put before him. He'd hated having to postpone seeing Annie last night because of work, but he decided after he got the note it might have been for the best. Sunday night had dispelled any remaining doubts he'd had about Annie's feeling for him, and, if Anthony had come up with a concrete job possibility, he could talk to her about their future together when he saw her tomorrow. That is, if the "position" paid more than he was currently making. *Hell, it couldn't pay less.*

After Nate paid for his share of the rent and supplies for the law offices and his room and board, there was hardly anything left over. Yesterday, he'd again broached the subject with his uncle of looking for an additional partner to share the law firm's expenses and bring in more lucrative clients. Once again, his uncle had said they would talk about it later. *Uncle Frank might find that later was just too late.*

Since Sunday, visions of a future life with Annie had dominated his thoughts, almost to the exclusion of everything else, fueling his impatience. Work at the law firm consisted of boring clerical work and the petty concerns of men like Suttlerly, the octogenarian Nate had met with last night. Men whose lives had narrowed down to trying to preserve their power beyond the grave through minutely detailed wills. This wasn't why he'd chosen the law as a profession. Too young to prove himself in the war, uninterested in following in the footsteps of his father and be a rancher, Nate had thought law would be where he would make his mark. Defending the innocent and establishing new legal precedents had been his goal, not writing out wills, deeds of property, and articles of incorporation.

However, a position in the state attorney general's office, or even better, working in the city attorney's office, would be a lot more stimulating. In addition, experience on the prosecuting side could be very helpful later if he wanted to set up his own law firm concentrating on defense. The investigations he did last summer with Annie had given him a taste for criminal law.

And, he had to admit, this investigation of the Framptons was turning out to be quite intriguing. He had thoroughly enjoyed uncovering the séance tricks on Sunday. Then there was the personal satisfaction of the all too short interlude with Annie in the cabinet. He supposed when Annie married him and quit her work as Madam Sibyl she might find life a little dull until the children came; but he would be sure to share with her the more interesting parts of his own work. She had a keen mind, and he was sure she would give him good advice as he moved forward in his career.

Entering the first floor of the *Chronicle* offices, Nate had to push his way past a line of people who were putting in classified ads and work his way down a narrow space between a counter and the wall to a swinging door that let him behind the counter. The *Chronicle's* new offices were impressive, and he could feel the pounding of the gigantic steam press engines in the basement under his feet. Several men stood outside of Charles de Young's office at the rear, talking loudly about the newest scandal in Nevada mining shares. The chief editor himself was still missing, rumored to be hiding out in Mexico until the furor over his attempt on the new mayor's life died down.

Nate took a detour when he noticed that his friend, Tim Newsome, was lounging at the subscriptions desk, chatting animatedly to the young female clerk. Nate hoped that the clerk knew Tim was both a hopeless flirt and hopelessly in love with his own wife.

Newsome looked up as Nate drew near and said, "Hey, Nate, you old rascal, come here and meet Amanda Fitchings, who has the loveliest copperplate handwriting in the whole building. Miss Fitchings, meet Nate Dawson, Esquire. And to what do we, of the Fourth Estate, owe the pleasure of your company?"

"Miss Fitchings, pleased to meet you, although I hope you will not hold my friendship with Mr. Newsome against me. Tim, I'm looking for Anthony Pierce; he asked me to stop by. Do you know if he's at his desk?"

"Not in yet. This is a little early for Pierce, usually doesn't come in until afternoon. What's he want to see you for? Got something I might be interested in?"

Tim Newsome draped his arm around Nate's shoulder and began to direct him back to stairs in the rear that led to the reporters' offices on the second floor. Tim was a tall Swede, with pale blond hair cut short, a silky mustache, ruddy complexion, eyes the blue of a deep fjord of his native land, and a mischievous smile that had made a devoted friend out of a young, homesick fifteen-year-old Nate Dawson when they'd first met.

Newsome specialized in stories about the state's agricultural and fishing industries, and Nate thought that Annie might find a lot to talk about with his friend. *I'd bet she'd like Lydia as well; they'd rail about "votes for women" to their hearts' content.* Having again conjured up an image of Annie, she never seemed far from his mind these days, Nate decided to ask Tim for information about Mr. Abraham Ruckner and the San Francisco Gold Bank and Trust. Wouldn't hurt to have a tidbit of information to bring with him when he saw her tomorrow, in case his expectations about Pierce's proposition didn't pan out. He smiled, thinking how unusual she was, a woman who would prefer a little inside financial information over flowers from a beau.

"Nate, my boy, you look very much like the proverbial cat with the cream. What have you been up to?" Newsome asked as they wove their way through the large second-story room, crowded with mostly empty desks, Pierce not being the only reporter who didn't come in this early.

"I'm helping out a friend, just doing some background checking on a local medium and some of her clients," said Nate, not wanting to get into his love life with his friend this morning. Tim had a wicked sense of humor.

"So that's why you want to talk to Pierce. I wondered if he was going to do a follow-up on that series. It was a real winner. Circulation went up, and the Chief was right pleased. I'm afraid stories about the wheat crop just don't get that kind of recognition."

Nate said, "I bet they don't, though I always try to read your columns last thing at night, best sleep aid I've ever used. But you might be able to help me out. One of the clients I'm interested in is Abe Ruckner, one of the owners of Gold Bank and Trust. I understand the man recently lost his wife. That sort of thing can shake a man, affect his business sense, don't you know."

Nate was amused to see the change his question produced in his friend. Newsome straightened up, his head pushed forward, like some hunting dog on the scent, and he stood for a moment, very still.

"Well, well, now that you mention it, I do remember hearing something about the wife's death," Newsome said. "But not that it was having a negative effect on Ruckner and the bank, just the opposite. The wife was a McCormick, so he inherited a pretty penny in Harvesting Machine Company shares. He's going to see a medium, is he? Can I quote you on that?"

"Tim, no. I don't have firsthand knowledge about this, and, anyway, the poor man just lost his wife. If I do learn anything concrete, I'll let you know."

"Same here, just promise me if there is anything, you'll tell me, not Pierce. I don't want to be stuck on the farm and fish beat forever. Just what do you need to talk to him about?"

"He told me last week that he would try to get me a meeting with the incoming state attorney general, see if there might be something for me in Sacramento."

"Pierce's pretty well-connected, so I wouldn't be surprised if he could. With the new state constitution and the shake-ups on the state level, there's bound to be some openings. Thing is, Nate, be careful. Pierce has a nose for corruption, and he writes damn good stories, but he's made enemies along the way, and some of his friends aren't all that savory. We all operate along the principle of 'you scratch my back, I'll scratch yours' or in your profession's terms, *quid pro quo*, but I've heard that Pierce can extract a pretty high price for favors rendered. He can be awfully hard to read, never know when you end up on his bad side. He did just come back from his mother's funeral, so he's been especially touchy. Why are you interested? You aren't thinking about leaving your uncle's firm, are you?"

Nate removed a stack of papers from the chair next to Newsome's desk and sat down. "Tim, you know how much I owe Uncle Frank. Damn it, we both do since most of the time when I was young and he had to rescue my sorry hide, he rescued yours as well. Thing is, ever since Haranahan died, the firm has begun to stagnate. Old men and their wills seems to be the only business he brings in, and if I don't start to get some trial experience, I'm not going to do any better. I'd hoped he would find a new partner this fall while I was away at the ranch, someone with a reputation and some big clients, but as far as I can tell he's done nothing."

"Have you asked him what his plans are?"

"I've tried, but he keeps putting me off. I think he still sees me as that raw-boned whelp he took under his wing nearly fifteen years ago. Doesn't occur to him I'm a grown man with plans of my own."

Newsome leaned over and said, "Plans of your own, you devil. So who is she? Lydia's just been saying we haven't seen you since you got back in town. Used to be you came hanging around every Saturday night, looking for a decent home-cooked meal."

Nate tried to keep the smile off his face but couldn't. "It's not a done deal, so don't you go spilling the beans to anyone. She's a widow; I met her at the end of the summer. Never known anyone like her. Independent to a fault, which, of course, made me think that your Lydia would get along with her like a house afire. Uncle Frank even approves of her, so you'd expect he would understand why I need to make more money. I just think he's been a bachelor for so long, never occurs to him I might want something different."

"I wouldn't be so sure of that, my fine friend. Just last Sunday, I took Lydia for a ride in Golden Gate Park, and I saw your Uncle Frank tooling along in a rented phaeton with a very lovely lady, a Mrs. Matthew Voss. He seemed in fine fettle, and I wouldn't be so sure his bachelor days aren't going to be soon over. Say, weren't there rumors that old Mr. Voss was tied up with some fortuneteller? Couldn't be that's what you are working on, is it?"

"Mrs. Voss . . . fortuneteller, where did you get . . ." Nate had just begun to ask Newsome to explain, when a hand clapped him heavily on the shoulder, and he turned to see Anthony Pierce at his side.

"My boy, glad you waited. Sorry I'm late. Hope Farmer Timothy there hasn't bored you to death with his grain reports. Come on over to my desk and sit awhile."

Nate nodded to Newsome and followed Pierce across the room to a desk that was scrupulously neat, with blotter, inkstand, and stack of papers all perfectly aligned. Since it had always been Nate's impression that reporters, by nature, were messy packrats, this seemed unusual. Pierce, himself, was spectacularly untidy this morning, and the strong smell of stale alcohol and tobacco drifting in his wake suggested he hadn't been home after what had been a nightlong revel in some dive. Yet when he sat down across his desk from Nate, his brown eyes were bright, his ugly face animated, and he showed no lack of energy as he smiled broadly.

"Dawson, glad you could come. Attorney General Hart got into town Tuesday evening. I met with his chief of staff, Jaffry. Good man. Turns out his wife came from my hometown in Missouri. Small world. Lots of social affairs were planned for this week. All the wives in town were showing off their parlors. Jaffry was ready to bust out last night after all that tea he'd had to down." Here Pierce's smile turned wolfish. "Man has appetites, I'll say that for him."

Nate nodded ambiguously. "I was glad to hear from you. You said you had a proposition for me?"

Pierce's smile widened. "Now, young man, let's not be hasty. Got to do the preliminaries."

He then opened up his bottom drawer and fetched out a bottle of bourbon and two tumblers, filling them up and pushing one across the desk. Nate hated drinking this early in the day, but he felt he couldn't turn the man down. He knew that politics and hard liquor went hand in hand, even among Republicans. If this was the world he wanted to enter, it behooved him to play the part. So he took the glass and drank the amber liquid down, feeling the hot flash of instant well being.

Pierce refilled Nate's glass and then leaned back in his chair, holding his own glass up to the sunlight and saying, "Tell me, any new developments in your investigations on the Framptons? Client hasn't decided to give it up, has she?"

Nate sipped at the drink, trying to bring his mind into focus. "I wish to hell she would. I mean, I haven't turned up any evidence strong enough to interest the police, but my client is pretty determined. Feels sure that Simon Frampton and his wife are involved in some sort of swindle. Can't say I disagree. There's just nothing on which to base a criminal complaint. People don't always understand that even though something's wrong, it isn't always against the law." Nate thought he should try that argument on Annie tomorrow night if she went back on her agreement to make the séance on Friday her last.

Thinking of Annie, Nate shook his head slightly, suddenly impatient. "Tell me, Pierce, what's the story? Did you talk to Hart about me?"

Nate noticed Pierce was frowning, and he thought, *God damn it, Tim told me to watch it. Damn bourbon.*

He tried to frame his next words, but Pierce intervened. "That's what I like to see, enthusiasm. Next best thing, I talked to Jaffry, who really does all the vetting for appointments, and I puffed you up plenty. He's interested, real interested. But, like Hart, he's a busy man, so you're going to have to jump when I get the word to you he's got time for a meeting. Don't know whether it will be sometime tomorrow or Saturday. I'll send a boy round with a note, give time and place, and you better come on the double."

Nate's first thought was this might mean he wouldn't be able to honor Annie's request that he accompany her tomorrow night in the place of Kathleen. If he couldn't go, Annie couldn't either. It was time she gave up her part in the investigations anyway. Surely she'd understand this meeting takes precedence. *After all, it's her future as well as mine at stake.*

With this thought, Nate stood up and leaned across the desk to shake Pierce's hand, saying, "Sir, thanks so much. You can count on me. Send word and I will be there. No matter what else is going on."

Chapter Thirty-eight
Thursday morning, October 30, 1879

"L. Pet Anderson, Medium, 850 Market, Developing class, Tues evenings"
—*San Francisco Chronicle*, 1879

Annie sat at a table with Mrs. Rowena Nickerson in the restaurant at Woodward's Gardens and tried hard not to let her mind stray to the last time she was here, with Nate. That day had been cold and rainy, but today the sun had quickly burned off the fog, and they were able to sit comfortably on the outdoor patio. She hoped the warm weather persisted so that the Halloween party tomorrow night could safely spill into the backyard. As of this morning, the number of young people who were going to attend had climbed precipitously when Kathleen got word her brothers and some of their friends were going to come. She had fussed about them being proper hooligans, but Annie could tell she was pleased.

"Mrs. Hunt and her friend, Mrs. Gordon, seemed quite taken with my Evie May, don't you think?" Mrs. Nickerson's question brought Annie back to the here and now.

Evie May's mother continued. "I remember ever so well when Mrs. Hunt traveled to Lynn to speak, right before the war started. She was so young and beautiful. I went with my husband, Mr. Sewell Nickerson. Since his father owned one of the biggest boot and shoe factories in town, we had special seats, right up close to the stage. Nothing was too good for me back then. Of course, I was quite young myself. A child bride, you would say. And to think that Mrs. Gordon was also a medium when she was young. Her name was Laura de Force? I think I remember hearing about her. I am so pleased that they are taking an interest in my Evie May. You said Mrs. Gordon is also a famous journalist? Good heavens, wouldn't it be too wonderful if she wrote a piece about my Evie May for the papers? I have been telling Simon, dear man, that we need to get more press for my darling girl."

Annie chose not to tell Mrs. Nickerson that Laura de Force Gordon was no longer the editor of the *Oakland Daily Democrat*. Instead, along with Clara Foltz, another local San Francisco woman, she had plans to be the first woman admitted to the California bar. Mrs. Nickerson might not be as excited about associating her "darling girl" with anyone quite so controversial.

Annie, on the other hand, had been delighted when Mrs. Hunt had introduced Mrs. Gordon this morning. Nate and she had talked about Gordon and Foltz this summer when the newspapers reported on their success in getting the "Lady's Lawyer Bill" made part of the new constitution. Perhaps she could arrange a meeting between Nate and Mrs. Gordon. He kept talking about how old-fashioned his Uncle Frank was concerning the law; maybe Mrs. Gordon could be their new law partner. That would shake things up.

Annie smiled and shook her head. *I need to stop thinking about Nate and concentrate on Mrs. Nickerson.* Annie had missed the last thing Evie May's mother had said, but she simply murmured agreement, which she had discovered was all that was necessary to keep Mrs. Nickerson's words flowing. But, now that Mrs. Hunt and her friend Mrs. Gordon had taken Evie May for a walk to see the animals in the Zoological Gardens, she should work harder to direct that flow into useful channels.

"Mrs. Nickerson, do tell me a little more about yourself. You said you were from Lynn, Massachusetts? Is that where the rest of your family still lives? You do have other children besides Evie May?"

The other woman's perpetual simper dimmed slightly at this question, and she patted at the frizz of hennaed bangs on her forehead, as if to assure herself they still held their curl, before answering. "Oh, yes, I had four children in all. The two boys, Sammy and Tom, high-spirited lads, went out at a young age to make their own mark in the world. Nan, my oldest girl, married young and left home when Evie May was just a little tyke. I couldn't complain. I married near the same age, so you might say she took after her own mother. But I miss them all sorely. Thank goodness for my precious Evie May."

Here Mrs. Nickerson took out a handkerchief and fluttered it in the direction of her eyes, which remained stubbornly dry.

Annie noted that none of the names of the older siblings matched the names of Evie May's "protectors" as she patted the woman's hand sympathetically and said, "I can imagine she must be a real comfort to you, particularly after you lost your husband. How old was Evie May when her father died?"

"He passed on over two years ago. A sad blow to us both. My husband may have had trouble with his boys, but he treated his girls like princesses. Nan's marriage hit him hard. He didn't feel the boy was worthy of his precious girl. But I told him, a girl like Nan, everyone said she got my looks you know, can't stay forever in her father's pocket."

Annie noticed this last statement had the ring of a well-practiced complaint, and she wondered if there had been some jealousy between Nan and her mother. Annie mentally replaced Mrs. Nickerson's hideous orange-dyed hair with a natural shade of red, stripped away the thick layer of powder to imagine a porcelain complexion, looked at a face bloated by water retention for the delicate features hinted at by the neatly shaped ear and chin, and concluded that, in her prime, Mrs. Nickerson might have been quite a beautiful woman. Her light-green eyes were still striking and could have outshone even those of Arabella Frampton if they didn't always look so desperate.

"Quite right," Annie agreed, to what she wasn't sure. "After your daughter Nan moved away, I expect that Evie May became the apple of your husband's eye." *Why is it that I keep speaking in clichés when I'm talking to Mrs. Nickerson?*

"Oh, yes. He cosseted her so. In the evenings, he trained her to bring him his slippers and pipe and dram of whiskey. Then she'd sit on his lap and they'd whisper together. I'd ask them what the joke was, and they'd never tell me. Made their own little world they did. That is until Evie May started having the fits."

"How distressing," said Annie, wondering if the "fits" were the strange blank interludes she had witnessed when Evie May was deserted by one spirit and not yet inhabited by another.

Mrs. Nickerson started, as if she hadn't realized that she had been speaking out loud. "Simon has explained to me that this was just Evie May beginning to communicate with the spirit world. I wish my husband could have understood that. He got extremely angry with her, and she would disappear for hours, days at a time, leaving me alone to fend . . . it wasn't a pleasant time. But then he became ill with a chronic bilious complaint, completely bed-ridden for the last four years of his life. Seeing him so weak, delirious at times, when he had been such a strong, handsome man, just broke my heart. As you may well imagine, I was prostrate with grief. Evie May took over. She was so good to us both."

Annie was appalled at the thought of Evie May taking care of a sick father and a malingering mother, at what age? She would have been no more than nine or ten when her father became ill, even younger if her mother was being truthful about her daughter's age.

"Oh, Mrs. Nickerson, didn't your husband's family do anything to help you out?"

"No, they did not." Mrs. Nickerson stiffened. "His father was a pig-headed tyrant. Soon after we married, he completely cut off all support. Heartless man, he didn't even come to Sewell's funeral. My mother-in-law tried to help a little from time to time, but she wouldn't openly go against her husband. She gave us just enough to keep us from starving. It was awful."

For the first time, Annie had a sense of kinship with this woman, remembering with bitterness how her own father-in-law had treated her after her husband's death. No wonder Mrs. Nickerson and Hilda Hapgood had developed an odd sort of friendship; they both had disinheriting fathers-in-law to bond over. But Evie May, what effect had all this wretched experience had on her?

"However did you manage once your husband died?" Annie asked.

"The spirits guided Simon Frampton to us, and he became our savior." Mrs. Nickerson smiled and sighed heavily. "Evie May and I had moved to Boston and into a dirty, crowded boarding house when one day I insisted to Evie May that we just had to have some pleasure in our lives. With the few pennies I had left, we went to the local theater where Simon and his wife were giving a public demonstration. Evie May volunteered to come up on stage ... well, you could have knocked me over with a feather, this wasn't like her at all ... and the spirits possessed her. She began to declaim such beautiful poetry. I had never seen nor heard the like. Simon came to us after the show and explained to me about the spirits and Evie May's talents, and he just took us under his wing."

"How did Evie May feel about all this?"

"She is ever so grateful. Simon is like a father to her, better than her own father, in fact. If only that woman wasn't so jealous. Just because she didn't want to have any children, she begrudges Simon the chance to raise Evie May as his own, train her talents."

To raise Evie May as his own? Did this mean Simon planned to adopt Evie May? As her guardian, he would have full control of her and any money she would make. He wouldn't need Mrs. Nickerson anymore. *I wonder if Mrs. Nickerson understands the implications of that, or is she so deluded that she thinks that it will be Arabella he won't need anymore?* How foresighted of Flora Hunt to have Mrs. Gordon, an expert in California law, come to this meeting. Annie hadn't thought that there might be legal issues involved in trying to protect Evie May from Simon Frampton, or her own mother for that matter, but clearly there were.

Annie noticed that Evie May was walking back towards their table, chattering excitedly to both Mrs. Gordon and Mrs. Hunt, who each held the girl by a hand. It was a striking difference from when Evie May and her mother first arrived at Woodward's Gardens. Then, Evie May had been very shy and non-communicative. At least her mother had dressed her appropriately for her age and sex today. Her outfit was a loosely cut Basque top and contrasting gored skirt made of a soft light-brown tweed, trimmed with dark-brown velvet, and her hair was held back with a matching velvet bow. As she watched the girl tell her mother about seeing the camels, and the bears, and the huge buffalo, Annie thought to herself that this was the first time she'd seen Evie May just being Evie May.

Until the girl, taking advantage of her mother's attention being claimed by Mrs. Gordon, turned to Annie and in Eddie's distinctive tones said, with a cock of the head and a wink, "Maybelle sends her love and said to tell you to watch out. The bad man isn't very happy with you."

*****

That night, the girl sat in the large armchair, wearing a loosely fitting white dress of a vaguely nautical cut, white stockings, and black three-button shoes. A man was standing over her, and he reached down and tipped her head up with his index finger so that she was staring up at him. He spoke slowly and distinctly, staring back into her eyes until her eyes closed.

The second man, standing in the shadows at the edge of the room, shifted his position. The girl's eyes flew open, and she twisted around in the chair until she was staring straight at him. Her thumb popped into her mouth, and she turned away to drag the china doll out from behind the chair's back cushion. She began to cradle the doll, humming.

The first man shrugged, took the doll from her, and again tipped up her now tear-stained face, speaking slowly until her eyes began to flutter closed.

Chapter Thirty-nine
Friday Evening, October 31, 1879

"Mrs. McDonald, Medium. No 9 Mason st. and Market. Sittings daily; meetings Tuesday and Friday evenings, 50 c 8 o'clock p.m."—*San Francisco Chronicle*, 1879

Annie's heart steadily thumped, filling the darkness with a regular beat in counter syncopation with the soft exhalations of breath from the men who sat on either side of her. It was her last séance, and she thought how oddly comfortable she had become with the strange ritual of sitting in the dark, holding hands with relative strangers, temporarily sightless, waiting. For a brief time, she had attended a Quaker meeting with a school friend in New York, and she was reminded of the long slow minutes of sitting silently, her mind, like a caged monkey, swinging and shrieking from idea to idea, image to image until, exhausted, it stilled, and she had felt at peace.

Tonight there would be no peace, because tonight, spirits, whether real or not, would soon arrive to shatter the silence and drown out the beating of her heart. *Spirits, real or not? Could Eddie or Maybelle be the spirits of some little children who have passed on? If not, who or what are they?* These thoughts had possessed Annie since yesterday morning when she recognized Eddie peeking out of Evie May's eyes.

"On this night of All Hallow's Eve, the spirits of the departed are closer to us than any other part of the year," intoned Arabella, dressed in a pale-rose satin gown that glowed in the red light emanating from the cabinet room. An odd dissonant tune from the piano upstairs began to play, soon joined by a slow, soft drumbeat. *Albert and his wife are busy tonight,* was Annie's first thought. She recognized that she found it easier to mock the obviously manufactured spirit manifestations of the Framptons' séances than to contemplate the possible existence of real spirits. Spiritualists like Flora Hunt believed that all souls lived on after death, in an afterworld where they continued to develop and progress as spiritual beings, capable, in time, of providing ethical and moral guidance to the living. For Flora, Spiritualism brought peace and an explanation for the strange voices that had spoken through her all of her remembered life. There was no hell or evil spirits in her belief system; All Hallow's Eve would hold no fears for her.

Annie could see the attractiveness of Flora's beliefs, but she was seriously troubled by the idea that her dead mother, or father, or heaven forbid, her husband, might live on in perpetuity, struggling to find some way to reach out and communicate with the living, with her. *But what of her lost daughter? Would it bring her any peace to think that, like Maybelle, she might still exist in some form, searching for her mother?* Annie didn't know if she could accept that idea. She also didn't know if she believed in heaven and hell. In her experience, evil came from the living, not the dead. This was one of the reasons she didn't believe it was the spirit of Charlie who tried to frighten his mother about her unborn child or pressure his father into betraying his employer. The evil came from the Framptons, not the afterworld. But if Charlie wasn't a real spirit, what was the explanation for Maybelle or Eddie? Round and around these thoughts had gone, always coming back to who or what inhabited Evie May.

To her left, Ruckner spasmodically clenched her hand as the volume of the music increased and Arabella commenced to moan, the now familiar signal for a spirit to manifest itself. The lights from the room behind began to flicker, a new phenomena. When the music stopped, a deep male voice rang out, saying, "'Ding dong dell, Pussy's in the well.' Do you hear me, little puss? It's your grandfather, come to speak with you."

Mrs. Larkson shrieked. Then the voice softened. "Isobel, Isobel, don't be afraid, my little puss. Remember how we changed the old song? 'Ding dong dell, Puss is Isobel, Who loves her best? Pa more than the rest.' Don't cry, little puss."

Annie heard the sound of Isobel Larkson weeping. Detecting a smile on Jack Sweeter's face as he leaned over to whisper in the distraught woman's ear, she thought she caught a whiff of evil in the air, and it didn't come from the spirit of Isobel's grandfather. Something must have happened since last Friday, because the lively young woman Annie met two weeks ago had been replaced by a woman who looked haunted, her laugh brittle, her clothes hanging loosely as if she had lost weight overnight, and her eyes darting fearfully around the room.

The spirit's voice continued, as Sweeter was successful in getting Isobel to quiet her sobs. "Little Puss, don't cry. My little Bell. I just want to remind you of how important family is, now and forever. That's all Granny and I ever wanted of you, to remember who your blood is, who you owe your allegiance to, and we will rest content and bother you no more." The final words became so soft Annie had trouble hearing them. "Ding dong dell, Puss is in the well. Who'll get her out? Little Jackie Stout."

Annie shivered. Could it be that simple? Jack Sweeter wanted something from his cousin Isobel. Money? A job in her husband's factory? Her complicity in some criminal enterprise? Would he be willing to pay Arabella to have the spirits frighten his cousin into compliance? Maybe he paid the Framptons by exchanging information, for example, about Nate's connection to her. Thinking back to what Esther Stein had learned about Isobel's life, the years nursing her grandmother and then her mother-in-law, Annie doubted this woman deserved whatever was now happening to her. Yes, this was evil, and Annie felt she must find a way to stop it.

Ruckner again moved restlessly beside her, probably impatient for his turn with the spirit of his dead wife. But a musical interlude had commenced, and Arabella was back to swaying and moaning. On the way to the séance, Nate had told her about Ruckner having inherited a great deal of money from his wife, which would certainly make him a good target for blackmail. She prayed that Arnold Vetch hadn't succumbed to the pressure Simon was putting on him to reveal information about Ruckner and the bank. If this had happened, would she be able to tell based on what the spirits had to say to him tonight? Earlier in the week, she had told Miss Pinehurst all about what she and Nate had found in the Framptons' house on Sunday, hoping the information would help convince Sukie the couple were frauds, but she hadn't heard back from her. Annie prayed this information had done some good.

Since she still hadn't figured out how to tell Nate about the incident with the barrels, she'd been relieved that on the car ride to the Framptons', there hadn't been time to do more than discuss what he had learned about Ruckner. Nate had agreed that he shouldn't accompany her all the way from the car stop to the séance house since the conversation they had overhead on Sunday suggested it was her connection to Nate that put her in the greatest danger. The plan was that he would walk up the few blocks to Market, stop by a little cafe he knew about, and then get a cab to pick her up at the corner of Sixth and Harrison. They would then go to the boarding house to join the Halloween festivities that would be well underway by the time the séance was over.

Annie found her attention pulled back to the séance at hand when Simon did his usual rigmarole about the departed ones. Right on cue, the lights in the back parlor strengthened, and the Judge eagerly left the table to join Evie May in the cabinet. This, of course, left Mrs. Mott and Nurse Herron to join hands, and as Arabella segued into another spirit voice, the two women vied to claim it as their own. Annie again felt her concentration drift. She had worried that Nate would be upset that she had put off seeing him all week or that he would want reassurance from her that tonight would indeed be her last séance. However, he'd been suspiciously agreeable. Preoccupied was a better description.

A raised voice caught her attention, as Nurse Herron shouted, "No, no, it wasn't my fault. I wasn't on duty. You have to believe me. I would never have left that day if I had thought it was to be your last." Nurse Herron was rocking back and forth in distress.

Annie, shocked at this outburst, wondered what the spirit, who was definitely female this time, had said to prompt this denial from the nurse, who had always before seemed to enjoy having little chats with former clients. Unfortunately, she hadn't been listening. *Drat. I need to concentrate. This may be my last chance to figure out if there is anyone besides*

Arabella who might be so upset by my investigations that they would try to hurt me. Despite what Annie had implied when she told everyone this was her last séance, she knew she wasn't entirely ready to give up on her investigations. She no longer believed that, even if Arabella was behind the threatening notes and the barrels, it was just jealousy. If she or someone else was frightened enough to threaten Annie's life, then there must be some sort of serious crime involved, and she couldn't leave it alone until she found out what it was and exposed it.

Mrs. Mott, in her gruff voice, spoke out, indignantly addressing the spirit. "I think that we have had quite enough from you, whoever you might be," she said. "You are obviously not very evolved. Good heavens, you are acting like a school child's idea of a haunt. Be gone, and don't come back until you have learned something in the afterlife."

Annie bit back a giggle and felt Simon stir beside her. Clearly, the séance had gotten out of hand. She wondered why Arabella would have chosen to have a spirit accuse Nurse Herron of some sort of dereliction of duty, if not something more serious. It had been Annie's impression that the nurse was a good source of information about potential clients and, therefore, treated gently in the séances. Perhaps she had become less cooperative.

Simon spoke up at this point, and, as Annie had come to expect, he brought the séance back under control by asking for everyone to sing a hymn. She thought this was also the signal for Evie May to dismiss the Judge, and, sure enough, he slipped back into his chair as the song ended. Annie's heart began to beat faster, wondering if she would be next. So she was relieved when Arabella, after the necessary swaying and moaning, began to speak to Mr. Ruckner. To her further relief, nothing Ruckner's wife said seemed to indicate anything threatening, no vague suggestions about the health of the bank or indications that Ruckner should be feeling guilty about anything. Either Arnold Vetch had held his ground, or he didn't know anything worth blackmailing the banker about.

The spirit of Mr. Ruckner's wife didn't stay around long, and the ambient light dimmed considerably while the music swelled. Annie felt her tension rise accordingly since she expected it was her turn to be called into the cabinet or to confront one of Arabella's spirits. She had told Simon at the start of the séance that this was to be her last, saying something vague about feeling she had found the solace she had been looking for in her conversations with her loved ones. Simon gave her one of his intense stares and then said how sorry he was, but to Annie he appeared more relieved than upset. The conversation she had overheard on Sunday confirmed her belief that Simon had never seen her as much of a threat; however, Simon might not be as sanguine if he knew she was trying to remove Evie May from his influence.

Annie jumped at the sound of a large crash, accompanied by a bright flash of light, followed by silence and complete darkness. Neither Arabella nor Simon made a sound. This time, the darkness no longer felt comfortable to Annie; instead, she experienced a strong feeling of menace. As the minutes ticked past, the scent of lilacs became so strong as to feel like a concrete presence in the pitch-black room. Next she heard the tap, tap, tap of what sounded like a cane, coming closer and closer. The room behind them was suddenly flooded with light, prompting at least two of the women around the table to cry out. Harold Hapgood was caught in a beam of the light, his mouth stretched into a silent scream.

Annie turned around and saw Evie May in her cabinet, illuminated by the light from above, which now had a bluish tinge and turned her skin to a deathly hue. Annie had never seen this Evie May before. She sat bolt upright, her shoulders square and her legs spread wide in her skirts, creating the illusion that she was a much bulkier person. Her head was sunk into her shoulders and wobbled to and fro, as if her neck was too weak to hold her head sufficiently straight. One of her arms was outstretched in front of her, holding a cane with a single round orb at the top. While she was dressed in her usual white, the cut of her clothing looked old-fashioned, as did her hair, braided up into a coronet. Around her neck were strand after strand of white beads.

She rapped once, very loudly, with the cane. Then she stretched out her other arm, her index finger pointing straight at Annie, who, bewildered, tried to figure out what departed relative of hers this Evie May was supposed to represent, until she realized the girl was looking past her at someone behind her at the table. When the girl began to speak, despite the ugly high-pitched whine of her voice, she left no doubt at whom she was pointing.

"Harold. Harold Hapgood. You don't deserve to live."

Annie heard a moan come from behind her.

"Six sons I was given, five were taken away from me. Six sons, but only five were worthy of a mother's love. Six sons, but all save the last died. When you were born, you were my most precious child, the son of my old age. You were supposed to be my staff and my support. But you were weak, led around by your nose by that stupid simpering miss, turning your back on your flesh and blood."

"No, mother, I never did. You turned your back on me." Harold's anguished cry rang out.

The cane came down hard, twice, in rapid succession, as Evie May screamed defiantly. "Don't you dare contradict me. I am your mother, and you will listen to me. I sat there in my room while you and your hussy were out on the town. I sat all alone while the fire went out and my hands and feet went cold. I sat alone and I called and called, and you didn't come. Wife gone to goodness knows where, you laid out in a drunken stupor. Can't even hold your liquor, can you? What kind of man are you? You killed me with your neglect. Left me all alone, suffocating to death."

"I'm so sorry, Mother." Harold's voice was barely above a whisper. "I never meant that . . . I didn't know . . . oh, God, can you forgive me?"

"Forgiveness is for your maker, not me. Six sons, all dead but you. And you don't deserve to live." Evie May tugged viciously at the strands of beads, which broke and flew everywhere.

The lights went out, and Annie couldn't see anything, but she heard exclamations and curses, the sound of retching, and a woman sobbing. The table began to rock violently while the piano from above swung into what Annie recognized as the closing hymn. In time, led by Simon and Mrs. Mott, the people around the table joined in singing, and the table's shaking slowly lessened and then stopped as the hymn ended.

Simon released her hand, left the table, and then threw open the doors, letting in the blinding light from the hallway. Annie turned to look at Evie May, but the girl had vanished from the cabinet room. When she turned back, she saw that Simon was leaning towards Harold, who was hunched over, his head in his hands. When Simon whispered something to him, Harold reared back and scrabbled out of his chair, shouldering his way through the knot of people who were moving towards the door. Annie saw Hilda Hapgood move towards her husband as he entered the hall, but he roughly pushed her aside and ran to the front door, wrenching it open and disappearing in the dark night of All Hallows' Eve.

Chapter Forty
Friday evening, October 31, 1879

"The feast of All Saints, which was ushered in Friday evening by the old-fashioned games of 'All Hallows' E'en, was yesterday celebrated in the Catholic and Episcopal Churches."
—*San Francisco Chronicle*, 1879

"Welcome to our celebration of *Oíche Shamhna*," Mrs. O'Rourke cried out as Nate followed Annie into the boarding house kitchen. Annie's cook and housekeeper was standing next to a large punch bowl, waving a ladle, and Nate had never seen her look quite as lively. Her pink cheeks, the wisps of gray hair that had escaped from the bun at the top of her head, and the breathiness of her voice had Nate speculating on what exactly was in the punch she was dispensing and how much of it she had already imbibed herself. Until he noticed the swirl of a fiddle coming from the back yard and realized Mrs. O'Rourke had most likely been dancing a jig!

A undetermined number of young people, none of whom Nate recognized, were milling around the kitchen, some getting punch to drink, others working at the stove stirring large pots of what smelled like spiced cider and ale, others putting some pans of cake in the oven, and all of them chatting in that musical lilt that signaled their membership in the Celtic tribe.

Nate was glad to see Annie smile as she ran over and gave Mrs. O'Rourke a hug. When Nate had helped her into the cab after the séance, he'd been struck by how grim her face had looked in the lamplight; and on the short drive home, she had stuck to monosyllabic answers to his questions. As they left the cab to mount the steps to the boarding house, he'd asked directly what was wrong, and she had only said that they would talk later.

"Mr. Dawson, it is good to see you again," said Patrick McGee.

Nate shook the hand of Kathleen's beau and said, "Officer McGee! How are you? Haven't seen you since this summer. I trust that the department isn't too upset over Kalloch's win as mayor. Chief Detective Jackson told me that Patrick Crowley is slated for Chief of Police. How do the men feel about that?"

"Actually, sir, they just made the announcement of his appointment official this morning. Those that worked under him in the sixties when he was Chief before say he's a straight shooter. Be good for the department to have an experienced man at the top. Rumor is there's even to be money for some new hires and new uniforms, blue like in New York City. The men are right excited about that."

Nate looked at the pale gray police uniform McGee was wearing, which always reminded him painfully of the Confederacy and his older brothers' deaths, and he nodded. "Have you come off patrol, or are you still on the night beat?"

"I did get put on day patrol last month. However, seeing that it's All Hallow's Eve and there tends to be mischief done this night, some just harmless pranks, some not so harmless, we were asked to beef up patrols. I go on at eleven. I can wear the uniform off-duty, long as I don't have on the badge or gun. I locked them up in Aunt Bea's pantry, till it's time for me to leave."

Annie had come up to him and Patrick during this last interchange, and she said, "Patrick, your aunt asked me to give you this bowl of apples to take outside. I gather that we are about to have a round of 'snap the apple.' Are you going to use the apricot tree again this year?"

"Yes, ma'am. Kathleen's middle brother, Aiden, has already shimmied up and tied the rope. Aunt Bea won't let us do the candle, says there'll be no singed faces at this party, so we'll put an apple on each end of the stick. Doubles your chance to get one, although with Aiden swinging the rope, I doubt it'll be all that easy. Ma'am, sir, I best get out there." McGee bobbed his head and threaded his way through the crowded kitchen.

"Candle?" Nate asked Annie.

"Yes, evidently an 'old country' variation on the game. Last year, Patrick's older brother put a lighted candle on one end of the stick and the apple on the other. One girl had already set her bangs on fire before Beatrice heard what was going on. You should have seen her! She sailed out of that kitchen and into the yard like a fully gunned frigate and smacked the young man upside the head with a wooden spoon, calling him every kind of fool. I gather he wasn't invited to come tonight. I just hope he isn't out creating some of that mischief Patrick was speaking about. Would be a shame if he has to arrest his own brother."

"Can I get you something to drink before we go outside?" Nate asked.

"Please do, and why don't you get us some of those little round cakes that have just come out of the oven?"

Annie then turned away from him to greet Jamie's mother, who accompanied the two spinster seamstresses, Miss Millie and Miss Minnie, into the kitchen. Nate bowed politely and moved over to say good evening to Mrs. O'Rourke and get the refreshments. He always had the uneasy feeling that these two former Southern Belles, who had to be in their late sixties at least, compared him to the gentlemen friends of their youth and found him wanting.

While Nate piled a plate high with small nut-filled cakes and oatmeal cookies, Mrs. O'Rourke handed him a glass cup of punch and said, "Please drink up, Mr. Dawson. I think you will find there is just a hint of rum alongside the fruit in this punch. A recipe that Annie's Uncle Timothy, God rest his soul, taught me when I was just a young kitchen maid. Made it the night our Annie girl was born, right in this house, right in the room she now has for her own. Annie's mother and father were fine folks, and they'd be so proud of their little girl."

They both looked over to where Annie and Mrs. Hewitt were getting the two old ladies settled in the chairs next to the fireplace. Biddy, the Framptons' servant, brought them a plate of cakes and some punch. Just then, Dandy ran into the kitchen, yipping excitedly, followed by Jamie, who had come to drag his mother outside to see him try his hand at snap the apple. Nate became aware that the fiddling had stopped, and there was much clapping and laughing coming from the back yard.

"Master Jamie, you put the leash back on Dandy before he trips up someone," said Mrs. O'Rourke. "That's right, and hand the leash over to your ma if you're going to try for the apple. I'll be out in a second to watch."

Mrs. O'Rourke glanced around the kitchen to make sure everything was under control, and then, with a small frown, she turned to Nate and said, "I worry if Dandy is underfoot that someone won't see him, he's so small. But I couldn't tell Jamie to leave him up in his room, with him being the hero and all for saving our Annie."

Annie appeared at this moment at his side and said, "Good, you got the cakes. Let me take the cups. We need to go out and watch Jamie. You come too, Beatrice." She grabbed the two cups and was on her way out, shooing Mrs. O'Rourke in front of her, before Nate had a chance to ask what Mrs. O'Rourke had meant about Dandy saving Annie.

Nate paused at the door, stunned at what he saw. Annie's aunt and uncle had the good fortune to buy the property on O'Farrell in the 1850s, before the city lots had been sub-divided, so they hadn't been forced to build one of the narrow row houses that dominated most of the city. Not only did this mean there was actually a tiny bit of space between the house and its neighbors but also the back yard was comparatively spacious, and every inch had been transformed for this party.

Snaggle-toothed jack-o'-lanterns leered down from the tops of both side fences, and two torches placed at the end of the lot added to the light that spilled out of all the back windows. The large garden plot at the back of the lot, stripped and readied for winter, now hosted a traditional All Hallow's Eve bonfire, carefully tended by several older men, who, Annie whispered, were Kathleen's uncles. The laundry lines were down, and the right side of the paved yard had been turned into an improvised dance floor, with chairs and stools and crates pushed to the edges for seating.

On the left was the apricot tree, and a dangling rope was tied around a lower limb, ending in a stick with apples stuck on both ends. A young man, probably Kathleen's brother Aiden, was in the tree madly swinging the rope and twirling it to the frustration of a younger boy and the general laughter of the watching crowd.

"The boy trying for the apple is Kathleen's youngest brother, Ian," said Annie. "She is determined that he stay in school, not be apprenticed like her other two brothers. She says he's the smartest of them all, and he should be given the chance to get a profession. She gives most of her wages to the uncle who took him in when her father died, so that he won't send him out to work. She's hoping that Ian and Jamie will take a shine to each other, thinks Jamie would be a good influence on him."

Nate smiled, thinking about the friendship he had developed with Tim Newsome and the scrapes they got into, and he wondered who would influence whom. Ian finally got his apple, to great cheers, and came over to slap Jamie on the back and push him into the circle for his try. Looked like Kathleen might get her wish.

While they sipped their punch and ate their snacks, Nate and Annie stood with Barbara Hewitt and watched the younger children try for their apples. Mrs. O'Rourke disappeared into the kitchen at some point and then came out with a large cake on a platter, which occasioned a shout and much pushing of young ladies to the fore. Kathleen, Biddy, Biddy's cousin Tilly, and about six other girls of varying ages, whom Nate didn't recognize but assumed were some of Beatrice's nieces, stood in line, each getting a slice of the cake.

Annie leaned over to Nate and said, "It's *barmbrack* cake. Beatrice has baked a ring in it, and tradition has it that the girl who gets the slice with the ring will marry within the year. Oh, my, look at Patrick, he seems to be taking a great interest in who's going to get the prize!"

"Saints preserve me, I've got it!" shouted Biddy, waving the ring in the air. "Nearly swallowed it, don't you know. I hate to think what that would have foretold!"

One of the older lads, who had been anxiously watching the girls eat their cake, came over to Biddy and whispered in her ear. When she laughed, he pulled her over to the dance floor, where couples were congregating as the fiddler began a tune. Nate asked Annie and Mrs. Hewitt if they wanted to take a seat around the edge of the dancers, but Mrs. Hewitt said she needed to check on Jamie, and Annie looked up at him and said she would rather join the dancers. Nate readily agreed, mentally thanking Tim's wife Lydia for the lessons in Irish country dancing he'd gotten at her family parties. What followed was a lively interlude where he got to swing Annie repeatedly in his arms.

Laughing, Annie finally pulled him from the floor, saying, "Nate, that's all I can do. Let's leave it to the youngsters."

"I guess you are right; there goes the youngest one at the party." Nate followed her, making sure to keep his arm tight around her waist as he pointed to Mrs. O'Rourke, who had just been cajoled by one of her brothers-in-law to join the dancing. Soon the pavement was crowded with the older generation, who were now showing the younger ones how a true Irish jig was performed.

Dandy, who had somehow gotten away from Jamie, came trotting up and sat beside them, staring at the dancers as if entranced. Annie picked him up, which reminded Nate of what Mrs. O'Rourke had said earlier about Dandy being a hero. He was just going to ask her about this when she turned and said, "I'm going to take Dandy into the kitchen and see if Mrs. Hewitt is there. I want to check on Miss Minnie and Miss Millie, and I will get us more punch. I'll be right back."

Nate stood and watched her weave her way through to the kitchen, stopping and chatting with everyone as she went. He couldn't help but think how useful she would be if he ended up with a political career since making people feel at ease had never been a social skill he had developed. He'd promised himself he wouldn't mention the prospective meeting with Hart or his aid and his hope he might get a job in the state attorney general's office, in case it fell through. Thankfully, he hadn't gotten any summons tonight, and he assumed his meeting would be sometime tomorrow.

"Mr. Dawson, I am so glad to get a chance to see you," said Mrs. Esther Stein, who had just come up beside him. "Annie told me I could find you out here. She is supervising the kitchen while Mrs. O'Rourke is having her fling. There are several giggling girls in there, peeling apples and professing to see the initials of their intendeds in the parings, and I was afraid that my presence was putting a damper on their high spirits."

"Mrs. Stein, how good to see you. Are you well? And your husband, he didn't want to join in the festivities?" Nate always felt a bit ill at ease with Mrs. Stein, very much as he would probably feel talking with a prospective in-law. He knew if the Steins objected to his courtship of Annie, it would be hard going. Mrs. O'Rourke and Kathleen seemed very much in his corner, but Esther Stein, he wasn't so sure of.

"Herman likes to put his feet up after a big meal. We were trying out the new restaurant that has opened up on Kearney. I must say this party is a good idea; it gives the young people something positive to do. The number of young boys and some girls we saw running around the streets tonight on our way home was distressing. Too easy for good fun to turn into bad judgment, with some broken windows and broken heads as a result."

Nate murmured his agreement, again thinking ruefully of his own boyhood pranks with Tim and his uncle coming to the rescue, not something he cared to share with Mrs. Stein. Instead, he asked her if he could bring her a chair, and she in turn suggested that they take a seat on two chairs that were located near the bonfire since the air was getting chilly.

When they were both seated, Mrs. Stein turned to him and, in a very serious voice, said, "I am glad to have this chance to talk to you alone. I was hoping to enlist your help in convincing Annie that she must stop these investigations into the Framptons. She could have been killed Tuesday night, and nothing you can say will convince me it was an accident. I think she has gotten too close to something dangerous, just as she did last summer, and I fear for her safety."

Nate's head swam, and for a moment he wondered if there hadn't been a bit more than a touch of rum in the punch. "Mrs. Stein, whatever are you talking about? What happened to Annie on Tuesday night? This is the first time I've seen her since Sunday, and she didn't mention any accident. Wait. Mrs. O'Rourke said something I didn't understand about

Dandy saving Annie, save her from what?"

Mrs. Stein then told Nate, in some detail, about Annie's close call with the beer barrels, Jamie's claim to have seen a man run away from the cart, and her own conviction that the incident had been deliberate and life threatening.

"Then, when I learned that she not only attended another private sitting with that odd sounding young girl, Evie May, on Wednesday, but she arranged a meeting with the girl and her mother and some other local Spiritualists on Thursday, I became seriously concerned. Mrs. O'Rourke said you accompanied her to the séance tonight, and I couldn't help but wonder if she had told you about what happened, since I thought you would be too sensible to give into her if she were really in danger. I know it is hard to say no to Annie . . ."

Nate interrupted her, rising from his chair. "Mrs. Stein, I knew nothing about all of this, nothing at all. I can assure you if I had, I would have . . ." Nate paused, then bowed to Mrs. Stein and said, "If you will please excuse me, I need to talk to Annie this instant. I'm sure you will understand." He then strode across the yard towards the kitchen.

Chapter Forty-one
Friday evening, October 31, 1879

"Miss Leland, the Greatest fortuneteller, gives correct information on stocks, love. Wishing charms and lucky tokens given; happiness in families remedied; fee $1"—*San Francisco Chronicle*, 1879

Annie was standing near the kitchen stove talking to Biddy when Nate came in and grabbed her hand, pulling her out of the kitchen.

"Nate, whatever are you doing?" she said, laughing. "I promised Mrs. O'Rourke I would oversee the girls." When she looked over and saw the grave expression on his face, she said more sharply, "Nate, slow down, what's happened?"

By this time, they were now up the short flight of stairs to the front hall. Annie heard the sound of the piano and singing coming from the formal parlor, so she wasn't surprised when Nate turned and opened the door to the small study directly to their right. This was part of Madam Sibyl's domain and, as such, would be off-limits to everyone else in the house, so it was a good choice if Nate had something private to discuss. Annie followed him into the room, feeling more and more disturbed by his behavior. After he had closed the door behind them, she moved up to him and took his arm, asking again what was wrong.

Much to her surprise, he pushed her away, then simply stood there, looking at her as if he were afraid to open his mouth.

"Nate," Annie said, her concern sharpening to fear, "whatever is wrong, just tell me."

"What's wrong is I just found out you were almost killed on Tuesday and, odd person that I am, I'm upset. So, Annie, just when were you going to tell me about what happened?" Nate stopped speaking and glared at her.

Oh, dear, I really should have told him about this earlier, she thought. *He has every right to be upset.* Feeling her face flush with guilt, she hurried to try and explain, saying, "Oh, Nate, I am sorry. I was afraid someone would mention it before I had a chance to talk to you. I know you must be angry, but there just hasn't been the time or privacy this evening. I had hoped when the party died down, but never mind, we can talk about it now." She again reached out to touch his arm.

Nate took a step back and said, "What about before this evening, for instance, the next day? And don't tell me it was my fault because I couldn't come Wednesday night. I bet you were delighted when you got my note since then you could go ahead with your plans for the week, without having to explain why you would continue to put your life in danger. You know, if you had sent word, I would have come round immediately. So don't tell me there just wasn't time. You didn't make the time!"

Annie, shocked, put up her hands to her cheeks, which now felt like they had been flayed by each angry syllable. Nate turned away as if he couldn't stand the sight of her. Then she saw his shoulders rise and fall, and he turned back.

He began to speak again, but his apparent attempt to appear calm soon faltered. He said, "Annie, I'm sorry. I was too harsh. But when Mrs. Stein told me . . . Annie, you have to understand I've seen what that sort of accident can do. I . . . I imagined you ... your body ... damn it, you could have been killed." Nate stopped, breathing heavily.

Esther, how could you? You have no idea the potential damage you have caused, Annie thought angrily. She looked away, trying to regain her composure, trying to find the right words to say to make Nate understand she hadn't meant to upset him so.

She again reached out to him, putting her hand on his arm, and said, "Of course I understand. I would feel the same way if it had been you who had such a near miss. And, much as I would like to pretend it was an accident, the more I see of the Framptons, the more I can believe that *our* investigations, and Nate you have to admit you have played a part as well, have stirred something up. I know at first I didn't really take the threat seriously. The note in my coat pocket seemed so melodramatic, even childish. I could see Arabella, or her lady's maid, or even Mrs. Nickerson, if she thought I was a threat to her daughter's future success, writing the notes. Heavens, it could have been Evie May in the form of one of her 'protectors,' like Eddie, who pushed me off the horse car. I can see him thinking it was a lark. But Tuesday's incident with the barrel . . ."

Nate broke in, "Pushed you off the horse car? What the devil are you talking about?"

"Oh, yes," she said. "I forgot I hadn't told you. I didn't really tell anyone because it seemed so silly at the time. Then Mrs. Stein gave me such a talking to about Sunday's excursion that I didn't want to give her any more ammunition." Annie paused.

"Exactly what *did* happen?" Nate said between clenched teeth.

Annie decided that nothing but full disclosure was going to satisfy him at this point. So she told him about the downpour on the way back from her meeting with Miss Pinehurst, the crowded horse car, and then the shove as she started to get down at her stop. She finished by saying, "I wouldn't have thought anything of it, beyond someone trying to make their way off before the car started up. But then I found another note in my pocket, like the first one."

"Another note? What did it say?"

Annie, remembering that she had put the note in the desk in this study, turned, opened up the small desk drawer, and extracted a small piece of paper, handing it to Nate.

"Stay away or else," Nate read the words out loud. "And you didn't think this was serious enough to tell anyone about? Annie, that's ridiculous!"

"But you see, Nate, at the time it seemed part and parcel with the first. There is no chance that being pushed from a stationary horse car was going to do anything more serious than what did happen. I fell in a puddle and got wet, for goodness sake. Just the sort of prank I could imagine Eddie doing, for that matter."

Nate shook his head and said, "Annie, I don't understand. You keep mentioning Eddie. Who is Eddie?"

"Eddie is one of Evie May's . . . Flora Hunt calls them protective spirits . . . anyway, I told you about him showing up at the end of my first private sitting with Evie May. He said he was her brother. Then there is Maybelle, I told you about her, too, and Miss Evelyn, who Kathleen has met, as have I, and Edmund, the young man Kathleen ran into last week."

Nate held up a hand to stop her and said, "You keep talking about all these, whatever you call them, as if they were real. I thought you didn't believe in spirits and trance mediums."

Annie had to smile. She knew how ridiculous she must sound, and confusing, because she was confused. She tried to explain, saying, "When it comes to Evie May, I just don't know. Is it all simply make-believe by a troubled young girl? Or are these spirits of real departed people or some kind of angels sent to protect her, as Flora Hunt believes? I have gone around and around in my head, and I just don't know what I think. But I do know Arabella is a fraud, and Simon is trying to manipulate whatever is happening with Evie May to his own ends, and that those ends are evil. I need to tell you about tonight and what happened at the séance."

Nate put up his hand again, and she realized that he hadn't really been paying attention to her when he said, "No, Annie, what happened tonight is not the point. The point is that after you almost got killed, and, particularly in light of this second note, you shouldn't have gone to the séance tonight. You should have put a stop to all your activities connected with the Framptons."

He paused, looked down at the note, and then he said, "Annie, apart from this note, do you even have any concrete evidence of criminal activity that the police would take seriously?"

Annie saw this as an opportunity to try and get him to see things from her perspective, so she chose her words very carefully. "The Framptons are most certainly engaged in blackmail if you consider what we know about what Simon said to Mr. Vetch. In addition, Mrs. Larkson is falling apart, and you can tell that her cousin and Arabella Frampton are working together to put pressure on her to do something. Mr. Hapgood, the poor man, is at the breaking point. Tonight, Evie May, in the form of his mother, practically accused him of being responsible for her death. In fact, even

Nurse Herron was threatened by the spirit that addressed her."

"But this is all hearsay and circumstantial at best. Is there any evidence of blackmail, proof that the Framptons are benefiting in anyway beyond the fees they are collecting? Do you think Mrs. Larkson or Mr. Hapgood would be willing to swear out a complaint? Without that, I just don't know what you could do that wouldn't simply put your life in more danger. I'm not convinced this note, or the barrel incident, would be taken seriously by the police on their own."

Annie said, "No, we can't go to the police just yet. First of all, Mrs. Hunt told me that we need to be careful that Evie May doesn't get caught up in any police investigation. It might be disastrous for her. Flora needs a little more time to win Mrs. Nickerson's trust, in the hope she can get them both out from under Simon Frampton's control."

Nate said, "So there is nothing . . . "

Annie interrupted him. "Nate, I didn't get a chance to tell you yet. On Thursday, when Mrs. Hunt and I met Evie May and her mother, Mrs. Hunt brought along Mrs. Gordon. You remember, the woman who worked with Mrs. Foltz to get the state constitution to permit women to become lawyers. Mrs. Gordon is quite remarkable. She was a trance medium herself at one point; she's very active in suffrage circles, was a newspaper editor, and now is studying for the California bar. I really want you to meet her. I think you will be very impressed."

Nate again shook his head impatiently and said, "You aren't listening to me. I need to know if you have any evidence that the police could act on if we went to them."

Annie sighed. "Not really, nothing concrete."

Nate folded his arms and said, "Then that's it. I can't see that going to more séances or sittings or whatever you call them will do any good. You need to tell Miss Pinehurst you have done all you can, and you need to make it very clear to Simon Frampton, if you haven't already, that you will no longer be availing yourself of their services. In addition, you need to stay away from everyone connected to the Framptons, including Evie May. Let Mrs. Hunt and her friend handle that situation. They seem eminently suited to deal with it."

Annie's frustration rose at his unwillingness to take what she had been saying seriously. "Nate, I *have* agreed to stop going to the séances. I told Simon Frampton tonight, but I can't just let this go. At least two, if not three, of the members of the séance I attended are being deliberately frightened, most likely as a part of blackmail schemes. As is Mr. Vetch, so goodness knows how many of the others who have come under the Framptons' spell are in the same situation. You were the one who said we need to get someone to be willing to swear out a complaint, and that is only going to happen if I can meet and speak with them, try to get them to do so."

"Annie, Mrs. Larkson and Mr. Hapgood, or any other person who has voluntarily paid money to commune with spirits, are not your responsibility. But if you continue to make contact with them, it doesn't matter if you stop going to the séances. The Framptons will find out. Either they, or whoever is working with them, will take action, and the next time Dandy might not be there to save the day."

"But, Nate."

"No, Annie. Mrs. Stein is right. There were reasons you put your life in danger this summer. We all understood why. But this is not your problem. You have done as much as you can to help Miss Pinehurst, but she would never have asked you to help if she thought it would endanger your life. Who knows what further meddling on your part might do; it could even endanger her sister's life if the person behind the attack on you figured out the connection. You have been down this road before."

Annie felt like Nate had just slapped her. *How dare he? There was no comparison! How could he think this of her?*

She was fighting back tears when Nate reached out, grabbed one of her hands, and said, a clear note of pleading in his voice, "Please, Annie. I just want you to be safe. Not an unreasonable position for a man to take toward the woman he hopes will someday be his wife."

Shocked, Annie looked up at his face to see if she had been mistaken in what she had heard, and she saw that he was looking very earnestly into her eyes.

He rushed on, saying, "Look, I know I shouldn't be talking about this now, not yet, but I can't stay silent anymore. Annie, you must know how I feel about you, and I have held off saying anything because I just couldn't see my way clear to support a wife the way things are at the firm. But now there is a real chance that all that is about to change. Pierce has gotten me a meeting with Augustus Hart, the new state Attorney General, to talk about going to work up in Sacramento. This could give me invaluable connections with the Republicans, lead to who knows what. Maybe if the Republicans get back into office in the city in two years, I could get a job in the local city attorney's office, or I would have made enough of a name for myself to start my own firm. In any event, I would be financially secure enough to marry then."

Join the Republicans? Move to Sacramento? What is he talking about? Annie felt like he had just begun to speak in some foreign language.

When she opened her mouth to ask him to repeat himself, he raised his hands and said, "Please, let me finish, Annie. I've seen how exhausted you get, managing the boarding house and everything, and don't think I haven't noticed your growing dissatisfaction with having to work as Madam Sibyl."

"Nate, please . . ."

"No, Annie, don't pretend you don't feel uncomfortable with the pretense. No wonder you've gotten so upset with what the Framptons are doing. But that is what I want to save you from. If I get this job, and even if I don't and I have to find a job in a better paying firm, in a few years I will make enough so that you can stop working, sell the boarding house if you want, and have your own home and family, with me. You deserve that, and I want to give it to you."

"Nate, what are you . . ."

Again he ignored her and rushed on, and she heard him say, "...and because I care so deeply for you, because I hope that you will be my wife someday, I can't stand the idea of you being hurt. Surely, if you also care for me, you would want to consider my feelings in this, accept my right to ask you to stop doing anything that puts you in danger."

Without warning, there was silence, but the words kept reverberating in her head, stoking her anger. Bile rose in her throat, and she knew if she didn't get the words out, she would choke.

"I can't believe what I just heard," Annie said, snatching her hand from his. "Sell the boarding house, stop working? You don't understand me at all, or you would never ask that of me. So I get tired, and I have doubts about being Madam Sibyl. But how could you think I would want to hand over my life and my independence to anyone, even to you? I did that once, and it was nothing but hell on earth, for me and for him. And you want to join the state Republicans and kowtow to men like the Big Four railroad tycoons who fought the new state constitution? Just so you can support me? Work yourself into an early grave for some corrupt politicians, so I can sit by and do . . . what? Let my skills and brain atrophy? Nate, what were you thinking?"

Nate practically shouted at her. "I was thinking how much I love you, Annie."

"Love me? Nate, how could you?"

Suddenly, Annie knew if she didn't get away this instant, from this man who had turned into some stranger in front of her eyes, she would suffocate. So she turned, pulled open the door, and fled.

Chapter Forty-two
Saturday morning, November 1, 1879

"The Past is dead that was so sweet, Lost is the love, we called our own;
Our life has reached its noonday heat, The road is rough for weary feet,
And yet we walk alone." *Divided Lives—San Francisco Chronicle*, 1879

Saturated with unshed tears, Annie's head pounded as the old alarm clock rattled out the message that it was six in the morning and time for her to get up. Without opening her eyes, she swatted it silent. At least she had gotten a few hours of sleep. She had insisted on helping Beatrice and Kathleen clean up after the party, for her sake as well as theirs. She had calculated that if she worked hard enough and fell into bed late enough she would be too exhausted to think or feel and would fall right to sleep, which is what happened when she dragged herself up to her room at two in the morning.

She had sent Beatrice off to bed at midnight because she knew, no matter what, her friend would get up in time to produce a full breakfast for the boarders this morning. Biddy's cousin Tilly had stayed to help and, in fact, slept over, since Annie was not about to let her go home alone. This meant that Kathleen could sleep past her usual five o'clock rising time because Tilly would be here to help out this morning.

I really must figure out a way to hire her for at least twenty hours a week. She is such a help to Kathleen, and the training she will get will be invaluable.

That thought led too closely to the fantasy she had been building of a shared life and shared income with Nate that would have made hiring Tilly a much easier proposition, so Annie sat up and opened her eyes. The sun hadn't risen yet, and, filtered by fog, the light from the gas lamp across the street had only succeeded in turning the room a ghostly gray. She closed her eyes and remembered the bright colors of last night: the red, orange, and yellow flickers of the bonfire flames, echoed in the garishly carved pumpkins that lined the fence; the ruddy red of the pile of apples, gleaming in the light of a full moon; the rich browns of cakes and cookies, filled with walnuts and figs and raisins; and the flashes of blue, green, and scarlet from the dresses worn by girls who had shed their somber servant garb for their "night out" best.

Then she opened her eyes again, and all the color of her world was gone, snuffed out by reality.

When Annie had left Nate in the study, her intent had been to flee upstairs to her own room, but halfway up the first flight of stairs she ran into Kathleen, who had been looking for her. Some of the older guests were leaving and wanted to thank her for hosting the party. Once she was back down in the kitchen, she realized she didn't have the luxury of indulging her emotions, so she moved into a place that had become quite familiar territory when she lived with her in-laws, where there simply was no connection between what she felt and how she acted.

As she stood near the back gate, giving hugs and handshakes to various members of Beatrice's and Kathleen's families, Nate had walked up to her and said stiffly that he was afraid he needed to leave but that he hoped she would be available if he called on her the next evening to continue their conversation. Annie hadn't been able to do anything more than nod and watch him disappear into the night.

That was when the colors of her world had disappeared.

She dreaded today. Last night, she had managed to forestall any questions by Kathleen and Beatrice as to why Nate had left so precipitously. When Esther started to come up to her at one point, Annie simply shook her head, and the older woman had looked distressed but turned away. Today, the questions would come, and Annie didn't know what she was going to say to the three women who cared so much about her. She couldn't tell them Nate asked her to marry him but that he had ruined any chance that this would ever happen.

Esther, why did you have to meddle? How different things might have been if you had just let me tell him about the barrels in my own way.

She really had planned on telling him last night, when they had some privacy, and she had hoped that she could convince him that if she stopped going to the séances she would be safe. He wouldn't have been so upset and angry; he wouldn't have felt he had to justify his anger by telling her that he hoped to make her his wife. *He wouldn't have told me that he wanted to marry me to rescue me from my life. Save me, that's what he said.*

But wasn't it good that Nate's true feelings came out? What if she had been fooled a second time by a man's professions of love? *Sell the boarding house?* How could he imagine she would want to sell this house? What would happen to Beatrice and Kathleen? Did he not even care about them? Or did he simply expect that they would be happy to come work for him in the grand house he'd build in the Western Addition with the new vast wealth he was going to amass, feeding at the Republican party trough?

She knew he was unhappy with his work at the law firm, unhappy that his uncle wasn't taking any of his suggestions seriously, but she never imagined that he would be willing to sell out and work for either political party. She was sure he had agreed with her distaste for the political corruption that seemed inevitable in a state so dominated by the wealth of the Nevada Silver Kings and the Central and Southern Pacific Railroad.

But maybe everything he had said had been just to please her, while he was busy thinking that it would all change when they married. Isn't that what men did when courting, tell the woman anything to get her to say yes? John certainly had. All the claptrap about being partners in life, when he'd clearly thought she was some sort of idiot who would be content to defer to him in everything, even as he systematically gambled away her fortune. She'd thought Nate was different.

I can't believe Nate expected me to quit working. How could he know me so little?

She supposed she should be impressed he was sensitive enough to have caught her growing disillusionment with being Madam Sibyl. She wasn't sure anyone else had figured that out, but to think she wanted to quit working altogether? He'd seemed genuinely shocked at how she had responded. He'd thought that the fact that he loved her was enough.

Why isn't it enough? Because I don't love him? But was that true? If she didn't love him, why did she feel like her world had turned to ashes at the thought of him leaving the city, moving to Sacramento, being away for years? She had hidden, even from herself, how hard it had been the month and a half he had been at his parents' ranch. She had told herself that it was the emotional backwash from the events of the summer that had drained the joy from her days, not his absence.

But love isn't enough, not if I don't trust him, and how can I trust him if he doesn't respect who I am, the life I have made for myself? If he thinks I need to be saved from that life ....

She had given him permission to call on her tonight, but she couldn't imagine that it would make any difference, and she hated the idea of having to go through another emotional upheaval. If she knew anything about human nature, the blow to his pride would have festered, and he'd try to bully her into admitting she'd been the one at fault, that she had misinterpreted what he'd said. Maybe he'd cancel, be too embarrassed to come. After all, he'd said he loved her, and she hadn't said she loved him in return. How could a man with Nate's pride ignore that? Maybe he'd never come again, just send round a note and end the relationship by mail. Wouldn't that be easier for them both?

*****

The note came two hours later, as Annie prepared to meet with her first client. She was sitting in the small study, putting the finishing touches on the wig and cosmetics that turned her ordinary coloring and features into those of the exotic Madam Sibyl. Kathleen came in and handed her an embossed envelope, delivered by messenger.

He'd sent his regrets. He had another engagement that had to take precedence. He'd signed it, "Sincerely, Nathaniel Dawson."

Then, and only then, did Annie cry.

*****

A flash of pale light stabbed up from the floor, and the trap door slowly opened and was thrown back. The girl emerged and carefully lowered the door closed. The room glowed dimly with morning light. She went over to the trunk and opened the lid, pulling out a warm jersey and a pair of pants. Stripping off her nightgown, she changed and then rooted around for a cap, a pair of stockings, and shoes. When she found them, she first pulled on the cap and then put on the stockings and shoes. She next went over to the window facing the back yard. She tugged at the window, getting it to move up with great effort. She took a rope that was lying coiled on the floor, found the end that had a slipknot already tied, and looped the coiled rope over her shoulder. She stood and looked out the window for a few minutes. Abruptly, she climbed onto the windowsill and disappeared.

Chapter Forty-three
Saturday evening, November 1, 1879

"In Monday's *Chronicle* was a full exposure of the Calabasas Land and
Mining swindle, whereof George C. Perkins, Republican machine and
railway candidate for Governor, is a leading director."
—*San Francisco Chronicle*, 1879

Nate stood and looked with discontent at his reflection in the mirror.
He had to stoop down to get a full view of his face, just one of the myriad
inconveniences provided by his room in Mrs. McPherson's boarding house
on the south side of Telegraph Hill. Others included a bed that was too
short, a rag rug that seemed to have been made out of scraps of burlap, a
three-legged table with mismatched legs that frequently dumped off the
piles of books he placed on it, an easy chair that was so low to the floor his
knees practically rose up to his ears when he sat in it, an oil lamp that
smoked, a wardrobe that was too short for his topcoats to hang without
bunching at the bottom, and a ceiling that sloped to such a degree that half
the room was unusable unless he crouched over like an orangutan.

His Uncle Frank had moved into this boarding house perched on
Vallejo Street nearly thirty years ago, and he had a well-appointed suite of
rooms on the second floor. When Nate had come up from the ranch to live
with his uncle while he attended Boys High, he had been given this room,
one of four carved out of the attic. For some reason, no one, himself
included, had questioned that he would return to it six years ago when he
came to work in his uncle's firm after finishing his Harvard law degree.
What had seemed a spacious palace to a boy, who had previously shared a
small room and a bed with his brother, now felt like a shabby prison cell.

A prison with a distinctly unpleasant odor, compliments of the boiled
cabbage the cook was making for dinner. A dinner, thank the Almighty, he
wouldn't have to sit through because Anthony Pierce had sent round a note

this morning asking Nate to join him at Franklin's Steak House, where local Republicans were celebrating their state-wide victories against the Workingmen's Party and the Democrats. A dinner where Nate was to be given a chance to meet with either Augustus Hart or his chief of staff, Jaffry, about a job in the attorney general's office. *If only the dinner had been last night, the disaster with Annie might have been avoided.*

At least it got him out of having to call on her tonight. He'd regretted having asked to see her as soon as he had left the party yesterday evening. When he got the message from Pierce this morning, he'd sent her a note canceling their appointment. She was probably relieved, and he didn't know what the hell he would have said to her anyway. What was there to say? He'd poured out his hopes and dreams, told her he loved her, and she'd acted like he had insulted her. If she wanted to see him, let her make the first move.

Nate brushed his hair back behind his ears and grimaced at his reflection. The bright light from the oil lamp threw his features in stark relief. Features that supposedly came from some maternal ancestor and had caused his brother Billy to call him Tecumseh, after the Shawnee leader who had come from their home state of Ohio. Billy, of course, had inherited their father's good looks: regular features, blond hair, and normal height. *Would she have reacted differently if I looked like Billy?* Nate stood up straight and turned away from the mirror, angry that he'd even had the thought. He respected Annie too much to think that his appearance or some part of his bloodline had anything to do with her rejection of him.

Checking to see that he had his pocket watch, he then pulled on his tailcoat, grabbed his top hat, and left his room, negotiating the narrow attic stairs. He'd told his uncle earlier in the day that he wouldn't be home for dinner, so he felt no need to stop off and see him in his rooms on his way out. He had noticed his uncle had been very distracted, showing no interest in the news that Nate had been invited to a Republican Party event, and Nate couldn't help but wonder if he had been preoccupied with thoughts of the newly widowed, and very beautiful, Mrs. Voss. How ironic if his uncle's love life was flourishing while his own lay in ruins. *Damned ironic.*

He left the boarding house, crossed the street, and turned left, going the half a block to where the incline became so steep on the way to the top of Telegraph Hill that the cross street that should have been Kearny was simply a set of stairs going down to the intersection at Broadway. Nate nodded to a young man leaning over a fence at the top of the steps, enjoying a cigarette and a breather from the climb. Then he made his own careful descent down stairs that were barely illuminated by a gas lamp at the bottom. Pierce had written that the dinner was to start at seven, and he was a little late, so once he made it down the stairs he lengthened his stride to make up time on the six blocks down Kearny to California, where he came to Franklin's Steak House.

As he approached the entrance to the restaurant, he could see a crowd of men, all in formal evening wear, chatting as they made their way through the door. He noticed there seemed to be some sort of functionary vetting the new arrivals. He was about to ask the man in front of him if he was supposed to have brought an invitation when Anthony Pierce slid in line beside him, clapping him on the back.

"Dawson, glad to see you could make it. Got you a seat at one of the back tables, going to be a lot of big wigs here tonight, was lucky to get seats at all. You would think that the Republicans actually just won the citywide races, given the turnout. Maybe they see this as the start of the push to retake the city." Pierce just nodded to the man at the door and in they went.

The low roar of male voices, the haze of cigar smoke, and the distinct smell of grilled beef assaulted Nate as he followed Pierce into the main floor of the restaurant. Several tables had been pulled together at one end of the room for the most important attendees. Nate recognized two of the Central Pacific Big Four, Stanford and Crocker, sitting there. Huntington was probably off lobbying in the nation's capitol. With a start, Nate remembered Hopkins had died in the spring. Andrew Hallidie, whose cable car had made it feasible for both Stanford and Crocker to build their mansions high up on Nob Hill, was also sitting at the table, as was William

Alvord, new president of the Bank of California and the last Republican to hold the mayor's office.

As Nate caught up to Pierce, who was leaning over and talking to a dark-haired man with a very bushy black beard, he noticed that there was one man at the front table he didn't know. When Pierce straightened up, Nate nodded towards the front of the room and said, "Pierce, who's the young fellow up there? I don't recognize him."

Pierce chuckled. "If all goes as planned, that's your new boss, Augustus Hart, not a day over thirty. One of the reasons I thought you and he'd get along; you're both young bucks out to make names for yourselves. Here, take a seat next to Smitty; he knows everything about everybody. I've got some business to attend to, but I'll be back after the speeches, take you up and introduce you. I don't see Jaffry, but I'm sure he'll be around later. He's the man to see."

Before Nate could respond, Pierce disappeared behind him. Nate nodded to Smitty and sat down just as a waiter delivered the first course to the table, fresh rolls and chowder. Smitty introduced all the men at the table, who represented nearly every local newspaper, and Nate realized he was at the press table. He wondered if he was sitting in Pierce's seat and, if so, where was Pierce going to eat? Looking around, he noticed the ceaseless motion in the room caused by a number of men who seemed to be less interested in dining than in wandering from table to table, shaking hands, swapping jokes, and whispering urgently into other men's ears. Pierce, no doubt, was doing the same.

Without asking, Smitty took the carafe sitting next to him and poured him a glass of red wine, saying, "Franklin's spending a bundle on this dinner, can't see what he's going to get out of it, with Kalloch and his crowd in power for the next two years. Of course, must be damned near a hundred men crammed in here tonight, and if even half of them come back and bring their wives, he'll be judged a success. Chowder's not bad, but the proof will be in the steak."

Nate nodded, thinking that anything would be better than the meals his landlady served. Smitty, throughout the next three courses, provided a steady stream of sarcastic remarks about the men in the room: how much they were worth, who had a mistress, who had lost money when the Comstock mine shares dropped, who had gotten a chance to meet privately with Grant when the former president was in town, and who hoped to get a job in Sacramento when Perkins took over the governorship. At this point, Smitty had looked at Nate and winked and continued on about Perkins' various business interests in railroad and steamship companies, cattle ranches, timber, and mining investments.

I wonder if Annie knows about Perkins' oil exploration? I'll have to remember to tell her, Nate thought, then the sirloin in his mouth turned to sawdust. He'd only courted a woman once before, the sister of a law school friend, and that was eight years ago. After Miss Foster had rejected his offer of marriage, he'd never seen her again, much to his relief since he'd found the whole experience one of mortal embarrassment. *Is that what is going to happen with Annie?* Would he never see her again? A wave of nausea threatened to overwhelm him, and he reached out to drain the glass of wine. There had to be a way to fix this. He just needed to figure out what went wrong.

The sound of a glass being tapped began to penetrate the noise that had steadily risen as the wine had been consumed. Eventually, the conversations around him died down, and the former mayor began to make a speech. Nate looked around the room again, struck by the self-satisfied look on the faces of the men, satiated by Franklin's steak and vintage wines and congratulating themselves for having weathered the series of economic blows the city and state had undergone in the past decade. Then he remembered the frustration Annie had expressed that so many of the city's wealthiest citizens showed no pity for their workers when the bad times came and then worked against the new constitution because it included the mildest of reforms.

Why in heaven's name did I assume she would be pleased about my plans to join up with men like this? No wonder she was upset. Although Annie came originally from this segment of society and spent a good deal of her time as Madam Sibyl advising men and women of this class, she had been scathing in her condemnation of the corrupt domination of state politics by the railroad and silver millionaires and their allies. There he'd been daydreaming about how, with her social skills and background, she would be able to help him in his political career, when throwing dinner parties and acting the gracious hostess to men like these would have been an anathema to her. And just how was that supposed to work if they were men who had been to Madam Sibyl for advice? She must have thought he wanted her to quit working as a clairvoyant because he didn't want it to hurt his political ambitions. That wasn't what he had been thinking, was it?

Nate looked at Hart, a lawyer only a year older than himself, sitting at the front table with men like Crocker and Stanford, and he wondered how Hart had gotten to that exalted position so quickly. Had he been born to that class, and did family connections get him there? Or had he done something for one of these men that resulted in a payoff in the form of political office? Maybe he was being too hard on the young man. Hart could be an idealist, hoping to clean out the excesses of the previous Democratic administration, but how could a man in politics today afford to go against the interests of the powerful men sitting at the table with him? Wouldn't Hart have had to make certain promises even to get nominated for the office, much less elected? What sort of promises would Hart expect of Nate?

What in the hell was I thinking? Nate asked himself as he pushed his chair away from the table and stood up. Smitty looked up in surprise but then turned back to the speeches when Nate mumbled something about a call of nature. He looked briefly for Pierce. He owed him some explanation for leaving, but when he couldn't find him, he left the restaurant anyway.

*****

In less than twenty minutes, Nate was standing in front of Annie's door, his heart pounding. There was enough light coming from the parlor window for him to check his watch, and he saw it was just a few minutes past eight. Hopefully, not too late to call. Hopefully, not to late to explain what a fool he had been.

When Miss Kathleen opened the door, she looked so surprised that Nate had the terrible thought that Annie might have given instructions to be permanently "not at home" when he called.

He had just begun to ask if Annie was available when she blurted out, "Mr. Dawson, whatever are you doing here? You just missed Mrs. Fuller."

He thought, *That's odd. Where would she be at this time of night? Is she just being kind, not telling me that Annie won't see me?* Not willing to give up, Nate said, "Miss Kathleen, is there any chance I could wait for her? Do you know when she is going to be back? It's imperative that I see her."

"But Mr. Dawson," the young maid said, looking puzzled. "She's gone to meet *you*. Mrs. Fuller didn't leave but five minutes ago."

"Meet me? What do you mean? I sent her a note earlier telling her I wouldn't be able to come tonight, but . . . wait, that wouldn't explain . . . are you sure she said she was meeting me?" Nate's confusion increased.

"Yes, sir. I saw the telegram. It asked her to meet you at Nielson's Restaurant at eight-fifteen. Something about the Framptons."

"That just doesn't make sense. I didn't send any telegram, and I certainly wouldn't ask her to go across the city to meet me at some restaurant. Damnation! Oh, excuse me, Miss Kathleen, but what mischief has your mistress gotten herself into this time?"

Chapter Forty-four
Saturday evening, November 1, 1879

"HOW TO RIDE A BICYCLE: Practical Instructions for Managing the Steel Steed."
—*San Francisco Chronicle*, 1879

Annie got off the car at Bush and Montgomery and looked around, momentarily dazzled by the bright lights and crowded thoroughfare. This intersection was at the heart of the theater district, and carriages intermingled with venders hawking flowers and salted pretzels. Meanwhile, small dogs and boys ran shouting after a few young men who were riding down the street on high-wheeled bicycles, ridiculous contraptions that were probably as dangerous as they looked. Annie shuddered, thinking of what would happen if Jamie got it into his head he wanted to try one. She didn't think his legs would be long enough, but that never stopped a boy from trying.

The sidewalks were, if anything, more crowded, with throngs of pedestrians weaving around jugglers, hurdy gurdy men, and fruit sellers. In the midst of all these people, Annie felt suddenly conspicuous, the only unaccompanied woman she saw, without a husband or beau at her arm or even a female friend to lean on. *I'm just being stupid, feeling sorry for myself,* Annie scolded herself.

For some reason, all day she had let the mixture of anger, embarrassment, and deep sadness she had been feeling cut her off from her friends in the boarding house. What did it matter that she no longer could plan a future of visits to Woodward's Gardens or carriage rides in Golden Gate Park with Nate? She could still look forward to cozy chats with her friends in the kitchen. And there wasn't any reason why she and Barbara Hewitt couldn't expand their friendship to include Saturday night strolls along Kearney and Montgomery, looking at the bright store fronts, buying one of those tasty pretzels, or even saving up to splurge on a matinee at the Belle Union Theater.

She noticed a bright yellow Omnibus car slowly climbing up Sansome and moved to the corner to be ready to climb on board. Since most of the traffic was coming the other way, she was able to find a seat on the car. She looked at her watch and saw that it was ten after eight; she would be late.

Serves Nate right. Whatever possessed him to send her such a cryptic telegram at the last minute, giving her not a moment to spare if she was going to meet him on time? Now that she had nothing to do but wait for the Omnibus to make its slow way to Vallejo Street, she finally had time to think about how odd it was for Nate to ask her to meet him at a restaurant. Why couldn't he have just come to her house if he had learned something important about the Framptons?

Maybe he felt embarrassed, assuming that she would have told everyone about what occurred last night. It couldn't be pleasant for a man to think that other people knew he had proposed and been rejected. But was that even what had happened? While she certainly hadn't responded the way he had wanted, had she actually said no? How could she, when he hadn't really proposed, just told her he wanted to marry her?

You really made a mess of it didn't you, Nate? she thought, now able to see a glimmer of humor in the whole ridiculous situation. No wonder he didn't want to come to the house. Could the reference to the Framptons have been just an excuse to get her to meet elsewhere? He wouldn't be that devious, would he? Or stupid. Surely, he'd realize how angry she'd be if it turned out to be a ruse. Then again, last night he had proved how little he understood her, so maybe he was being that foolish.

Sell the house, quit working! All she had to do was think about this and her blood began to boil. Yet, absurdly, it was his blithe assumption she wouldn't mind if he moved away to live in Sacramento for years before they married that had gotten her most upset last night.

Annie closed her eyes for a second, feeling sick when she remembered the panic and pain she'd seen in his face, knowing that, however misguided he had been about what she wanted, he did care for her and that her response had hurt him.

No, I will not go into this meeting feeling sorry for Nate Dawson, she chided herself. He had said he had information on the Framptons, and she would make sure they stuck to that topic. They would be in a public place, and it would be completely inappropriate to talk about anything personal. *Yes, that's the approach I will take.*

Annie noticed that the car had made the turn on Washington, and they were now going right through the middle of China Town. This early in the evening, lights still streamed out from every storefront, and the narrow sidewalks and alleys were crammed with people and livestock, illuminated by brightly colored paper lanterns. She thought of Wong, the one resident of China Town she knew, and how wonderful it would be to see him, with his grave smile, get on the car. Would he be shocked if she sent him a letter? When the car turned to go up Stockton, they left China Town behind, and the incline began to steepen somewhat. As the car slowly rumbled through the intersection with Broadway, she got up and made her way to the front of the car, ready to get off at Vallejo where Nielson's was located.

She wondered whether Nate had chosen this restaurant because it was near the boarding house where he and his uncle lived. Could someone who had been attending the Frampton séances have agreed to meet him at his home to talk to him? Perhaps he thought he could then convince this person to meet her at a nearby restaurant, knowing she would be reluctant to have anyone come to her house but be equally unwilling to meet them at his home. In those circumstances, the restaurant made sense.

When she stepped down from the car and watched it continue on its way up Stockton, she noticed how much darker it was here in the residential section of the city. The street lamps were further apart, the few stores were shuttered, and only an occasional beam of light spilled out from the narrow row house windows. Ready to cross Vallejo, she looked to the left and had her breath taken away by the sight of what looked like a ladder of lights climbing into the sky. In a moment, she realized she was looking at the gas lamps climbing up the steep eastern front of Russian Hill. When she looked to the right, she saw a similar effect as Vallejo made its way up the slope of Telegraph Hill. From comments Nate had made about the steep climb to his boarding house, she concluded that he lived three or four blocks from where she was standing.

However, he was probably already at the restaurant, and she really should get going. She began to walk quickly towards Nielson's, which was on the corner of Columbus Avenue and Vallejo. The restaurant had a nice green-striped awning and gilded sign that glittered under the corner street lamp, and there was a couple just coming out of the entrance, letting loose a burst of conversation and clinking china. Annie hesitated when she got to the door of the restaurant. She had assumed that Nate would be waiting for her outside, and she didn't want to go in if he wasn't there yet. Looking at her watch again, she saw it was now almost twenty-five minutes after eight. Given how late she was, he might have simply gone inside.

Just as she put out her hand to grasp the brass door handle, a young boy ran up and said, "Mrs. Fuller? The gentleman asked me to give you this and said could you come straight to the house. He's waiting there."

The boy was just a little taller than Jamie, and he wore an enormous cap that nearly covered his eyes. She noted that his hand was very grubby as he thrust a small folded square of paper at her, which she took with surprise. She looked at the paper and then thought she ought to give the boy a coin for his trouble, but when she looked back up from her purse, she saw he'd flown, running down Columbus, quickly disappearing from view.

How odd! It's not like Nate to be so rude. Maybe this is his way of throwing my desire for independence in my face.

She unfolded the paper and saw the number 506. This must be the number of his boarding house, and it would put the house well up the hill. She picked up her skirts and, waiting impatiently for a hansom cab to pass, she crossed Columbus and walked quickly by a large imposing cathedral, which she registered distractedly as St. Francis of Assisi. Once she crossed Grant, she stopped to look for the numbers on the doors to her left. There wasn't another street lamp between the one she was standing under and one way at the top a very long and steep block, and the moon wasn't visible yet, so she wanted to get her bearings before she went any further. She was definitely in the right block.

She began to climb past a series of row houses, whose front stoops came right down to the sidewalk. Both sides of the street featured the same architecture, as if they had all been built at the same time, and there didn't seem to be anyone out and about at this time of night.

A disconcerting slab of emptiness loomed ahead, as if one of the houses had disappeared, and Annie found her heart beating more rapidly until she figured out that it was the entrance to a tiny alley. She hurried past the dark void and felt better when she saw by the house numbers that she was more than halfway to her destination. She was surprised to see the entrance to a second dark alley, just about six houses up from the first, but was heartened to see that several yards up one of the houses had a lighted lamp next to the door. *I bet that's Nate's boarding house. He would have certainly made sure the light was on for me.*

Chapter Forty-five
Saturday evening, November 1, 1879

"October: On the 11th an unknown man died in the City Receiving Hospital from injuries received at the hands of parties unknown."—*San Francisco Chronicle*, 1879

Nate was out of breath, cursing at what just three weeks out of the saddle and behind a desk had done to his stamina. He'd gotten a horse car pretty quickly to take him back to the center of the city, and there he'd made the decision to head up two blocks on foot and pick up Columbus Avenue, the new street that cut diagonally up from Washington to North Beach, like a miniature Market Street. Assuming that Annie had taken the Omnibus, which ran on tracks that still followed the old indirect zigzag path, he hoped to reach the restaurant about the same time she did. Within sight of his destination, he looked at his watch and saw it was twenty-five after eight. He had certainly made good time, but he was feeling winded and very disheveled.

Coming up to the intersection at Vallejo, he couldn't see any sign of Annie standing outside Neilson's. Maybe he had actually made it here before her. As he crossed the street, he looked west to see if she was walking up from the stop on Stockton, but the sidewalk was empty. However, as he looked to the right to make sure there weren't any carriages coming down the hill, he saw the figure of a woman pause under the street lamp at the corner of Grant and Vallejo. He was sure it was Annie; he would recognize that erect carriage and absurd hat anywhere.

Why was she going up Vallejo? Would she be looking for him at his boarding house? Could this all be some elaborate scheme on the part of her matchmaking friends to get the two of them together?

Nate smiled at the thought. He could believe it of Mrs. O'Rourke, Mrs. Stein, and Kathleen to plan something this outrageous. They were formidable women. *But, oh, how angry Annie would be!* Yet it really didn't make sense that they would trick her into meeting him at his home. They were much too careful of her reputation.

Nate's anxiety, which he had been holding at bay ever since Kathleen told him about the telegram, spiked, and he picked up his pace. Annie was now almost half way up the hill, just past the first of the two alleys that branched off Vallejo, and she seemed to be speeding up. He was now close enough to shout, and he had just opened his mouth to do so when a dark figure darted out of the second alley, and, in a blink of an eye, Annie disappeared.

Time first slowed to a nightmare pace as Nate sprinted up the half a block to the second alley, then it sped up as he rounded the corner and saw Annie struggling with a man trying to pull her deeper into the dark shadows of the alley. His only thought was to distract her attacker, giving Annie a chance to escape. So he came at him from behind and wrapped his arms around him, pinning the man's arms and using his own greater height to lift him off his feet. He felt more than saw Annie break away because suddenly the man felt lighter and began to twist and kick in his arms. Nate shouted at Annie to run as he threw the assailant to the ground, just as he would do with a calf ready to be branded. He followed the man down and was trying to grab his arms and flip him so that he would be face down when he felt a sharp stab down his left side. Nate, seeing the knife in the man's right hand, worked to get control of that arm while the assailant began a series of sharp jabs at his kidneys.

Nate had never tried to do serious damage to another human being; in fact, most of his fights had been with Billy, and he was always trying not to hurt him. But when he heard Annie scream and realized she was still in danger, he knew this was a fight he needed to win, at all costs. So he smashed his right fist into the man's face and, using the brief disorientation this caused, grabbed the wrist that held the knife and snapped it, taking the knife from the now useless hand and throwing it down the alley.

Annie's attacker, who was now screaming in pain, head-butted him in the face and kneed him in the groin, the combination temporarily weakening Nate's concentration. Before he regained his breath and his focus, the man lurched out from under him, gave him a savage kick in the ribs, and then ran down the alley, disappearing around the corner. Nate as trying to straighten out of the fetal position and stand when Annie appeared at his side. He gasped out, "Help me up. I need to follow him."

"No, Nate, let him go. You're hurt and in no shape to run after him."

With sheer will power, he refrained from checking his privates and got to his feet, using Annie's shoulder to help him rise to a semi-standing position. His head swam, and he thankfully leaned on Annie, taking shallow breaths to combat the nausea that threatened to overwhelm him. In a few moments, he felt able to stand up straight, and he cupped her face with his hands, whispering, "Annie, love, are you all right? Did he hurt you?"

She rubbed her cheek against his left hand, like a cat, and said softly, "I'm fine, just shaken. Oh, Nate, who was he? Who would have known about your telegram telling me to meet you here?"

"Annie, I swear, I never sent that telegram. Thank heavens I happened to come to your house right after you left, and Kathleen told me about the message. This was clearly a trap of some sort."

Having noticed a streak of dark wet material along her cheek, he said anxiously, "Annie, is that blood? You *are* hurt. He had a knife. Did he cut you?"

"I don't think so. We need to get in better light. Nate, it's your hand. There is a deep wound. We need to get you to a doctor." Annie pulled out a handkerchief from her coat and pressed it into his palm, closing his fingers over to keep it in place.

She then began to tug at him, pulling him out of the alley onto the sidewalk. "Hurry, Nate, where's the nearest doctor in this part of town?"

Nate put out his hand to slow her. "Annie, I'm sure it's just a scratch. Look, my boarding house is right up the street. Let's go there. One of the other boarders is a medical student. He can take a look at me, and we can make sure you are all right as well. Would that be acceptable? I will ensure that my landlady attends us. It will be entirely respectable."

Annie turned quickly, gave his arm a little shake, and said, "Nathaniel Dawson, you are the most absurd man I have ever met. You just saved my life and almost got killed in the process, and you are worried about propriety? Sometimes I want to kill you myself. Now hurry up. If you bleed to death, I swear I will never forgive you."

*****

For Annie, the next few minutes were a jumble of confused thoughts that mostly focused on her unfavorable impression of Nate's boarding house compared to her own. A faint unpleasant smell of cabbage overlay a mustiness that suggested a house where windows were seldom opened or carpets cleaned, and the front parlor that Nate led her into was crammed with very ugly furniture, which appeared to be from the previous century. The maid that Nate summoned was slow to arrive, surly, and only when Nate yelled at her did she grudgingly go upstairs to get the medical student and the owner of the boarding house to come downstairs.

When the servant finally left the room on her errand, Annie rounded on Nate and exclaimed angrily, "How can you and your uncle live here? This is awful. I would be ashamed to charge anyone room and board for such dismal surroundings and service."

Later, Annie admitted to herself that her anger really came from her mounting terror that Nate had been badly hurt. While he insisted that she take off her coat in order to check to make sure she hadn't been cut, she knew he was the one who had suffered grievous harm. She could see a trickle of blood coming down his brow, a swollen bruise already appearing along his right cheekbone, and the handkerchief clutched in his left hand was bright red. When he reached up to pull the cord for the servant, he had winced and put his hand to his side, shoving aside his tailcoat. She'd had to swallow a small scream when she saw that there was fresh blood on his shirtfront.

In a mercifully short time, the medical student, a short stocky fellow with an enormous ginger handlebar mustache, came clattering into the room, satchel in hand. He took one look at Nate and said that they had best go to the kitchen since this looked like it might be a messy business. That was where Mrs. Randall, the cook, and Mrs. McPherson, the boarding house owner, found them a few minutes later.

Annie wasn't sure which woman was more outraged, but this was something she could handle while the medical student, Mitchell—she never did learn whether this was a first or last name—attended to Nate. Annie told the cook, using her mother-in-law's most imperious voice, that she needed to get a basin and fill it with hot water. She then directed the maid, who had just straggled into the room, to get some of the clean kitchen rags. Finally, she announced that the two servants would then assist Mitchell in any way he required.

She then turned to Mrs. McPherson and thanked her profusely for offering to stay with her while Mitchell attended to Nate, saying, "I didn't know what else to do. We were just leaving Nielson's and looking for a hansom cab when this man accosted us, and Mr. Dawson bravely fought off the assailant. As you can see, he was hurt, and I didn't feel I could wait until we got to my home to attend to him, yet he was worried about my reputation if we came here. I assured him that no one would question *your* propriety and that all would be quite right if I was under *your* protection. Therefore, I am quite in your debt. I couldn't stand to leave until I know that Mr. Dawson's injuries have been attended to, but with *your* presence here, no one would dare say a word. Thank you so much."

Of course, Mrs. McPherson hadn't agreed to act as chaperone, but Annie had long ago discovered if she told someone how wonderfully they were behaving, they were usually too embarrassed to do anything else but comply with her wishes. Although she longed to go over and supervise Mitchell, she saw that the cook had stepped in and was holding the basin while Mitchell seemed to be cleaning the wound on Nate's hand.

Instead, she asked if Mrs. McPherson could direct her to the facilities so she could clean herself up. Mrs. McPherson nodded graciously and announced that "the girl" would show her and then would make them both a nice cup of tea.

After washing her face with tepid water and re-pinning her hat in front of a dusty, smudged mirror, she returned to the kitchen to discover that Nate was now sitting shirtless while Mitchell was wrapping a piece of gauze around his palm. The cook and the servant were standing by looking quite appreciatively at Nate's well-muscled torso, and Annie confessed to herself it was really quite an imposing sight. She wouldn't think that a man as tall and lean as Nate would be so well proportioned. No wonder he had been able to pick up that wretched man and throw him down like he weighed nothing.

Mrs. McPherson moved in front of her, clearly taking her chaperone duties seriously, and directed her to a chair, where she would be sitting with her back to Nate and his ministering angels. Then, as the landlady poured out a cup of tea, she kindly told Annie that Mitchell had said that the wounds on Nate's side and his hand were shallow and that, although the side would need a few stitches, no important tendons or blood vessels had been damaged.

By the time Annie had finished her drink, Mitchell had completed his work, and Nate had come up behind her to thank Mrs. McPherson and to say that he would now be escorting Mrs. Fuller home. He put his right hand on Annie's shoulder and squeezed hard, and she shut her mouth. Just this once she would take his lead without arguing. The poor man certainly had had a difficult night. It was the least she could do.

While Annie was thanking Mrs. McPherson and her servants for their support, a sharp exclamation from Nate caused her to turn around swiftly, and she saw him standing looking down at his hands, which held her coat. She said, "Nate, I mean, Mr. Dawson, what's wrong?"

Nate looked up at her, shook his head, and said, "Excuse me, I need to run upstairs and change out of this shirt. I will be right down." He then left the kitchen.

Annie laughed and said to Mrs. McPherson, "How like a man, he took my coat with him, will probably put it down somewhere, and we will be delayed looking all over for it." She then went over to shake Mitchell's hand, saying in a low voice, "Thank you so much for everything you've done. He's going to be all right, isn't he? Will it hurt him to take me home?"

"He won't want to walk very far, but otherwise, he'll be fine," Mitchell replied. "I'll check on him when he gets back. Mostly he's going to be very sore in the morning." With that, Mitchell smiled, closed up his bag, and left.

Annie was forced to use the time waiting for Nate to continue to flatter his landlady, which required her to utter a series of whopping great lies, praising the good taste of the house's decor and the efficiency of its servants. She was enormously relieved when Nate returned and they were able finally to leave.

As they stepped onto the sidewalk, she experienced an unexpected wave of fear. Clutching Nate's arm, she said, "Oh, dear, you don't think there is any chance that man is still around, do you?"

Nate put his arm around her and said, "No chance at all. You see, I broke his wrist. He won't be doing anything until he gets it set. And he'll no doubt have to report to whoever sent him after you. But we must talk, now, before we get in a cab. I need to know exactly what the man said, what he looked like, and we should consider whether or not to go to the police."

"*No police!* Can we even be sure he was after me specifically? It wasn't just a robbery?"

"That's what I want to determine," Nate said. "Look, if we go up Vallejo to the top of the hill, there is a bench that overlooks the Bay. We would be private. After our talk, we can walk back down to Columbus where, at this time of night, there should be plenty of cabs. It's only a quarter past nine. I could still have you home by ten-thirty."

Annie agreed but began to regret this decision when she saw how slowly he was walking up the steep hill and how stiffly he was holding himself. As they reached the bench at top of the street, she barely registered that they had a view of the whole moonlit Bay from this vantage. Instead, she focused on the ragged sound of his breathing.

This was a bad idea. I should insist that he take me right home so he can go to bed, she thought. But she wasn't ready to leave him. She was still too shaken. She couldn't yet get the images out of her mind, Nate struggling to grab the knife and then being savagely kicked as he lay curled on the ground. *Whatever would I do if he'd been killed?*

Annie moved in close and felt Nate's arms encircle her, and she stood there, listening to the beatings of their hearts.

Chapter Forty-six
Saturday evening, November 1, 1879

"A Night Ambush: Murder of C.L. Peterson by Unknown Assassins: An Unknown Woman and a Half-emptied Revolver the Only Clues."—*San Francisco Chronicle*, 1879

The moon had climbed considerably higher by the time Annie stirred in Nate's arms and said, "If you still want to ask me questions, you'd better start. If I am too late getting home, Beatrice is going to start worrying. Shall we sit down?"

What she really wanted to do was lift her head to be kissed, but that would make a declaration she wasn't prepared to make yet. The events of this evening had changed everything and nothing. She did know that now was not the time to examine her emotions or act on them.

Nate sighed and stepped back, leaving her chilled. He said, "Let's sit here. Will you be warm enough?"

"Yes, this is a wool coat. I'll just button it up." Annie walked around the bench to sit down. "That's odd, one of the buttons is missing. I hadn't noticed."

"That's not all you didn't notice."

Nate's voice sounded strange to Annie. Harsh, angry. She started to ask what he meant when he took her right hand and placed it over her heart. Shocked by the intimacy of this gesture, his hand, heavy and warm, pressing her hand against her left breast, Annie didn't register at first what her fingers were encountering, until her index finger snagged on an opening in the material.

"My goodness, my coat seems to have a tear in it! Must have happened when that man first grabbed me. I wonder if the Miss Moffets will be able to repair it?"

Nate had removed his hand from hers as soon as she began to speak, so she was able to pull the coat material out to look more closely at it.

"It's not a tear," he said sharply. "I had a good look at it when I went up to change. It is a slit from your assailant's knife. I think it must have caught on your button, which probably deflected it. Otherwise, you might have been severely wounded, even killed."

Annie sat down heavily on the bench, stunned. "You don't think it was just a random robbery, do you?"

Nate sat down beside her. "No, I don't. Did he say anything about taking your purse?"

"No, he didn't. He just said my name." Her heart rate accelerated. "Oh, he knew who I was! I had forgotten that." Annie paused, trying to recreate those first moments when the man had appeared at her side and grabbed her, his hand over her mouth, her feet scrabbling to get some purchase, her arms pinned to her side.

Nate said, "Annie, I think we have to consider the possibility that this was a deliberate attempt on your life."

Annie burst out, "I just have difficulty believing that! Maybe it was another attempt to frighten me off."

Nate shook his head sharply. "Look, I could buy that the notes, the push off of the horse car, maybe even the barrels were all designed just to frighten you, scare you away from the Frampton séances. But tonight was different. Someone arranged that you be in that place at that time, so he could stab you."

"A trap, you said that earlier," Annie said, her words no more than a whisper.

"A trap, because I didn't send the telegram. Someone else did, obviously someone who knew that a message that mentioned the Framptons would get you out at this time of night. I guess by picking a restaurant near my home, they hoped to convince you it was legitimate. But why were you going up Vallejo?"

"Oh, I forgot to tell you. When I got to Nielson's, a young boy ran up and asked my name, and then he said you wanted me to come to the boarding house. He gave me a piece of paper with your house number written on it. Then he ran off."

"So all your attacker had to do was wait in the alley for you to pass by."

Annie thought about this and said, "It makes sense that the Framptons, or someone working with them, would use a telegram from you to lure me since they know we are working together. But what if you had been visiting me this evening, as was planned? How did they know you weren't at my place?"

"Because the man who assaulted you followed me tonight," Nate said, sounding surprised at his own conclusion. "It seems obvious to me now. You see, when I left home tonight, I noticed this fellow loitering on the steps that lead down to Kearny. I would swear he was the same man as the one in the alley. If he followed me, he would have seen me enter Franklin's Steak House. I was attending a Republican Party dinner. All he would have had to do, once he saw me go into the restaurant, is continue down two blocks to the Western Union office and send the message."

Annie frowned, trying to picture the sequence of events. "But it all seems so risky. I might have not been home, or I might have refused to respond to the telegram or decided to take Kathleen with me," she said.

Nate shifted on the bench, as if in pain, then he said angrily, "Don't you see? If you didn't come, there was nothing lost. He would have simply tried something else another time; and, if you had brought Kathleen, I don't suppose someone who was intent on murdering you would quibble at killing your maid."

The image of Kathleen's lifeless body, imposed on the real memory of a battered Nate sprawled on the ground in the alley, shattered Annie's delicately constructed calm, and she began to tremble.

Nate gathered her in his arms, saying, "Annie, love, it's all right; he didn't succeed. You're safe."

"Because you were there to save me," Annie whispered into his shoulder. "If you hadn't come, I would be *dead*."

"But I did come," Nate replied and pulled her closer.

Some time passed, and Annie's breathing gradually slowed. She then remembered the question that had been nagging at her, and she pulled back from his arms and said, "But why *did* you come? You said you arrived at my house right after I left, which is why you knew where to look for me. But why were you there?"

Nate looked out over the Bay, the moon bathing his face in soft light, reminding her anew of how the chiseled lines of his face made him look like a bird of prey. He moved uneasily next to her and didn't answer her question. After a few moments, she tried again, saying, "Nate, you said the man followed you to a Republican dinner, which I assume would have gone on for some time. So why did you leave early and come to my house?"

"Because, as I sat eating my steak and listening to the speeches, I realized what a prime fool I had been, and I needed to tell you right away. A fool to even think twice about getting involved in politics, to think you would be impressed if I did. I know you better than that. I know myself better than that. Looking at Crocker sitting up there, being praised for his brilliant business acumen and statesmanship, all I could think of was the poor Chinese workers who died building the Central Pacific and that petty spite fence he just built up on Nob Hill."

Nate turned back to her and continued. "I know there are good men in the Republican Party, even good men sitting at that dinner, but I also know full well that once a man asks for a job or a favor from the party leadership, he's expected to put party above principles. That's not the kind of man I am or want to be."

"Oh, Nate," said Annie, moving back into his arms, "I didn't think you were. But I still don't understand . . . Nate, what is that?" She pulled back again, shocked at encountering the feel of a leather holster at his side. "Are you wearing a gun?"

"Yes. I thought it best to be prepared, so I got it when I went up to change," Nate said, matter-of-factly.

Annie, pulling his coat open, made out in the moonlight the polished wooden handle of a revolver sticking out of an unadorned holster attached to a leather belt around Nate's waist.

"An 1860 Colt?" she asked, thinking she recognized the firearm her father always had in his saddle holster.

"My brother Frank's. He died at Shiloh. How did you know?"

"My father. He taught me to shoot with one. Said I couldn't ride alone on the ranch until I could defend myself against rattlers."

Annie remembered that when she first met Nate, he had reminded her of the strong, laconic ranch hands from her childhood. This first impression had faded, and she had begun to think of him as primarily an urbane gentleman. The colt turned the man beside her into someone both more familiar but also more dangerous than she had previously imagined.

"What do you think? Do we go to the police?" Nate asked after a few moments of silence.

"I don't know. What would we tell them? You said last night that there wasn't enough concrete evidence against the Framptons for the police to act on. Since they hold séances on Saturday evening, they would be sure to have firm alibis for tonight."

Annie looked out over the San Francisco Bay and sighed. "We don't even know for sure that it was the Framptons who were behind this. Why would they be? I already told Simon I was no longer going to attend the séances. It just doesn't make sense. And why aren't they going after you? It must be something from the séances themselves."

"I agree. So what if you exposed their methods? At the very worst, they would have to move on, which is what they probably did when they left England. You must have been close to uncovering a serious crime by them or someone else connected to the séances."

Nate paused and then continued, "If we could find the man who assaulted you, find out who hired him, that would help. But I don't know how to do that without bringing in the police, and I know you don't want that kind of exposure. I could leave *you* out, just tell them *I* was assaulted."

"I can't ask you to do that. Maybe Beatrice's nephew, Patrick, could help us. If you described the man, he might recognize some local hoodlum. Then we would have something specific to take to Detective Jackson."

"That's a good idea. We should also go over everything you've learned so far with Patrick, see if there is anything we've missed that would explain why you pose such a threat that someone would try to have you killed."

Annie shuddered. Every time Nate said those words, she felt a blow to the framework of her existence. How did she become a person whom someone wanted to kill? How did she go about her day, knowing some unknown person was out there plotting her death? *Some bad man.* In her mind, Annie heard Eddie, sitting across from her at Woodward's Gardens, telling her that Maybelle wanted her to watch out, because "the bad man isn't very happy with you."

Was it possible that Maybelle really was her own protective angel, her own lost child? For one moment, Annie wished fiercely that was true. Then her more rational nature kicked in, and she had a sudden frightening thought. If Evie May, even in one of her incarnations, knew who was behind the attacks on Annie, might not she be in danger as well?

Chapter Forty-seven
Sunday afternoon, November 2, 1879

"A Row between the Spiritual and the Material—The Dark Séance and
Paraffin Circle Exposed"
—*San Francisco Chronicle*, 1879

Annie sat at the small round table in her bedroom and looked at the
neat list of names that she had just written on a piece of paper, entitled
"Motives." Usually on Sundays, Annie attended the substantial mid-day
dinner with her boarders, the only meal during the week she routinely took
with the rest of the members of the house. Today, instead, she'd slept in
and had Kathleen bring a light luncheon to her room, thereby avoiding any
contact with either Beatrice or Esther.

She knew she was hiding from her friends, but she wasn't ready to
handle the outpouring of love and concern that would follow any attempt
to tell them about the events of last night. Consequently, she had main-
tained the distance she had established after the party, simply telling
Beatrice, who was nodding off in the kitchen rocker when Annie got home
around ten, to instruct Kathleen not to disturb her in the morning and to
convey her intentions to skip dinner to Mrs. Stein.

When Beatrice had started to ask about Nate and the telegram, Annie
had hardened her heart and told her it was simply a mix-up but that she
was very tired and was going right to bed. This was pretty much what she
said to Kathleen this morning when she prepared her bath. Thank
goodness, the young maid hadn't pressed her further and, since she was
needed in the kitchen, hadn't been there when Annie got into the bath and
discovered the bruises on her shoulders and ribs from the man's initial
mauling.

She had asked Kathleen if she had plans to see Patrick this evening
when he got off patrol, and when she told Annie he was stopping by the

house around seven, Annie then told her that Nate was coming over after supper and that the two of them hoped they would be able to speak with Patrick. Annie smiled to herself, thinking that this snippet of information would have to satisfy her friends for the rest of the day.

Meanwhile, she had promised Nate she would try to figure out which of the people she'd met at the séances might have committed such a serious crime that they would try to have her killed rather than risk exposure. Last night, she had thought that it would be difficult to find anyone who would have a sufficient motive. Today, she wasn't so sure.

First, there was Mrs. Larkson, with a grandmother who had conveniently died, leaving her money, and a mother-in-law, whose death must have been devoutly wished for. Mr. Sweeter could have been an accomplice to either of these women's murders or simply a blackmailer who wouldn't be happy with the idea of Annie's meddling. Then there was Mr. Ruckner who, according to Nate, had inherited a good deal of money from his wife, and Harold Hapgood, whose parents died and left him a thriving business. She supposed either of those men could have been murderers. Judge Babcock probably hadn't killed anyone, but he might be deranged enough to try to have her killed if he thought she might be interfering with his access to his beloved daughter.

Even Nurse Herron might have been responsible for the death of one of her patients, either on purpose or through negligence. Annie had trouble imaging Mrs. Daisy Mott as a murderess, but she certainly had a passel of dead relatives, and, who knows, maybe she would kill to preserve that special recipe for plum pudding. Of course, there was the fact that Maybelle warned her of a "bad *man*." However, she wasn't going to try to convince either Nate or Patrick that they should rule out all the women as suspects based on a message from Evie May or one of her protective spirits.

Annie was just trying to figure out if Mrs. Nickerson would have any reason to wish her dead when she heard a sharp knock on her door. Wondering if this was Mrs. Stein and if she could put this dear woman off any longer, Annie opened her door to see Miss Pinehurst standing there.

Her boarder appeared quite breathless as she said hurriedly, "Mrs. Fuller, I'm sorry to disturb you, but I just had to speak with you."

"Dear Miss Pinehurst, don't apologize. Do come right in and sit by the fire. You look positively frozen," said Annie. While Miss Pinehurst must have stopped in her own room next door to remove her hat and coat, it was patently clear she had recently come in from outside. Her usually neat hair was windblown, and her dark wool skirts were decidedly damp.

Annie ushered the clearly agitated woman over to sit in the armchair next to the fireplace, and she asked her if she could make her some tea, pointing to the cozy covered teapot sitting on the table where she had been working.

"That would be lovely, Mrs. Fuller. I am afraid I was so anxious to get back here to tell you my news that I walked all the way from Sukie's, and it's begun to drizzle."

As Annie added more hot water to the pot from the kettle that sat on the grate, Miss Pinehurst leaned forward, stretching out her hands to catch the warmth from the fire. Annie thought that, despite her disarray, the older woman looked particularly attractive. The cold air from outside had turned her usually pale cheeks pink, the dampness had coaxed her soft chestnut waves to frame her face, and her dark brown eyes positively snapped in the firelight. With shock, Annie realized that Lucy Pinehurst looked happy.

Putting the cup of hot tea down on the small side table next to Miss Pinehurst, she offered her cream and sugar. When this was declined, Annie pulled a chair over, sat down, and said, "Miss Pinehurst, please tell me, what's happened?"

"Mrs. Fuller, I don't know how I can thank you. Sukie has decided not to go to the Framptons, ever again, and it would have never happened without your help and God's blessing. Oh, Mrs. Fuller, after all these months, my Sukie's come back to us, and we finally prayed together for Charlie and her new baby. Truly her healing can now begin."

"Miss Pinehurst, I am so pleased. But tell me what caused this change of heart?"

Miss Pinehurst delicately dabbed at her now-moist eyes and then took a long sip of her tea. Leaning back in the chair, she said, "I believe all the details you gave me from your investigations on Sunday were the beginning. I wrote Sukie a letter; I knew she wouldn't listen to me in person. Mr. Vetch, her husband, said, although she threw the letter into the fire, she did so only after she read it. She again pleaded with him to come with her to the next séance, and he said that he would but only if afterward she would be willing to listen to any concerns he wished to express."

"She agreed to those terms? I'm surprised," said Annie.

"Mr. Vetch confessed to me later that he suspected that this had been a false promise on her part. Nevertheless, he could tell during Thursday's séance that she was paying close attention to the music and lights. He said, 'Your sister is not stupid. Once she knew how the tricks were done, it was hard for her not to see how fake everything was.' Of course, Sukie is also stubborn, so afterward she said that whether the lights and music were fake or not was irrelevant, because Charlie spoke through Evie May, and that was real."

"That was what I was afraid she would say. From my own experience, I can tell you that Evie May is hard to dismiss."

"Yes, but that is what was so unexpected. It was Sukie's private meeting on Friday afternoon with Evie May that shattered Sukie's belief that she was really communicating with Charlie."

Miss Pinehurst stared into the fire for a second, then continued. "Mr. Vetch did agree to go with her, but he told her that he could not believe that any son of his would ask him to betray the confidence of his employer and that if Evie May asked any questions about Mr. Ruckner or the bank, he would refuse to answer, and he would never come again."

"Oh my, what did she say?"

"Evidently, Sukie was so sure that Mr. Vetch had misunderstood what Simon had said to him that she promised she would stop pressuring him to come to any more séances if Charlie's spirit asked him to do or say anything unethical. You can imagine how upset she was when the supposed spirit of their son immediately began to ask his father questions about the financial soundness of San Francisco Gold and Trust Bank."

Miss Pinehurst laughed dryly and went on. "How absurd, to think of our dear six-year-old Charlie using terms like 'capitalization rate,' 'mining funds,' and 'secured personal loans.' Her husband is correct, Sukie is not stupid, and I can just picture how upset she must have been. Mr. Vetch said she angrily asked Charlie why he was talking this way. Didn't he want to tell his father how much he missed him, tell him about the lovely gardens he played in? Then she started to cry."

Annie said, "My goodness, the Framptons seemed to have overplayed that hand. They must have sensed that this might be the only chance they had to find out any information about Ruckner. I haven't heard a whiff of scandal about this bank. Makes me wonder what they know that I don't about the financial soundness of Gold and Trust?" *And is it important enough to kill for?*

"They are certainly up to no good. Even that child who pretends to be Charlie said so. Mr. Vetch told me today that when Sukie started to cry, the girl began talking in an entirely different voice and tried to comfort Sukie, saying that she was sorry, that the bad people had told her to say those things."

Annie started. "Bad persons? Did Evie May say 'bad people' or 'bad man'?"

Miss Pinehurst frowned. "I'm not sure, maybe it was 'bad man.' Anyway, just at that point Mr. Frampton whipped open the curtain, and Mr. Vetch said the two of them were hustled out of the room and the house, without any explanation."

"And that's when your sister accepted that the Framptons were frauds? How devastating for her!"

"Yes, her husband told me he feared for her life Friday night, she was so distraught. She couldn't stop crying, moaning that she had lost Charlie forever. He then remembered the kind note that Mrs. Hunt had sent him last week, asking if she could be of service. He sent for her first thing yesterday morning, and she came immediately. Mr. Vetch couldn't tell me exactly what she said to Sukie because they met in private. But he said when Mrs. Hunt led her out of her bedroom, Sukie looked at peace for the first time since Charlie died.

"Oh, Mrs. Fuller, she went to church this morning. When she slipped in beside me and held my hand throughout the service, I knew God had answered my prayers. I don't know how I can thank you, for you were surely his instrument in this."

Annie watched uncomfortably as Miss Pinehurst began to weep. She was happy for her, getting her sister back and having her faith confirmed, but it made Annie uneasy to accept any part in a miracle. She was trying to think of what to say when there was a loud rap on the door, followed by the precipitous entrance of Kathleen into the room.

The young maid looked startled to see Miss Pinehurst, who was hastily wiping away her tears, and she stood for a moment, speechless. Noticing Kathleen was wearing her good outfit and, like Miss Pinehurst, looked chilled and damp around the edges, Annie assumed she had been to afternoon mass. Annie also concluded that, like Miss Pinehurst, the young girl had news of some import to convey.

Annie got up and went over to her, saying quietly, "Kathleen, dear, what is it?"

After a brief curtsy, Kathleen blurted out, "Mrs. Fuller, you'll never believe it! Mr. Hapgood tried to commit suicide yesterday morning. Biddy said he drank down a whole bottle of laudanum and nearly expired, but his wife found him just in time. Do you think those spirits from the séance drove him to it?"

Chapter Forty-eight
Sunday afternoon, November 2, 1879

"Arthur R. Watterson, Massachusetts, aged 41, poisoned himself with
laudanum"
—*San Francisco Chronicle*, 1879

As Annie turned left on Hyde Street, she realized she had completely forgotten the promise she made to Nate that she wouldn't go anywhere in the city unescorted. When she'd learned from Kathleen that the Hapgoods lived only a few blocks away on Hyde, she had simply made the decision to go alone since this was officially Kathleen's afternoon off. She told herself she would stop in quickly, leave her card, and be home before anyone, including Nate, was the wiser. She doubted that Hilda Hapgood would see her, but Annie wanted to reach out to the poor woman, express her sympathy.

Kathleen had told her about meeting up with Biddy at afternoon mass and how Biddy described what she heard about Harold Hapgood's suicide attempt from Mrs. Nickerson the day before. This was Biddy's last week-end of work for the Framptons; she'd given notice last Monday. Evidently, Evie May's mother had gone to the Hapgood's for a planned visit yesterday morning and found the household in chaos.

The Hapgood's parlor maid, who had opened the door to her, had poured out the whole tale to Mrs. Nickerson, describing how her mistress had returned from the store that morning and found her husband lying in the upstairs bedroom, an empty laudanum bottle by his side, looking "dead as a doornail."

The maid had boasted that it had been her own quick thinking to run and get the doctor whose surgery was just "two doors up" that had saved him. Mrs. Nickerson had finally been forced to leave the Hapgood's home without seeing Hilda, but she had announced to the Framptons, in Biddy's hearing, that she was going to go back this morning to support her dear friend.

In less than ten minutes, Annie found herself at the Hapgood's home, an older Italianate, with the typical flat roof and cornice brackets. The whole house was a nondescript, light-brown color, with oddly contrasting black trim, and the flower boxes under each window were empty. Since this was Annie's own neighborhood, she knew the house had probably been built in the 1850s and would have a substantial yard hidden in the back. In the front, however, there was only a small portico over a front door that was only a few steps away from the sidewalk. Annie felt uncomfortably conspicuous standing under that portico, using a black iron doorknocker to announce her presence.

When the young parlor maid opened the door, Annie had her card ready to hand over. At Mr. Stein's insistence, Annie had calling cards printed up when she had opened up the boarding house, although she'd protested that she couldn't imagine she would ever again be involved in the elaborate social rituals of calling and exchanging cards. In the past year, she'd only used about ten of the fifty cards she'd had made. The maid took the card and, unexpectedly, asked Annie to step into the front hall while she went to inform her mistress of her presence.

Annie couldn't believe that Hilda Hapgood had told her servant that she was "at home" to callers. What was the girl doing? Trying to embarrass her mistress? Or just hoping for another audience for her tale of how she saved the master of the house from certain death?

Even more unexpectedly, Hilda Hapgood followed the maid down the stairs, grabbed onto her hands as if she were a woman drowning and Annie her life raft, and urged her to come and have a seat in the front parlor.

Once the maid had been sent away to get a tea tray, Mrs. Hapgood turned to her and said, "Dear Mrs. Fuller, I am so glad you called. I have been desperate to speak with you. You have heard about my husband?" Here she faltered. "How he tried to take his own life?"

Annie's heart went out to Mrs. Hapgood, whose pale good looks had turned gray with fatigue, and she reached over and patted her hand, saying,

"Yes, I heard, and I wanted to express my sincerest sympathies. I know how worried you were about his state of mind. Please tell me how I can help."

"If you could just tell me what went on at the séance on Friday night! I couldn't think whom else to ask. You saw how he left so quickly? He didn't even acknowledge I was there. Harold didn't come home until dawn, and then he was so drunk I couldn't get a word out of him. I'm afraid I was extremely angry. I just put him to bed and went on to open up the store, giving the maid instructions not to disturb him. Thank goodness, midmorning I remembered I had asked Mrs. Nickerson to tea, thinking that Harold would be at the store. My brother Karl said he could handle the clerking alone while I went home to leave her a note. I almost didn't go up to check on him."

At this point, Mrs. Hapgood broke down, and Annie moved over to sit beside her on the sofa, putting her arm around the woman's shoulders, rocking her gently, and remembering a morning six years ago when she, too, had returned to her own home and found that her husband, like Harold Hapgood, had been out all night, drinking. She'd returned from shopping and saw his coat on the hallstand, but she had just gone on through to the kitchen to put away the groceries. All she had wanted to do was sit down and rest her aching feet since she'd been up before dawn, trying to bring some order into her disordered household.

She'd had to dismiss Susan, their servant, months earlier. There just wasn't enough money, and no matter how hard she worked, John criticized her housekeeping. He got angry when there were too few courses served at dinner or there was a wrinkle in the tablecloth or he found dust on the mantel. When John got angry, he drank. Of course, by that time he was always angry: at the plummeting stock market, at the failing banks, at the bad run of cards, at the horse that didn't cross the finish line. Mostly, however, he was angry with her.

She remembered putting the kettle on, sitting down, and putting her feet up, thinking with disgust that John was probably passed out, fully clothed, on their bed. She was sorely tempted to just let him be, let him wake up in his own filth. But, when the kettle sang, she'd poured him a cup of tea and dragged herself up the stairs, responding to some remnant of her sense of marital duty.

She also remembered being puzzled when she had opened the door to their bedroom and found it empty. The smell emanating from the small study had then hit her. Burned gunpowder and raw flesh. Like Harold Hapgood, her husband had tried to take his own life; but, unlike Harold, he hadn't permitted any chance of rescue, no chance of redemption. Instead, a gun shot to the head was John's final, angry act against the wife he must have known would find his shattered body.

The servant's return with the tea tray brought Annie back to the present and prompted Mrs. Hapgood to compose herself. Wiping her eyes, Hilda directed the maid to come in and deposit the tray, then asked her to leave and ensure they would not be disturbed.

Turning back to Annie, she took a deep breath and said, "I'm sorry for my outburst, Mrs. Fuller. I guess I hadn't let myself consider how close I came to losing him. But I am frightened that if I can't figure out what caused him to decide to take this step, he will only try again. You see, this has happened before, when he was young; he tried to commit suicide when he was in college. I am so concerned; he won't talk to me, and he just lies with his back turned to the room, restlessly picking at the sheets. The doctor said that this is a normal response to an overdose of laudanum, but I know it is more than that."

"He certainly was upset by what happened at Friday's séance," Annie responded. "Unlike previous séances, this time it was the young medium, Evie May, who spoke to him, channeling the spirit of his mother. Somehow, she conveyed the impression of being a large woman, sitting in a chair. She had her hair up in a circle of braids and strands of beads around her neck. Her voice was quite shrill, and she had a heavy cane she kept pounding on the floor."

Hilda Hapgood gave a small cry, and she looked around the room, as if she expected to see the spirit of her mother-in-law appear in the parlor. She clutched at Annie's hands and said, "Tell me exactly what she said."

"Near as I remember, she first said that your husband deserved to die. Then she went on about having six sons and something about five of them dying and that your husband was the baby, her most precious child, until he turned his back on her. He cried out at that, said she had turned her back on him." Annie noticed that Hilda nodded vehemently at this last statement.

Annie paused, trying to recall what Evie May, as the old woman, said next. "I think she complained that you and your husband left her all alone while you went out on the town. Then she seemed to be describing the circumstances of her own death. She said she was cold because the fire in her room had gone out, that you were gone but that your husband was in a drunken stupor downstairs. Finally, she accused him of causing her death, that she died of neglect . . . I think she said that she suffocated, and then she very dramatically broke her necklace."

Hilda Hapgood moaned and then whispered to herself, "Oh, Harold, it was her. I didn't believe you, but there isn't any other explanation. She blames you, they all blame you, and they won't let you rest until you're dead. What should I do? What can I do?"

Annie, shocked at what she was hearing, tried to calm her down. "Mrs. Hapgood, please, even if it looks like this was the spirit of your husband's mother, I am sure there is a rational explanation. You need to tell me the precise details of your mother-in-law's death, and then we can figure out how the Framptons learned those details and who might benefit from using them to frighten you and your husband. Tell me, exactly how did your mother-in-law die?"

Mrs. Hapgood shuddered and then began to speak. "The doctor said it was heart failure. She had a very bad heart, but she continued to indulge her appetites. She weighed nearly three hundred pounds and hadn't walked on her own in years. With help, she primarily moved back and forth from her bed to a chair in her room. Harold and I had to wait on her hand-and-foot. She would pound that cane on the floor, morning, noon, and night. God, how I hated that cane. She'd hit you with it, if she felt you weren't moving fast enough to serve her.

"The morning of the day she died, Harold and I had a terrible fight. She'd hit me, hard, on the back when I brought her breakfast, and I'd told him I couldn't stand it anymore. I said we needed to move out of this house, live on our own again. We were already paying for a full-time cook, parlor maid, and nurse; we didn't have to live in the same house with her. I didn't care if we lived in a hovel, as long as I didn't have to live under the same roof as her."

"How did your husband respond?"

Hilda shook her head. "As usual. He repeated that he had promised his father he would take care of his mother, and he couldn't break a promise. I told him I was leaving, going back home. I even packed a small bag."

"Oh my," Annie murmured.

"I left, but I didn't go to my parents. I knew they would just say that I had to return; it was my marital duty. Instead, I walked around the city, and then I took the horse car out to the Cliff House and walked on the beach. It was a lovely June day; the sun didn't set until nearly eight. When I came back to the city, I had a late dinner at a small restaurant in North Beach. Then I came home. I had simply needed some time away."

Annie nodded encouragingly.

"When I got to the house, it was around ten o'clock. I found Harold passed out in this parlor. He hadn't had a drink in four years. I blame myself. He must have been devastated when I left. I ran up to check on his mother, to make sure he had put her to bed and given her the heart medicine she took every evening. There wasn't anyone else to do it because it was the nurse's night out, and our maid had been gone for much of the week because her mother was ill. And the cook doesn't live in. Harold told me later she went home around seven when he got back from the store and told her he wouldn't be wanting any supper." Hilda Hapgood stopped speaking.

Annie waited while the seconds slipped by, then she said quietly, "When you went up to check on your mother-in-law, she was dead, wasn't she?"

*****

The girl stood, holding onto the back of the chair, as if this was the only thing keeping her upright. She picked up a doll from the chair and held it fiercely to her chest, whispering harshly. She then looked up, glared, and pointed a finger at the man who stood, looking back at her, his face filled with curiosity. She said, her voice shaking so badly with anger as to make her words nearly incomprehensible, "You won't succeed. He tried to hurt our girl, but he failed. You'd better watch out, or your end will come very, very soon."

Chapter Forty-nine
Sunday, late afternoon, November 2, 1879

"J.D. Fay's Death: A Belief by Some of His Friends That He Was Murdered."

—San Francisco Chronicle, 1879

Annie knew she was pushing Hilda Hapgood to reveal a potentially damaging secret, but she also knew that this secret could reveal who was trying to torment Harold Hapgood to death and perhaps even who had tried to have her killed last night. So she waited, praying the woman beside her on the couch would give up her secret.

After what seemed an eternity, Hilda let out the breath she had been holding and said, "Yes. When I got upstairs, my mother-in-law was still sitting in her chair. At first, I thought she was just asleep. But when I said her name and gave her shoulder a little shake, her head flopped to the side. It was horrible! I ran and got the looking glass from the dresser, put it up to her mouth, and there was nothing. She couldn't have been dead long. Her skin was still warm to the touch even though the fire had gone out."

"What did you do then?"

"I know it's terrible, but all I could think of was the possible scandal if the doctor felt her death was due to my husband's neglect. So I went downstairs and, after much effort, roused Harold. When I got through to him that his mother was dead, he sobered up enough so that he could help me undress her and move her to the bed. While I can imagine this sounds awful to someone else, the whole process didn't differ much from what we went through each night. Afterwards, I straightened the room, picked up the pearls that had scattered, and . . . well, then we went to bed."

Mrs. Hapgood stared into space for a few moments as if she was reliving the experience. She then resumed speaking. "Marta, our nurse, returned from her night out early the next morning, and it was she who discovered her. We called in the doctor, and he said she had died of heart failure, which he had been expecting. He actually told Harold that our good care of her had probably given her an additional six months of life."

Annie said, "How did your husband react? Did he accept that his mother's death was inevitable, or did he feel responsible?"

"At first, we both felt such tremendous relief. We had been given our lives back, after eight long years, first taking care of his father, who had been bedridden by stroke, and then taking care of his mother. But then Harold got the invitation to go and attend his first séance. That was the beginning of all our troubles. When he came home that first night, he said that the spirit of his father had visited him and blamed him for his mother's death. He kept going back, and after a few weeks he began to say to me that if he hadn't gotten drunk and missed her medication, his mother would have lived. He even said the spirits also blamed me, for threatening to leave him, causing him to drink. I . . ."

Annie held up her hand, stopping Hilda. "Wait a moment. I can understand how the Framptons might have learned details about your mother-in-law, how she looked and acted, and the kinds of general complaints she made about the two of you. The servants, the nurse, or even friends of the family could be the source of that information. Even your husband's drinking problems might have been generally known. But who would have known the details about that night, that you were out of the house and your husband was drunk?"

Hilda shook her head, twisting her handkerchief in her hands. "Oh, Mrs. Fuller, no one. I've not told a soul until now. Only his mother would know, and she is dead. That's what frightens me. Harold is convinced it's the spirits of his parents and brothers who've been speaking to him. I kept telling him he was being foolish, but now, given your description of the last séance, I don't know what to think."

"Could Harold have told someone else, confessed to someone about your fight, his getting drunk, his mother's death?"

"Maybe. He has admitted to me that when he drinks he blacks out and can't remember much. But even he didn't know about the necklace. You said the girl broke her necklace and the beads scattered? You see, my mother-in-law always wore these multiple strands of pearls, and they had broken and fallen all over the room. I didn't notice them at first, and I must have picked them up on my shoes, because later I found a number of them all the way down the stairs and near where Harold was sleeping on this sofa. While Harold was drinking the cup of coffee I had fixed him, trying to sober up, I picked up all the pearls I could find, down here and up in her room, and I never told him about her broken necklace.

"I figured she must have had some sort of convulsion when she died, which caused the necklace to break, since her footstool and the table beside her chair were also knocked over as if she had thrashed about. I had to pick up all the little knickknacks that slid off. There was even a pillow from the bed on the floor."

Hilda paused and then said, "That's strange, I hadn't thought of the pillow before. How did it get on the floor behind where she was sitting?"

Annie pictured the room as Hilda described it, and she began to feel the stirring of an idea. She said, "Hilda, if someone, like the nurse, had come into that room the next morning and found it the way it was before you straightened up, the furniture turned over, the pillow on the floor, the pearls broken, they might have concluded that there was something suspicious about your mother-in-law's death, particularly if they found you missing and your husband blacked out on the sofa downstairs."

"What are you saying?" Hilda put her hands up to her mouth.

"I am saying that it would have looked like the pillow was used to suffocate your mother-in-law, and, in the struggle, the furniture was kicked over, the necklace broken. The doctor might not have just assumed she had died of natural causes, and he would have examined her more closely. If so, you and your husband could have become suspects in her murder."

"No, no, you're wrong. Harold would never have deliberately hurt his mother. How could you say that?" Hilda stood up and was looking down at Annie in horror.

Annie stood as well and put her hands on Hilda's shoulder, saying, "Mrs. Hapgood, please, listen to me. I am not saying I think your husband killed his mother, on purpose or accidentally. What I am saying is that it is possible someone else did kill her and wanted your husband to be blamed. Someone who knew you were out of the house, that your husband had blacked out and would probably not remember what had happened, someone who would have benefited in some way from either your mother-in-law's death or Harold being accused of it."

And someone who would try to kill the nosy woman who was helping a lawyer investigate the Framptons if they thought she was getting too close to the truth, Annie thought, remembering that the accident with the barrels came the day after she had visited Hilda at the store.

Annie drew Hilda back down on the sofa. Seeing the shock in the woman's face, she poured her out a fresh cup of tea, putting in several lumps of sugar, and handed the cup to her.

"Trust me," Annie said firmly, "the spirits conjured up by Arabella Frampton are not real. In addition, if your husband didn't know the detail of the pearls, and you haven't told anyone but me, then the logical explanation is that someone else was in the house that night. That person must have been the one who told the Framptons and asked them to use the information to terrify your husband in the séances. If one of your servants, perhaps the cook, came upstairs or your maid returned that day and saw what the room looked like before you cleaned it up, it is possible they might try to blackmail you and your husband. Has that happened? Is the maid who opened the door the same one who worked for you back then?"

"Yes, Betsy has been with us for four years. She isn't all that bright, but both she and the cook have been quite loyal to us these past months, despite our troubles. We pay them well, and their duties are so much more pleasant now that my mother-in-law is gone. But there hasn't been a hint of them having a secret or trying to get anything from us. Marta, the nurse, is actually one of my cousins, and I absolutely can't imagine her as a blackmailer. I also don't see any of them as murderers either."

"I would agree," Annie said. "Even if one of them acted out of anger, and your mother-in-law certainly sounds like someone who might drive someone to strike out, I can see no reason why they would be funneling the details to the Framptons. No, I think it is very possible someone deliberately killed your mother-in-law in the hope that you and your husband would be blamed. But, when you came home, which was not expected, and moved the body and cleaned up the room, so that the doctor declared it a natural death, they were stymied.

"Normally, a murderer would be delighted to have gotten away scot-free. But in this case, he or she might have seen the murder as a means to an end. The end being your husband's death. If they couldn't get your husband executed for murder, they hoped to drive him to take his own life. It has to be someone who knows about your husband's history with suicide. When your husband wasn't accused of murder, the real murderer must have turned to the Framptons, fed them the details about that night to create such fear and guilt in your husband that he would take his own life or, at the very least, drink himself to death.

"Mrs. Fuller, this is fantastic. Who would do such an evil thing? My poor Harold never hurt a soul."

Annie sat back, worried that Hilda was correct and that she had let her imagination carry her away. "I know the motive does seem to be the weak link. I suppose someone could have a secret hatred for your husband, but money is usually the motive, and I can't see how anyone but you would benefit by the death of both your mother-in-law and your husband."

"Mrs. Fuller, I may have disliked my mother-in-law, but I never wanted her dead, and Harold, how could you . . ."

"No, Mrs. Hapgood, you misunderstood me. I simply meant that I assume that you would be the one who would inherit if Harold died."

"Oh, no. The business and the house are all part of a trust, which Harold, in conjunction with the bank, administers. If Harold were to die, I wouldn't get anything beyond a few personal bequests."

"Really? How extraordinary. What happens when Harold dies? Who gets everything?"

Hilda frowned. "I think if we had a child, the child would inherit. But I haven't been able to conceive. Another reason my mother-in-law disliked me so." Her voice trembled. "In my heart of hearts, I believed that once we were finally out from under his parents' roof, we would be blessed by a child. Now, I just don't know."

"But if there were no child, what then?" Annie asked, feeling a pang of sympathy for Hilda, whose marriage seemed to have held nothing but unhappiness.

"I think that Harold said when his mother died that his father's sister and her offspring were named as the next beneficiaries. Harold felt badly about the terms of the will, that despite all the time and effort I had spent caring for both of his parents, his father had still cut me out of any inheritance. I tried to explain to him that I didn't care, that I hadn't married him to become wealthy."

"Does Harold's aunt live in San Francisco?"

"No. I think she lives in Missouri. You can't possibly think she is behind any of this. She must be in her eighties, and her son says she's in ill health." Hilda sounded shocked.

"Her son?"

"Yes, Harold's cousin Tony, he lives in San Francisco. He's really Harold's best friend, and he has been very kind the last few months, trying to help me turn Harold's mind away from his troubles. He came by immediately yesterday when I sent word to him about what Harold had done, and he talked to him a long time, trying to get him to see how foolish he'd been."

Annie said, "Is it possible that Harold might have told him about what happened the night his mother died? Or might he have stopped by that evening?"

Hilda looked uncertain, but she said, "I can't believe Tony would do anything to harm Harold."

"Does that mean that Harold might have confided in him?"

"Tony would be the one that Harold would turn to if he was upset. In fact, I wasn't surprised when Harold told me later that he thought he remembered seeing Tony sometime on the day his mother died, but Tony said later he'd been out of town, which is why he didn't hear of my mother-in-law's death for several days. He travels a lot as part of his job."

Annie's suspicions grew, and she asked, "What exactly does Tony do?"

Hilda said, "He is really quite famous. In fact, this morning when Mrs. Nickerson stopped by, she recognized him from this photograph of him and Harold."

She stood up and walked over to pick up a framed picture off the mantel, handing it to Annie and pointing to a short, squat man with a wild mane of hair, straggling mustache, and broad smile. "His name is Anthony Pierce. You may have heard of him. He is a featured reporter for the *San Francisco Chronicle*."

Chapter Fifty
Sunday evening, November 2, 1879

"Michael Shannon, a native of Ireland, aged 38, died in the city Hospital from the effects of a knife wound, inflicted by unknown parties. No arrests have been made."—*San Francisco Chronicle,* 1879

When Hilda Hapgood told her that Harold's cousin Tony was the journalist Anthony Pierce, Annie felt like someone had just leaned over her shoulder to put in the last piece of a puzzle, revealing for the first time a complete picture.

Anthony Pierce! Who better to work as partner with the Framptons? As a reporter, he could move with ease among his fellow San Franciscans, both high and low, and he would know where all the skeletons were buried: who had cheated on their spouses, neglected their aged parents, had a drinking problem, skimmed a little money out of the till, or fallen asleep when they were supposed to be watching a patient. In exchange, Simon probably gave him a cut of their proceeds, alerted him to possible scandals that might be turned into stories for the *Chronicle*, and did him the favor of directing a series of spirit messages to his cousin, Harold Hapgood.

She wondered if Pierce had made his arrangement with the Framptons before he planned the murder of Harold's mother, if it was even planned. He couldn't have foreseen Hilda leaving on that particular day and Harold getting drunk for the first time in four years. No, if her understanding of what happened was correct, this had been an impulse killing. He may have been looking for an opportunity for years, perhaps from the moment he had discovered that he would eventually inherit the Hapgood's fortune if both Harold and his mother could be gotten out of the way.

Then, as fate would have it, everything was handed to him, the perfect constellation of events. Hilda gone, supposedly for good after a fight over her mother-in-law; the servant and the nurse out of the house; Harold conveniently having imbibed to the point of blackout, probably encouraged by his dear cousin Tony. All Pierce had to do was go upstairs, suffocate the old woman with a pillow, leaving the evidence scattered about (she wondered if the trail of pearls down to the sleeping Harold had been his touch or just an accident), and let himself out.

As a journalist with police connections, he probably thought he could nudge the police in the right direction if the doctor didn't immediately alert them himself. But Hilda had come home, cleaned up all the evidence, and the doctor obligingly called it a heart attack, and any nudging of the police by Pierce would make him look suspicious. No, the Framptons must have simply been a fallback plan.

She wished she knew more about Pierce. What was his motive? Pure greed? Annie wondered how long Pierce would have been willing to pursue this indirect route, waiting for the spirits to drive Harold either to commit suicide or drink himself to death, before taking matters into his own hands and arranging an accident for his cousin. Perhaps he didn't feel the need to hurry events along while his mother was still alive and he was just a contingency beneficiary. But Nate had told her that the reason Pierce hadn't been able to meet with him at first was he was back home attending his mother's funeral. No wonder the spirit attacks on Harold had gotten worse in the past two weeks. The inheritance was now right within his grasp if Harold could just be gotten out of the picture.

Annie found herself curling her hands into fists at the thought of how Pierce had manipulated Nate. Had Pierce known from the very first that she was investigating the Framptons? She knew that Nate had been careful not to mention her name, but then he had shown up at the Framptons to escort her home. That had been at the end of the same séance when she found the first threatening note. It was possible Pierce had immediately made the connection between them if he had been at the Framptons that night. He had done that series of articles on local mediums and for-tunetellers, and he may have even checked Madam Sibyl out and remembered that she lived in Mrs. Annie Fuller's boarding house.

This would explain why Simon seemed to know about Madam Sibyl but didn't find the connection particularly worrisome. Pierce must have simply warned him that Mrs. Fuller had already had some dealings with a local rival. On the other hand, Nate's stated purpose in investigating the Framptons and finding out if they were engaged in criminal activity would have been what concerned Pierce the most at the start. When he learned of the connection between Nate and Annie, then she would have become more dangerous.

Oh, heavens, Nate would be so upset when he discovered that Pierce's promises to get him a job in Sacramento had probably just been a way to distract him from further investigations into the Framptons. Annie was glad Nate had already come to the conclusion he didn't want the job, less humiliating that way. For a moment, she let herself get distracted by the sweet memory of last night when he apologized for how seriously he had misread her. Thank goodness he'd come to that conclusion when he did and left the restaurant to find her, or she might be dead!

But why try to have Annie killed? Why not Nate? Pierce must have felt pretty confident he had been successful in distracting Nate. Annie, on the other hand, had persisted in coming to the séances, despite the threatening notes and the push off the horse car. She then reminded herself that the barrel incident happened the day after she visited the Hapgood's store and spoke to Hilda. *Oh my!* Hilda had mentioned a cousin who was bringing her husband home from the Monday séance. Annie would have to ask Hilda if she had mentioned her visit to Pierce. If so, Pierce would feel she was getting too close to guessing the truth.

This would mean the barrel incident really had been an attempt on her life, and the man that Jamie saw run away was most likely the same man who assaulted her last night. Not hard to imagine the reporter having connections with local hoodlums, any one of whom could be hired to do the actual killing. How upsetting for him when, despite the scare with the barrels on Thursday, she had showed up the next night for the séance, thereby witnessing Evie May's performance, which was obviously the climax of the campaign against Harold and would have been successful if

Hilda hadn't checked on her husband when she did.

Thinking of Evie May, Annie felt a spurt of anxiety. Once again, she couldn't get out of her head Eddie's message to her from Maybelle, warning her to watch out for the "bad man." If the "bad man" were Pierce, and he suspected that Evie May had been talking to Annie outside the confines of the cabinet, then he might see Evie May as a direct threat. Equally upsetting was the thought that Evie May's mother might have come to a similar conclusion as Annie had about the connections between Pierce, the Framptons, and what had happened to Harold Hapgood.

Hilda had told her that when Mrs. Nickerson saw the photograph on her visit earlier today that she had been quite excited and said what a surprise it was to discover that Harold was related to Pierce. Hilda described her as becoming very distracted and said she left quite quickly after that conversation. What if Mrs. Nickerson had decided to confront Pierce?

Her fear that Evie May and her mother might be in immediate danger had prompted Annie's decision to take a horse car straight to the Framptons, rather than to walk back to her boarding house so she would be on time to make her meeting with Nate. Having spent over an hour trying to explain her suspicions to Hilda, she knew it was going to be hard to convince Nate, or the police, for that matter, that Anthony Pierce was a murderer.

Oddly, what had finally persuaded Hilda that Pierce was behind everything was the discovery that his mother had died over two weeks earlier and that he hadn't mentioned this to either her or her husband. Annie couldn't count on Nate making a similar leap, and she didn't feel she could postpone her conversation with Mrs. Nickerson. As a result, Annie was hoping to talk Evie May's mother into removing herself and her daughter from the Framptons' house as soon as possible, for safety's sake.

Annie looked at her watch and saw that it was after six o'clock. Since it was Sunday, the Framptons' cook should have left the house by now, and everyone but Biddy should be above stairs getting ready to go out. If she went round the back to the kitchen, Biddy could let her in and maybe get a message to Mrs. Nickerson without alerting the Framptons. While it was possible Simon and Arabella had no idea that they were helping a murderer, Annie had no faith that they would care. All they would be concerned about was any threat to their source of inside information about San Franciscans or any negative publicity that might come their way. No, Annie didn't want to run into Simon or Arabella Frampton. Maybe she should just hang around outside the house until Mrs. Nickerson and Evie May left and follow them to wherever they were going to dinner.

Getting down from the horse car, Annie began to walk up Harrison, and when she had crossed Fifth Street she halted, seeing a great deal of activity going on in front of the Framptons' house. The sun had set about an hour earlier, and the moon hadn't risen yet, so the street was dark between the gas lamps. She moved nearer to the storefronts on her right and cautiously crept along until she was able to stop in the darkest part of the sidewalk, equidistant between the lamps on her side of the street.

Looking across the street, she could see that there was a wagon pulled by four strong dray horses and a large, four-wheel hackney, both illuminated by several lanterns hung on their sides. The wagon looked to be filled with boxes, and while she watched, Albert came out of the house at a trot, a large trunk on his shoulder. He was followed by a woman, who Annie guessed must be his wife, Arabella's lady's maid. She had two smaller valises that she handed to an unknown man, probably the cab driver, who began to strap them to the back of the hackney.

The woman returned up the steps to the front porch, and Annie saw Arabella in the light of the porch lamp move out of the house to meet her. She had on a hat and coat and was carrying another small valise, which she handed over to her lady's maid, confirming Annie's conclusion that she was witnessing the rapid decampment of the Framptons and their servants.

What could have happened to force them to leave so precipitously? Could they have known about the attack on Annie last night? Maybe Nate had gone ahead and reported the assault to the police. He had said that he could do so without involving her. The police could even have stopped by, spooking the Framptons into making the decision to leave town before an investigation went any further. Or could this be a reaction to Harold Hapgood's suicide? Certainly having a client try to kill himself wouldn't be good for a medium's reputation if it got out. But they had known about the suicide for over a day, and the activity going on in front of her looked like a very hastily organized affair.

Annie felt her heart spasm. Could this be the result of something Mrs. Nickerson said or did when she returned from visiting the Hapgoods earlier today? Where were Mrs. Nickerson and Evie May? The cab in front of the house wasn't large enough to carry six, but maybe Albert and his wife were going to ride on the wagon. Annie couldn't imagine Simon abandoning the young medium; she was too much of a financial asset to leave behind. And Biddy? Was she in the house helping with the packing?

Annie moved out of the dark and began to cross the street, impelled by an overwhelming need to find Biddy and Evie May and make sure they were all right. As she stepped onto the sidewalk, she saw Simon come down the steps, pulling on gloves. They must have been about to leave. As she walked up to him, she saw a start of surprise on his face, then a crooked smile that didn't quite reach those intense gray eyes of his.

He said, tipping his hat, "Mrs. Fuller, or perhaps I should call you Madam Sibyl? Why am I not surprised to find you here just in time to see us off? I am afraid that from the beginning I underestimated you, despite my lovely wife's misgivings. Was it just professional jealousy that motivated you? Surely there are enough good people in the city willing to part with their money that you didn't need to meddle in our affairs?"

So someone finally made that connection, Annie thought.

She said, "Mr. Frampton, I am sorry to disabuse you, but I have never considered us to be in the same profession. I don't make my living using other people's grief to blackmail or defraud them or drive them to suicide."

Simon shook his head vehemently. "No, you're wrong. I had no idea that this was his plan. What kind of fool do you think I am? If I'd had any idea . . ."

"Shut your mouth," hissed Arabella, who moved out of the darkness and grabbed Annie by the upper arm. "My stupid husband is forever being fooled by a pretty face. Don't think I don't know what your game was, with your private sittings and your outings to the Gardens? You wanted to set up your own business with the little bitch and her mother. She's all yours, much good she will do you." Arabella let Annie's arm go and started to pull Simon away, saying, "Leave her. We need to finish bringing out the suitcases. Albert is nearly done with the boxes."

Annie moved to follow them, saying, "Mr. Frampton, where is Evie May? You aren't taking her with you, are you?"

Simon didn't respond but followed his wife up the steps and disappeared into the house. Annie hesitated a moment, then went up the steps herself. The front door was wide open, and light from the lamps in the hallway spilled out onto the porch. She stood in the doorway until she saw Albert barreling toward her, his arms filled with boxes, and she then moved in and stood to the side. When Albert didn't say anything to her as he went by, she decided to investigate further.

She first looked into the séance room, which had been stripped of drapes, tablecloth, and candles. The furniture, which probably came with the rental of the house, remained, except for the cabinet. This was gone. Annie assumed it was an integral part of their equipment and was constructed to be easy to dismantle and transport. She then moved through to the back hallway, into the kitchen, looking for Biddy.

The kitchen was in much greater disarray. Cabinet doors were ajar, a canister of flour was on its side, dishes stood drying in the sink, and the lady's maid was on her knees methodically wrapping up pieces of china, using a stack of towels, sheets, and other linens to do so. When she asked the woman where Biddy was, she simply said, "Gone," and went on with her packing. The single-minded activities of Albert and his wife and their complete lack of interest in Annie reassured her. Annie left the kitchen, relieved that at least Biddy was safe, and she went up the back stairs to the second floor.

Here, there were additional signs of hasty packing. The doors to the rooms on both sides of the hallway were open, and what she could see of Albert and his wife's room suggested that everything of value had already been removed, except the furniture. Since she could hear Simon and Arabella talking in their room, Annie turned back to look in the room that Evie May shared with her mother. This door was closed, so she knocked. When there was no answer, she opened the door and was relieved to see that there hadn't seemed to be any attempt to pack in this room.

So Simon did intend to leave Evie May and her mother behind. Was it possible that Mrs. Nickerson didn't even know the Framptons were leaving? Annie had trouble believing that Evie May's mother would let Simon go without a fight. Maybe Simon was taking advantage of her absence to sneak out of town. She could very well imagine he would do almost anything to avoid the inevitable scene that the besotted woman would cause. Maybe the hastiness of this departure was nothing more than Simon's desire to escape Mrs. Nickerson's hysterics. No, all this activity felt like a desperate flight from some greater danger than a clingy woman, something she imagined Simon was used to handling.

And again, why leave Evie May behind? Could he be trying to re-move the girl from her mother? She looked more closely at the room and noted that none of Evie May's toys or clothing seemed to be missing. As she was about to leave the room, however, her attention was caught by a sound over her head. She then remembered there were steps that led to the cupola at the top of the roof and that Biddy had mentioned that Evie May used this square room as a sort of playroom.

Annie went and checked the door, which, unlike last Sunday, was unlocked. She opened the door slowly and listened. When she didn't hear anything more, she moved onto the first step and looked up, seeing a square of light at the top of a set of stairs that were so narrow and steep they seemed more like a ladder.

She must be seeing the opening of a trap door, and the light suggested someone might be in the attic. She hitched up her coat and skirts with one hand and began to move up the stairs, holding onto the steps above her with the other hand to counter the feeling she was going to fall backwards at any moment. Every few steps, she paused and listened. She heard nothing until she was about to reach the top. Then, just before she let her head rise above the opening, she heard a strange animalistic noise, a kind of growl that brought the hairs on the back of her neck upright.

Annie slowly took one more step up, putting her head above the level of the floor, breathing in a miasma of musty scents overlaid by a sharp metallic odor. At first, she was partially blinded by the bright light cast by a lantern that was sitting on the floor to her right, but as her eyes adjusted she began to make out a bundle of clothing about three feet directly in front of her. *No, not a bundle of clothes.*

With dawning horror, Annie realized she was looking at Mrs. Nickerson, lying on her side, her face whiter than any face powder could make it, her green eyes staring fixedly at Annie, and a thin trickle of blood, as red as the dead woman's hair, in a trail across the floor. A scream had begun to coalesce in her chest when she saw a hand holding a knife descend to touch the floor in front of Mrs. Nickerson's chest, followed by the bloody visage of Evie May, who laid her face gently down along her mother's face and smiled at Annie.

Chapter Fifty-one
Sunday evening, November 2, 1879

"Burned to Death: While O'Neil was absent from the house…his wife
upset the lamp, setting the house on fire, and she perished in the
flames."—*San Francisco Chronicle*, 1879

"Hello, nice lady," lisped Maybelle. "Eddie said your name was
Annie, and you aren't my mother. Annie's a pretty name but not as pretty
as Maybelle." As Evie May spoke to Annie, she sat back up behind the
body of her mother, and Annie could see by the light of the lantern that
blood was smeared down the front of the girl's white dress.

*Smeared as if she had clasped her mother to her chest, not spattered
the way the blood would look if Evie May had stabbed her*, Annie found
herself thinking, and her terror ebbed.

"Maybelle, dear, can you tell me what happened to your mother?"
Annie asked, slowly moving up the stairs so that she was now about
halfway out of the square opening.

"My mama left me. She said Papa could only have one princess wife,
and if he chose me, she would leave. So she went bye-bye."

Annie, confused, as she often was speaking to Maybelle, said, "I
don't understand, Maybelle. If she isn't your mother, who is that woman?"
She pointed to Mrs. Nickerson.

"Eddie says she's our mama, but I know better. Mamas tuck you in
and sing you songs, and they don't let bad men hurt you."

Annie restrained her desire to rush over and take the child into her
arms. Could Mrs. Nickerson possibly have been an impostor? No, if Eddie
said she was really Evie May's mother, that was more likely the truth.
Annie remembered Mrs. Nickerson's tale of woe about her husband's
illness and death and wondered once again if during that time Evie May
had suffered something more terrible than simple neglect. Was that when

she stopped seeing Mrs. Nickerson as her real mother?

Annie put her hands down on the floor in front of her and pulled herself to a crouching position, not wanting to stand up and startle the girl. She then said, "Maybelle, can you tell me what happened to the woman lying there?"

"She's sleeping with the angels," Maybelle said, gently patting the shoulder of the dead woman.

Annie gathered up her skirt and coat and shifted her weight in preparation to standing as she said very softly, "Maybelle, sweetheart, I would like to come over to you. Is it all right if I come and take your hand and help you come downstairs?"

"Yes, Annie, I would like that."

Annie stood up and had just moved carefully around Mrs. Nickerson's body when Maybelle continued, saying, "I'm glad you came. I don't like being here with the bad man."

Annie froze. Before she could say a word, Anthony Pierce walked out of the shadows and swung down to stand on the top of the stairs, the light from the lantern turning his odd features into a gargoyle level of ugliness.

He said, "Well, well, Mrs. Fuller, we finally meet."

Evie May stirred at her feet, prompting Annie to crouch down and put her arms around her protectively, saying, "Leave this child alone."

Pierce laughed. "Madam, I can assure you, I have no more desire to remain with that devil's spawn of a child than she has to stay with me."

Enraged, Annie nodded down at the body at her feet and said, "You killed her, didn't you? Just as you killed Harold's mother."

"Oh, my good woman, I think you will find it very difficult to get anyone to believe you. Don't you know that my dear, selfish, heartless bitch of an aunt died of natural causes? Of course, if you insist in revisiting that conclusion, my drink-addled cousin may be charged with contributing to her death through neglect, or even worse. As for the ridiculous nuisance of a woman lying before you, I think the fact that her completely demented daughter is holding a knife and is covered by her mother's blood will make her a much more likely candidate for the charge of murder. A fact I tried to explain to my dear partners, who have instead panicked and are scampering away like some frightened rabbits, breaking up the perfectly good business arrangement we had going."

When Annie shifted her weight, Pierce pulled a small derringer out of his pocket and said, "Please, no heroics. I do believe it is time to depart. Since you have been able to fool the usually wide-awake Simon, drive his beautiful wife into a jealous rage, as well as ensnare that stupid lawyer fellow, I suppose you must have a fascinating side to you; but I am afraid I can't stay and further our acquaintance."

Reaching over to pick up the lantern, he then began to back down the steps, keeping the gun steadily pointed at her. Finally, he pulled the trap door down behind him, plunging the room into darkness.

*****

"Sir, there are two ladies below to visit you. I have put them in the parlor."

The maid sketched a curtsy and gave Nate a speculative look before disappearing from the door to his attic room. He stood up from his chair and carefully put on his coat. Mitchell had redressed both his hand and his side this afternoon, but he could do nothing for his bruised ribs, which hurt like hell when he breathed deeply or made a sharp move. *Two ladies?* That was odd; he couldn't think of any woman who would be visiting him except Annie, but she had asked him to come to the boarding house at seven, so why would she be here at twenty after six? Accompanied by another lady? Mrs. Stein perhaps?

Since he was due to leave for Annie's momentarily anyway, he picked up his top hat and coat, taking them downstairs and hanging them on the hallstand before entering the parlor. There, he encountered two complete strangers sitting and talking with his Uncle Frank. All three stood up as he entered, and his uncle introduced the women as Mrs. Flora Hunt and Mrs. de Force Gordon. Mrs. Hunt was a tiny blonde who reminded Nate for some reason of a fairy sprite, and Mrs. Gordon was a tall, striking brunette, with a kind, round face and warm smile.

Nate shook hands with each woman, saying, "Mrs. Hunt, how pleased

I am to meet you, and I want to thank you for being such a help to Mrs. Fuller. And Mrs. Gordon, I am honored to meet you. I have followed your fight for women in the legal profession with great interest."

Nate's uncle put his hand on his shoulder and said, "Nate, my boy, why don't you go over there by the fireplace and sit with Mrs. Hunt while I continue the interesting conversation I was having with Mrs. Gordon about naturalization law?"

Nate, ignoring his reflexive irritation with his uncle's dictatorial style, graciously bowed and led Mrs. Hunt to the other side of the parlor, waiting for her to be seated before sitting down. As he did, he noticed distinct signs of agitation on Mrs. Hunt's part in the way she sat perched on the edge of her seat and fidgeted with her purse, so he skipped any conversational small talk and went right to the point.

"Mrs. Hunt, how may I help you?"

"Mr. Dawson, I am very concerned about our mutual friend, Mrs. Fuller. As you may know, I have spent my life with spiritual protectors, and just half an hour ago I got a strong message from one of them directing me to come to you and ask for your help on her behalf. Mrs. Gordon was visiting me. I looked you up in the city directory, and she and I just hailed a cab and came here as quickly as we could. Do you know of any danger that Mrs. Fuller is facing?"

Nate felt a brief flicker of anxiety, then, remembering he didn't believe in Spiritualism, he smiled and said, "As far as I know, she is safely at home, waiting for me to arrive for an appointment we made at seven." He paused and, seeing that Mrs. Hunt didn't seem to be reassured, continued, "However, just last evening she did confront a real danger. A man tried to kill her in an alley, just a few houses away from here. Perhaps this is what your . . . ah . . . spirit guide was telling you about."

Mrs. Hunt frowned and closed her eyes for a moment. Then she reached out and clasped Nate's hand, swaying slightly. Her eyes flew open, and she stood up, pulling Nate up with her.

"This isn't in the past. I see darkness, and there is a strong sharp odor of blood. She and the little girl need you. We must go."

Nate, startled at her vehemence, said, "Go where?"

Mrs. Hunt shook her head and said, "I'm not sure. You say she is supposed to be at home? Let's start there. Something terrible is going to happen. We must get to her soon."

*****

Oh, Nate, Annie thought, her heart pounding, *you are going to be so angry with me for getting into this predicament. And you'll be right. What was I thinking?* Gradually, Annie's eyes began to adjust to the darkness, and she became aware that on all four sides of the cupola there were sets of windows, letting in some ambient light. The girl leaned back against her, humming a familiar-sounding nursery rhyme. Remembering the knife in Evie May's hand, Annie fetched her handkerchief from her coat pocket and then let her own right hand move slowly down the girl's arm while she said, "Dear, may I take this from you?" Evie May nodded, and Annie carefully reached around with the handkerchief, pulled the knife from the girl's fist, and wrapped it firmly in the handkerchief. She then placed it in her coat pocket, not wanting it loose but feeling better having some sort of weapon at hand if Pierce should come back.

She looked around again, noticing a chair silhouetted against the windows to her left and a bulky, rectangular shape she thought might be a wardrobe to her right. She turned her head and saw a large trunk behind her. If there were any other objects in the room, they were lost in the deep shadows. The attic wasn't much more than ten feet square, and, since the windows all seemed shut, the air felt close and stuffy and the smell of blood unpleasantly strong. She also noticed a smell of excrement, her stomach turning as she flashed on the image of Pierce stabbing Mrs. Nickerson.

Annie wanted to go over and see if there was a way to lock the trap door or move something on top of it so Pierce couldn't get to them, but she didn't want to leave Evie May sitting next to her dead mother. She told the girl they were going to get up, and she could sit in the big chair where she would be more comfortable. When Evie May didn't respond, just kept on humming, Annie got on her knees and, with some effort, got to a standing position, wishing her long skirts in perdition. Next, she gently pulled Evie May up and guided her around the body on the floor. When they reached the chair, Evie May suddenly bent over and picked a ragged china doll and climbed onto the chair and started rocking it, reminding Annie she was probably still dealing with six-year-old Maybelle, not the older Evie May.

Annie watched her for a few moments and then walked slowly to the center of the room where the trap door should be. Kneeling down, she felt around for a handle, which she found quite quickly. However, there didn't seem to be any sort of locking mechanism. She decided to pull it up a crack to see if she could hear any movement in the room below, but when she began to pull, nothing happened. Tugging harder and harder, Annie realized that the door was not stuck but was locked from below.

Two can play that game, she thought, having little desire to descend to the rest of the house until its occupants were well on their way to wherever they were going. What she didn't want was Pierce to change his mind and return to the cupola, so she stood up and went to the trunk and carefully dragged it around Mrs. Nickerson's body and placed it squarely over the trap door. She then made her way over to the unexpectedly dust free front windows to look down into the street.

The combination of the street lamps and the lanterns on the wagon and hackney lit up the scene below as if Annie were watching a play from darkened balcony seats. The wagon was now piled high with boxes and trunks, and Albert was climbing around, strapping everything down with ropes. Evidently, he wasn't doing it to his good wife's satisfaction because the lady's maid was standing in the street, gesticulating vigorously.

Finally, Albert jumped down from the wagon, threw a coil of rope at her feet, and stomped out of view. Annie could practically hear the curse words that must have filled the air. Only a moment later, he returned with suitcases in each hand, which he handed over to the hackney driver who was standing at the back of his cab, looking at the growth of appended cases and trunks that had sprouted at the back and top of his vehicle. Annie felt a pang for the horses and hoped they weren't going any further than across town to the docks.

Then Simon walked into view, and the three men seemed to be conferring over where best to place the suitcases when their heads all turned in unison to the lady's maid, who was pointing upwards at the house. Annie took a hurried step back and then realized there was no way that anyone could see her in the darkened room. She moved back to the window and saw that Arabella had joined the other four, and all of them were clustered in the middle of the street, pointing and shouting, clearly upset by whatever they saw in the house.

That was when Annie first smelled smoke.

Chapter Fifty-two
Sunday evening, November 2, 1879

"Record of the Alarms Sounded During the Year: There were 274 alarms given, of which 223 were fires, 7 second alarms, 17 false, 20 chimneys, 6 bonfires, and 1 falling building."—*San Francisco Chronicle*, 1879

Kathleen ran down the alley to the gate at the back of the boarding house, laughing because she'd beat Patrick there.

"Slowpoke! And don't tell me it's because you have been on your feet patrolling all day." She stretched up on her tiptoes to give the young, red-haired police officer a kiss on his freckled nose.

Patrick grinned and scooped her up in his arms, planting a warm kiss on her mouth, and she playfully drummed on his shoulders with her fists, noticing how broad he'd become in the last six months they had been courting. *Courting!* How grand that sounded! She'd started out just having fun teasing Beatrice's nephew, who had the habit of stopping by to cadge sweets from his indulgent aunt. With his carrot top, freckles, and ready smile, he'd just seemed like a good-natured boy. As he'd become more attentive, shyly asking her to accompany him to a dance or a walk down to Market Street to the confectioners for some ice cream, Kathleen had been careful to let him know she'd no interest in getting serious, ostentatiously walking out with several different boys.

Then this summer when they helped Mrs. Fuller and Mr. Dawson with their investigation, Kathleen had become more and more impressed by his quick wit and ambition. He had a drive to better himself, carrying around books to read when he took a break on patrols, studying the rulebook on his off days. She was proud of him.

Patrick put her back down on her feet, frowned, and said, "Miss Hennessey, a penny for your thoughts!"

Kathleen felt herself blush, but she laughed and said, "Mr. McGee, my thoughts are worth a good deal more than a penny. Besides, we'd better go on in. Mr. Dawson should be here by now."

As they walked through the gate, Kathleen could see into the kitchen window and was surprised to recognize Biddy standing there, waving her hands around excitedly. A deep foreboding hit her, and she ran across the yard and pushed the back door open.

Mrs. O'Rourke, who was standing in the center of the kitchen, whipped around and said, "There you are. Biddy's come to say that the Framptons are packing up to leave town in a mighty hurry. She thought Mrs. Fuller should know, but she isn't in her room, wasn't here for supper. Do you know where she is?"

Kathleen's mind raced. She'd stopped by the boarding house after mass, around 3:30, and found Mrs. Fuller in her room talking with Miss Pinehurst. After Kathleen had interrupted them to tell her mistress about Mr. Hapgood, she had left the house by the front since she was late to a planned meeting with her younger brother and didn't want to get delayed talking to Beatrice. Kathleen figured Mrs. Fuller would tell Mrs. O'Rourke the news if she wanted to. It wasn't for her to be the go-between. But that was nearly four hours ago. Mrs. Fuller should certainly be back from any visit to the Hapgoods by now.

"Girl, what are you keeping from us? Spit it out," Mrs. O'Rourke said, fear lending a sharp edge to her words.

"Ma'am, I'm sorry, I was just surprised. Did Biddy tell you about Mr. Hapgood's suicide attempt?" Kathleen asked. Beatrice and Biddy nodded, so she went on to explain about stopping back at the house and Mrs. Fuller's plan to go to visit the Hapgoods to see if there was anything she could do.

"I asked if I should accompany her, but she refused. She knew I'd promised to meet Ian and take him to the docks to see the Pacific Mail China steamer come in. Mrs. Fuller said it weren't more than a ten-minute walk down to Hyde and Eddy, where the Hapgoods lived, and she would enjoy the outing. She thought it most likely that all she'd be able to do is leave a card but looks like she stayed."

Beatrice said, "Not after dark, not without sending us word she was going to miss supper."

Kathleen's anxiety increased. "I know, ma'am. But she told me to bring Patrick here at seven. She and Mr. Dawson wanted to have a word with him, so surely she'll be back any minute."

The peal of the bell connected to the front door made all four of the kitchen's occupants jump, and Kathleen tore up the stairs, hoping to see both her mistress and Mr. Dawson on the front steps, although it would be unusual for Mrs. Fuller to forget her keys.

She threw the door open and was disappointed to see it was just Mr. Dawson and some woman she didn't know.

"Miss Kathleen, we're here to see Mrs. Fuller. This is Mrs. Flora Hunt," Mr. Dawson said as Kathleen backed up and let the two of them enter the hallway.

"Oh, Mr. Dawson, she's not here. We're ever so worried. She went out this afternoon to see Mrs. Hapgood, sir, whose husband tried to kill himself, and she's not come back. Please, would you mind coming down to the kitchen? Patrick and I just got here, and Mrs. O'Rourke is in a rare state."

As Kathleen led Mr. Dawson and Mrs. Hunt to the kitchen, she briefly told him about Mr. Hapgood's suicide attempt the day before and Mrs. Fuller's plan to visit that afternoon. "And now Biddy's here with news that the Framptons are doing a runner, and Mrs. Fuller isn't here. Whatever can have happened, I don't know. But the mistress is probably right in the middle of it all. You know her, sir."

As they entered the kitchen, Kathleen announced, "Here's Mr. Dawson and Mrs. Hunt, ma'am, here to see Mrs. Fuller. He doesn't know where she is either. Biddy, tell 'em what's going on at the Framptons."

Kathleen then moved to stand with Patrick, whispering, "That little blonde must be the famous Spiritualist that the mistress says is helping her with that strange Evie May I were telling you about."

Biddy, after solemnly shaking Mr. Dawson's hand and curtsying to Mrs. Hunt, swiftly told them about what had happened when she went to work at the Framptons' that afternoon. She described finding the house in an uproar, with the cook in high dudgeon because she had just been dismissed without notice and Arabella's lady's maid running up and down the stairs shouting orders to her husband. "She told me to go down to the cellar and get boxes they had stored there and then wash up all the dishes, ready to be packed. Then I was to go into the study and help the master."

Mr. Dawson interrupted Biddy. "Did anyone say why they were leaving in such a hurry?"

"No, sir. I asked the lady's maid, and she just snapped my nose off. I could hear the mistress cursing at the master at one point but couldn't tell what she was saying. When I went into the master's study, he looked sick, all white-faced, but he didn't say much, except to tell me which books he wanted packed. He was piling together papers and putting them in special boxes, burning some stuff too."

Mr. Dawson broke in again and said, "Miss O'Malley, did Mrs. Fuller or anyone else come to the house while you were there?"

"No, sir. Not Mrs. Fuller, sir. I did think I heard a man's voice, weren't Albert or the master, but I might've been mistaken because I didn't see anyone. Fact is, didn't see Mrs. Nickerson or her daughter either, and no one seemed to be doing anything to pack up their room. Then at six-thirty, the master came into the study where I was still packing books; he thrust some banknotes at me and told me to leave. I came here straight away, because I was sure Mrs. Fuller'd want to know what was happening. Surely looked like they were trying to outrun the coppers."

Mr. Dawson looked over at Patrick and said, "Officer McGee, have you heard anything about a police action against the Framptons?"

Kathleen felt Patrick stand up taller as he said, "No, sir, I haven't. But then my beat's the Western Addition, so I might not hear about a raid planned south of Market. I could find out for you if you want me to run to the local station house?"

Mr. Dawson hesitated then said, "No. I've got to think what to do."

"Sir, may I ask what happened to your face?" Patrick burst out, and Kathleen tried to shush him, although she'd been wondering the same thing since they had come into the brighter light of the kitchen. The poor man had a dark bruise on his cheek and a black eye.

"Happened last night when Annie, I mean Mrs. Fuller, was attacked," Mr. Dawson replied.

Kathleen knew she wasn't the only one in the room who gasped, but it was Mrs. O'Rourke who first spoke.

"Mr. Dawson, what do you mean, our Annie attacked, by whom? Oh merciful heavens, why didn't she tell me?" Mrs. O'Rourke rounded on Kathleen. "Never tell me you knew about this!"

"No, ma'am, I didn't. She's been as closemouthed with me as you since the party Friday night. Mr. Dawson, please tell us."

Mrs. Hunt, who had until this time stood silently near the back door, suddenly walked into the center of the room and spoke. "Mr. Dawson, we don't have anymore time. The danger is increasing. We must go find Mrs. Fuller."

"But where? Do you think she is still at the Hapgoods?" Mr. Dawson asked.

"I feel the spirit of the little girl, very strongly. Wherever Mrs. Fuller is, she is with Evie May. Oh, dear, the fire burns! We must go now!" she cried out and then swayed. Patrick darted over and steadied her.

Kathleen turned to Mr. Dawson and said, "Sir, what does she mean?"

Instead of answering her, he said, "McGee, you and Miss Kathleen go to the Hapgoods, see if she is still there and, if not, find out if anyone knows where she went." He took out a wallet and handed over some money to Kathleen, saying, "If you don't learn anything, get a cab and meet Mrs. Hunt and me. We will go straight to the Framptons' house. We have a cab waiting out front. Now go, there's no time to waste."

*****

In the dark of the attic cupola, Annie couldn't see any smoke in the air, but the smell increased with every breath she took. She went back and pushed the trunk to the side and tried the trap door again, but it remained stubbornly shut. She returned to the front windows and tried to pull each of them up, but they seemed warped shut. She hurried over to the windows to her right and found them equally stuck, although with great effort she was able to open one of the top windows a few inches. This mitigated her sense of panic somewhat. Continuing to move clockwise, she next tried the windows that overlooked the backyard, relieved when she found that she could pull up one of the two windows about a foot. The last two windows, however, were stuck closed. She felt a tickle in her throat and suppressed the desire to cough.

Annie groped her way back to the chair where Evie May sat rocking the doll. When she couldn't get a response from her, she simply pulled the girl to her feet and walked her to the now-open window and pushed her to a sitting position. The girl recommenced rocking and singing, and Annie noticed with a start that the tune was "Hot Cross Buns." *How odd.*

Sitting down with her arm around Evie May, trying to believe she was getting some fresh air, Annie wondered if she should check to see if the trap door was now unlocked, but she worried that the smoke was being produced by Pierce in some fashion to force her to come out of the attic, straight into his hands. She found it intolerable to sit and do nothing, so she got up again and made her way back around to the window facing the street. She saw that Simon was still looking up at the house, with Albert and Arabella clearly remonstrating with him. She wondered if they were arguing about whether or not to go into the house to try to put out whatever fire was causing the smoke.

Could they know Evie May and I are trapped up in the cupola? Annie turned to check on Evie May, and a flicker of light to her left caught her attention. Moving over to that window and looking across to the abandoned house next door, she was confused, thinking at first that she was seeing people wandering around the upper floors of that house with candles. Then in dismay she realized she was seeing bright flames reflected in the neighboring house's window, flames that had to be coming from the house in which she and Evie May were effectively being held prisoner.

With a rising sense of fear, she ran back to the side of the cupola overlooking the street and started to bang frantically on the windows and shout, but she saw that no one was looking back at the house any longer.

The hackney driver was up in his perch, and Albert was pulling Simon towards the open carriage door. She yelled and banged again with more force and thought that she saw Simon turn and look up at her, but then another man came walking up to him, arresting his attention.

Annie stopped banging, recognizing Pierce. Simon was gesturing upwards to the upper stories of the house. Annie saw Pierce shrug and Arabella drag Simon to the carriage. The door to the hackney hadn't even had a chance to close behind them when the driver cracked the whip, and the hackney moved smartly down the street. Annie saw Albert and his wife were now up on the seat of the wagon, which began to move more slowly forward.

Surely the neighbors would have noticed the fire by now, she thought, but then with dismay she remembered that the house to the west was unoccupied, and overgrown trees obscured the one to the east. The shops across the street were boarded up and empty, so they would be no help. Who knew how long it would take for any one further down the block to notice? Meanwhile, the air was getting perceptibly smokier, and her cough worsened. Frantically, Annie looked around the attic, trying to see something she could use to break the glass. However, the easy chair and the trunk, the smallest objects she could see, were certainly too heavy for her to lift. Instead, she pulled off her coat to drape over her hands before beginning to pound on the window again.

She stopped for a moment and saw that Pierce had moved across the street and was standing underneath the gas lamp. He paused, looked back up as if he could see her standing in the cupola, and he tipped his hat before walking swiftly up Fifth to Market. She then noticed a flicker of flame coming from the flat roof under the window where she was standing.

With Pierce no longer a threat, Annie moved towards the center of the room, hoping that he had unlocked the trap door before he left the house. She was finding it harder to breathe, so she started to reach into her coat for her handkerchief to put over her nose until she remembered it was wrapped around the bloody knife. She was also having more difficulty seeing as her eyes began to sting and tear. The smoke in the room seemed to absorb the little light that came from outside.

She went down on her knees and crawled, feeling for the trap door handle. A searing pain in her right hand caused her to rear back. She had touched one of the metal hinges, which was extremely hot. Again using her coat for protection, she felt around until she found the bump of the handle through the cloth of the coat, and she pulled hard. The door didn't budge. She tried again but stopped when her head began to throb with her effort. *Probably just as well. With the hinges that hot, the floor below must be engulfed with flames, and the windows won't help since the roof is on fire now.*

Completely blinded by the smoke, she started crawling to where she had left Evie May sitting under the partially opened window. Annie's thought was that the access to some fresh air would help clear her head so she could think of what to do next. Her hand encountered something soft, which rolled, and she cried out, having run right into the body of Mrs. Nickerson.

Scrabbling sideways away from the body, she thought, *How could I have forgotten the murdered woman was there?* Realizing she had become so disoriented that she wasn't even sure anymore where Evie May was sitting, she sat up and wiped her eyes, trying to see something in the impenetrable haze. She could hear the fire now, too, an ominous, crackling, popping sound.

Despair replaced the panic that had been pushing her forward. She wasn't a fool, and, like any person who lived in a city, she'd seen how quickly fire could consume a house. Even if a neighbor had called the fire in and the fire engines were on the way, if the origin of the fire was in the rooms directly below, the firemen would have no way to break through to the cupola.

I should have told someone I was coming here. How could I have been so stupid? Oh, Nate, I promised I would keep myself safe, but I didn't. And I never told you I loved you.

Annie had started to get back on all fours when she became tangled up in her skirts and the coat she still held in her hands, tumbling flat, her cheek banging painfully into the floor. Then a flame hovered in front of her eyes. Annie screamed and struggled up, thinking that the cupola floor must have caught on fire. As she wiped her eyes, she saw a young boy now standing next to her, holding a candle aloft.

Not just any young boy but Eddie. Somehow, Evie May had replaced her dress with a jersey and pair of knickers. She was also wearing a pair of boy's high-buttoned shoes and a large cap, into which she had pushed her hair.

"Lady, we've got to get out of here. Take my hand. Mind the body. Shame that, but she was such a dunce about men. Thought that Simon was gonna marry her. So stupid, thinking she could use what she learned about that ugly bastard as leverage. Bastard killed her. Maybelle shouldn't of had to see that, poor mite."

Annie stood up, feeling dizzy from the smoke, and said, "Eddie, the trap door's locked, and while you might be able to slip through the crack in that window, I think the roof may be on fire. Besides, how would we get down off the roof?"

Eddie pointed to a coil of rope he had looped over his shoulder and said, "I've got that covered. You bring that coat of yours. That might help protect our feet a bit."

He then pulled her gently around Mrs. Nickerson's body to the back window. While she was estimating whether there was any way she would be able to crawl through the opening, given her voluminous skirts, Eddie pushed the window down and shouted for her to step back, giving her a shove. Then he picked up what looked like an iron bar and swung it at the window, which shattered, glass falling outwards.

A rush of hot wind went past her face, and the sound of the fire seemed to increase. Eddie then swept the bar around the window frame, knocking the remaining jagged pieces out.

"Here, hand over the coat," he said, reaching for it and laying it over the edge of window frame. "I'll go out first, see if it's safe for you," he said, disappearing into the night.

Annie moved over to the window and gulped a lung-full of fresh air, causing her to cough again. Eddie had been gone what felt like an interminable amount of time when he reappeared and said, "Gotta move now. Use my shoulder, and mind the frame at the top."

As instructed, she put one hand on his shoulder to steady herself. Then, picking up her skirts with the other, she put her right foot up on the window edge and went up and over, keeping her back curled as she went through. She would have stumbled to her knees if she hadn't been holding onto his shoulder. He then pulled the coat off the windowsill and put it on the roof, instructing her to stand on it. She realized her feet had already begun to feel the heat because there was immediate relief when she stepped on the coat.

The boy said, "I had a hook I used to tie the rope to when I scaled down the side of the house, but the roof on that side's already burnt through. Looks like going down the back is the only chance. If you can get to the edge of the roof, I'll brace up against the gutter and lower you down. I think I can jump down behind you."

Annie nodded and, grabbing the coat, ran beside him, sending out a prayer that the roof wouldn't collapse under them. When she got to the edge, she threw down the coat, and the two of them hopped onto it. Eddie handed the looped end of the rope to her and sat down on the coat at her feet, putting his legs up against the foot high wood cornice. She stared down at him for a moment, then her mind suddenly cleared, and she thought, *Eddie may think he's strong enough to lower me down, but after all, the body he's inhabiting is that of thirteen-year-old Evie May, and there's no way she's strong enough to handle my weight.*

"Eddie, this isn't going to work. I'll hold on to the rope. When you get down to the overhang over the first floor, maybe you can get to the woodpile and jump down. If you make it to the ground, run to the front, which is where the fire engines will show up, and get them to bring a ladder back here. Now, do as I say."

Annie pulled him up, handed him the looped end of the rope, took the coil from him, sat down on the coat, and braced her feet. He nodded to her once and then climbed over the cornice, and she felt a strong tug on the rope that she tried to counter by pulling sharply backwards. In an instant, the tension of the rope evaporated, and she gasped, going to her knees to look over the edge. He stood firmly on the two-foot overhang, waving cheekily, so she let go of the rope, which slid down to his feet. He moved sideways and was soon out of her sight.

Annie cocked her head, finally hearing the clanging of bells she'd been waiting for. *Thank goodness, help is on the way.* Standing there, listening to the bells come closer, she looked out at the old carriage house at the back of the yard and felt a moment of hope, until she realized that she was able to see that structure so clearly because it was illuminated by the fire at her back. She turned and saw through the open window the cupola up in flames. *Oh God, Mrs. Nickerson's body!*

The sound of an explosion filled the air, and the roof under her feet shuddered. Looking down, she saw that smoke was rising from the coat beneath her feet and a red line of flames were spreading along the cornices to the left and right of her. Mesmerized, she saw the flames turn the two corners of the roof and begin to move at a steady pace toward where she was standing. She closed her eyes and pictured the two lines meeting and her life being snuffed out. If only she were Flora Hunt and could believe that this would simply be a step into another existence. She would even like to believe in protective angels who would sweep her up to safety. But the only protective angel she knew was Eddie, and he was gone.

An odd-sounding thump caused Annie's eyes to fly open, and she looked down at her feet and saw the ends of a ladder reaching above the cornice, followed instantly by the battered face of Nate Dawson, who broke into a grin and said, "Well, a young boy who said he was Eddie told me I'd find you here. I don't suppose you would mind being rescued for a second time in two days, would you?"

Annie grinned back and said graciously, "Why, Mr. Dawson, what a surprise to meet you here. Now if we could have a little less talk, I do believe my shoes are about to burst into flame," and she reached down to be taken in his arms.

Epilogue
Sunday, November 16, 1879

As if the city wished to offer up one last glorious warm day before the winter storms began to sweep across the peninsula, the sun was out, there wasn't a hint of clouds in the sky, and even to the west the usual line of fog had evaporated. Annie only needed her shawl to keep warm sitting in the closed chaise, which was opportune since the Moffets hadn't yet finished making her new wool coat, her old one having been entirely consumed by the fire two weeks earlier. She was thankful that she'd had on one of her older black dresses that night, because she'd had to get rid of every stitch of clothing she'd been wearing since everything was so permeated by smoke. Even the soles of her shoes had cracked from the heat.

Thank heavens she'd had a little emergency savings put by, because her investigation into the Framptons on behalf of Miss Pinehurst had been pretty hard on her finances. Between the cost of replacing the lost clothing, several canceled sessions for Madam Sibyl, the extra money to hire Tilly to cover for Kathleen, and the Halloween party, October had turned out to be a very expensive month. Miss Pinehurst insisted on reimbursing her for the cost of the séances themselves, which had been kind of her, but she hadn't felt right in asking for anything more of her boarder. Annie had meant it when she said the satisfaction of knowing how well Sukie was doing was compensation enough, but she wished she felt as sanguine about the overall outcome of her investigations.

"Was that a sigh?" asked Nate, who sat at her side, driving the team of horses. They were on their way to meet Flora Hunt, her husband, and Evie May at the Conservatory of Flowers, one of the first structures built from William Hall's grand plan for Golden Gate Park. As usual for a sunny Sunday, the park roads were packed with vehicles of every sort, so their pace was quite slow.

Annie glanced over at him, glad to see that the bruising on his face had finally faded. He was wearing gloves, but she didn't think his left palm was bandaged anymore. When he had helped her into the carriage, he'd moved with ease. She hoped that this meant the wound on his side had healed as well. She'd been afraid that his daring rescue of her from the fire had torn the stitches, because she had noticed blood soaking through his shirt when they made it back to her house just short of dawn.

Realizing by the puzzled look on his face that she'd not responded to his question, Annie said, "I find I have been doing a lot of that of late. Sighing. Every time I think about the events of this past month: the Framptons, Pierce, Evie May, the Hapgoods, Mrs. Nickerson's death . . . it's like I keep needing to take a deep breath to clear my mind."

"If you think you're confused, imagine the police. Even when I left out the most bizarre details, like the fact that I made it to the burning building just in time because the famous Spiritualist Mrs. Flora Hunt had a vision that you were in danger, they have had a hard time understanding the ins and outs of this case. For example, they are understandably puzzled about who the little boy was who came running out of the fire and how he was related to Evie May, the daughter of the woman whose body they found in the ashes of the burned building.

"Thank goodness Mrs. O'Rourke's nephew Patrick showed up and took the initiative to use the police call box to summon Detective Jackson. Only the fact Jackson had worked with me on the Voss case made him willing to take my word on what had happened. Otherwise, the Framptons and Pierce might have slipped through the fingers of the police."

"Is Detective Jackson charging the Framptons with anything?" Annie asked.

"Since they were seen fleeing a burning building in which a dead woman was found, he's threatened to charge them as accessories to arson and murder. The coroner did find cuts on Mrs. Nickerson's ribs, which supports your claim she had been stabbed. The cuts evidently matched the blade of the knife they found among the ashes. Jackson's intention seemed to be to frighten the Framptons into turning against Pierce and confirming your story that it was Pierce who killed Mrs. Nickerson and tried to kill you. The strategy worked just fine, and both the Framptons and their servants are falling all over themselves to blame Pierce for everything.

"Simon Frampton told the police that he'd overheard Mrs. Nickerson trying to blackmail Pierce the afternoon of the fire. He admitted that Pierce had an arrangement with them to funnel information about prospective clients, but he swore he didn't know exactly what information Mrs. Nickerson had on Pierce. He said that when his butler discovered that Pierce had killed her, they had panicked. Simon insists, however, that they had no idea that you or Evie May were still in the building when they left."

"The first part of that statement was probably the truth," Annie said. "And if their evidence will get me out of having to testify in a trial, I will even forgive the obvious untruth of the second statement."

Annie knew she wouldn't be able to completely escape police scrutiny. Even Nate couldn't hide her involvement, since the entire fire engine company had witnessed her rescue from the roof of the burning building. She'd also known that if she kept silent about Pierce, he might get away. As soon as Nate got her safely down from the roof, she told the fire captain and the local police constable about Mrs. Nickerson's body and that she and the dead woman's child had been locked in the burning building by the local reporter, Anthony Pierce, who had murdered the woman.

Annie would never forget the look on Nate's face when she told her story to Jackson when he arrived and Nate realized Pierce was the person who been trying to have her killed all along. If he had gotten his hands on the *Chronicle* reporter that night, she'd wasn't so sure Pierce would have survived.

Annie sighed again and then said, "I assume Jackson is still buying the story that I just happened to come to the Framptons' house that evening because I wanted to take Mrs. Nickerson and her daughter out to dinner, having been so impressed with Evie May during the séances I had attended?"

"Yes," Nate replied. "He did mention to me that he was glad to have finally met the elusive Mrs. Fuller, who had played such a mysterious role in the Voss affair. However, the Framptons didn't contradict your statement, and it helps that Mrs. Hunt and Mrs. Gordon were willing to testify to your interest in Evie May, including your outing with her and her mother to Woodward's Gardens."

"Well," said Annie, "I'm certainly glad I took your advice not to bring up my theories about Mrs. Hapgood's murder or the man who assaulted me."

"So far, Jackson hasn't mentioned the Hapgoods to me or questioned your story that you were just an innocent bystander."

"That's good, because I'm not sure if Harold could hold up to questioning by the police at this point," Annie said, going on to tell him about her visit last week to the Hapgoods. Hilda asked her to describe in detail to her husband what Annie thought Pierce had done to his mother, his partnership with the Framptons, as well as what had happened to Mrs. Nickerson.

"Harold seemed very frail and quite bewildered by what I had to say, but Hilda was optimistic. She said that in time her husband would be able to accept that it hadn't been the spirits of his relatives who had been speaking to him, and he would find some peace."

"I hope she appreciated why you didn't tell your suspicions to the police," Nate said.

"Oh, yes, and she was also extremely grateful for your offer to give them legal advice if Pierce does decide to drag them into his troubles."

"At least if they end up needing a good defense attorney, it looks like I would have the expertise of a first-rate lawyer to help me, if I am to believe Uncle Frank."

Nate had already told Annie about his uncle springing on him the news that he was not only bringing an experienced trial lawyer into the firm but that he was in negotiations with Mrs. Gordon and Mrs. Foltz to share office accommodations.

There was a pause while Nate maneuvered the chaise onto the North Ridge Road, the most direct route to the Conservatory, whose gleaming glass dome they could now see rising above the rolling hills of the park.

Once he was safely on the new road, Nate said, "I guess I should be glad that Uncle Frank was listening all those times I complained, although I'm not sure it isn't his desire to have more time with Mrs. Voss that primarily motivated him to take on another partner."

Nate paused and then said angrily, "But Annie, why did he have to keep me in the dark, as if my opinion didn't matter? I can't help thinking, if I'd known, I would never have listened to Pierce, and maybe the attack on you wouldn't have happened, and we wouldn't have had that fight . . ."

Nate's voice cracked, and for an instant she shared his anger at his uncle. Then she shook her head and said, "Nate, don't get mired in what might have happened. Pierce would have just found another way to get you out of the way, one that might have worked better, and as for the fight . . . I believe it was for the best. We were moving too fast. When you think about it, almost all the time we have spent together since we met in August, we've been wrapped up in investigating other people's problems, not talking about our own. It's not surprising that we don't really know each other that well."

Nate pulled the chaise over beside the road and stopped the horses; he then turned to her and said, "What do you mean?"

Annie's heart sped up, and she picked her words very carefully. "I am trying to say that some of the statements you made the night of the Halloween party, and how I reacted to them, revealed that neither of us knows the other as completely as we thought we did. Before we move forward, that needs to change."

"Annie, I know I messed everything up, but . . ."

"Nate, please, listen to me. I once made the mistake of moving too fast, and I ended up married to a man I hardly knew. The result was disastrous, for him and me."

Nate shook his head fiercely and said, "I'm not like your husband. I would never . . ."

"Never what? Don't you see? You don't even know what John did to hurt me. Or how marriage to him changed me, because it did, sometimes I think irrevocably. These past few weeks, I've discovered some things about myself that frighten me. You need to know me better before you can make any decisions about a future with me. And I need to know more about you before I can let go of my fears about being dependent, not just on you but on anyone. I not only didn't keep my promise to you not to go anywhere alone, but I even pushed Beatrice and Kathleen and Esther away this time, not telling them where I'd gone, and it almost cost me my life. But that desire for independence has become such an ingrained part of who I am that I am not sure I can change, and I don't know that it would be fair to you if I can't."

Nate looked down at his hands and took a deep breath. When he started to speak, he kept his eyes lowered, and she heard a tremor that tore at her heart.

He said, "I'm not asking you to change. I love you the way you are. No matter how much you infuriate me sometimes. But if you don't love me, I don't see how time is going to change how you feel."

"Nate, look at me," Annie said, putting her hand out and physically turning his face towards hers. "I didn't say I didn't love you. I do, and believe me it scares me to death to say that, but I owe you that truth. I'm just not sure love is enough. My father loved me, but the decisions he made, even though he thought they were in my interest, hurt me more than I can tell you, and . . ."

Annie, shocked that this particular betrayal still hurt her so, fought back tears until Nate took her in his arms, and then she let them fall.

Minutes later, Annie sighed once more. As she pulled away, she said, "See, Nate, somehow I end up revealing more to you than I have ever revealed to anyone, ever before, and it unnerves me. I just know if we go too fast, I'll either lash out at you with my wretchedly sharp tongue, or I'll run."

Nate smiled and shook his head. "All right, you've convinced me. We will go more slowly. But tell me, Mrs. Fuller, what does going slowly mean? Are you saying that I can't see you as often? In the future, will a carriage ride such as this be out of bounds? Am I not allowed to take you in my arms when you start to cry? Or . . . oh my heavens, you don't mean we can only see each other under the chaperonage of the Miss Moffets!"

Annie laughed at the real sound of outrage in this last question and said, "I personally think a little traditional courting wouldn't be amiss. And, if you need the presence of the Moffets to remind you that simple conversation is how we will get to know each other better, then so be it."

Annie was still chuckling, her heart feeling lighter than it had since All Hallow's Eve, when they pulled up to the lawn that stretched out in front of the Conservatory. Annie wasn't sure why Mrs. Hunt had asked Nate and her to meet them this Sunday, although she assumed Evie May would be the subject of their conversation. The night of the fire, Detective Jackson had given Flora Hunt permission to take Evie May home with her when it became clear that they weren't going to get anything coherent from the girl. Evie May had subsided into a near comatose state as soon as she became the focus of attention. With her mother dead and the Framptons in police custody, Jackson didn't know what else to do with the odd child.

As Nate looked for a place to tie up the horses, Annie asked if he knew the purpose of this meeting.

"When I talked with Mrs. Hunt on Wednesday at the office, she said that it would be good for Evie May to see you outdoors for the first time, since the trauma you both went through happened in such close quarters," Nate replied.

"That makes perfect sense. You mentioned seeing her in your office? Does Mrs. Hunt feel she needs legal protection for Evie May? Has Jackson tried to interview her again?"

"No, he hasn't. Frankly, after I told him a little of the girl's history and her strange behavior, he decided that any testimony he did get from her wouldn't hold up in court."

Nate got down from the carriage, tied the horses to the rail, and then came around to help Annie alight.

As Nate grabbed her around the waist to lift her down, she slid her hands up his arms, feeling the strong muscles he'd used to free her from her assailant and later to carry her down a ladder out of a burning building, and she felt an unexpected warmth, not entirely attributable to the autumn sun. When she was back on her feet, she said, "Tell me, why were you meeting with Mrs. Hunt?"

"She has asked me to work informally with Mrs. Gordon to draft up papers of adoption for Evie May on behalf of her and her husband."

"I am so glad! If anyone can help that young girl, Mrs. Hunt can. I don't know what horrors happened in her childhood or while she worked for the Framptons, but something terrible happened to make her the way she is. And then to see her own mother killed."

"Yes, Mrs. Hunt feels that given her own history and their financial resources, which will help her get the girl the medical help she needs, they are the best persons to care for her. I think the court will agree."

"Is there any chance that relatives might come forward to contest the decision?"

"Mrs. Hunt has, on my advice, hired a local detective firm to make enquires back east, but even if she located Evie May's siblings, she has the resources to challenge them in court. No, the most troublesome threat to adoption might come from Judge Babcock, who has made noises about becoming the girl's guardian."

"No, that would be terrible," Annie exclaimed, her stomach turning at the idea of Evie May under the control of that clearly deluded man.

"I think that his claim that Evie May is his reincarnated daughter will probably not go over well with the court, and Mrs. Hunt seems to have satisfied him by promising that he can visit Evie May, with the girl's permission and under strict supervision."

As they walked up the hill to the Conservatory, Annie saw what looked on the surface to be a perfectly normal family grouping, Mrs. Hunt and her husband, sitting on a bench and looking fondly down at a young girl, perhaps twelve or thirteen, playing on the grass at their feet with a silky-haired spaniel. Annie realized she was very nervous about this meeting with Evie May, not knowing what to expect or whom, for that matter, she would meet.

As Nate went over and shook hands with the Hunts, Annie came and lowered herself to the ground so that the puppy was between Evie May and herself. She said in as pleasant and neutral a voice as possible, "What an adorable dog. Does she have a name?"

Evie May ran her hand along the dog's ears and said happily, in Maybelle's voice, "Yes, I named her Annie, after you. She's got the same brown hair and brown eyes as you, can't you see?" Startled, Annie looked up at Flora Hunt, who said reassuringly, "Evie May has decided to let Maybelle come to the park today. She wanted to tell you about the puppy."

Putting her hand on Evie May's shoulder, Mrs. Hunt said to the girl, "Mrs. Fuller is very flattered that you named the puppy for her. We think Annie is a beautiful name. But would Evie May herself feel comfortable spending some time with us?"

Annie watched in fascination as the girl straightened, stared at nothing for a split second, and then pulled her legs around to sit more demurely. She reached out a hand to Annie and said with the self-conscious politeness of a maturing girl, "I am so glad to see you, Mrs. Fuller. Mrs. Hunt has told me that I have much to thank you for, not the least for introducing me to her. I hope you don't mind that we named the puppy for you, but it made the child happy."

Annie shook the slim hand that was offered her and said, "It is my pleasure, Evie May, and I am delighted to have such a lovely namesake."

For a moment, nothing was said as both she and Evie May played with the puppy, who had turned over to offer them her belly. For some reason, Annie felt sad, sitting with this very proper girl, and once again that afternoon she found herself sighing.

Evie May looked up at her with those odd hazel eyes, glanced over at Nate, who had come to sit down next to Annie, and suddenly grinned, a very familiar grin. Eddie then winked and said, "Lady, mighty glad to see you're doing all right. Maybelle and I, well, we think someday when you decide to get hitched, you will make a great ma."

Annie leaned against Nate's shoulder and smiled.

The End

About the Author

M. Louisa Locke, a retired professor of U.S. and Women's History, has embarked on a second career as the author of novels and short stories set in Victorian San Francisco that are based on Dr. Locke's doctoral research on late 19th century working women. *Maids of Misfortune* and the sequel, *Uneasy Spirits,* are best-selling historical mysteries, and her short stories, *Dandy Detects* and *The Misses Moffet Mend a Marriage,* offer a glimpse into the lives of minor characters from the novels. The third book in the series, *Bloody Lessons* features the teaching profession in 1880 San Francisco.

Check out http://mlouisalocke.com/ for information on Locke's journey as an indie author and a deeper glimpse into the world of Victorian San Francisco, and, if you enjoyed *Uneasy Spirits*, please let the author know at mlouisalocke@gmail.com and post a review.

CPSIA information can be obtained
at www.ICGtesting.com
Printed in the USA
LVOW12s0852081017
551660LV00002B/329/P